THE DEAN OF

WITH KISSES ON THE BOTTOM

By

Dee Vee Curzon

Copyright © Dee Vee Curzon 2023
This book is sold subject to the condition that it shall not, by way of trade or otherwise, be lent, resold, hired out, or otherwise circulated without the publisher's prior consent in any form of binding or cover other than that in which it is published and without a similar condition including this condition being imposed on the subsequent publisher.
The moral right of Dee Vee Curzon has been asserted.
ISBN-13: 9798861595261

This is a work of fiction. Names, characters, businesses, organisations, places, events and incidents either are the product of the author's imagination or are used fictitiously. Any resemblance to actual persons, living or dead, events, or locales is entirely coincidental.

CONTENTS

CHAPTER 1 *The Graduation of Emily Govan* 1
CHAPTER 2 *In which Celia needs a Service* 21
CHAPTER 3 *Eva Regina Buchman and the Rowing Club Fall-out* 34
CHAPTER 4 *Eva, Nina and Yuri Duly Punished* 55
CHAPTER 5 *In Which The Mistress Is Mastered!* 90
CHAPTER 6 *Melanie Needs A Wake-Up Call* 113
CHAPTER 7 *Freya and Natalie thought it would be a laugh* 123
CHAPTER 8 *Kerry is too old for a spanking* 153
CHAPTER 9 *Kerry: Five Days Later* 170
CHAPTER 10 *In Which Felicity Wants her mummy* 182
CHAPTER 11 *Like Mother, Like Daughter* 214
CHAPTER 12 *In which Olivia gets a lesson in sportsmanship* 247
CHAPTER 13 *Philippa Becomes Enlightened* 268
ABOUT THE AUTHOR 319

CHAPTER 1

THE GRADUATION OF EMILY GOVAN

Another year, another graduation ceremony, thought the professor as he stood on the vast lawn of Central Court as the graduated students mingled, drifting in and out of the huge marquee with their beaming, proud parents, guardians and close relatives. The year's cohort returned for the three-day event as the city celebrated its cerebral success by default. The University had turned this autumn event, between academic years, into a massive occasion and a huge economic boost for the area and its hotels, hostelries, guesthouses and private lets. The retail sector likened this to the Christmas shopping period, rammed into one week in September, as tills everywhere rattled in celebration of academic achievement. For many of the students, their hour of glory in the graduation ceremony was just a minor formality, in this final hurrah that most dragged out from Monday to Saturday as they held on to clouds of love, memories, friendship and success. The next week really was the start of the rest of their lives; reality would bite, careers would need to be developed, new relationships were to be formed, and adulthood would truly begin.

Several young ladies approached him with their parents, always an entertaining moment for Stones, as often the students who had suffered the most from the college's specific, and nowadays highly unusual method of applying discipline and adherence to rules, were, oft unbeknown to them, offspring of mothers whose unfrocked derrières he had also known close encounters with.

Stones' face failed to register the emotions he felt as Emily Govan and her eminent parents passed civilities. Emily was due her graduation at tomorrow's final ceremony, her parting shot and her final, formal act in college. As her parents drifted away to chat with some known associates just spotted in the distance, Emily turned to Stones and spoke quietly.

"So, Professor Stones, once I have received my degree from the chancellor of the University I have graduated and therefore I am no longer a current student member of the college?"

Stones looked at her knowingly as he answered.

"That is correct, Miss Govan, you will become alumni, a lifetime college member, but your undergraduate days and terms and conditions of that status will have come to an end."

Emily looked at him coyly.

"So in theory you could no longer punish me for something I had done!"

Stones sighed. He could see where this was going and could not resist playing along.

"Correct, Miss Govan. I will be powerless to impose any punishment or take disciplinary action against you once you pick that certificate up. However, as I believe that I have told you before, I do get requests for assistance from occasional ex-students who call for my input in the form of what I like to term as life coaching. You have something on your mind, young lady, so get to the point, please."

Emily's face was now pink and she was clearly aware that he had already seen where this was leading.

"Sir, in my first year, I once stole bottles of expensive wine from a crate in the catering store. I think that they assumed it was an internal theft by one of the staff because there was never any fuss or public announcement, and I have worried that someone might have got into trouble over it. I am very sorry, sir, and feel that you should know, as you have been so good to me during my time here. I am sorry that I had failed to come clean about this disgraceful act before and wanted you to know in case you feel that this deserved to be dealt with before I graduate."

Stones resolved not to allow any sense of amusement or interest to show in his face or in his voice as he contemplated her words.

"Excuse me, young lady, but you have just admitted to theft of college property, today of all days, and apparently feel that this will be expunged from my memory if you offer up your scrawny backside for a seeing to."

Emily blanched, giving him the reward he had been looking for.

"Um. Er. Well sir, sorry, sir. I know, sir. Um. I am sorry, sir." Her rather incoherent apologetic response was gist to his mill.

"Presumably in your plan was me just happening to be free at the correct time to be able to punish you this evening, and no doubt there's a plan that involves your parents having alternative arrangements!"

Emily nodded. "Yes, sir, they are out for evening dinner and I told them I would be meeting up with friends, sir. Oh shit! I've screwed up again, haven't I, sir? Sorry, sir."

"Emily, you are a disrespectful and disreputable woman and you do make me despair sometimes. As it happens, I am free this evening, before meeting the mistress and the senior tutor for drinks and dinner with some rather important donors to impress. You will be outside my rooms with an essay admitting your guilt and your request for justice to be dispensed. You will volunteer what form that punishment will take and you will arrive in a freshly showered and fully prepared state. Oh, for goodness' sake, you know the drill. Be there at 17.30 hours, fully ready for a final thrashing on your bare backside. Now be off with you, and be thankful that this issue will not be officially reported, as it would not have been too late to stop you from graduating. Go!" Stones fairly barked at her, causing slight concern to nearby guests and more than a mere tremor down the spines of one or two students in earshot. A red-faced Emily scurried away.

As he expected, Emily reported to him at the agreed time, her essay in her hands. Stones barely glanced at it; he could see words 'such an irresponsible, theft, rule-breaking, criminal act' and then quite predictably the apologies and remorse followed by a plea to be punished severely to help her atone for her guilt and find improvement through chastisement.

"I suppose I should be grateful that it does not say that you are in love with me and want me to fuck you!"

Emily's mouth dropped open, on two accounts, Stones suspected, the first being that he had actually spoken those actual words out loud, and secondly because he had used the F word in her presence. He certainly was not convinced that she would claim that it was not true!

"Oh, close your mouth, you look ridiculous. I note that you have failed to stipulate which instruments of chastisement you feel should be used, but I accept that you have asked for a severe and thorough punishment to take away from this institution as a reminder of how bad behaviour has repercussions, and I commend you for that. Please remove your clothes and bend over, legs apart, hands on ankles for a hygiene check."

If he needed any confirmation that her presence in his room was prompted more by lust and passion than a genuine request for contrition, then Emily's smile told Stones conclusively so. With minimal clothing actually on, it took Emily seconds to divest herself of everything and with a rather flamboyant twist she presented Stones with her bottom clad in a white string before slowing pulling the panties down her legs and bending with her legs wide apart.

"Would you like my cheeks pulled further apart so you can inspect me properly?" Emily's voice was husky and quite breathless and Stones realised that she was extremely turned on already. The point of the hygiene inspection was twofold, initially to avoid any unpleasant aroma in dealing with unwashed and unprepared students, but far more importantly to immediately put his misfits on the back foot, confusing them, horrifying them, disgusting them and ultimately causing them massive humiliation, degradation and embarrassment. He knew that none of this applied to the confident and most forward

Emily Govan, and decided that he needed to take control of the situation.

"Actually, Emily, I am so sure that your preparation for this session will have been of the highest level in terms of service cleanliness and hygiene standard that I will pass up the need to get close and personal with you. However, you do unaccountably appear to be damp between your legs, so perhaps you could take a tissue and dab your wet labia dry, please."

Emily spun round and up, clearly annoyed at being thwarted and basically ridiculed, grabbed at the proffered tissues and folded them between her legs. He watched as she struggled to control her renowned quick and fiery temper, knowing full well that he had bested her yet again. She marched over to the bathroom, giving him a perfect view of her bottom in motion, and flushed the tissues down the lavatory. She hesitated, before washing her hands and then returned to face him, hands going to her head, her breasts thrusting prominently, her neat and obviously recently coiffured pubic bush displayed in all of its glory.

"Would you like to select the first two implements from my cabinet that you feel would be most appropriate articles to use for the beginning of your thrashing? Remember that this may be an historical act that you have confessed to, but it is still theft and as such I do need to ensure that you pay the cost in pain and suffering."

She spun around and marched to his cabinet and returned within seconds holding the riding crop and his bat-shaped wooden paddle.

"I think a bloody good whipping with crop – excuse my language, sir – after a quick hard hand spanking and then twenty firm slaps with the bat should set me up nicely for the grand finale of your choice, sir. I would hazard a guess that the wicked thick strap is going to make an entrance, being your favourite application, sir. Thank you for your consideration and time, sir, I hope you approve of my selection?"

Stones could hardly say not. She had indeed chosen well and had slipped in that she was expecting to go over his knee as well.

"Fair enough, Emily. I prefer that we go with the padded bat and a cane before finishing with the thick strap, so you can replace the crop. I think you can go over to my cupboard and fetch one of the bamboo canes. About time that you experienced one of those again, I feel. The one with the red-taped handle please, it should look familiar as it is the bamboo used on you by Chloe and Zoe that memorable evening. The braided knotted lash I will hold in reserve for now."

Emily collected the cane from the selection of long bamboo canes that stood in his cupboard, which sat alongside the spanking machine and dreaded table that he had designed, with its strap and pulley system to configure how he saw fit to expose his victims, when delivering the ultimate thrashing experience. Stones was delighted to see that looking at it now still sent a shiver of fear coursing through her body.

"I hope I don't find the need to use my contraption again with you, Emily. It is clearly for the most severe punishments, however the spanking machine could be a different story should our paths cross again."

The light returned to her eyes with those last few words, and Stones' inference of future meetings had added a spring to her step as she reverently handed him the bamboo that had wreaked havoc on her bottom a year ago.

Stones settled down on the sturdy wooden chair he had bought years before, chosen purely on the grounds of the design being perfectly suited for over-the-knee spankings. He patted his legs.

"Over you go, young lady. Assume the position, please. Put the paddle within my reach in case I opt to move on to that straight after. Good girl."

Emily obeyed immediately and holding on to the bottoms of the chair legs, raised her bottom high.

"Like this, sir?" she asked in her most coquettish voice.

He didn't answer but released an avalanche of slaps to the backs of her legs. Apart from the tiniest of yelps, Emily accepted the spanking in virtual silence. Stones progressed to her buttocks and began concentrating on the creamier white skin on either side of her bottom crack, which had obviously been bikini clad. Once he had turned the visible area red, he placed one hand on her left cheek and gripped hard, pulling her cheek aside, and unleashed well-targeted blows to the normally hidden inner skin of her bottom crack. He switched hands and repeated the avalanche of blows to the inside of her right buttock. With her arsehole twitching open and closed and her breathing heavy, he was not at all surprised to see her labia moisten again. He ignored her lust as he then went to work on the tanned skin framing her bottom. He was well aware that he had become erect and that she was trying very subtly to move her groin to rub against his hardness, but decided that at this point in their strange relationship he would allow them both to enjoy the moment.

After a hand spanking of 200 slaps he picked up the cricket-bat-shaped paddle and brought it down hard across the centre of her seat. Her grunt of pain was satisfying and he began a slow methodical stinging beating. His eyes were riveted to her bottom and he was well aware that she aroused him in a way few students ever had. He loved her rebellious character, her humorous quips and her fortitude in taking a very hard thrashing. That in combination with her stunning athletic body and striking attractiveness with her pretty face and long blonde hair made her a joy to be with for a man of his tastes. Of course, her stunning breasts and sensitive nipples, the very neat bush and full labial lips of her gorgeous vagina helped. To have, in his eyes, the absolute perfect bottom with an arsehole that he felt was a work of art, worthy of his worship, topped it off. He had never succumbed to the charms of a student in all of his disciplinary days but Emily was definitely the one to have caused his temptation to waver the most. In truth, he rather adored her, but that was an emotion he vowed he would not share with her.

One hundred times his arm rose and fell, the heavily varnished wood meeting her porcelain cheeks with a resounding slap every time, her bottom a deep glowing red all over, her quiet whimpers, occasional sobs and haphazard breathing, the signs of her hurt and discomfort. She continued to gently grind herself against him throughout her ordeal and he suspected that without that sensation she would have been in much greater distress. He cast the paddle down and with his large hands on either cheeks continued to move her body against him. Her yelps of pain turned quickly to a mixture of signs and grunts of lust and pleasure. He spreads her cheeks further so that her arsehole and vagina were just inviting holes in front of his eyes. One a dark spider web of neat crinkles amongst little off-blonde curly hairs around her dank hole, a hint of bright pinkness just showing within, the other a moist haven of interwoven plump lips moulding into one another, amidst the trimmed blonde pubes, the layers glistening with droplets of her secretions. He could see how much she wanted his touch and gently ran a finger along the wet crack and up into the crevice where her dark hole twitched open and closed at him. He leaned down and put his fingers in her face; she automatically knew what he wanted and she sucked them enthusiastically, coating them with her saliva. The wet fingers went straight to the neat, entrancing arsehole and as he ran one finger around her rim, she felt him drip her spit into the relaxed opening. His thumb slid into her pussy and she jerked her body but held on to his calves as she retained her position of surrender and subjugation. Stones switched and Emily now had two fingers in her pussy and his juice-wet thumb rimming her arsehole. He knew they were in tune with each other and that she knew he was biding his time, working her open to accept the intrusion. That she wanted him so much was obvious as she was able to relax herself and his thumb slid smoothly in, through the tight opening with little resistance.

"Oh yes, oh yes, oh yes. Do it, sir, do me, sir. Please do me with your thumb. Go on, sir, please fuck my arse."

Stones was aroused by the pathetic pleading note in the voice of this strong and independent young woman. He felt her need to have him embedded in both of her intimate holes. He imagined that it was just the thought of what he was about to do that gave her an immediate shuddering orgasm as she bucked her body up to force his thumb firmly and fully into her most private and personal place. She flinched as he spat phlegm into her bottom crack to ease the way for his thick digit. He slowly eased his thumb out to allow his spittle to dribble into the open hole before his thumb slid back inside of her wanton darkness and his fingers started to frig her pussy more deeply. His other hand now tweaked a nipple, and she howled in her ecstasy and he felt her push her groin down to rub hard against his erection. She climaxed, leaking into his lap and coating his trousers, as his fingers increased their motion in and out of her sodden sex, the squelching sound adding to both of their excitement and her total and abject surrender. Her orgasm repeated. Her head shook from side to side, her body bounced, her guttural screaming was primal and without reservation. Finally, she slumped exhausted and his dampened hands moved back to stroking her throbbing buttocks, the pain of which, he assumed, was now coming back into her consciousness. There was more to come and her lustful behaviour would not distract him from his primary focus.

The screaming was higher pitched now, as the paddle suddenly came down savagely on her cheeks. Stones launched a sustained barrage of blows on the unprotected buttocks before him and allowed Emily no time at all to recover, as the wood slammed down twice every second. Her howls were sustained, and of great distress but this mattered not a jot to Stones, whose heart could be made of stone when he was beating a miscreant. He had a very good idea of exactly how much pain Emily could take and he was determined to push her to her limits. His grip needed to be firm as the strong young woman tried frantically to escape his hold. Striking at the tops of her legs, he achieved his goal as Emily screeched like never before, with blow after blow striking the sensitive and vulnerable skin below her buttocks. It had been the longest, and most comprehensive paddling he had ever dispensed. As the last smack landed, at the end of a flurry slamming across the very tops of her buttocks, he felt he received his just reward, as her body slumped down, all resistance broken. Two hundred and fifty times his arm had raised and fallen and the blazing, mottled, dark red discolouring of her bottom paid a compliment to a mission fulfilled successfully. He stayed quiet and unmoving as she sobbed and bleated for several minutes in the aftermath. His only act was to reach over and then hand her tissues as the tears fell onto his carpet. Eventually, when her movements became less agitated and the crying subsided, he placed his hands gently on her beleaguered globes and began to rotate them, circling over and over the swollen mounds whilst he hummed melodically.

"Hush now, sweetheart, hush now," he whispered. His hands travelled down her legs, and then up again.

"Oh my, Professor Stones, oh my. That was something," she responded in kind, between long breaths as she struggled to regain some sort of composure.

"Harsh but fair, I would say. Sadly I am still waiting for your official response." His disappointed tone was deliberately targeted to encourage the response he required. Emily, as he suspected she would, did not let him down in her eagerness to please him.

"Oh, sorry sir, it was fucking amazing. Wow!" she says. "Just fucking wow. It stung so much, sir. Exactly what a worthless creature like me deserved. Now it feels wonderful though, sir. I truly love the burn that comes afterwards, sir. Thank you, sir, thank you, thank you, thank you. Would you like to make love to me now, sir?"

Stones smiled in response and continued his stroking of her glowing cheeks.

"Oh no, dear, up you get and clean my hands of your filth with the wet wipes, please. Then we will get on with the caning and the delights of the tawse!"

"Sure you wouldn't like me to relieve you of that erection, sir? It would be a privilege for me to assist you, sir."

Stones was aware that she had begun forcing her midriff down to rub against his hardness, and felt tempted by her offer. However, his resolve held and the iciness in his tone as he responded brooked no argument.

"Seems like you are looking for extra strokes with the thick strap. Is that what you would like, Emily?"

Emily went silent for a moment. The thick strap, along with the braided lash, were her most dreaded implement of punishment, and Stones knew the threat would work.

"No, sir. Sorry, sir. I am ready to be caned, sir. As always, I am at your service, sir, in any way you desire."

"There's my girl. Let's just have you bent over hands on ankles. No restraints for you with the bamboo cane needed, I hope?"

"No, sir, I am happy to adopt the traditional position, sir."

Emily smiled at him, spun on her heels, opened her legs wide and bent perfectly from the waist, presenting her red buttocks, taut and round, her arsehole peeking between her open cheeks, her still-wet lower labial lips on display.

Stones drank in the view. This could possibly be the last time he caned the magnificent bottom of his favourite student and he wanted to relish and enjoy the experience. He strongly suspected that she would be one of his returning culprits, but he knew from the past that so many things happen in life that could affect any ongoing relationship.

Crack. Crack. Crack. Crack. Crack. Crack.

He went hard and fast with the cane's first six strokes from the top of her bottom to the lower fleshier cheeks. Emily's breathing changed but other than that, she showed no signs of distress or vexation from receiving the harsh contact. Stones was impressed but also content and confident that he would break that stoicism and reduce the resilient young woman to a blubbering wreck within a few minutes. He drew his arm back and swung the cane with force as he targeted the earlier stroke marks accurately.

Crack. Crack. Crack. Crack. Crack. Crack.

Each of the six strokes produced grunts and small murmurs in response and her knees almost buckled but she held position as the weals thickened and swelled.

She shivered as he ran his hands over the swollen lines.

"Well taken, young lady. Ready for your final eight cane strokes?"

Emily sighed.

"You know me, sir. Hate the impact, live for the afterburn. Do your worst, do your best. Swing that cane and thrash my arse, sir. Please, of course."

Crack. Crack. Crack. Crack.

The first four went to the tops of her legs and Emily squealed and staggered forward but maintained her hold on her ankles impressively. Stones let her settle and then landed the final four.

Crack. Crack. Crack. Crack.

The four strokes landed across the sensitive strip of skin at the top of her bottom cleft, each one on top of the previous. Each blow enticed a louder grunt from Emily than its predecessor and her knees finally buckled as final stroke landed.

Struggling back into position, Stones was delighted to hear her voice wracked with sobs.

"Thank you so much, sir. I am so grateful for your efforts to improve me. Ready for any further punishment, sir."

Stones walked over and picked up the strap.

"Just the matter of your old friend, my lovely thick strap. Stand up and kiss all along the leather length to show your love for it, my dear."

Emily rises and goes over to him, takes the strap and kisses it up and down its length before her tongue snakes out and she licks it coating it with her saliva. She goes to his table, grins at him and opens her legs, settles her pudenda on the protruding mound and bends forward stretching her arms out to grasp the wooden edges.

"Thrash me, Professor Stones. Make me burn, make me scream, make me come."

She starts to rotate her hips and Stones knows that she has placed her groin perfectly to enable her to grind against the mound to simulate sex.

He brings the thick strap down with force and she squeals and shuffles but otherwise holds her stance.

"Stay still Emily. If I have to stop to strap you down then the ten strokes will start from scratch again. You will receive five more strokes evenly spaced across these rather spoiled and disfigured buttocks and then I will overlay the final four across those tramlines to try and cause maximum pain, soreness and bruising. Here we go then."

The strap whistled through the air before slashing Emily's lower buttocks, causing a strangled scream from Emily, her hands scrabbling to hold on to the desk. Stones wondered if she could really maintain this pose without restraints. The strap was definitely her nemesis, and he respected the fact that she embraced the challenge and was attempting to conquer and cross the pain barrier. He would not go easy on her, however, as the punishment was agreed appropriate to the misdemeanour and original offence, and he appreciated that she wanted and needed this thrashing to be real and brutal. He struck her rapidly with three lashes to test her resolve; her body flinched and her knees buckled, as she screeched in pain. He was not fazed by the sound of Emily displaying total despair. He delivered the sixth stroke as she just about regained her appointed position, causing the tears to flow and her body to almost slide off the edge of the table. He allowed her to pull herself together and work through the fearsome pain he unleashed. She was writhing now and he could see she was desperate to find some kind of rhythm to her movement that would allow her to work herself against the raised mound. He viewed dispassionately her obvious search for sexual relief and distraction from the torment.

He whipped the seventh stroke diagonal down from left to right, disrupting her sexual rocking as she rose up before slumping down, her gasp of agony a strange gurgling noise. He let her settle again, her tear-sodden face falling back to the table, before unleashing number eight diagonally crossing the previous stroke. Emily howled and jerked, screaming out.

"No! No! Fucking hell, oh, oh, oh. Fuck! No! Oh. Gaaarrrgghhh!"

She rolled her hips, stamped her feet and bent at the knees, before slowly pulling herself back into position.

"Two more to go, Emily, so can I have a little more decorum and control shown, please? These two will be memorable, I hope. Please make the most of them. Now present properly, legs further apart, bottom up, anus open and pointing at me, please."

"Yes, sir. So sorry, sir. Please strap me as hard as you can, sir. Go on then, sir, give me your best shot. Make me holler, sir."

Stones possibly loved the young woman before him more than ever at that moment. He knew she dreaded the fearsome sting of the thick strap and that her carefree words were virtually a proclamation of her servility, adoration and loyalty to him. He went very low and pulled up at the last moment to slam into the lowest part of her cheeks, and as she wailed and scrabbled against the desk he swung high and brought the strap down for the last time with a resounding splat across the highest point of her buttocks. It caught Emily unaware and her scream was earth-shattering and she crumpled to the ground clutching her buttocks. Stones had never been accused of not being a man of his word, and Emily was now experiencing what he had promised.

"Well, young lady, you have failed to keep your position again and while I was prepared to turn a blind eye to any minor indiscretions earlier, this latest disobedient display is not acceptable. So go to the wall and put your hands out to take your weight, now walk your feet backwards until your shoulders are in line with your hips. That's it. Bottom out, nice and proud, legs and buttocks apart. Lovely. Six punishment strokes hard and fast coming. Hold tight."

Emily was compliant but clearly suffering and struggling to cope with the anguish and torment of the pain of her red-raw cheeks. She took a deep shuddering breath and just issued the two words that Stones would always appreciate hearing.

"Ready, sir."

Stones thought her capacity for punishment admirable and wondered how close to her absolute limit he had taken her. He was certainly aware of the state her buttocks were now in, and was very conscious of the soreness and bruising he had caused. He raised the tawse and swung his arm rapidly to apply the six strokes to the sensitive strip of skin just beneath her lower bottom dimples where just a couple of cane lines were standing proud. She screamed and wept copiously but more or less held the demanded pose, no pleas for mercy, no begging, no words beseeching or imploring him to desist. She took her dues and Stones felt respect and love for his graduated pupil now finally stepping out from being under his authority.

Amidst the tears, she spluttered her words of supplication and subservience.

"Thank you so much for my thrashing, sir. I am so sorry for my behaviour."

He pointed at the bathroom.

"Bidet. Iced water. Ten minutes."

Emily obeyed, and he laughed when he heard the sharp intake of breath as her bottom met the cold water. In her absence he produced a luxurious rug from one of his many adjoining rooms and laid it on the floor. He placed his chair at the edge of the rug, fetched a jar of his moisturising cream and a glass of his favourite Malbec and settled to wait for Emily's return.

Several minutes later she was standing with her back and bright red bottom to him.

"So, Emily, I noted you did not manage to pleasure yourself to climax whilst taking the tawse. As you have generally behaved yourself in my rooms and today is an important day in your life, I will allow you to masturbate to orgasm in front of me."

He put his hands on her hips and moved her backwards onto his lap. He pushed her forward, forcing her hands to stretch down to the floor. As she settled with her bottom in front of his face, her cheeks parted, exposing the damage-free inner cheeks and her butthole. He covered his fingers in cream, staring into the enticing crevice before him. She squeaked in delight at his delicate touch, as he gently rubbed the soothing cream into the welts and weals he has caused. His thumbs dipped down, barely grazing her swollen wet lips and he could smell her arousal. She was breathing deeply and trying to rub herself against his knee; he held her cheeks apart and took a long look at her exposed arsehole and couldn't resist leaning in to give it a brief kiss. He pushed her to the floor, saying, "Show me how you do it."

She turned to face him, smiling, running her slender hands over her breasts, tweaking her nipples, her eyes sparkling and wide. One hand snaked down between her legs and a finger delved into her wetness, and he could see the moment she touched her clitoris. Other fingers slipped inside and she began the dipping in and out as her frigging fingers replicated the motions of a man's cock. She was pinching a nipple hard enough to turn her areola bright red, her back arching, her pussy slurping as two fingers drove all the way inside of her and then all the way out. Her head shook and her hair was wild. She lifted her bottom off the ground; her body rippled as her knees bend and spread wide apart as she displayed her self-abuse to him. Her hand now covered her whole mons and he saw all four fingers flicking and twitching in and out of her soaking wet folds. Emily started to moan and cry, her voice becoming unearthly and croaky as she began the journey towards the relief and release that she craved. She turned round, pointing her battered buttocks at him. He could no longer see her arm but she arched her back so he could see the splayed lips as three fingers plunged in and out, her knuckles giving the friction to her clitoris that built the explosion of her climax that was so plainly about to happen. He tried to take it all in, aware of his cock ramrod straight and stretching the fabric of his trousers as it stood proud. He longed to sink to his knees behind her. He could not stop the thought of his tongue invading her pussy, his nose embedded in her arsehole, before slamming his cock deep into her wet hole and filling her with his spunk while his hands yet again spanked those sore twin globes of her arse. His eyes were drawn to her twitching arsehole as she started to lose control. He felt bewitched by the intricate lines and darker skin surrounding the opening and closing dark hole. She screamed and screamed, her head and free hand rucking up the rug as she reached her goal.

"Fuck! Fuck! Fucking fuck, fuck! I am coming, sir, I am spurting my love. Aaaargggghhhhhh! Yes! Yes! Yes! Oh, Professor, frigging, fucking yes! I love you. Here we go again. Yaaaar! Look at my fingers, Professor Stones, covered in my come for you. Oh yes, yes, yes."

Her voice subsided and she sank her haunches down to the floor. Her body bucked twice and then she relaxed, sprawled sated at his feet, her breathing beginning to calm. She took a moment then turned to face him, her face flushed to match her bottom, her eyes wide with a look of wonder and possibly enlightenment. Stones could see the longing written all over the face of Emily and knew it was time to put her out if her misery.

"I will say to you, Emily, as I have said to others before you. I understand your desires and am willing to listen to entreaties to allow your return to this office to facilitate further improvement. I would advise you to keep a notebook in which you jot down any misdeeds, grave errors or rash and irresponsible behaviour. But, and I warn you quite seriously, this needs to be an accurate record free of fantasy, creativity or embellishment. Any sense of this and you will find that I am completely unavailable to you. However, if I deem that your documentation illustrates a need for improvement, resolution or forgiveness via the use of corporal punishment then I will send for you. So yes, Emily, of the big wide eyes and rather swollen wet vulva, you will have your bare bottom flogged and flayed to suit your wrongdoing, to appease your guilt, to improve you and put to rest your shame. Now get your slutty rags back on and get out of my sight."

Stones sensed, now fully dressed, Emily's reluctance to leave him. He could see her steeling herself to say something of great importance to her and had a fair idea of what was coming.

"Now is the time, Emily, spit it out, or you will never say it!"

She gulped loudly and the words came out in a torrent.

"Sir, I so want to make love with you, sir. Sir, if you please, sir, I want to give myself to you absolutely, sir. I want it all, sir, everything, sir, and sir, I offered you my anal virginity once, sir, and sir, I still have not done it there, sir. Not with a man's cock, sir. I really would love for you to be the first one there, sir. Oh God, I've said it now, sir." Emily fell silent and Stones just allowed the words to hang in the air as she squirmed in embarrassment before him.

"You are a brazen and captivating young woman, you are delightful company, a joy to look at, and your beauty is unarguable. You are without doubt exceedingly pretty and have a truly divine body, proportionately perfect. You are fit, sporty and in good health. I have seen your kindness and your generosity, the reports from tutors support that you are inclusive, engaging and a great debater. However, you are a lustful and wanton, highly sexed young woman, thirsty for carnal knowledge of all types. You most certainly have a penchant for taking punishment, and a desire to have substantial pain applied, generally on your bare bottom. Reports from the tutors also say you can be wilful, argumentative and stubborn to the point of rudeness. You have a foul mouth, a quick temper and you like getting your own way far too much."

Emily's face betrayed a range of emotions as he spoke. Actually Stones could see that she was digesting and contemplating the points he was making. He hushed her as she went to speak.

"Now, my dear, listen to me, do not speak. The point is not necessarily to change you, your character and personality are what they are and what makes you the fine adult you have developed into. No, what you must learn to do more is to recognise your reactions and emotions and take better control of them. You need to understand yourself and the way your mind works. There is no shame in passion, lust and sexual desire but you need to channel your feelings correctly to ensure that you get want you want from life with no detriment to others. I repeat, you have turned into a fine adult and one that I am proud to have known, your flaws are acceptable, but it is how you adapt and reflect on them that is so important. Interestingly, in this more equal, less sexist world, you have a slightly worrying trait that one normally associates with the male sex. You seem far too often to think with your wet, wanton sex organ rather than your brain, young lady. This voracious appetite for sexual stimulation has its undoubted charms and positives but also makes you potentially vulnerable and closed-minded. You must be more cautious, Emily, or trouble awaits, and I care far too much for you to let you walk into this dangerous world without due warning." Stones stopped, slightly taken aback to see the tears flowing down Emily's face.

"You do know that I love you with all my heart, Professor Stones. God, it's not just love, I worship you, I adore you." She stopped as Stones put a finger to her lips.

"Yes I know, my sweet girl, but it is pure infatuation, and however real it feels now, it will pass. It is not something to bemoan, though. Please embrace your feelings and take on board my advice, and always know that I will never close my door to you. You are now off to train in your chosen field of physical and psychological therapy, albeit I understand that your parents wish you to have a grounding in the legal profession before you venture out on your own. I hope that you appreciate that the college are supporting you in your endeavour and, as an institution, will be available as ever to assist you on your career journey. You may take it that I will follow your fortunes closely, and offer you personally, my own independent support."

Emily beamed at him.

"You are really not helping, sir. I am horny and wet just listening to you. I will go back to my room now and frig myself off looking in the mirror at the state of my arse and imagining you licking and kissing it better."

Stones leant in, kissed her on the cheek, and ran his finger under her chin, raising her eyes to his.

"Sweet dreams, Emily. I shall look forward to our paths crossing again. Take care, my dear, take care."

He turned her around and with a gentle push urged her towards the door. He watched as her shoulders dropped in resignation but was pleased to see her straighten and head from his room without a backward glance. He had no doubt that they would meet again.

CHAPTER 2

IN WHICH CELIA NEEDS A SERVICE

"Are you free later?" questioned the email from Dr Celia Ford, the college's Senior Tutor. "Full service, please. I would like the full works, please, Edward. I think I am overdue for the complete and extensive version."

Professor Edward Stones, the Dean of Discipline at St. James' College, smiled to himself. Overdue indeed. It was halfway through the summer vacation at the college and things were quiet. No students, and even the graduates, those students who had stayed on after attaining their degree, to study for Master's degrees, Doctorates or purely for sponsored research purposes, had left for a summer break. Most of the college's fellows or dons, the senior teaching scholars, had departed for retreats in the country or long holidays abroad, and the staff had gone down to its usual skeletal level between university years.

"I am free at the usual 3pm. Bring me something new to use on this project, please. You will not need briefing, I presume. There is just a single item on board to discuss. Yes, the complete package will be waiting. Do not be late." As always using the diplomatic wording that Celia had become accustomed to, Stones being alert to security issues and data protection for everyone's safety and benefit.

He knew that Celia would understand that she was now booked in for a thorough thrashing, in which he would humiliate her verbally as well as physically punish her, followed by a bout of lovemaking. The professor was very careful about any sexual encounters himself in college, but he and Celia had shared many episodes, incidents and experiments together and there was a solid trust and unbreakable bond between them built over a relationship of many years. However, their partnership had been on a slightly different footing since Stones had had cause to severely punish her officially, and on record, after she had broken one of the college's golden rules of behaviour concerning relationships with students. A humiliating and very painful experience that, several months on, still caused Celia much shame and embarrassment whenever Stones made casual allusions to the day, forcing her thoughts to stray to the memory. She may well have been forgiven, but she would know that the episode was one that would never be forgotten by the professor. Nor, he was sure, would the fact that he had not allowed her to identify the involved guests allowed in to watch and participate in her shaming, be something that she would ever be comfortable with.

He had no doubt that Celia would correctly interpret his message, as always, and would realise that the instruction was to bring him something original to beat her bottom with, to wear no underwear and just a single covering garment. *Don't be late* meant exactly that, for fear of additional punishment strokes. He was also sure that Celia would interpret that as a disguised suggestion to her to flout his request and give him reason to cause her greater discomfort with an increased punishment. Celia might not like to think of herself as a masochist as, like a lot of aficionados of the fetish and sexual lifestyle that she actively partook in, she usually found the reality of the thrashings to be somewhat challenging to cope with. However, the anticipation, the thrill of handing over complete control to a trusted partner and the throbbing heat afterwards were the things that, Stones knew for certain, drove her desire. There were times during a discipline session that she would be begging for mercy, not that he would ever grant such a request, as he set her thighs and buttocks afire and made sure that the pain level approached unbearable. However, Celia could not deny the amazing climaxes she reached during these sessions with the professor. Lovers for many years, they both knew exactly what turned the other on, and both had thoroughly explored their sexual fantasies and lusts completely over this time.

As he fully expected, the security camera picked Celia up at just after five past three as she entered his back garden through the discreet passage hidden amongst the greenery at the back of the college. She beeped the intercom and waited for the door mechanism to allow her in. A full 30 seconds later there had been no response so Celia tentatively buzzed again, looking expectantly at the small camera placed above her head. The door immediately sprang open and she walked into his lobby, then pushed the door that opened into the huge lounge and study wherein Stones 'entertained his guests', as he liked to jest. As she entered a large hand grabbed her by the neck and pulled her across the room before throwing her down over his desk.

"Keep me waiting, then stand there buzzing impatiently, you tardy excuse for a woman," Stones said as he yanked her summer dress up over her back and head, exposing the uncovered glory of her bottom unadorned by panties. He snatched the bag she was carrying out of her hands, put one giant hand down hard on her back, preventing any escape, and then started to systematically spank the backs of her legs. Fully aware that this was a very painful way to begin a beating, he ignored her bottom so that her sexual desire wasn't fuelled, and was not at all surprised to hear her scream and beg for mercy.

"Please, Edward, not there, it hurts, it stings, it's too early for that," she implored.

"Should have thought of that before you tried playing games with me, shouldn't you? And I'll remind you to call me Dean, Professor Stones, or sir, you irreverent little hussy," shouted the professor as his hand came down again and again on the backs of her scarlet thighs.

Celia conceded defeat, lay bent over the table, stunned, struggling to get her breath, tears still rolling down her face, confirming the professor's ability to still manage to inflict unexpected pain on her after the many sessions they had been though together. She would have had no qualms about why she was there, of course, and Stones had long ceased trying to understand what drove her to long for this fake, abusive, and quite violent treatment from a colleague who, in truth, was a dear and trusted friend. Clearly she recognised that there were joint rewards for both of them in this relationship and that they trusted and respected each other implicitly. Stones had learned very quickly how to read her and always deliver what she wanted from him, albeit she had admitted that she did not necessarily know it was exactly what she wanted at the time! At the moment her legs would be stinging phenomenally but even so, Stones could see that despite her protestations implying that there was no sexual gratification on her part from this treatment, her vagina was decidedly telling a story all of its own. As he paused in his administrations he looked down at the slickness shining from her thickening labial lips, in awe of her sexual wantonness despite the clear distress he had caused her.

"You slovenly, ungrateful and horrible little hussy," he roared, as she stood and turned.

The flimsy dress fell back into place, although not for long as with one massive paw Stones grabbed a fistful of her dress and ripped it from her body. Tossing the torn garment aside, he continued to berate her.

"Look at me, not at your whore's outfit. No knickers, no shame, no morals. What a dirty little slut. Come over here now." He dragged her across to a clear space in the room and peeled back the rug to access two covered little compartments built into the wooden floor. Within seconds Celia's ankles were cuffed to the exposed metal rings beneath the wooden hatches, her legs spread apart, her hands forced to the top of her head as she struggled to keep her balance. Stones went to his desk and flicked at his keyboard, causing two chain cuffs to drop from the false ceiling. Moments later Celia stood vulnerable, posed in a crucifixion stance, spread-eagled upright and virtually unable to move.

"No blindfold for you today, bitch," he snarled. "I want you to see exactly what is going to happen to you. I want you to fully appreciate the swish of the lash, the flight of the cane, the rushing, oncoming breeze of the thick strap heading towards your naughty little backside. Oh, how you are going to sob. How you are going to shriek. How you are going to suffer. You filthy, disgusting little pig."

Professor Stones turned to his cabinet, selecting the item he called his lash, a thin belt-like strap of leather with three twisted cut ends that was often assumed to be a touch lighter on impact than expected. The three ends made it similar in look to a cat of nine tails, but the strips of leather were thicker and, if used correctly, the effect of the three ends landing could be quite substantial. Raising the lash high above his head and out of Celia's view, Stones brought it down unexpectedly across the top of her shoulders. Completely unprepared, Celia shrieked with shock and pain and then immediately again as the next stroke followed across the backs of her upper legs without giving her any chance to prepare. He showed her no mercy as the next stroke then landed on her lower back before the fourth finally cracked across the more expected target of her buttocks. The next four strokes followed exactly the same pattern with Celia now streaked with multiple vivid red stripes from her neck to her calves and helplessly weeping. The last four strokes were lashed with force across her bottom, which bucked pointlessly, attempting avoidance as her bindings held her in place.

"That's your first twelve then, slag. Now thank me properly."

Celia took a deep breath, controlled her crying and spoke calmly. "Thank you so much, sir, for my whipping that I truly deserved. If sir wishes to thrash me more, then I would very much like to receive further punishment that my disgraceful wilful attitude and conduct deserve, please."

She tensed in anticipation as she heard the professor return to the cabinet.

"Oh dear God, what am I doing? Oh my word," Celia whispered as she heard the clatter made as her tormentor swapped over his punishment tools.

She almost screamed as Stones leant in and began gently kissing the back of her neck. His arms snaked around her and he held her breasts in his hands, kneading then lightly and then beginning to twirl her stiff nipples between his fingers. Celia relaxed, his intention for her to assume that he had not brought an instrument of torture over from the cabinet fuelled by both his hands bring occupied, little realising that there was a long, flat, thick wooden paddle in his trouser belt. Celia tried to push her bottom back into his groin as her arousal grew and her sexual state heightened, her recovery from the pain of a beating as impressive as always.

"I am so wet for you, my love," were probably not the finest choice of words for that moment as she let her guard down.

In one sweeping movement Stones stood back, pulled the paddle from his belt and landed it squarely across her bottom.

"Yaaaaar! No, you utter bastard!" Not the wisest retort which soon earned her three quick hard slaps on each cheek and a rapidly reddening bottom.

"Waaaaaaaaaaaaaaaaah!" became one long scream of agony as the harsh pain of the six strokes registered. He made Celia wait for the final five strokes, biding his time, swinging the paddle backwards and forwards behind her, the rushing air cooling her cheeks but making her keep tensing in expectation.

"Just ask nicely when you want them," he tormented her. "I am happy to wait for your request for me to continue."

As he knew it would, her desire soon won over any battle with her discomfort.

"Please spank me, sir, please beat this naughty girl's bottom good and hard."

He didn't hesitate and brought the paddle down onto the middle of her bottom, on exactly the same spot, five times as Celia's strangled screams of anguish filled the room. Slumping to the degree that she was allowed by her bindings, Celia drooped, beaten and conquered again by this man of scorn and ridicule, this defiler of her body, this splendid monster of a man, this brute, her hero.

"Do stand up straight," he ordered. "Standards are important, let's have some decorum. I'll fetch the cane now, shall I?"

Celia straightened up, gulping for air.

"Oh lord, yes sir, please sir, I would like to be caned now, Dean, if you would be so very kind."

Normally caned bent over, her skin tight across naked buttocks, as Professor Stones had always demanded, meaning little padding or fat protection as her cheeks would be stretched taut, Celia might wonder whether the impact would be seriously lessened in her current upright position, her full cheeks softening the blow. As the first stroke whistled through the air and struck home high on her bottom at beginning of her arse crack, she would have no future cause to ponder on this point. Taking the cane on the highest point of her buttocks put paid to any thought of a caning of less severity. The breath shot out of Celia as the pain etched into her brain, causing her to issue a low guttural groan. She would not have been surprised to find that the next whistle was followed with the cane striking her at terrifying pace on the very lowest point of her cheeks. Stones was certain that without the restraints she would have been unable to hold any sort of standing position, as her body bucked and twisted pointlessly in an attempt to avoid the cut of the cane.

"Fucking hellfire!" was her response as again tears began to flow.

The next eight cracks of the cane landed full onto the central part of her splayed buttocks. Closely grouped together, the welts joined forces to form one long ridge of raised, angry flesh across her rear. This was Stones giving her what she most desired; he knew Celia's favourite form of corporal punishment was to be caned and with her low mewing as he applied the cane, he recognised the signs of her rising sexual desire. The last two strokes replicated the first two, landing high and low on her cheeks again, the searing pain evidenced by the high-pitched scream in response.

"A good thrashing, well delivered, my sweet, if I say so myself.

What do you say now, slattern?"

Stones grinned wickedly as he watched her struggle to pull herself together and override the burning sensation in her bottom to force out an answer.

"Oh, my. Thank you, Dean. Thank you so much for caning my naughty bottom, sir, and please, sir, now would you like to give me a thorough flogging with the thick heavy strap, sir? A naughty girl needs to be beaten hard, sir."

He was impressed as she nearly choked on the words but still managed to deliver them with stoicism and resolve as he stroked her throbbing buttocks and murmured the kind of endearments she rarely heard, but so longed to hear from him.

"Of course I will, sweetheart, especially as you have been such a good girl so far in taking your punishment," causing Celia to sigh at the combined soothing hands now slipping between her legs to toy with her pussy and the loving words that, as usual, had the power to seduce her. As always, though, he lured her into a false sense of security, even as he so softly fingered her well juiced and slippery clitoris and reached around her to stroke a breast he quietly continued. "Yes, as you've been such a good girl I am going to flog you extra hard and, as an additional treat, I will try my hardest to place every stroke of the strap on the same place to intensify the sensation."

Celia's response was a tremor that ran through her whole body. She, like virtually all others who had suffered the heavy strap, the professor's favourite improver, was in awe of its bite. Her fear apparent at the prospect of twelve on the same spot, but well used to his ways, she automatically answered with the words to appease him. Her lengthy and humiliating punishment at his hands most recently had included a thrashing with the heavy strap that had brought her to tears at the end of the most severe flogging she had ever suffered. This, however, was a thrashing that incorporated sexual activity and blissful erotic moments, unlike that punishment beating, and they both knew that the pleasure of the experience would outweigh the pain as Celia had long ago accepted that the two were entwined as far as her sex life requirements went. That said, Celia had admitted to him that she still masturbated at the memory of that incredible severe beating combined with the additional factor of a superb orgasm being given to her by an unknown female guest, whom the professor had brought into the session whilst Celia was bound and blindfolded. Celia could not deny the fact that the more severe and painful the punishment the higher her sexual desire was driven, and the more exhilarating the climax that followed.

"Oh yes, sir. Thank you, sir. I am ready to be flogged now please, sir," Celia replied, even though that meant he would remove his hands that had taken her close to orgasm.

Stones smiled in satisfaction. He sometimes viewed her as a star pupil that he had trained to perfection.

Without further ado he marched over to the cabinet, unhooked the thick strap, and returned without breaking stride, swinging it straight away hard and true across her bottom. Before Celia had managed to let rip the first of many screams he hit her again, repeating the blows at rapid speed with all twelve landing precisely, as intended and targeted, on the already swollen central ridge across her buttocks. The air was filled by a screaming Celia, bucking and wriggling as the first lashes landed and continuing throughout the phenomenal harsh and severe beating, and for several seconds after Stones had actually returned the strap to its hook. Walking past the wailing woman, the professor went straight to the kitchen and came back with a full-sized pizza board in his hand.

"I am waiting for your thanks, young lady," he snarled threateningly.

"Oh, sir. So sorry, sir. Oh, sir, it hurts it hurts, sir. Oh my. Ooooh, sir. Sorry, sir. Jesus and Mary, of course I thank you, sir, yes thank you. Oh my poor bottom, sir. Shit, fuck and bullocks."

"Hmmm. Slovenly, Celia. Slovenly and rather offensive actually. However, I think we will just round up to the overall fifty mark with a final two. Pull yourself together. Good girl, hold tight and…"

With that he landed an almighty slap on her bottom with the pizza board, which was as big as the target area.

Celia reacted as though she had just sat on an oven top as her whole bottom experienced the stinging pain all over. The professor paused, allowing her to recover, and then with an almighty swing applied the final blow, causing her buttocks to completely flatten and Celia to screech in banshee fashion. It was a minute or two later before she was able to speak and gasp out her final platitudes of gratitude.

"Oh, sir, can I thank you sincerely and honestly for such a beautiful beating, sir. It was wonderful, sir, thank you so much."

Stones released her from her bindings.

"Good girl. The bidet is full of iced water so go and sit in it for a few minutes to calm your buns. I will get us a glass of nice wine and take it through to the bedroom. You may join me and come and sit on my face when you are ready, Celia."

When she entered the bedroom, her bottom calmed and cooled, a naked Stones was laying on his back, his erection standing tall and proud. Ignoring the explicit pornographic film playing on the huge screen at the bottom of his bed, Celia climbed on top of him and slowly dropped her red and beaten flanks towards his waiting face. Stones grasped her sore bottom cheeks firmly, parting them to peer at the dark centre of the valley of her cleft, and the sheer forest of black curly hairs that hid the secret entrance. It was like being reacquainted with an old friend, thought Stones lustily as he positioned himself to first lubricate his nose by plunging it deeply into the wet treasure trove above him, and then adjusting to allow his mouth access to her moist pussy while his nose settled, as it had done in the past so many times, snugly into her bottom crack, his nose tip just nestling against her lovely, soft and welcoming arsehole. With a free hand he picked up the remote and switched off the anal sex scene and its accompanying soundtrack. *No need to fantasise when the real deal is at hand*, thought Stones.

In a state of pure ecstasy he breathed the raw and primal smell of her in. Each woman's private areas carried their own specific scent, Stones had long ago realised, and to his mind, Celia's was a very strong and pungent smell of moistened skin, sexy sweat and damp soil after rainfall. His tongue began to greedily lap at Celia's slick, hot pussy while his nose edged further into her bottom. Slowly the professor started by gently licking and teasing her outer swollen lips, before working his tongue between them, seeking out the warm, pink, sweet-tasting inner folds. Celia sighed in appreciation, pushing her pussy forward into his face, greedily wanting more. With his face smothered by her love holes, Stones gurgled in pleasure as at last he felt Celia's fingers wrap around his straining hard cock and was able to feel her breath as she knelt to sensually lick the helmet. In heaven with his hands tweaking her nipples, his nose now planted deeply into her arsehole, his tongue darting in and out of her pussy as his chin rubbed against her mound and the small hard nub that forced itself against him as her thrusting body began to settle into the momentum she desired to achieve her orgasm.

Celia noisily sucked the length of his huge cock, struggling to contain the mounting groans building inside, as she lost herself in her increasing intense pleasure, showing that she was ready to let forth her love juices. The professor felt the flutterings of her inners as the flavour changed and he enjoyed that glorious sensation of her pussy sprinkling his tongue with the sweet come of her ejaculation. Her juices almost gushed from her wanton pussy as Stones withdrew his nose from the heat of her dark bottom tunnel, watching in fascination as she treated him to a twitching, palpitating and jiggling display by her arsehole as it conducted an orgasmic dance complementing the shuddering of her climatic pussy. Celia bucked and rocked on his face with a freedom and enthusiasm that he adored as she tightened her lips around his cock and started the hard sucking motion that she knew he loved and that would bring him soon to the edge of his own moment of ecstasy.

As they both paused for breath and Celia's orgasm subsided, Stones gently pushed her down his body as she reached beneath to slip his cock into her in the reverse cowgirl position he loved. He always felt that the length and girth of his cock seemed so out of proportion to the narrow tunnel of her sex but as always he slid straight in, filling her perfectly. He marvelled at the sight of his cock sliding in and out of her dripping fanny whilst she was unreservedly exposing her fully open, beautiful arse crack. He very much doubted that this was a view he would ever tire of. He wetted a finger with saliva and ran the wet digit around her anal ring which immediately twitched and opened in response.

"Yes," she commanded. "Stick it in," and then, "fuck, fuck, fuck, fucking, fuck it, fuck!"

Celia was now yelling incomprehensibly as he did as she wished and unceremoniously rammed his finger to the knuckle up the dark, dank passage before him. His body tensed and then he slammed his flanks upwards, impaling her on his rod as he forced himself deep inside of her. Celia came again to join him in the special moment as he snatched his finger from her arsehole, causing her to scream at that wonderful sensation of pain and pleasure combined and merged into something that was just pure animalistic sex. He slapped her bottom hard as her pussy muscles squeezed and drained his cock.

"Aeeooooww!" she screamed. "Yes, you bastard, spank me, hurt me you fucking cunt."

Celia's obscene sexual vocabulary never ceased to amaze them both during these steamy sessions, as she was known as such a quiet, cultured and reserved lady amongst the college's inhabitants. He duly obliged and spanked her as hard as he could, wondering at her endless appetite for this special pain on her poor thrashed cheeks. As the spanks rang out in the room she pushed down hard, grinding her pussy against him as she reached for yet another orgasm. A final flurry of well delivered spanks to her bottom crack and a few finger flicks to her spasming arsehole, as her muscles contracted involuntarily, caused her to come again, yelling obscenities and insults before slumping down on him.

Feeling his own moment approaching, Stones pulled her off him and threw her onto her back, his arms underneath her spread legs. He lifted them up and wide, Celia grabbed his cock and guided it in to her splayed pussy. Holding her legs high and forced back towards her head, Stones rammed his large penis deep inside her and started to pump, finally searching for his own climax.

Celia was already there yet again. "Yes, yes, yes, oh fucking hell, yes, yes," she screamed as she began a protracted and quite violent orgasm, coming deliciously and copiously, her head spinning, her sore bottom far from her mind but knowing in truth that the intensity of climax owed much to her blood-reddened cheeks. Stones juddered and jerked inside of her, spurting his come deep into her receptive pussy, emptying himself ferociously like a man half his age.

Sipping their wine later they gently kissed and snuggled together, enjoying the moment knowing that they would shortly part company, slipping back into their professional relationship until the next time.

CHAPTER 3

EVA REGINA BUCHMAN AND THE ROWING CLUB FALL-OUT

A new year and a new term, yet only weeks in, serious mischief had taken place and once more the Dean of Discipline was called into action.

Stones assessed the student before him dispassionately and objectively. Eva Regina Buchman, daughter of alumni member Esther Goldstein, celebrated rower at college and now a famed German banker. A 21-year-old economic undergraduate, following her mother's footsteps as vice-captain of the college's rowing team, rugby player and also long-distance runner of note within the wider university. Her physique was admirable, undoubtedly extremely high fitness level, not too far short of a six-footer, broad shoulders and bulging thighs beneath her Lycra. A formidable challenge when it came to corporal punishment, that would appear to be no doubt, although Stones was well aware that some of the hardest nuts he had had to crack, over his long years in charge of college disciplinary procedures, were often not the most physical looking specimens he had dealt with.

"So young Eva, let's hear what you have to say, if you would be so kind. Explain what you did, why you did it and what you think we should do about it. Come on, girl. Expound, please."

Eva took a deep breath and then spoke clearly.

"Sir, I allowed Yuri to pull my strings and reacted to being wound up by resorting to physical violence. I am very sorry, sir, and have apologised to Yuri. It was disgraceful behaviour, especially as Yuri is younger and much smaller than I am. I was completely in the wrong, sir, no excuses and I deserve any punishment deemed to fit the crime, sir. I am aware that this is viewed as a sending down offence, sir, and I am sure that you already know that I have vowed to do anything, anything at all, to avoid that. I have been advised, sir, that if I can convince you that it was an aberration, a most definite one-off, against my natural and evidenced normal behaviour, then sir, you might be kind enough to have mercy and find another way to punish me. Not to beat around the bush, sir, I am volunteering to be thrashed, spanked, caned, whatever. Sir, would you like me to drop my trousers and knickers and bend over now, sir?"

Stones shot a slightly annoyed look at her.

"To start with you can slow down. Things do not just get sorted in minutes, Eva. There's a little journey to take first. However, as you have requested to defrock then yes, strip naked, please. We do not do bottom halves only, here. Fully naked, please, my dear."

There was not a moment of hesitation from the student, so eager to throw herself on the professor's mercy with the gift of retaining her place in the college supposedly on offer. Her previously Lycra-clad body was naked in seconds and Stones found himself having to control his reaction to the sight of the stunning body standing before him. No attempt at covering herself was made, her arms dropped beside her hips, her straight back accentuating the jutting breasts and prominent nipples, her stomach a six pack of absolute perfection in definition, a shaven groin displaying full and bulging labial lips with a protrusive slit housed between muscular large thighs and long athletic legs.

Needing to tear his eyes away from the outstanding beauty of this glorious specimen, Stones gestured for her to turn round. True, he was keen to see the back view of this Adonis but equally because he needed to keep his composure and not let the student notice his admiration and desire. He let out a silent sigh of appreciation at the blemish-free back that rippled with muscular artistry and the two round, taut buttocks that looked as though they had been sculpted from marble.

He decided to let her sweat it out while he gained total control of himself.

"Before you go and stand in the corner to contemplate your situation, I would like to give you an opportunity to explain why you acted as you did."

Half-turning towards him to reply, Eva took a long, deep breath, which Stones could not help thinking enhanced the beauty of her breasts even further.

"Oh, sir, it was nothing. Just changing room banter. Caught me on an off day and I over-reacted. Trivial stuff, sir, I cannot even remember what she said now. Certainly nothing to absolve me from my disgraceful and unforgiveable action. There is certainly no blame to be attached to her. She is a novice rower, sir, and I am much more experienced, I really cannot excuse my behaviour."

Stones studied her for a few seconds. No doubt her response was admirable but his information was that Yuri had been spiteful and malicious in her teasing of the older student. She might have forgiven her but Stones was keen to find out how culpable Yuri had been.

"Into the corner, hands on your head, legs apart, nose to the bookshelves. You can stand there for a while and think about how you have let yourself and the college down with your foul behaviour while I contemplate the limited options that are available to me to deal with such a disgraceful specimen." Stones could not help but grin at the spectacle before him and the thought of the pleasures ahead in applying corporal punishment to such a perfect bottom.

Stones had of course already received the detailed reports from Nina Sparkes, who for the last few years had held the position of Head of River Sports, traditionally known at St. James' as 'Boats'. He was also aware that Nina had not reported the incident directly to him, and he had also summoned her to attend his rooms, to explain her inaction in the matter. This was the second incidence of physical violence at the rowing club boathouse in the space of eight months. Having previously dealt with a rather feisty and truculent student, Olivia Harland, most severely, he was not inclined to believe there was any acceptable reason for him not being informed concerning a similar aberration. Word had reached him through the grapevine, a grapevine that he worked hard to keep active and pertinent, that the incident had been covered up and it had taken a direct email from him to Nina raising the matter before he received the report in response.

An undergraduate who had returned to study first for her Masters and then for a Doctorate, she was one of the handful of St James' students who had been at the college for approaching ten years. Her previously unblemished records as 'Boats' and the success of their rowing teams in University competitions, had assisted greatly in her tenure being extended and the college's willingness to grant her wishes to continue her studies. Albeit Stones was not the only senior figure who ruminated on whether her sporting prowess was given too much weight considering her not so spectacular examination results and feedback on her research projects from some of her tutors.

As Stones tapped out emails and texts to begin the process of Eva's punishment he was impressed to note her steady stance as she stood almost statuesque in the corner of his room for over an hour. He found himself occasionally in a hypnotic state as he feasted his eyes on the glorious form of her bottom and was relieved when his door buzzer sounded and they were joined by the first of his summoned guests.

"Ah. Welcome, Celia. Welcome, Philippa. Do join us and take a seat, just waiting for a couple more to join our little gathering before we get to work on this little issue."

While Celia took in Eva's situation in a glance, a knowing smile on her face, Philippa blanched and looked quickly away from the naked student before colouring as she noted that Stones was taking in her reaction. He was impressed to see no real indication from the student that she was the least bit perturbed or intimidated at the additional presence of senior college personnel in his room. It was not often that one of his unfortunates faced up to their fate and embraced the idea of corporal punishment in such good stead.

"Thank you for attending. The silent embarrassment in the corner is young Eva Regina Buchman who I am glad to report has willingly offered herself up for improvement and retribution by way of a sound thrashing. Very keen to proceed she is too, hence her nakedness already. A fine form and good solid buttocks that look made to take a firm beating, don't you think, Philippa?"

The look of desperation on the face of the college's Graduates Manager, as she attempted to curry favour with the professor, amused him but he kept that emotion inside as she voiced her approval.

"Indeed, Professor Stones, indeed. I only know the briefest detail of her behaviour but thoroughly support you in your aim to nip these problems in the bud. Yes, yes, she must be made to pay for her sins with a good hiding, sir."

Philippa could not hide the wildness in her eyes that belied the conviction of her words, but Stones appreciated that she was at least making an effort to curtail her previously displayed lack of enthusiasm for his methods of chastisement.

"Excellent, Philippa. There might well be an opportunity for you to enforce those fine words with some active participation dependent on how things progress with our expected visitors. It will be useful augmentation to assist in cementing your commitment to our beliefs and ideals, don't you think?"

Her cheeks now bright red, much to Celia's unconcealed joy, she stuttered out a response.

"Oh, um, yes sir. Active participation, I see. Yes, of course, it would be my duty and an honour, sir, thank you."

His grunt was not designed to take away any of her uneasiness in his presence.

The buzzer sounded, much to the obvious relief of the discombobulated Philippa, and Stones moved to release his door electronically. Yuri Ivanov, the victim of Eva's action and a rueful looking Nina Sparkes entered rather tentatively. Both froze when they spotted the naked back view of Eva. Yuri in particular looked ready to run from the room. Stones stepped in quickly using his most perfunctorily tone.

"Right, you two. In the room and over here before my desk. I have some questions to run through concerning the disgrace of Eva. If you could both tear your eyes away from her nakedness and focus on me, please."

The two decidedly uneasy women obeyed without question with nervous glances towards the two senior female staff seated, although Stones was interested to note that Yuri looked the more terrified. He decided to hit hard and fast.

"Right, Yuri. Eva Regina Buchman's university life is hanging by a thread because she got so angry that she slammed you up against a wall in a changing room and had her hands around your throat before throwing you to the floor. Of this I suspect there is no contest from Eva, or indeed our Head of River Sports, Nina?"

Both entranced women nodded in response.

"The question that seems most pertinent to you, Yuri, is why on earth did she do that? I would like to hear from your mouth, what exactly you did to cause this outburst, young lady."

Yuri blanched and Stones knew that his words, carefully chosen as they were, had done the trick and led the student to believe her knew far more than he did. Yuri's rather despairing glance at the naked form of Eva and Nina beside illustrated her rising panic.

At Stones' nod, Celia joined the discussion.

"Now Yuri, take a step forward, please. I don't think you need to be looking at Nina for support. Both myself and Dr. Stanford have been carrying out our own investigations into this matter and I think it is now time for you to come clean and have this matter aired fully."

Stones was thankful that Philippa's surprised response was not noted by Yuri. This was a perfect example of Stones and Celia's intuitive manoeuvring honed by many years of enticing the truth from students.

Yuri took the bait.

"Oh, sir. I am so sorry. I did not mean anything. It was just that I felt that she had been bossing the newbies around all section and I was exhausted and fed up. My mouth just ran away with me. I did not mean it."

Stones stroked his chin as he studied the trembling youngster. A fierce glance across to Nina, whose face was betraying her own growing panic, added to the air of guilt that Stones was sensing from both of them.

"Please do not think of interrupting, Nina. You will be given a chance to speak shortly. We are all eager to hear your explanation for your behaviour in this matter, too."

The loud sob from Nina seemed to be the straw that broke the camel's back as Yuri blurted out her confession.

"I am sorry, sir. I know that my language was appalling and offensive, sir. I did apologise and accepted my punishment. I knew it was wrong, sir."

The sharp intake of breath from Nina earned her a look of such ferocity from Stones that her eyes filled with tears and he could see that her inclination to speak had died under his stare.

"Yes, please expand, Yuri. I wish a complete confession on the words spoken and a brief outline of the punishment imposed. Nina, this will be the last warning I will give you. If you interrupt I will suspend you from the college pending further investigation. No, whatever it is you wish to say will wait until I give you the opportunity to give us an explanation into your actions when dealing with this matter."

A single tear made its way slowly down the trembling student's face. Considered above reproach by so many of his colleagues for far too long in his opinion, Stones had long been keeping his watchful eye and inquisitive ear on the comings and goings at the college's boat club and it looked like his attention was about to bear fruit. Nina mumbled an apology and her head bowed forward in submission as Celia moved to stand close beside her, earning herself a nod of approval from the professor who could see the move had intimidated Nina further.

At a questioning glance from Stones, Yuri continued.

"Oh, sir. Sorry, sir. I used some unforgiveable language concerning Eva's heritage and nationality, sir, which provoked Eva, sir... Oh."

Stones had moved to within a few inches of her, bringing her up short.

"You also need to listen carefully, young lady, or you will find that any punishment you may have received for your offensive outburst will pale into significance with a return to these rooms. I wish to know what Eva did to cause you to react so disgracefully the words that you spoke to her in response, what she did to you and the reason that you received a punishment whilst Eva did not. That is all. Just the truth in a succinct manner. Now please continue."

Yuri's eyes now wide open, Stones could see that she was now determined only to please him and give him what he wanted.

"Oh my, I am so sorry, sir. Yes, of course. All Eva did was drive us hard, sir, and wind us up by insulting us if we did not achieve the targets she set us, sir. I was just exhausted one morning and reacted childishly and rudely, sir. I told her she was a bullying Nazi, sir, and that she would be at home in the SS, sir. It was extremely offensive and rude, sir, as I now know that Eva is of Jewish ancestry and that her family suffered so much during the World War years, sir. Eva just got very cross, sir, and grabbed me by the throat and slammed me against the wall, before throwing me to the ground, sir. As you can see, I am no match for her physically, sir."

She paused as everyone turned their heads to momentarily take in the sight of the muscled rear view of the naked female, who continued to stand stock still in the corner of the room.

Yuri continued, "Then, sir, she pulled me around the room by the hair, shouting at me and slapping my face. It was all my fault, sir, and I knew I was in trouble straight away. I did apologise, sir, to Eva, and Nina when she came in and took Eva away. I understood completely that I was the issue and when Nina said that I could either take a 'Boating' or leave the club, I immediately volunteered to take the punishment, sir."

Stones interrupted her.

"Nina, perhaps you would just explain to all present exactly what a 'boating' consists of. I appreciate that it is an old club tradition for you rowers but let us have your version of what happened to Yuri, please. Try and pull yourself together, Nina. This is the big girls' club now. I will not tolerate you playing the crying for sympathy card."

Nina took a big breath and shook her head a couple of times, before she spoke.

"This is for when there is a serious rule breach in terms of the togetherness of the team, Professor Stones. It is so the club can maintain its own disciplinary code without invoking college processes and the college hierarchy. A 'Boating' is given when the seniors determine that it is necessary to punish a member, instead of the member being expelled from the club and banned from rowing. Yuri volunteered to accept this, sir, so she was stripped naked, tied over an upturned rowing boat and she was beaten on the backside with an old broken oar paddle, sir. She was given six strokes, sir."

"Hmmmm," pondered Stones. "You say that she was given these strokes, Nina, but who by and who else was there?"

"Oh. Er. It was me, sir, and nobody else was present, sir, to save her from more embarrassment."

Nina shuffled from foot to foot and Stones exerted the pressure.

"So, you, a mature and older post-graduate student, asked a young first-year student to strip naked, tied her down over a boat and then proceeded to beat her with no witnesses to ensure fair play. Did you enjoy that then, Nina? Do tell."

Nina stammered, her face now bright red. Yuri was wide-eyed and Stones held his finger up to stop her from interrupting.

"No, sir, of course not. It is just our tradition as a club, sir. The paddle hangs in the clubhouse as it has done for years now, sir. The miscreants' initials are engraved on after the beating, sir, as a sort of badge of honour. It is just to keep discipline in-house, sir, and not get students into more serious trouble. I thought it was fine to do, sir. I did not think the college had a problem as long as the students accepted our process and traditions. I really thought it was the correct thing to do, sir, and Yuri seemed happy to go along with it so that we did not end up, well, like we are now, sir."

Stones moved closer to Nina, further disconcerting the already flustered woman.

"Nina, you seem blissfully unaware that I have been keeping an eye on you since the incident with Najia Ahmed at the start of last year. So let me remind you what occurred. A final-year student, thankfully now graduated with flying colours and already embarking on a good career in medicine, incurred your wrath by continually failing in her duty to prepare the boats properly and was guilty of poor timekeeping. Eventually the team got docked points and this was unarguably Najia's fault for her sloppiness. The team were enraged, and you, as Head of River Sports, felt your authority challenged and acted to discipline Najia to appease her teammates and re-establish your control. Najia accepted the decision to submit to a beating to save her position in the rowing squad. A fearsome beating was handed out as I understand it, with a dozen of you administering two strokes each of the paddle. Your attempts to cover this up were, to say the least, amateurish. A fall down the stairs hardly likely to have caused the extensive damage to her buttocks that the college nurse eventually treated. Najia's silence is to be commended, and never once did she breech her commitment in her misplaced loyalty to the team. Unbeknown to you, Elizabeth, the college nurse, took photographs of the damage, which I have seen. You may sob now, Nina, but my sympathy is with the young lady who suffered a sound thrashing and a total humiliation at your hands over what was basically nothing but minor rule breaches. For your information, I have since had a first-hand account from one of the dozen who delivered the strokes. Luckily, for you, my decision on that matter is that without Najia, the victim of your action, being prepared to speak against you, then, in theory, no rule breaking can be proven to have taken place. Therefore, although that matter has had a bearing on this further issue coming to light, I did not find that I had grounds for disciplinary action in that instance. Today, however, I am having a very differing view. I am very much bothered by the fact that you chose to chastise a fellow student by physical beating, using your position of authority to manipulate her acquiescence when you had her at a distinct advantage. I am not questioning the need for punishment in this scenario, I am not questioning Yuri's decision to accept that the punishment should be of a physical nature considering that the option was expulsion from the club, and I am not questioning that Yuri deserved to be thrashed. However, I do very much question that you took it upon yourself to have Yuri strip naked, that you tied her down and that you beat her with no one else present to ensure that everything was conducted above board. There is nothing in the constitution of the college or the river sports organisation that allows this action to take place, albeit a blind eye may have been turned to action in-house previously. All disciplinary matters come under my auspices, and corporal punishment is only permitted by my hand or under my instruction. Therefore, I find you, Nina Sparkes, guilty of a serious rule breach and ask, at the very least, that you formally and voluntarily submit yourself for disciplinary action to correct and improve your behaviour and help you find redemption. May I take it that you accept my findings and agree to submit to such punishment?"

All composure gone now, Nina looked around at the two senior female members of staff, eyes pleading for help and support.

"Nina Sparkes, do not expect help or indeed mercy, from any member of the team in this room. We are all of one mind here. You have brought disgrace to your position by abusing the powers entrusted in you. You now need to show contrition, own your disgraceful behaviour and seek to make some amends by requesting redemption, correction and improvement. Dr Ford and Dr Stanford are fully behind your defrocking and will assist me in bringing this matter to some conclusion and dispensing a fitting punishment to all concerned."

Stones paused. Celia immediately took her cue.

"Absolutely, Professor Stones. I am disgusted to hear of such behaviour from a long-standing post-graduate student and feel that the only recourse is the highest level of punishment that is within our hands. Clearly our trust has been betrayed and restitution must be sought. Her position is this college, let alone her position with river sports, must be questioned."

Those last words brought forth a loud sob from Nina and a desperate look at her mentor at the college, the post-graduate tutor, Dr Philippa Stanford.

"I am sorry, Nina, but this is unacceptable behaviour. The beating of one student by another is not something I could ever support. Your record at the college in my time here has been impressive, most impressive on the sporting front, although academically you have not excelled. Allowances have been made for you in the past due to your success in the leadership of the rowing team in particular, but I am most disappointed to see evidence of you misusing your authority in this way. To my mind, being sent down and formally dismissed from the college should be the first option in this case and I have little sympathy for you. You have let everyone down and behaved in a manner that I find reprehensible and quite shocking."

Stones' glance at Philippa was one that did not bode well for any post-meeting discussion and she blanched at his clear lack of approval of her words and quickly attempted to dissipate any anger directed at herself.

"So I must second the words of Professor Stones and Dr Ford and recommend that you now be subjected to the full force of disciplinary proceedings. Professor Stones, I of course support any decision you take, whether it be removal of her duties on the river, suspension from the college or the most severe physical chastisement if that is an option available in this instance."

Stones knew full well that Philippa struggled with the college's commitment to corporal punishment as a means to an end, so was pleased to see her rescue her position and gave her a nod of approval. He turned back to the now totally distraught Nina, who was sobbing openly and clasping a tissue to her face.

"Right, young lady, pull yourself together, please. We have a need to have a discussion about where we go from here. Now, as the six of us are together, we can save time by resolving this matter today. I have some busy weeks ahead and it would suit me to take this off any future agenda. But first I am only too aware that poor Eva has been standing quietly and very obviously naked in the corner for a while now. This seems unfair as she now appears to be just one of three very naughty girls, rather than the single miscreant. So if we are all in agreement I believe we should correct this imbalance. Eva, please go and stand beside the chair where your clothes are placed. Everyone agree that she should not have to be on her own in her naked humiliation?"

As Celia turned her head to hide her smirk, knowing full well that Stones was toying with the unfortunate students, and with Philippa nodding in agreement, Stones turned an enquiring look at Yuri and Nina.

"Agreed, ladies?" he enquired.

Both Yuri and Nina spluttered out their affirmative words. *Hook, line and sinker,* thought Stones.

"Excellent, so we are all agreed. Right-ho, get your clothes off quickly and then the three of you can line up in front of us."

Realisation dawned immediately on Yuri and, without hesitation, she began to strip. Nina looked aghast and was decidedly wrong-footed by his ploy.

"But. I thought you meant… Oh no. No. No. No. In front of everyone, surely not. Oh no."

"Quite honestly, Nina, I am having to restrain myself from ripping your clothes off and thrashing your bare backside right at this very moment. So, unless you wish to be escorted back to your room to pack your belongings and leave this institution, you will get your clothes off and do as you are told for the next few hours."

Seconds later the three students were naked, standing with their legs apart and hands on their heads. Yuri gently weeping, Nina trembling visibly and doing her best to control her pitiful sobbing, whilst a much more stoic Eva continued to set the example, her demeanour of one who had already come to terms with her fate.

After a quick conversation in a side room off the main central room, the three senior college figures took their seats in front of the students.

"Firstly, I would like to see the state of Yuri's bottom. I presume that as this only occurred very recently you still have some physical evidence on display. Yes, girl, turn around and bend over, let us see."

A rather red-faced Yuri turned slowly around and bent over. She was a slight, slim brunette with small perky breasts that hosted very small dark nipples, her pubic hair sparse and very wispy. As she bent forward in front of Celia, Stones assessed her buttocks, noting the small firm-looking cheeks and the tight narrow cleft between. As with her pubic hair she had little growth between her buttocks, fair down just tapering down to a small dark slit of an arsehole. There was clear bruising and mottled red marks that suggested that she had been hit with some force. As Celia leaned forward to probe at her injured cheeks, she flinched and yelped in distress.

"Thoughts, Senior Tutor? If she wished to volunteer for the

option of a physical punishment for her part on this debacle, would you think it would be appropriate?"

Celia smiled as she ran her fingers backwards and forwards over the flesh before her. She slapped her right cheek and ordered her back upright and facing her.

"Turn round, girl, and stand up straight. Professor, I think that a damn good over-the-knee spanking would be an adequate punishment taking into account her previous beating. She needs a good wash first, though, rather reeks down below I'm afraid."

Stones smiled approvingly at Celia's words as Yuri's face went through contortions of embarrassment mixed with anger. Yuri was not to know that this was a speciality of the professor. Undermining, demeaning and belittling the unfortunates who crossed his path being a massive part of the ordeal he insisted on putting them through.

"Fair point. If they wish to opt for physical chastisement then they can all have a couple of hours to freshen up. Give them time to think long and hard about what is to come. Always helps to focus their minds first. Yuri, my sentence is that you are to be gated for the rest of term, so no leaving the college grounds between the hours of 8pm and 8am. So, you will be suspended from all sport and all evening social activity for three months. You will therefore lose your place on the rowing team. Do you accept this? Or do you wish to request the option of taking physical punishment in the form of a thrashing applied to your bare buttocks this evening?"

The blood had drained from Yuri's face as he spoke. As Stones had suspected it would be a devastating punishment for her to lose her sports and social privileges. The short sharp shock option had already been taken when Nina had punished her originally so Stones was not at all surprised to hear her decision made quickly and without much thought.

"Oh please, sir. I would like to be thrashed, sir, as my punishment, please. I am so sorry. Yes. Yes. I volunteer to take a beating, sir. Please do not suspend me from the team."

"Eva has already requested a sound thrashing for her part, albeit we have allowed that there was provocation. The fact is that she physically abused a younger and smaller colleague and as such has to face a just punishment. Of course, it remains unexplained as to the reason why Yuri was given a beating by Nina, whilst Eva walked away scot free. Maybe now is the time to discuss what exactly has been going through Nina's mind in all this. Your misdemeanours appear to be mounting in number, my dear, and that means that any punishment you face is likely to be climbing in its level of severity. Take a breath, and compose yourself, Nina, then please enlighten us as to the reasons for your actions and how you feel you should be dealt with."

Nina took the deep breath as requested and Stones studied her. Medium height but as with a lot of the rowing fraternity, well-defined shoulders and an athletic build. Dark haired, with a plentiful growth of pubic hair surrounding quite prominent labia, her strong-looking legs, toned without appearing overly muscular. Her breasts were full and firm looking. Her nipples dark and obvious sitting amidst large pinkish areolae.

"Sir, Dr Ford, Dr Stanford. I am so very sorry that I have let the college down. It really was with the best intentions with a view of putting the team first as we strive to win the annual contest, sir, and earn our place at the national championships. I felt that Yuri had disrespected a senior colleague in the way that she spoke to Eva and I did not think that Eva's reaction was the main issue. Yuri apologised and did accept that she had committed a rules breach, sir, and seemed content that a physical admonishment was fair justice. I realise that I should have kept you informed, as Dean of Discipline, that the punishment had been determined and when it would take place. However, sir, I thought that if you were to agree and indeed attend, then the punishment would seem so much worse and more formal and official if I did so. For Yuri's sake I decided that I would deal with it on my own terms and then the matter could be consigned to history, sir. So, whilst I admit to not following the documented processes, which I agree that I signed up to when I took this post on, I hoped that my record of successful leadership and captaincy in the role had earned me the rights to make certain decisions without going through formal process, sir. It felt just and correct, sir. Yuri and Eva were satisfied with the outcome and until today I very much thought the situation had been handled to the best of my ability. I apologise for taking my role further than I should, sir, but maintain it was for the best possible reasons and for the good of the rowing club and the college, sir."

Stones allowed her words to hang in the air. As was the norm his face was impassive and he kept his eyes firmly fixed to Nina's as she swayed and bit her lip in nervousness.

"Sadly there is a complete lack of contrition, apology and remorse in your fine speech, Nina. Also, and perhaps more importantly, you appear to have opted out of taking the opportunity to offer yourself for punishment. You still seem to have failed to grasp the point that your behaviour was absolutely unacceptable and the main topic of conversation is to what extent you should be punished. So do I assume that you wish to deny culpability and guilt and do not wish to repent and pay your penance? Please enlighten us so that I can take the steps to determine whether you face removal from college, let alone sacking in disgrace as Head of River Sports. Speak!"

Stones had adopted the tone that brooked no argument and had breached the defences of more determined recalcitrant personalities than Nina Sparkes. She proved, as he had anticipated, to lack the will and courage to stand her ground. Her ground being rather flimsy, it was probably a wise decision.

"No, sir. Please. No, I did not mean that. Oh no, I do not know what to say. What do I have to say?" Her desperation was such that she turned to Philippa with pleading eyes. Stones had to smile. In most cases, she would decidedly be the sympathetic one of the three, but in this instance she had taken Nina's supposed treachery to heart.

There was no clemency to found in her heart, although Stones was not convinced that the graduate tutor would be happy to sacrifice the student's future if it avoided her having to play a role in a corporal punishment scenario. Her response was brutal.

"To my mind you should be frogmarched out of the college in disgrace for your appalling behaviour. Anything else is a let-off, a poor second, and far too lenient in my view."

Her words hung in the air, the silence only broken by Nina's weeping, as both Stones and Celia looked at Philippa with raised eyebrows.

"Oh, I am sorry, Professor Stones, I was not disagreeing with you. Well, I meant…" She dried up, her face showing clear signs of panic at the words she had used and the clear stance taken against Stones' rhetoric.

"Thank you for your opinion, Dr Stanford. Duly noted. We will save further discussions for your tenure review meeting, I think."

The comical effect of his words caused Stones to turn away as Philippa's mouth dropped open and tears filled her eyes at the barely disguised threat to her own future at the college.

"I am so sorry. Of course, she must be thoroughly thrashed, Professor Stones. Of course. Of course. She needs a harsh lesson and something to remember for a long time. Yes. Yes. Yes. She must be flogged!" Philippa's desperate attempt to curry favour earned her raised eyebrows from Celia and a look of clear disdain from Stones, her deepening misery at her incongruent words soon apparent.

"I think the important thing here is what Nina proposes. I am happy that Yuri has requested and agreed to a sound bare-bottom spanking and that Eva is willing to request a paddling followed by a hard caning for her part. However, the real villain of the piece is you, Nina. So, what do you propose for your own punishment? I have options such as my spanking machine that can deliver up to 500 strokes at a time, I have suspension and floor rings so that you can be spread-eagled in standing or bending-over positions for a series of thrashings with a variety of instruments. I have my caning desks that you can be tied down over, my gym horse that is excellent at adding to the tautness of protruding splayed buttocks for extra impact and I have my chain and cuff table that exposes you in all glory for an intimate flogging. Such a choice. What do you think, Nina? What do you deserve?"

Nina's face was a picture of horror as Stones moved around the room exposing his contraptions from their secreted places and opening his cabinet of punishment implements, which drew sharp intakes of breath from all three students. As he slowly unhooked his contraption, with the massage table and the hanging straps and chain, Nina began to tremble visibly.

"I see you are impressed by my special table here. I am very proud of this one, Nina, come over here and have a closer look."

Nina's steps were tentative and slow as she made her way beside Stones, weeping quietly. He decided to put her out of her misery.

"As it happens, I think that we will hold this little beauty in reserve for now."

Her responding face was one of such utter relief that Stones could not resist toying with her a bit longer.

"However, young lady, I think you should go through the motions of experiencing its delights even if we do not actually apply the actual punishment. Just so as you have an idea of what awaits if you again step out of line. Celia, Philippa can you assist and we will give Yuri and Eva a little show for everyone's benefit. Now Nina, as long as you are a good girl and do as you are told, then this is just for show and no punishment will be applied. So play along and let my colleagues here put you in position as though you are to face the music. Ho-ho, ladies, what fun!"

Stones chortled away as the terrified but acquiescent Nina allowed herself to be manoeuvred onto the structure that Stones lowered from its secreted cupboard door. Nina's squeaks of fear and panic-stricken eyes were exactly the reaction he had wanted and he gestured the other two naked females over to join them as Celia began to winch the supine Nina's spread legs up into the air.

As Celia propped Nina's head up and stood away, the horror of Nina's position obviously hit her. Three very senior college members and two aghast younger colleagues stood between her splayed and fastened legs, her knees pulled up towards her shoulders, her head propped up so that she was directly facing the peering faces, her bottom clear of the table and pointing up towards her audience.

"Excellent, excellent, Nina. Now ladies, you see how her bottom cheeks are pulled taut, her cleft wide apart, her anus winking and twinkling away amongst her little garden of hairs, her vagina fully on show, plump labia lips for the world to see. This is the target area." His hands stroked her cheeks. "Although if she is really naughty, I have a handy little knotted lash that can be applied to the most delicate areas. Not much of a treat, I can assure you." To a high-pitched yelp from Nina he ran a finger alongside her vagina and right around to the top of her wide open bottom crack.

"Anyway, enough of this amusing interlude. Unhook her, ladies. I think it is high time that these three sat down and wrote me a script for the punishments that they have chosen and volunteered to undergo. Nina, I hope you take the hint. I expect to see the desk, the rings and the spanking machine feature in your request. You have ten minutes to compose an acceptable written request for corporal punishment, citing your misdemeanour, your remorse and your proposal of chastisement to attain full forgiveness, contrition and behavioural improvement. No need to wax lyrical. A quick confession, apology and plea for punishment will suffice. If all is acceptable then we will reconvene in a couple of hours to sort things out and put things right. Off you go, ladies. No time to lose!"

The three scurried over to the desk where Celia had laid out pens and paper. Eva and Yuri started writing immediately while the forlorn and still crying Nina just stared at the paper.

"You seem reluctant to go along with things, Nina. Unfortunately, ladies, life is not always great, not always fun and we do not always get what we want. If you act atrociously then anguish is inevitable in response, you must learn to expect disappointment, it will come, people will let you down, misfortune is quite normal, success is exceptional and often a reward for effort. Attainment is earned, not given freely, patience is a virtue, frustration is to be controlled and violence is not the answer in everyday life. Punishment is essential to maintain control, order and civilised behaviour. That punishment is sometimes by nature and most appropriately of a controlled physical nature. Lessons can be learned, wrongs corrected, improvement made. Chastisement combined with humiliation can bring honour and humility, remorse and contrition. From this, a better understanding of how to deal with the upturns and downturns of life will be installed. A sharp lesson for the three of you now may lead to better decisions in the future. This is what we hope. Remember this and you will be more prepared than most people and maybe better able to cope. So, your bare buttocks will be soundly thrashed at your behest and with your permission, co-operation and approval. You will be in a great deal of discomfort and shame. You will feel inconsequential and you will suffer degradation. You will, however, be taught a valuable lesson. This is both your punishment and your reward. I would expect you all to be very thankful on completion."

At a nod from Stones, Celia began to whisper into Nina's ear. Stones did not need to hear the implicit threatening words as he saw Nina jolt, grab hold of the pen and finally begin to write.

CHAPTER 4

EVA, NINA AND YURI DULY PUNISHED

Several minutes later the three stood before the seated Stones, flanked by the standing Celia and Philippa, as Stones read out their finished papers.

"Good job, Yuri. I concur that a sound spanking on your bare buttocks is an acceptable offer. You will receive 50 spanks each from the hands of myself and Dr Ford, as requested. Eva, I accept your proposal that you receive a paddling of 30 strokes followed by a 20-stroke caning. Dr Ford will paddle your buttocks and I will unleash the cane immediately after. Nina, you will need to add in some more specific figures, but in principle, I am content that you have offered us an acceptable physical punishment rather than face expulsion. You will now make the following amendments to your script to meet the level of chastisement that fits your crime. You will specify that you would like to receive a 300-stroke beating from the spanking machine, followed by Dr Stanford giving you an over-the-knee spanking of 100 slaps, before I finish off by having you tied down over the gym horse for a sound dozen or so strokes from my favourite thick leather strap. You will arrive 15 minutes in advance of the other two reprobates to get your ordeal underway on the machine, and give them a good idea of what a thrashed bottom looks like, before I allow you to recover somewhat to prepare for your spanking. Do not speak, Nina, please, I can see you are struggling to maintain your dignity and I advise you not to stretch my patience any further. Dr Ford will take you back to the desk to finish your request to my satisfaction now. You two can put your clothes on and be back here at seven o'clock precisely, washed and scrubbed clean, empty bowels and bladders, suitably attired and without any electronic devices, all set for your requested discipline."

Yuri and Eva did not need a second opportunity, and with indecent haste threw their clothes on and scurried from the room. Nina forlornly returned to the desk with Celia muttering sharply into her ear as she picked up the pen once more.

Stones meanwhile had wheeled the spanking machine into position and proceeded to set up the apparatus, tormenting Nina by swishing the leather-covered cane through the air before attaching it to the equipment.

"One every six seconds, changing position each stroke, but repeating the landing target every 20 strokes seems a good programme, don't you think, Dr Stanford?"

"Yes sir, indeed. That will take a good 30 minutes, Professor Stones, a bit longer if you allow a break or two. I think she will remember that she has been beaten after that."

A sobbing Nina was handing Stones her rewrite, eyes fixed on a spot away from the machine as he flicked the switch and the cane whipped through the air. Stones held a cushion in front of the cane as it reached the pinnacle of its sweeping arch, the loud impact noise producing a yelp in response from the despairing looking Nina.

"Imagine that lovely thwacking sound decorating the atmosphere of this room 300 times, my girl. That is your fate, your punishment and your path to redemption. Yes, the backs of your legs and your buttocks will be ablaze. Yes, you will be in pain and discomfort for a long time. Yes, a damn good old-fashioned spanking by my colleague here, once you have recovered enough to feel the benefit, will reignite those feelings as you suffer the humiliation of being treated like the naughty little girl you have been. Yes, 12 strokes of my heavy strap will make you think that what has gone previously was a not such a big deal after all. But, my dear, and this is the important point, once this is complete you will have embraced contrition, salved your conscience, fulfilled your duty of paying for your sins and you will have been released from your guilt, your honour restored, and your behaviour going forward will illustrate the improvement that a fair and just chastisement brings forth."

There was not a thing in the demeanour of the stricken student that supported his flowery words but Stones was not daunted. His belief in the act of corporal punishment to improve behaviour was based very much on the records he could show to prove his point and the testament of former students who had incurred his displeasure over the years, taken their punishment and almost without fail had later acknowledged the valuable lesson they had learned.

His thought process though was interrupted by Celia, who had, unfortunately for Nina, overheard her muttered response to the professor's rather lyrical waxing.

"Oh dear, Professor Stones, Nina has expressed the view that what you propose is barbaric. Oh dear, oh dear, oh dear."

Aghast at her words being heard, Nina turned her distraught face to Stones.

"Oh no, I did not mean it. I am so sorry. It just slipped out. 300 strokes, sir, 300. It sounds an impossible punishment to bear though, sir. I am sorry. I am sorry."

Stones marched over to the student and spun her round.

"Dr Ford, bend her over, head between your knees. Nina, arms locked around Dr Ford's legs, bottom up. Dr Stanford, please sit down here and hold her legs wide open. You will now receive two hard strokes with my strap as a reminder of when to keep your mouth closed and your ignorant thoughts to yourself." Stones moved to the cabinet and unhooked his strap as he spoke.

Taking a step back, he tapped Philippa on the head to keep herself out of his line of sight and his arm went back high with the thick leather poised. As Nina began to sob and incoherently blubber pleas for mercy, he unleashed the strap.

Thwack!

There was a moment's pause.

"Aaaaaaaaeeeeeeeeee!" Nina's scream was ear splitting and Stones paused with his arm raised again. He waited for the moment that the trapped woman's legs ceased their trembling and Celia steadied her body within her iron grip, and he swung for the second time.

Thwack!

Two inches lower than the fierce red stripe already formed, the blow flattened the lower cheeks of the captive student.

"Aaaaaaaaaaaaaaaaaaaaaeeeeeee! No, aaaargh! Oooooooh!"

Stones strode over to his cabinet and replaced the strap.

"Release her, ladies, thank you."

Nina dropped to the floor and curled into a ball, weeping copiously, her hands now grabbing at her bottom.

"That should give you food for thought about what is to come. Now get your clothes on and get out. You have not much more than 90 minutes before we start the main course. You heard what I said to the others, washed and scrubbed up, bowels and bladder empty. Simply dressed, no electronic devices, just a compliant, ashamed and remorseful offender ready and willing to take her dues, pay the price and move on with her life. A life that hopefully will be more fulfilled and complete thanks to the corrective action we have put in place. Dr Stanford will now escort you back to your room and collect you later. We do not want you making matters worse by being late or reluctant to attend, do we now?" He chuckled away as Philippa took the half-dressed student by the arm and led her towards the door.

"Good idea, Dr Stanford. No harm in any passers-by seeing her taken from my quarters in a state, is there? We will see you back here shortly, Philippa, a coffee or a glass of wine will await to help us pass the time before we wreak havoc on the buttocks of our three miscreants. Indeed, indeed."

As arranged, Philippa brought a subdued Nina back at the agreed time. Stones decided not to prolong the terrified students' wait. He had planned the evening to ensure that Nina was part way through her initial thrashing when the other two were scheduled to arrive, and had another issue he wanted to take up with the college's river sports leader in the meantime.

"Please divest yourself of your clothing and stand facing us with your legs apart and your hands on your head," he snapped.

Nina's eyes were transfixed on the spanking contraption, the leather-wrapped cane poised high in the sir, as she slowly removed her clothes. Nothing was said as the red-faced student tried to compose herself and adopt the position as commanded. Opening her legs wide with her damp flattened pubic hair rather causing her prominent labia to be even more obvious than earlier, Stones noted that he was not alone in focusing his eyes on the blatant display of her sex. Stones wondered if she was aware of the rather stunning sexual exhibition this created combined with the full breasts, dark nipples and wide pink areolae.

"Pits and orifices, please, Philippa," Stones said as he tore his eyes away from the beauty before him.

Philippa's grimace was spotted by both her colleagues, but she rose and obediently sniffed at Nina's exposed armpits as she reluctantly played the game and tried to pass the test that Stones realised she was fully aware of, albeit neither would acknowledge it.

Philippa took her time moving her head down to Nina's pubic region, the student taking in a deep breath as she attempted to suffer the indignation without comment or reaction. An obvious deep intake of breath was taken before the college's Graduate Manager moved behind Nina and bent down once more.

"Please bend over, Nina, and make it easier for Dr Stanford to check you out." Stones' cold toneless voice brooked no argument. A gulp from Nina but no resistance as she acquiesced. Philippa's face coloured somewhat but adopted a resigned acceptance of her role.

There was a distinct pause before tentative fingers were placed on Nina's taut buttocks and Philippa dipped her head, taking a far less obvious sniff as her face dropped to Philippa's open anal cleft.

"All in order, Professor Stones. Rather citrus heavy all round, I would have thought." Patting Nina's cheeks to release her from the subservient pose, Philippa and Nina returned to their previous positions.

"Before we begin your thrashing, young lady, I just want to clarify a point that has been bothering me." Stones' words sounded innocent enough and Nina seemed to grasp at the opportunity to put off the moment when her punishment began, her facial expression of one eager to please. It was not to last.

"You are, I believe, a person who has been in single-sex relationships during your time here. Can you confirm this for me, please?"

Nina looked aghast. He sensed her quite natural response would have been to tell him to mind his own business, but she was naked and about to receive a monumental beating, and wisdom prevailed.

"Yes, sir, not at present, but I have had two lesbian relationships with other students in my time here. I am not sure why this is relevant, sir, if you don't mind me saying."

Stones smiled as he responded, "Oh, I don't mind at all. However, I was wondering how much of a sexual thrill it was for you, alone with a tied-down, naked, young student about to abuse your position and beat her buttocks. Had you been fantasising over what it would be like? Were you wet while you beat her? Did you masturbate at the clubhouse or wait until later back in your room?"

Stones was not in the least bit surprised to see the colour drain from the student's face. Her eyes filled with tears as she spluttered to deny his accusations.

"No, no, no, sir. It was not like that. I did not. I did not. Oh no. No, that is not right, sir. Please, sir."

Stones stroked his chin and indicated Celia beside him.

"You may not know this, Nina, but Dr Ford here, is an expert in body language and the science behind the human condition when lying. I believe that there are over 30 tell signs when someone is lying, Dr Ford, so shall we ask Nina some further questions to help you in your analysis?"

Celia's smile was enough to freeze Nina. Stones watched as the student seemed transfixed by the steely gaze Celia was imposing on her.

"Oh, she is undoubtedly lying, Professor Stones, but let us just see how long it takes for her to realise that honesty might be a good policy. You did indeed enjoy your little performance with the unfortunate Yuri. It was written all over your face when we spoke earlier. I am just not yet sure whether this was the plan all along and you were thoroughly abusing your position to an almost illegal level, or whether this was just an added benefit to what you saw as punishment. That is understandable, we are all sexual beings and Yuri is a very pretty little thing who deserved to be punished."

Stones could have applauded Celia's performance as he saw the light appear in Nina's eyes at the supposed understanding and possible sympathy in Celia's words.

"Yes, Dr Ford, that's it. I definitely had no intentions towards her and the punishment was just exactly that. But, I have to admit that it did arouse me somewhat when I was giving her the beating. I swear it was never intended to be a sexual experience in the slightest though."

It was obvious to the three academics the exact moment Nina realised that she had just been played and hoisted by her own petard. She stopped talking, her eyes flicked from each of them in turn, her face coloured further and her mouth dropped open. Celia continued the probing, her victim now completely on the ropes.

"Tell us how you felt, Nina. There is redemption here and you will not be in further trouble. You have just confirmed what we thought and I think you will find that your harsh punishment ordained is because Professor Stones has taken this into account already.

Honesty, and total honesty only, is the route now that will bring this matter to an end today. Any deviation from the truth that I see now will present us with further problems as to your future. So, take this final opportunity, Nina. How did you relieve the most impure thoughts that this incident unleashed? Full confession only accepted, last chance saloon, I think. Do you agree, Professor Stones?"

A curt nod from Stones and Nina grasped the lifeline hanging before her.

"I swear to you that I had nothing planned. It was definitely not sexual at all to begin with. I don't know what else to say. I promise you that there really was no sexual element to her beating, sir. It was a punishment. I realise that I should not have done it and maybe should have reported the incident now, sir. I am sorry. I did get it wrong but for the best of reasons."

Stones looked at Celia who took the hint and, with a dismissive gesture at Nina, rather sealed her fate.

"Started well, now avoiding the question and lying, Professor Stones. Any more chances, sir, or shall I strap her down? I presume that she is making a good case for the punishment to be doubled or possibly repeated at a later date until she can bring herself to tell the truth?"

The gasp from Nina earned raised eyebrows from Stones and an indication that she could speak. His gesture alone conveyed the message that she had just about run out of options to pacify him.

"Oh, lord. I am so sorry. Yes, yes. I was turned on once I had her strapped down and helpless, and I was aroused when I had completed the beating, sir. Yes, yes, I admit that I masturbated thinking about it afterwards, sir. I am so sorry but please believe me that it was not a ruse to be alone with her naked or anything like that. I know that it was inappropriate but that thought process started after I had agreed the punishment with her, sir. It was not pre-planned. Oh, lord. I am so sorry, I do see what it looks like."

Celia laughed and moved forward to take the sobbing student's chin into her hand.

"I wonder whether your dirty little fingers will be up your fanny wanking away tonight after we have finished with you. What do you think, Professor Stones? Are we not just giving her another sexual fantasy to wank herself off over?"

"Thanks for your input, Dr Ford. That will do for now. I think we all get the picture thanks to your graphic description. Nina, I will allow you to forego the promised spanking as a nod to your honesty, albeit rather belated and drawn out, but woe betide you if you do not behave during your punishment. I would be perfectly happy for you to have your spanking at any point. Let us proceed with the beating. Please strap Nina down now in place for my little machine here to start its work. Time is slipping away and I want her to be experiencing her requested chastisement when the other two arrive. Nina, I will ponder as we proceed on what you have admitted and consider whether or not this evening's process is severe enough to equate to the misdeeds committed and confessed to. Winch the seat up nice and high please, Dr Ford. That's it, wide open legs, bottom cheeks split and nice and taut all ready. Chin on the support please, Nina, we would like to see your face as you receive the strokes. All set and time for the off, I think."

Stones leaned forward and flicked a switch. He had programmed the spanking machine before her arrival and with a loud whirring sound the metal arm holding the cane moved back and then whipped down with force to land across the centre of the exposed and defenceless bottom before it. The double-wrapped leather surrounding the rattan cane, both protected the buttocks from the cutting edge of the wood and slightly cushioned the blow, so that it was nowhere near as fearsome as uncovered wood. It was designed for multiple blows that would blemish and sting but with no danger of cutting the skin. None of this mattered one jot to Nina, though, as the crack of the first impact hung in the air before she yelped as the bite registered in her mind. As promised the cane pulled back and slashed down every six seconds, each blow landing millimetres below the previous one as it began its programme. Stones moved and bent behind Nina, his facial expression one of pure satisfaction as the swish through the air and the crack of the landing of each strike brought higher pitched yelps from fastened miscreant. On the thirtieth stroke, which landed towards the middle of the backs of her legs, the machine visibly adjusted and then slashed down at the very highest point of the buttocks before it, a bright red line at the point of the start of her anal cleft. The resulting screech brought forth nods of approval from all three watchers. Nineteen strokes later, the first 50 were completed as the rod landed on the only tiny white strip left on her buttocks just above where the torture had started for Nina. Her bottom was now bright red, from the very top to halfway down her upper thighs and the howls and distraught facial features of Nina illustrated a job being successfully executed if not yet completed.

Stones paused and inspected the damage done to the embattled buttocks. The muscle-developing nature of the work that most of the members of the rowing club religiously performed nearly every single day of their time in college, meant that the women were strong and muscular and tended to carry very little spare fat. Not exactly an advantage when you are bent over, your skin is stretched tight and a cane is striking hard against unprotected flesh. Stones traced his fingers along some of the more prominent rising welts causing the sobbing Nina to flinch at his every touch. Celia moved forward with a box of tissues in hand to wipe Nina's tears and, always a humiliating twist that Stones enjoyed, hold the tissue close so that the miscreant could blow their nose and have it wiped dry.

"Oh please, Professor Stones, I have learned a lesson. Could we stop this now? It hurts so very much. I do not think I can bear much more." Nina ventured words that caused a loud snort from Celia and the cutting response from her tormentor.

"Please do not be so ridiculous, Nina. We have barely begun. Trust me, young lady, you have a long way to go before we reach an unbearable point. Now settle down, my little machine is primed to continue."

The whirring of the machine caused Nina to tense her bottom cheeks dramatically as the cane swished through the air to land at the exact starting spot from the previous series of strokes. Nina's screams began anew as the cane whipped down again and again, repeating the pattern of the previous set.

After 30 strokes Nina's head dropped down and the screams merged into one long low yell, broken only by spluttering gasps of breath. The buzzer sounded to announce the arrival of the other two unfortunates and Stones nodded to Philippa to allow them in as the machine continued its relentless abuse of the student's thoroughly flayed buttocks. To Stones' amusement Eva and Yuri both stopped at the same moment, frozen in place by the tableau presented as they entered. The sight of the split peach of their rowing coach's naked bottom covered in angry red lines seemed to jolt them, and Stones wondered if they thought the whole thing was some kind of strange fantasy until that moment. There could be no denying in their minds now that this was a serious punishment session and Stones could determine the different emotions playing through the two students' minds as they processed the scene before them. Eva looked distraught and was probably envisaging the landing of the cane on her own hindquarters whilst Yuri looked partly aghast and partly excited at seeing her mentor suffering for acts she had visited upon her own bottom. At Celia's snapped fingers the two quickly removed their own clothing and, hands on heads, were positioned behind Nina to give them full view of the last of the second session's strikes from the cane.

Stones encourage them forward to inspect the damage as he moved to the machine to change the setting.

"Feel the heat, feel the ridges. Can you appreciate the quality beating this scallywag is receiving? Good show, I say, top rate," chuckled the professor, keen to cause Nina more woe and belittling as tentative fingers touched the bright red cheeks.

"I have decided to up the ante a bit as Nina's cheeks are withstanding the burn better than I expected. Therefore, the next 100 strokes will be received at one per second and just targeted to the three areas of your bottom that are absorbing the blows best so far. Let us see if this helps bring about true repentance, absolute correction and an improved student that will bring pride rather than disgrace to her college. Tally-ho!"

Stones' cheery words accompanied the ominous whirring as the device started once more and the cane whipped down, swung back and immediately repeated. Nina's screams went to a higher level now as the intensity of the continuous beating allowed no respite, no moment to prepare, no easy breathing pattern to set as the bite and sting became constant.

As the last stroke of her second hundred landed, Stones leaned in to check the three rather prominent purple-coloured masses across the centre, upper and lower buttocks. His hands pinched and prodded the evident soreness causing a further series of yelps from the conquered female, her sobbing now bringing forth a waterfall of tears that Celia was struggling to mop up.

"I am going to give you a definite sitting down problem now, my dear. I doubt you will be rowing again for a couple of weeks. Your upper legs are about to get the stripping of their lives; 80 on the legs then a final 20 across the very top of your anal cleft where the skin is very tight and gives little protection. I believe that will send you a very clear message, my girl."

To the surprise of no one, there was no answer from the weeping, snivelling Nina. Her body language illustrated the broken spirit that Stones always desired in his victims. All resistance gone, the experience hopefully scarred into the misfit's mind forever. He had no sympathy, he was very much concerned with Nina's actions and had no doubt that the thrashing of Yuri was sexually driven, and wanted to imprint on Nina's mind that he was no understanding, kind, sympathetic uncle, more of an avenging angel, although he suspected that she would consider him closer to a devil!

"Yuri, you seem unable to tear your eyes away from your colleague's beleaguered buttocks. Do I detect an eagerness, bordering on enjoyment, in watching her suffer by any chance?"

Yuri's head jerked away from the sight she seem transfixed by, to face the professor.

"Oh, no. Sorry, sir. It is so bad, sir. I have never seen anything like it. I do not know how she is bearing this, sir." Her words seemed caring in tone, her eyes belied that and Stones suspected that she was enjoying being witness to the downfall of her rowing persecutor.

"Oh she can take so much more, my dear. You should be aware that this worthless wretch has admitted finding the thrashing of your naked backside a bit of a sexual turn-on. Hopefully, the next hour should be a lesson to her in keeping her perverse thoughts and fantasies to herself and not to abuse and bully those younger students that are left in her care."

Yuri's face had lost its sparkle now and Stones could see the look of distain that Eva directed at Nina.

"Now you two, we are resolving this today and the intention is that after you have all paid your dues there will be a line drawn and things will move on. Forgiveness comes through repentance, repentance aided by chastisement brings forth contrition and improvement. The three of you are all miscreants although your offences are of varying degrees. Nina is paying her dues by suffering a very severe and harsh thrashing. From this experience I believe that she will learn and develop, she will improve as a coach, as a student and as human being, otherwise my work is in vain. Now Yuri, come and sit in front of Nina's face and hold her head in your hands. You can watch and rejoice as she repents. After that you will receive your walloping and then the two of you can hopefully kiss and make up, all forgiven. We will see. Time to commence the final 100 strokes of this part of Nina's thrashing, so watch carefully, Eva, and imagine what your own bottom will feel like once I apply my full strength with a swishing cane. Trust me, young lady, the strokes will be superior in force and my cane thicker and longer than what Nina is being tickled with."

Once more, the whirring began, followed immediately by the swish of the cane and thwack of the impact before Nina screeched out into Yuri's face.

Stones allowed Yuri to get away with the single, "Dirty dyke," whisper at Nina as she howled, but caught her eye as a warning to her not to overstep the mark.

While Stones was not at all surprised to see a lack of concern and compassion on Celia's face, he was quite impressed, for all her anger at Nina and her behaviour, to see that Philippa was keeping a stoic and impassive expression fixed on her face. Albeit he could see that she was shying away from watching the landing of the cane as it stung Nina's legs again and again. Yuri's original anger at Nina seemed to have dissipated, however. Possibly thinking ahead to what was to befall herself in the not too distant future, she was now attempting to soothe the screaming student, whose legs had now developed an extreme tremor in reaction to the beating. Stones leaned in to keep an eye of the state of the targeted area. There was a point at which he would make the decision to stop if he felt that the purpose of the thrashing had been reached. He decided against calling a halt, though, and allowed the full 80 strokes to blister the backs of her legs. At last the machine fell silent and the professor moved slowly around to lift the chin of the weeping and wailing Nina.

"Just these 20 stingers to go, then. I say just, but I suspect that they are the ones you will remember most. They will be hard and fast and tightly clustered so the pain will be intensified. Bear up, young lady, bear up." He released his hold and the vanquished student's head just dropped and hung as Yuri moved to wipe her face.

With a quick adjustment the machine began its threatening signal of intent, louder now as Stones had changed the settings to deliver the final blows at the maximum speed. There was barely a noticeable sound through the air as the cane swung round in a blur, the crack of its impact much louder as it landed on the tight skin at the top of Nina's bottom. Once more a screech filled the air, followed by more strangled ones as the blows landed with no recovery time in-between and Nina's body barely completed its flinch from one stroke before the next one landed. To the watchers it was over in seconds, although Stones was sure that to Nina it hardly registered that the cane had stopped, as she continued to scream and thrash about within the limits of her constraints, her head shaking wildly in Yuri's grasp.

"Philippa, please assist Celia in adding some ice to the shallow cold-water bath I have prepared and we will give this wretch some blessed relief, although she may not initially think of it as such," Stones chuckled away. The iced water would undoubtedly benefit the blistered cheeks and legs of the thoroughly whipped student but it was doubtful she would appreciate the gesture designed to soothe the stinging and encourage the bruising to develop.

He sent Yuri and Eva to the corner to stand facing the bookshelves in the supplicants' position of hands on heads, knowing that their own dread would now be heightened, as their turn to bend and receive approached. He slowly released Nina from her bonds, watching fascinated as the muscles of her bottom cheeks continued their mini dance, clenching and unclenching as though more damage was to be afflicted. He hesitated as he put his hands on the buckles that held her ankles fast.

"Feels a bit remiss of us to have left you with such stark white skin between the fields of rosy scarlet," he murmured as he ran fingertips inside her unblemished bottom crack. "Certainly know where the target will be if you speak out of turn in your remaining time in this room this evening, won't we? I have a nice little knotted lash that would soon turn this virgin white skin crimson to match the rest of your nether regions. You have not got anything else to confess while we are here, have you? I could always give you a few strokes now to salve your conscience if so." Stones' teasing provoked the response he expected.

"Oh no. Please, sir. No ore, no more. I have been punished enough, surely. It hurts, it hurts," she begged.

He patted her bottom affectionately.

"Fair enough, fair enough. I think you have earned your ice bath. Ladies, take her away." Celia and Philippa had returned and took Nina under her arms to lead her to the bathroom, her legs buckling immediately as the pain of movement alone caused her to stumble.

He watched as the two academics lifted the protesting girl into the bath, the shock of the ice causing her to shriek out once more before a quick slap to the face from Celia stopped her mid-cry.

"This is for your own good. Behave or we will assume that you have not learned your lesson and return you to the professor." Celia's warning clearly sunk in as although there were some noisy intakes of breath and plenty of shuffling about as she adapted to the cold, she settled down into the bath.

"Twenty minutes in silence now while I deliver the damn good hiding our delinquent friend here has requested. Yuri, come here, girl."

Stones had pulled his chair out into the centre of the room and Celia dutifully took her place beside him ready to share the task of hand spanking the young student.

"Philippa, you will hold her head, tissues at the ready, to keep her stable and wiped clean as we impose this mildest of punishments. No fuss, please, Yuri, bend over, legs wide apart, pointing that little cutie of an anal hole up at me, please. That's it, no need to be shy, come along, nice and wide, there you go. Nothing to be ashamed of now you are all cleaned up and smelling very much of citrus fruits. Such a narrow little cleft and tiny anus, most attractive with those little wispy hairs framing it, don't you think, Dr Ford?"

Stones enjoyed deliberately taunting Celia so. She had made the error of letting Stones know, in an unguarded moment, that she did not approve his belittling of the students by emphasising and highlighting his thoughts on their private parts in particular. Since then he had enjoyed moments of toying with her, knowing that it could encourage her to speak unwisely and open her up to his sharp tongue at the very least. He acknowledged that some of her reservation was pure jealousy but that did not concern him in the slightest. In his view she should have got over her moments of angry envy by now, he had certainly delivered plenty of reminders to her own bottom for her to have got the message as far as he was concerned!

"Yes indeed, Professor Stones, very pretty arrangement between her legs all round, I would say. I am certain that I will enjoy spanking those tight little cannonballs."

Stones nodded, accepting his failure to provoke her, and raised his arm high.

"Let the fun commence. Listen up, Nina, the cause of all your discomfort is about to start her own little chorus, I suspect." As he spoke, his arm swung down and his meaty open hand walloped the already bruised right cheek of the exposed student.

He applied hard slapping strokes, alternating between her cheeks, pausing halfway through the quotient he had allotted himself to study her writhing buttocks and the developing bright red hue.

"Looks like I have managed to hide the remnants of your previous beating, anyhow. So that looks a lot healthier now, don't you think, Dr Ford? A nice spread in a lovely deep red glow. Beautiful. How is the top end, Dr Stanford? Is she suffering appropriately?"

A smiling nod from Celia and a hesitant response from Philippa as she tried to adapt to Stones' light-hearted conversational tone.

"Er. Well, she is making quite a lot of noise and is getting through the tissues. She certainly seems to be suffering, Professor Stones."

"Tally-ho, let us get on with it then. I will give the backs of her legs a touch of colour and finish on the tops of her buttocks to spread the love a bit further!" He chortled away and his arm rose and he began to slap the white legs hard.

They were not to be white for long and judging by the increased shrieking from the unfortunate recipient, the backs of her legs were very sensitive!

Twenty-five strokes later, Stones rose abruptly, jettisoning one howling student at his feet.

"Your turn, Dr Ford," he said brusquely as they swapped positions. "Make her realise that you are the easy second option here, please."

With Celia now aware that she was almost certain to replace him in the role of dean of discipline as he cemented his retirement plans, he knew that she would not want any thoughts spreading that his leaving would lessen the severity of punishments dispensed. Armed with an implement he was confident that she could be a match for him, but the disadvantage physically when it came to a hand spanking was definitely a challenge to overcome that he wanted to set Celia.

A grab of Yuri's hair and a forceful jerk was enough to send the student sprawling over her knees as she quickly took Stones' place on the chair. Celia allowed no time for Yuri to prepare and began her avalanche of stinging slaps immediately. Any lack of power in her administration of the spanks was countered by the speed and placing of her swiping hands as she concentrated groups of consecutive slaps at a time on a particular spot, going high, low, then right side to left side before catching even Stones out with her snapped remark to Philippa.

"This ends now, Dr Stanford. Yank those cheeks apart, these last ten are going to the virgin territory beneath her cheeks. Come along, Philippa, don't be shy, open her bottom up fully and stay still. I will not be amused if I find your hands in the line of fire and neither will Professor Stones."

Any reservation or argument Philippa may have pondered soon dried up on her lips as she noted the eagerness with which Stones had moved to allow himself a clear view of the spread cheeks of Yuri. No real reaction from the recipient herself as she was still howling in response to the salvo of stinging blows she had just taken. The first sensation of Celia's hand slamming down between the valley between her cheeks brought her to a fresh level of ferocious torment and she wrested against Celia's other arm holding her down, causing Philippa's hands to lose their grip on her buttocks.

Celia angrily forced her back into position.

"Dr Stanford, please pinch her cheeks really hard now to get a firm grip. Yuri, if you struggle like that again then I will punish you far more harshly. Professor Stones, may I please ask that you fetch your small knotted lash and give it to Yuri to hold as a reminder of what will be used down her bottom cleft if she does not submit to a spanking there."

Stones laughed out loud and clapped his hands.

"Of course, of course. Jolly good idea. Hopefully the feel of this between your fingers, young lady, will make you reconsider any inappropriate response to the rest of your punishment. If you, Dr Stanford, are unable to do as Dr Ford has requested, then perhaps I should take over. Please just say if you cannot cope."

Philippa's spluttered response and anguished demeanour suggested to Stones that she knew full well her support and compliance in this endeavour was not incidental to their doubts as to her full commitment to the disciplinary ethos of the college. She wrenched Yuri's cheeks apart with fingers that were digging in so hard Yuri screamed out in response. A smile from Celia was swiftly followed by her hand swinging down, to land her middle fingers dead centre on the sobbing and terrified Yuri's arsehole. Celia took her time, allowing Yuri to recover from each impact, noting that she held tightly onto the knotted lash as she did so, before her arm swung again. By the time she landed a final open hand on the inner cheeks of the sufferer's bottom, the whole area between her cheeks was a bright pink and there could be no doubt as to the distress the beneficiary of the punishment had been caused.

"All done, excellent. Up you get, young lady, here's a new tissue. Now get over to the wall next to your fellow reprobate, who has been very patient. I will take the lash back as you seem to be taking the message on board. It will always be here if called upon, though. Do not fret, Eva, your lovely bottom will soon be on fire too!" Stones gave her backside thunderous slap, for no other reason than he was eager to lay his hands on her superb bottom and was just giving himself an extra treat! Eva's restrained response suggested that she would be a worthwhile adversary and Stones was very much looking forward to applying his wares to the beautiful bottom of such a stoic and resilient student.

"Time to fetch Nina from the tub, Philippa. Bath time is over, ladies! Let us have her dried down, and then you can take her over your knees and apply some cream please, Dr Stanford. I think she deserves a bit of luxury on those poor ravaged cheeks and legs, don't you?" Stones handed a stunned Philippa a tub of his most expensive and decidedly luxurious moisturising lotion.

Philippa gulped before taking the tub from Stones, clearly reluctant to undertake the rather personal and intimate chore she had just been assigned.

"Of course," murmured Stones, "if you do not think that you can manage a simple, and generally pleasant task such as that, please do say. I am sure Dr Ford can take over."

Once more Stones could see the realisation dawn of yet another test she was not passing with flying colours, as she belatedly grabbed at the jar, before walking briskly off to fetch Nina.

Celia and Stones watched silently as an also mute Nina was escorted back into the room, a huge towel covering her body.

"Legs apart, arms up high, please, Nina. Allow Dr Stanford to dry you down ready for your pampering with the cream. There's a good girl. Get in the crevices and creases, Dr Stanford, mop up all the drips and drops now."

The humiliation in Philippa's eyes was totally obvious to the two conspiratorial academics as she knelt at the feet of the vanquished Nina, who obediently allowed herself to be towelled down most intimately without flinch or word.

Trying to maintain some sort of air of nonchalance, Philippa drew the acquiescent Nina to the chair and pulled her over her lap, before opening the moisturiser. The redness of Philippa's face almost matched that of Nina's bottom as she tentatively began to daub cream on the blistered cheeks before her.

"Nice and gentle to start with, Dr Stanford, then apply a bit more pressure as you proceed to rub the cream deep into her poor suffering little buns. Open those legs, Nina, you want to get the cream in every suffering crevice." Stones was thoroughly enjoying Philippa's awkwardness and was determined to push her through her reticence and embarrassment in both punishing and touching intimately the students who earned the college's wrath.

"Right, young Eva Regina Buchman, it is your turn to pay your dues, show your remorse, seek forgiveness and offer yourself for improvement. We have agreed and accepted your proposal for a 30-stroke paddling from the hand of Dr Ford, followed by one of my best and most effective 20-stroke canings. If you can continue your work on Nina's bottom for a couple of minutes, Dr Stanford, while we get Eva's paddling done and dusted, then you can strap her down and hold her head and administer the eye-wiping, nose-blowing duties produced by her caning."

A nod from Philippa was the response but Stones noted that her hands were now massaging Nina's buttocks in a way that did not suggest that she was finding the process unpleasant!

Without being asked, Eva had turned and walked towards Stones, her hands still on her head as she stood before him with no trace of fear or concern. Once more Stones took in the stunning view of the firm, young, protruding breasts, with the eye-catching nipples, above her muscular stomach and shaven groin emphasising the prominent labial lips and obvious slit. A cough from Celia jolted him back to the matter in hand, and she reached out for the student's wrist and pulled her to her side as she sat herself on the chair that had already seen plenty of similar activity that day. Eva placed herself over Celia's knees without a word, grasped the legs of the chair and pushed her parted legs high to raise her bottom. Celia, too, took a moment to appreciate the marbled orbs before reaching behind her to pick up her chosen paddle. She had opted for a thick leather model that promised a stinging experience but without the bruising effect of the wood. Stones had approved her choice; Eva's buttocks were muscular and not fatty so she had little padding to protect her from the harsh, unyielding effect of the wooden implements but also little protection from the fierce slapping and deeper bite of the flexible thick leather.

To the surprise of neither of them, Eva took the first blows of the swinging paddle with no reaction other than the tightening of the muscles in her shoulders, back and bottom. Three quick blows on the same spot on the highest point of her taut right cheek finally caused an audible intake of breath and a quiet groan. Encouraged by this, Stones noted Celia's eyes glow and she immediately applied the same treatment to the other cheek, and the strength of the blows increased. As the blows continued to rain down in very specifically targeted groups of three, Eva began to breathe loudly and her body began to jerk at each new impact.

"Finish with six of your hardest on each cheek where her bottom meets her thighs, double-quick time, Dr Ford, I want this reprobate in tears before she leaves your lap." Stones snarled out his implied threat as he moved to the other side of the chair and pulled up Eva's head by her hair, bending to look into her face at close quarters. He could see the tears that had already gathered in the suffering student's eyes, as Celia straightened her back and a look of steely intent entered her eyes. Stones knew that she would have been offended by the implication that she was not causing Eva enough distress and fully expected the next 12 strokes to be an onerous onslaught for Eva to endure.

It took until the fifth of her final dozen slaps before the resistance broke and Eva wailed loudly, tears suddenly spouting form her eyes. By the time Celia nonchalantly discarded the paddle, the defeated student was kicking her legs, calling for mercy and crying uncontrollably.

"Good job, Dr Ford. Good job." Their eyes met and the gaze held promise of extra mural activity for both of them.

"Right, Dr Stanford, enough of your handiwork on Nina's bottom, I can see you are both looking as though you are enjoying it rather too much. Nina, back to the wall and start thinking about the feel of my favourite thick strap lashing those very sore beauties, while we finish off giving Eva what she asked for. Let us get this one over the desk for her real punishment, then. Come along now, more work to do still."

The two female academics took an arm each of the weeping Eva, her stoicism gone, her spirit broken as she stumbled between them to the caning desk.

"Wipe her face, Dr Stanford, and make sure she does not deposit tears and runny mucus on my nice carpet please. Fine job at this end, Dr Ford. My, my, she is a sight for sore eyes. Goodness gracious, what a display!"

The rubber mound on the desk had forced her bottom up and her muscular build and sparse amount of pubic hair meant she was displaying her rather abundant labia lips to their full extent. Added the parting of her hard buttocks to show off her rather extensive valley between the mounds meant there was no hiding place for her totally exposed arsehole, with its spider's web of twisting and interwoven tiny layers of skin surrounding her anal opening.

"Delightful, delightful. This will be such a pleasure," Stones mused out loud as he tapped his cane against the solid cheeks.

"Yes, well, mind on the matter in hand, Edward." Celia's jealousy took hold for a moment and there was a long pause before Stones spoke in a cold and angry voice.

"Thank you for your advice, Dr Ford. Perhaps you will care to stay back once our guests have left to have a discussion with me concerning your uncalled for remarks and familiarity of address."

None of the three students seemed aware of the friction that had arisen but Philippa was looking at Celia with pure horror. As Celia blushed and looked away from the professor meekly, agreeing to his request, her face took on a more triumphant look and Stones could see she was delighted to see Celia put down in front of her.

"No need for you to look so pleased with yourself, Dr Stanford, it will not be long until we meet to sit down and discuss your future here. Your shortfalls are well documented, mainly by Dr Ford, who has considerable input on your possible tenure extension."

His words caused a rapid change in demeanour for both female academics, Celia firing a vindictive look at Philippa, whose bottom lip was now wobbling and tears had filled her eyes.

"But for now we will concentrate on the matter in hand, please, ladies. We have a job to do. Hold on to her head, Dr Stanford, tissues at the ready. Dr Ford, sit between her legs and hold those knees firm as she struggles against the restraints. Your view will be so much more enjoyable but do keep your head down. I would not want to crack you with the cane now, would I?"

The two muttered their acknowledgement, the atmosphere now charged between the three of them. Stones grinned, all grist to the mill as far as he was concerned. Looking at the heavenly sight before him, he could feel his arousal and the thought of a session with Celia to follow this most satisfactory chastisement session made his cock twitch.

He savoured the moment, swishing his cane through the air to taunt the waiting student.

"Turn around and watch, Nina and Yuri. See what a sound caning looks like."

The students dutifully turned, Yuri seemingly fully recovered and her eyes wide open and lustful looking as she stared at the fully exposed bottom of her colleague. Nina was still preoccupied with her own discomfort, snivelling and suffering. Her bottom would be reminding her of her downfall for many days. Stones smiled at the forlorn expression on her face, her eyes still fearsome, her teeth chewing her lip as she looked at the thick, long cane hovering in the air. Moments later both were to jerk back as the cane whistled at speed through the air and landed in the middle of Eva's bright red buttocks.

This time there was no pointless effort to remain resolute and courageous, or attempt to retain any dignity. A full-blooded scream rent the air, and Philippa's grip almost fell away as Eva tried to twist her head away from her in her torment. Repeatedly the stinging rattan cane landed onto the firm cheeks, each one eliciting an accompanying shriek of agony and shock from the beleaguered Eva. Soon she was begging for mercy, pleading for the blows to stop, apologising for her sins and promising total obedience from now on. None of this made any difference to the severity or number of strokes and Stones soon announced the final six, his derisive voice mocking her surrender to him and promising that these would be his hardest strokes. He waited as the quivering buttocks pulsed and twitched before his eyes, winking at Celia as he flexed his arm and prepared to deliver. Celia's answering beam and eyes full of pure wantonness promised a good evening ahead, thought Stones.

Swish. Whack! "Yaaaaarrrrggghhhh! No. No. No. Please."
Swish. Whack! "Yaaaaarrrrggghhhh! Fuck! Fuck! Fuck! Please stop."
Swish. Whack! "Yaaaaarrrrggghhhh! Ooooo! No. No. No."
Swish. Whack! "Yaaaaarrrrggghhhh! Fuck! Fuck! Fuck!"
Swish. Whack! "Yaaaaarrrrggghhhh! Fuck! Fuck! Fuck!"

The final strike was aimed at the very top of her buttocks where there was some mainly unblemished skin. It landed with ferocious force.

Swish. Whack! "Aaaaaaiiiiiieeeeeee! Yaaaaarrrrggghhhh! Fuck! Fuck! Fuck! Nooooo! No. No. No."

Stones replaced the cane in his cabinet, picking up his thick black leather strap as he did so.

"Now Eva, listen up, young lady. I am pondering the opportunity for you and Yuri to spare Nina's poor bottom the whole dozen with my strap. What say you, Eva? Do you think you should take a few on her behalf? Her bottom is very red, very badly marked and undoubtedly very sore. Yuri, how do you feel about that? Would you volunteer to spare Nina more agony? Just wondering if the three of you have bonded a bit and a show of magnificent benevolence is forthcoming."

Nina's eyes showed her hope, her eyes pleading with Yuri to go along with the professor's dangling carrot. Yuri dropped her head away from the desperate gaze of her fellow student but to her credit looked back to see Nina's face raised and alight from her newly tethered position, her face now wiped tenderly by Philippa, at this offer of a partial escape route.

It was Eva's voice that broke the tense silence that hung in the air after Stones' words.

"Sir, I do accept that I am possibly the catalyst that caused this situation to develop and as such, I am happy to take four strokes as my share of Nina's punishment." Her voice was clear and resolute, and Stones could not help but admire her acceptance of her guilt in the sorry episode.

"Excellent. Excellent. Well spoken. Admirable. But I doubt that you realise the impact my lovely favourite strap will have on these rather damaged beauties." His hands stroked the swollen and discoloured buttocks of the student as he spoke.

"However, it is an all-or-nothing offer so unless Yuri volunteers to join this little club then all bets are off. In fact I am considering bringing that spanking we had discussed back into play. Maybe I am being too soft."

With that, Nina burst into a fit of loud gasping sobs, her hands going to her face as she broke down, her spirit defeated and self-awareness a thing of the past as the tears fell copiously from her eyes.

"Okay, okay. I will do it, sir. I will take four as well. Oh my god, what am I saying?" Yuri blurted out, her face betraying her anguish at what she was signing up for.

Stones smiled. He loved it when a plan, particularly such a manipulative one, came to fruition.

"Right. Let us get this done with, then. Dr Stanford will sit on the chair, Yuri behind her with her arms around you. Hold firmly onto to her arms, please, Dr Stanford. I am going to lash these tight little walnut-cracking buttocks of yours standing up. Different type of sting when the cheeks are less tight and round. Help you appreciate the power of my strap."

As Yuri draped her arms, rather reluctantly, over Philippa's shoulders, she was not aware of the swinging arm and the leather flying through the air. The loud slapping impact certainly caused her to jump in surprise and shock as the blow landed. The feel of that thick leather hitting her at speed, sunk into her consciousness a split second later. The scream was one of surprise and extreme horror as she writhed and twisted against Philippa's hold. The movement was not her best decision, allowing the following blow of the pliable leather to wrap around her quite bony thighs, and this time the scream was far longer and much higher pitched. Not that Stones paused in his commitment and as the student moved her body the other way, in a pointless attempt to evade the next delivery, he just moved with her and exploded the cruel implement onto the underside of her bottom cheeks. The stroke was placed so perfectly that as she rose on tiptoes in her frantic twisting, the force seemed to lift her off her feet, and she rather draped her body over Philippa's, forcing the graduate manager to almost fall from the chair as she took on the burden of the thrashing student's weight. Again, this was no inconvenience to the professor as he moved forward, swinging the lethal strap, and it completed its journey across the top of her squirming buttock cheeks. Yuri may well have been very much regretting her courageous words as her scream rent the air once more.

"You are done, Yuri. Please cease that noise or else I will feel compelled to continue your beating."

It never failed to amaze Stones how quickly a howling distraught woman could pull herself together when the option of additional punishment was threatened and almost instantly Yuri ceased screaming and her face froze with just the tears continuing their trajectory down her cheeks.

"Eva, please take Yuri's position over Dr Stanford's shoulders. Yuri, stand clear and watch Eva show you how to take the strokes with decorum and gumption. Nina, concentrate please, just your four strokes to follow afterwards presuming there is no further misbehaviour to deal with. That's lovely, Eva, legs apart but not too stretched. I want those red cheeks nice and relaxed for these."

Crack!

"Yuuuur!"

The strap flew down as he spoke, catching Eva by surprise with the ferocity and timing across the tops of her legs. He drew back his arm and landed the next blow on her lower cheeks.

Crack!

This time Eva was more prepared and a strangled moan was the only response.

Crack! The third stroke landed across the centre of the sore globes and apart from a decided tightening of her buttocks there was no reaction.

Crack! Her final stroke hit home on the strip across the top of her bottom and again there was barely a whimper, although her lower torso went through the unmistakable dance of pain received.

"Well done, young lady, well done. Impressive, my dear, impressive." Stones stroked the undoubtedly throbbing cheeks, turned almost purple by his administrations that day. "Up you get and I think we can all enjoy savouring Nina taking the final four strokes of my lovely strap."

All four women stood alongside Stones as he raised his arm over the quivering bottom of a quietly sobbing Nina and swung down with force.

The thin red stripes from the cane were prominent and boded

badly for Nina as the leather headed for her severely marked bottom, and to no one's surprise the first below produced an ear-piercing scream from the beleaguered and restrained woman. He paused between each stroke, ensuring the student recovered before applying the fearsome and memorable admonishments to a student he believed required a serious lesson.

"Uncuff her, Dr Ford, and then the three of them can stand against the wall for an hour while they consider their actions, their shame and their disgrace. No further ice baths or soothing cream today, let these rascals suffer fully. Redemption is theirs as long as they have arrived at remorse and contrition. Improvement will follow, I am sure. Legs apart, hands on heads, ladies, if you would be so kind, and I expect no movement or words. That, of course, will include a complete lack of reaction if any visitors arrive. Do not look so shocked. Your ordeal here ends when I say so. There is more than one way to skin a goose, don't you know! You may not be proud of your berated buttocks, ladies, but we are." Stones went off into a hearty chuckle as the three miserable students with forlorn looks on their faces moved at different speeds to the wall. Nina, desperately rubbing her blistered bottom, the last and least eager to shuffle over into position.

Seconds later the three stood silently in line, facing his bookshelves, albeit Nina clearly still quietly weeping, their three naked backsides illustrating the levels of punishment and the different stages of recovery reached.

"Thank you for your assistance today, ladies. Dr Stanford, if you could draw up a chair behind our reprobates to ensure they stay still and in complete silence until the college nurse arrives to give them a quick check over. Dr Ford, you may leave and return here within the hour to chat through some of the aspects of today that need revisiting. If you could bring me back something appropriate of your choice to assist us in resolving any issues that would be most kind."

Celia grimaced and avoided Philippa's shocked face as she

reluctantly placed her chair as instructed. She quickly looked away, however, when she sensed Stones' gaze fall on her.

"Yes, Professor Stones, of course. It will be my pleasure, thank you." Celia's recovery earned her a nod of approval from Stones, her evening's entertainment finalised!

Celia stood before him an hour later holding out a long, slim package.

"Thank you, Dr Ford. Now if you would like to divest yourselves of your clothing and go and stand in the corner, please. I think we both know full well why you are here and what is now going to happen. Yes?"

Celia gulped but turned smartly and began undressing.

"Yes, Professor Stones. Of course. I spoke out of turn and require a thrashing to remind me of how to behave during a disciplinary meeting. I apologise profusely, Dean, and would be most grateful if you could teach me a harsh lesson to ensure that I do not let you and myself down again." She spoke as she dropped her skirt and Stones smiled to see the lack of underwear and the evidence of her readiness and keenness to be so acquiescent.

Stones' mood was further enhanced when he revealed the contents of her gift. A long leather strap with cut-outs in the shapes of pursed lips, denoting kisses.

"I hope you approve, sir. I hoped you would appreciate the chance to apply kisses to my bottom in your own inimitable style," she ventured expectantly.

Stones just rewarded her with a brusque nod of approval, although inwardly he was impressed with her inventiveness and such devotion to satisfying his sexual appetite in any way that she could.

"We shall see if this does the job. Feels adequately thick and flexible enough to make an impression. The cut-outs should assist with the speed through the air also. Yes, you have done well. The downside for you is that the cane I intend also to use to punish you will now have to be applied to the backs of your legs, so as not to spoil the intended outcome of your little pattern maker here. That will be painful but never mind, rather serves you right for being such a disappointment to me. Now in the corner to contemplate your sins while I just finish off some paperwork."

Her sullen face as she contemplated how once more he had turned things around so that any sense of self-satisfaction she felt in pleasing him had been undone by his words, was gist to his mill, his sadistic and domineering nature always being brought to the fore when dealing with Celia.

After several minutes, Stones beckoned her to his desk.

"I have formally annotated the punishment book with your indiscretion and the agreed chastisement. I presume that you have no reservations about signing it off to approve the actions I am about to take?"

Celia's face gurned and twisted as she suffered the additional humiliation of realising that her ordeal was being made a matter of record. Stones had twice before made a point of officially documenting her indiscretions and subsequent corporal admonishment and much as she in part despised him for shaming her in this quite public way, she also revelled in his totally mastery of their relationship. In reality very few would peruse the college's official punishment book, but it was signed off by the college mistress and available for the college council and governing body to view on demand. She was, however, wise enough to realise that there was absolutely no benefit in challenging him and that she could only make the situation worse rather than better. She gave out a long, shuddering sigh before finally answering him.

"Of course, Professor Stones. It is only correct that my sins should be formally broadcast, as a lesson to others as well as myself. Thank you, sir." She signed with a flourish, trying to maintain as much self-pride as possible considering she was naked, about to be flogged and had just been given soul-destroying news!

"Good girl. Now over to my chaise-longue. On your knees, legs wide apart, drape yourself over the back, fingertips to the floor, bottom standing proud."

As Celia arranged herself to his instructions, he took his thick cane from his cabinet and positioned himself behind her.

"A dozen strokes of the cane, six on each leg. Hard and true. Hold your position, please, Dr Ford, and accept your penance, your redemption and your improvement." As he voiced the final word, the cane swung down fast and landed just under her left buttock.

A sharp intake of breath and a tiny squeak were all that she allowed herself, to Stones' approval. He swept the cane down again, catching her an inch lower. More prepared this time, there was only a small body movement to acknowledge the fierce pain of the stroke. The next four were quickly landed, and just as accurate, as he striped her left thigh with six red lines.

"Well taken, Dr Ford. Well taken," he acknowledged, awarding her his approval as much to please her as to add to the gameplay. He gave her a moment to soak in the endearing words before adding, "I will try to up my game with the second six, my dear. I would not want to disappoint you by appearing weak." He laughed as she tensed and slashed down ferociously onto her right leg. Her squeal was high-pitched but short as she swallowed it down, the twitching leg giving clear evidence of its impact. Once more he laid them on quickly, before standing back to admire his symmetry and the blossoming of the vivid red massed stripes. Her sobbing was wholehearted now despite her attempts to stifle her reaction.

He handed her tissues.

"While you clean yourself up I will reward you for taking the strokes so well by supping at your divine vagina. We will then move on to enjoying your little present together." As he dipped his head, Celia pushed her torso back and then gurgled in pleasure as his tongue licked the length of her quim. She had always taken a beating as well as any person in his long history of practising the sadistic art form that he so loved, and his love for her was never higher than in the aftermath of having caused her to suffer so. As always her capacity for sexual pleasure, immediately following a thrashing, did not fail to amaze him, and as his hands slipped around her front she held her position as though tied in place. With one hand turned to allow her pubic mound to rub ferociously against his hard knuckles, the fingers of the other sought out her slippery hard clitoral nub and pinched it between them. As her flanks pushed back against his probing tongue his nose nudged against her unresisting anal opening and edged inside the dark hole. As always, she quickly arrived at the brink of orgasm, the blood flow to her beaten legs adding to her state of arousal, and Stones knowing her body so well, was able to pick the moment of her climax and release her completely as she started to come.

"Noooooooooooooooooo!" she wailed, her body thrashing against the furniture as she searched for a focal point to drive her on. Stones slapped away hands that strayed back over the top of the chaise-longue to force her to experience her moment without the contact between her legs.

Without the contact normally engaged, either by a lover or as a masturbatory practice, Celia could only thrust her midriff against the back of the chaise-longue, her hands thumping against the carpet as her whole body shook with the wave of pleasure that was delivered with a strange intensity with touch denied. Stones knew full well how this experience felt as a male but could only wonder at the true feeling and sensations that Celia experienced as her whole body tremored and she thrust her hips repeatedly, moaning and whimpering as she gradually worked through the furore that racked her.

He allowed her to calm, her breaths still coming quickly, rapid pants gradually subsiding, before he swung the leather strap down across her lower buttocks.

"Aaiiieeeeeooooww! Ah, you bastard." The element of surprise worked perfectly to enhance the impact as the white cheeks finally received their dues. Stones paused a moment to watch the pinkness spread and the white pursed lips shape to emerge amongst the developing soreness and then struck again.

"Yes, you sodding bastard! That's it. Beat me, my love, beat me."

Stones laughed. "True colours, Celia, true colours."

The strap swung down again. No more cries, just laboured breathing and sharp intakes of breath as Stones laid on the strap, finishing with a massive blow across the thin strip of skin along the top of her bottom that caused Celia's whole body to writhe but was taken in silence before she slumped back down. He dropped the strap and stood back to admire his handiwork. The white patches were distinctive in their defined lip shapes, the pale skin stark against the deep red background of her enflamed cheeks. He dropped to his knees and began to tenderly kiss the throbbing redness as once more his hands moved around her flanks, one travelling up to pinch an erect nipple, the other sliding back between her legs into her marshy wetness.

Celia started to moan immediately but stayed in her submissive position even as Stones forced his chin between her legs, lifting her to allow his tongue to lap at her pussy. For many minutes the only sound in the room was the subtle slurping sound of his active tongue and the quiet panting of Celia as she started the slow climb to another climax. Sensing the moment had arrived Stones moved quickly around in front of her, his twitching cock released as she automatically, so in tune was she with his sexual needs, engulfed him in her mouth, her tongue curling round and round his stem while he held her head and eased in and out of her mouth. With his cock dribbling with her spit he was behind her again in a moment, his hands on the insides of her legs as he wrenched her fully apart and open. Stones forced his cock with no great grace through the bulging, swollen and sodden pussy lips and up deep into her slippery and welcoming inner tunnel.

This final part of their lovemaking was quick and effective. They were both ready to come and the moment his ejaculation flooded her pussy she screeched in ecstasy and came with a heaving shudder that lasted many seconds.

Always ready to surprise her, she was to climax again seconds later when he slipped out of her and then enveloped her pussy with his whole mouth as he sucked his own come from her leaking quim. The smacking of his lips announced that he had completed the act and swallowed his own offering and Celia laughed out loud in her delight at his inventiveness. As she went to rise he held her buttocks firmly in place, saying, "Kisses on the bottom, indeed, Celia. Good call with the strap, well done, it looks quite lovely."

Finally allowed to rise she turned to embrace him, kissing him fully on the mouth, her tongue searching to see if she could taste herself within.

"Such a bastard, such a wonder. I love you so much, Edward."

"Indeed," was the only response she received as he released her and headed towards his bathroom. He looked back at her. The faintest of smiles on his face. Celia sighed and followed. There was more to come and Stones was confident that she had realised years ago she had to settle for what she got from him. Take it or leave it. She always chose to take it.

CHAPTER 5

IN WHICH THE MISTRESS IS MASTERED!

The planned visit to his quarters by Professor Dorothy Winslow-Bellingham, the redoubtable Mistress of St James' College, was long overdue and had been anticipated by Stones for some time. His reading of people was renowned and many years ago he had picked up on Dorothy's excitement when he had first suggested to her that she should have a live feed of what occurred in his room regarding the disciplinary dealings of the college. Once the electronics had been sorted out she was able to view on her laptop the many angles covered by the intricate CCTV system installed in his main room. It was subject to control by Stones and required him to switch the feed on, but she soon learnt that he would do this religiously every time an incident took place. He had made it clear that the only time he would not give her access was if he was 'entertaining' in a more social setting rather than on college business. Dorothy was well aware that this would generally be when he was alone with the senior tutor, Celia Ford. His relationship with Celia was something that Dorothy was fully aware of and completely comfortable with. They were both incredibly discreet with their business and very few college members were aware of the relationship.

Stones had always been confident that the day would come when Dorothy would no longer be able to resist giving in to the latent urge he sensed growing in her by the month. His computer's data clearly showed the amount of the punishment sessions she viewed in their entirety and there was ample visual evidence, in his eyes, that her level of interest was way beyond a professional capacity. The call from her to book two hours of his time one evening to discuss personal matters was therefore not totally unexpected and oblique and cool as she tried to be when making the appointment. Stones was aware that she felt the need to make sure he understood what sort of meting she was requesting, presumably to avoid any embarrassing misunderstandings. Although Stones would say he was rarely embarrassed by anything! Never one to miss the opportunity to begin a chastisement with his acid tongue and cruel wit, he set the tone of the path forward immediately.

"So let's just clarify please, Mistress, what exactly can I do for you? No beating around the bush. Unless that's what you want of course!" Stones chuckled to himself.

"Oh please, Edward, don't make this difficult. I find that I am in the need to scratch an annoying itch that has bothered me for many years. You, dear man, are the only person who I could accept or trust to take this on. You are a most perceptive man and I know that you will be one step ahead as always. Just guide me, please, Edward. I need to make this happen."

Stones did not want to let the opportunity to chastise the Mistress of the college pass by but was always careful to cover his back.

"You will bring me a handwritten and detailed report as to why you require my services, Dorothy. You will be clear and unequivocal, you will be honest and you will come to my room with it in your hand ready to face any consequences that the contents bring forth. You will prepare yourself for eventualities in the manner that meets my requirements. Do you understand and accept this?"

She murmured her consent, her eyes down now as though she had just realised what she had put in place.

"When you return, and let's not hang about as you obviously have a conscience to cleanse, you will address me as your superior, treat me with the utmost respect and obey my every instruction. Is 5pm acceptable?"

The look she gave him in response displayed a mixture of fear and excitement and Stones knew that he had a willing victim for his foible and felt a stirring of arousal.

"Yes Edward, oh, I mean sir. I have a drink reception at 8 with an important donor attending. But if that gives us time I would like to do this, please."

"Off you go then, Dorothy. You have a confession to write. Your punishment will be determined when I see how sinful and naughty you have been. You will then in all likelihood be given a thorough thrashing to purge your body of your misbehaviour and sins, if that is what you request. Be off with you and be at my front door at the time set and not a moment later. I presume that I do not need to state the expectations I have in regard to personal hygiene and cleanliness?"

Stones smiled in amusement as the renowned Mistress of one of the country's most respected colleges blushed in embarrassment and with a flustered demeanour fled from his room.

Stones busied himself in a mixture of the occasional feedback he offered to students who required his input into his fields of academic expertise and his organisational duties on behalf of the college and its endeavours in pursuit of the richest and most influential donors and benefactors. It was not unknown for Stones' input to secure multi-million-pound commitments for the college's latest academic initiative or expansion. He was nothing if not a patient man and much as he had secretly hoped for this particular set of circumstances to fall into place, he was happy to bide his time and intended to endure that Dorothy received the full experience, which certainly included being made to work to his timetable and not hers. His desire to see this impressive figurehead and leading scholar naked, vulnerable and at his mercy had definitely produced a full-on erection that he could hardly fail to be aware of, but he was a man who had mastered control of his desires over time and his hard swollen protuberance would not deflect him from the path he had formulated as Dorothy squirmed before him. When the buzzer rang, he left her to wait outside for several minutes before granting her entry and then amused himself by ignoring her irritated stare as she finally stood in front of him. He snatched the papers she held from her and waved her to stand in the centre of the room while he read through her proffered words.

Eventually Stones moved close to Dorothy before he waved her document of guilt in front of her face and roared at her. The regret apparent now on her face for the words forever scribed, as an imperious Stones lambasted her.

"You are an utter disgrace, woman. Using private CCTV footage to show off to your latest conquest amounts to invasion of privacy, breach of contract, sexual harassment, albeit of a student ignorant of the offence, abuse of trust, a gross misuse of our agreement concerning the restrictions of use of the CCTV footages of punishment sessions and a betrayal of the faith I have invested in our relationship. This is incompatible with the values of this college and I find you guilty on all counts. As such your punishment can only be of the most severe level particularly as in a position of ultimate responsibility you have chosen to act at a level unbefitting of your status. There can be no other option. You must be thrashed, and thrashed severely for your outrageous behaviour and appalling judgement. I assume I will have no argument that only the most brutal of beatings can be applied in response to this confession. I will deliver what you want immediately. Remove your clothing, you shameful and disgraceful creature, and present yourself properly for your just and most deserved chastisement. And take fair notice, no mercy should be expected or requested as I promise you that none will be given. Let the chastisement commence!"

The horror on Dorothy's face as Stones adopted his most severe and terrifying tone was joy to his heart. As much as she had watched him strip down his student victims layer of skin by layer of skin, she had not been in the least prepared to be in the firing line. His words tore into her consciousness and with the doubts that had plagued her from the moment she dreamed of this happening, now Stones knew her inner voice would be screeching at her to run, to deny, to beg.

Stones was not going to give her any such opportunity. He suspected that her description of this incident with a fellow academic from a nearby college was embellished somewhat. He had been aware that there had been a liaison of sorts between the two high-ranking scholars but had not suspected that she had allowed a visitor to her rooms to view a live screening of one of the many punishments that he had carried out.

"You have allowed your filthy lust to get the better of you. You have put your perverted little thoughts before your duty to this august institution. You are an absolute disgrace and an embarrassment. Hurry up, hurry up. Get those rags off and present yourself."

Dorothy's removal of her clothing was quick as her terrified face gave evidence of her realisation of the position that she had voluntarily left herself in. Naked, she turned to him, her eyes beseeching, her bottom lip trembling, demeanour already of the vanquished.

"On your knees, you disgusting cretin. Don't look at me with that pitiful expression. Redemption can only come through remorse created by shame and retribution. As you are well aware, I am very much a believer that humiliation and pain are the parents of redemption so let us be clear that there will be no pity on offer here. No mercy is deserved and no mercy will be given. A thoroughly flayed backside and a total shaming are the only solution. Apologies and contrition are incidental, remorse and regrets count for nothing. Pity does not exist, self-disgust is deserved. Flagellation as a penance is your only hope. There is no easy way out for you, you shameless creature. Nose to the carpet between my feet. Buttocks raised, legs wide apart. Grovel, wretch, grovel in your shame!"

Dorothy obeyed instantly, suppressing a sob as she desperately presented herself as he demanded, her supplication complete and unreserved.

"I am so sorry, Edward, so very sorry."

A slap across her buttocks was followed by the stony voice that he adopted when seeking to terrorise the miscreants he seemed to conquer and dominate. He could barely contain his excitement and seeing her thus exposed and helpless before him, his trousers tented alarmingly in his lust as he gazed down at the spread naked bottom of his only superior amongst the college staff. He had fantasised about this vision and almost went off script in his desire to sink to his knees behind her and gorge his desire on her flesh. He took a breath, adjusted his clothing discreetly to hide his throbbing erection and went back into character.

"How dare you. Address me as Dean or Professor, you irreverent and offensive cretin. I am so going to enjoy lacerating these buttocks with my improvers. Come on, legs wider apart, point that dirty and ugly old anus at me. Let's have a look at those worn out labial lips."

Her sobs increased as she rearranged herself, widening her legs and arching her back.

He bent behind her and took a loud sniff, his fingernails digging into her bottom cheeks as he ran his nose from the bottom of her lavish lips to the top of her anal cleft.

"Hmmmm. Smells like a freshly dug garden. Acceptable, acceptable. At least you have one thing in your favour, I suppose."

"Oh my word, this is awful. Please. I am sorry. What have I done? Oh my word. I am really so very sorry, Edward, oh no, I mean Professor, sir. Sorry, sir. Aaaaargh!"

A hard slap accompanied her unwise address and was soon followed by several more as Stones pulled her up by the hair with his left hand whilst administering rapid slaps with his right. Seconds later she was over his knees in the old-fashioned position of the errant reprobate and Stones' arm was rising and falling with pace and power as he proceeded to thoroughly wallop the generous buttocks splayed open before him. He was relentless and unforgiving, his large hand flattening her flesh as he methodically worked his way from the backs of her legs to the tighter stretched skin across the top of her bottom, turning the whole area bright red. Dorothy's sobs and gasps were heartfelt and without restraint as she finally received what Stones felt she had secretly dreamed of and desired for years. He very much doubted that it had played out quite like this in her sexual imagination, as he finally rested with hand on quivering red hot cheeks, 200 spanks duly delivered. She stayed in place, her bright red cheeks quivering dramatically as she struggled to absorb the sting of his large hand, her sobbing gradually subsidised to a quieter snivelling. Stones jerked his knees and deposited her on the floor at his feet.

"Up and over to the cabinet, you wastrel. Bring me a nice firm paddle, a thin whippy cane, my long hard cane and I think we had better have my thick strap to apply the additional punishment strokes that I am rather confident that you will earn."

His only response from a crestfallen Dorothy was a noise somewhere between a sigh and a gulp of dismay. Dorothy dutifully picked the appointed instruments of her coming chastisement and tentatively handed them over to Stones.

Stones moved over to one of his bookcases and, with a deft shuffle and rearrangement of the books, he exposed metal rings attached to the wall behind the units.

"Take hold of the rings and step back to that your shoulders are down to a level just above your hands, your legs are straight and your buttocks nicely rounded and pointed at me, please. Arch your back slightly, legs further apart so that your goods, for the little they are worth seeing, are out on display. Come on, come on. Anus and vulva on full view. That's better. Now just relax those tight cheeks so that when this wooden paddle first hits its target we get a real sound effect..."

As Dorothy obeyed automatically, Stones swept the wooden

paddle, which she had unwisely, he thought, selected herself, down onto the target area of her waiting cheeks.

The screech and buckling of her legs as she struggled to cope with what was, Stones was certain, an experience unlike any that she could have envisaged, brought a satisfied smile to his face. Not that he was going to spare her any of his refined skill at belittling the recipients of his particular form of reprisal.

"Oh boo hoo, is the naughty little girl's bottie hurting? You filthy whoring bitch, sucking cock and flaunting your worn out flappy mess with your gigolo, were you? Masturbating watching one of your students being beaten while your latest paramour was shoving his tongue up this monstrous crater of your depravity. Is that what you like, slut?" He rammed a hand into her groin, fingers flitting into and around her pussy and arsehole.

He didn't allow her time to answer before bringing the paddle down in a fusillade of blows that sent her down to the floor.

"Up you get, you pathetic excuse for a woman. I am inclined to get in touch with young Maisie Groningen. Since you have had the pleasure of watching her receive a thorough spanking, then it would only be fair for her to see you receive a similar comeuppance, do you not think?"

It took a minute for the blubbing, totally shaken most senior member of St James' College to get some sort of control and Stones' words to register.

"Oh no, no, no. Please don't, no. I am so sorry, please do not call her, I would have to resign, I could not continue. Please don't. Please, Edward, oh, I mean Professor Stones, sorry sir. Nooooo!"

The paddle came down hard across her upper thighs as she blathered on with her desperate begging. Stones had no intention of informing the student that her trust and personal privacy had been betrayed in such a manner, that road could lead to more complications than he was prepared to encompass. However, it was another handy weapon to hang over Dorothy's conscience. For now, turning the rosy cheeks before him a shade of angry scarlet was his aim. As Dorothy struggled to keep hold of the metal rings and twisted her body away from his blows, he deftly moved to allow the paddle to slam into her suffering buttocks. As the wood hit home for the 20th time her knees buckled once more and Stones grasped her hair and dragged her over to his caning desks, deposited her face down and kicked her legs apart without care or compassion.

"Come on, you pathetic creature, stretch those arms forward, stick that fat arse up, let's get this deserving tub of lard ready for a bloody good thrashing with the cane."

Her sobbing intensified as he picked up the cane and swung down it close to her face.

"Hold on to the edge of the desk right now, legs wide apart, point that bullseye of an anus up at me. Remember that this is the easy bit, just a taster. The serious stuff is still to come, so can I have some decorum and a display of some level of pride and dignity?"

Dorothy sniffed loudly and tearfully, but managed to blurt out a positive response.

"Yes, sir. I will do my very best. Am I presenting to your satisfaction, sir?"

Stones laughed.

"Good effort, well done. Your posterior and its accoutrements are indeed displayed in an acceptable manner. Brace yourself."

The swishy cane was built for speed and a cutting bite, and Stones knew exactly how to use it for the best effect and response.

"Now, are you going to pretend to be a grown-up and hold your position like an adult or am I going to have to tie you down like a naughty little strumpet with no pride, no shame and no self-respect?"

Stones began tapping the cane against his hand, enjoying the sight of Dorothy's trembling scarlet buttocks and the sounds of her sobbing.

The long breath that preceded Dorothy's response was shuddering and uneven but she managed to speak calmly enough, recovering some sense of composure to his approval.

"Oh my goodness, indeed, indeed. I will do my very best, Dean, to comply. I deserve this beating and I will continue to try to bear the burden of my dishonour with as much dignity and acquiescence as this occasion demands. Please proceed, sir. I am ready to accept a most deserved punishment and ask you to carry out your duty, please."

As was his usual habit with the small whippy cane, Stones applied the 50 strokes in a matter of seconds. Dorothy's response was muted; a low guttural moan almost without break came from deep within her as the cutting strokes flew down again and again. As he stepped back, Dorothy let out a long yell, screaming at him:

"Thank you, thank you, thank you. Yes, yes, yes. My word! Oh my. Oh my. Yes. Thank you, Dean."

Stones ignored her and swiftly swapped the canes over so that he was soon laying his long cane across the top of her trembling globes.

"Twenty hard strokes, good and true to come. Hold fast and take them well, Dorothy. Show some self-respect and remember your position. It is time to display fortitude and courage. Take them well, my dear, take them well."

The first five were laid on fast and keen with Dorothy managing to contain herself and restrict her responses to quiet yelps and sharp intakes of breath. It was not to last, however. Stones applied a real up and under, sweeping the cane down low before a flick of the wrist brought the thick wood against the underside of her lower bottom cheeks. His reward was instant, dramatic and loud as Dorothy screeched in pain as a new site was found to exacerbate her torment. Never one to miss an opportunity to subject his victims to the most discomfort he could impose, Stones repeated the stroke with relish. Again and again he raised his arm high and rained down six quick strokes, causing Dorothy to writhe and wriggle as she struggled to hold her position. Pausing to allow her to calm, he picked up a nearby tissue and wiped her tear-stained face.

"Another seven strokes to take, you pathetic wretch. How about taking them with a bit more propriety and deportment? All of this brouhaha is not necessary. Take a deep breath in and steel yourself, you naughty girl."

Dorothy gulped, her head hanging lower and lower, as she brought herself under control.

"Yes, sir. Sorry, sir. I apologise and ask you to forgive me my poor reactions."

Stones harrumphed in response and whacked her hard across the centre of her swollen cheeks.

She shrieked, her control loss complete, vanquished and defeated. The next strike went a fraction higher, the follow-up a fraction lower. Each howl was music to Stones' ears. He felt no conscience, no pulls on his heart, no mercy considered. She had opted to take this path and as far as he was concerned he was just delivering the means to quench her thirst and quell her desire. He raised and brought the cane down ferociously again, two quick strokes applied to her lower cheeks before applying the final two strokes across the sensitive band of tight skin across the very top of her buttocks where her crack began. The final crack of the cane echoed in the room for a second before it was drowned out by her banshee wail.

Stones stood in front of her and waited for the words of acceptance and gratitude that he required to complete the episode in his mind. It took several minutes before Dorothy's sobbing subsided and she was able to speak. He had not expected her to fail him and smiled in satisfaction as she delivered the acquiesced words that spelt out his conquest and power over her.

"Sir, thank you for my caning. I thoroughly deserved it and welcome the discomfort it has caused me. My thrashing was supreme, I am so very sorry and hope sincerely that you feel that I have been truly punished, and that you have accepted my comeuppance to your satisfaction. I ask for your forgiveness and hope you feel that I have earned it. Once more I would like to apologise for my disgraceful behaviour."

There was a sense of self-satisfaction to her words that she would have been best advised to keep to herself, as Stones drew himself up and loomed large over her.

"Oh, all proud of ourselves for managing to survive a proper caning, are we? Well, congratulations because all you have achieved is to ensure that that my application of this beauty will be all the harder to make certain that you are fully vested and beaten."

Stones picked up his thick strap and walked around to tap it on the desk top in front of her face. He doubted she would have the fortitude and resilience to hold her position for the prescribed six strokes. His taunting was just part of the gameplay that as far as he was concerned, she had fully signed up for with her confession. His anger at her was only part play; she had taken advantage of her position for sexual titillation and possibly, he surmised, to show off the power she had to her paramour. It was a dangerous act and he felt very unbecoming of a woman in her position, the college's reputation having been put at risk as the climate in the country moved further and further against the act of corporal punishment. Their ability to hold to their principles was dependent on the continual stream of successful women out-achieving other institutions and possibly over-achieving their own targets. Every generation of women that left the college and went on to establish themselves as leaders, movers and shakers was fundamental to their survival and very existence in a world that had turned very much against the very philosophy ingrained in the day-to-day operation of the college. Very few alumni ever raised the issue of corporal punishment being a negative component of their education, albeit that the reality was only a few students each year actually felt the wrath of the Dean of Discipline in a physical sense. But the tradition was known and fully understood by virtually everyone that passed through the hallowed gates of the insular and self-serving institution. The college's support and promotion of its graduates was paramount to this and almost to a body it wrought loyalty and devotion from the grateful recipients of its influence and reputation. True, he was honest enough to admit, not every recipient of his specific form of discipline was convincingly grateful for the delivery served up by his right arm, however almost without fail they recognised the benefit of corporal punishment over a form of chastisement that would have affected their education in a more detrimental manner. Professor Stones was convinced that it clearly helped that most students were offspring or close relatives of former students, that they did not matriculate until they were 19 years old with a working year behind them, and they were forewarned of the ways and traditions of the college as far as the control of their behaviour operated.

Dorothy took a long, deep breath and Stones was pleased to see that she was making a real effort to obey his instructions and adhere to the rules. He knew that he would break her down but was pleased to see her gain some control and fight to retain some dignity. Her buttocks looked raw and ravaged and he recognised that he had laid on the cane very harshly, with none of the restraint he often practised when punishing errant students. In his mind, this older, hardened woman, who had watched over and implicitly approved of his many chastisements, had to take and accept a thorough beating to avoid an accusation of hypocrisy and a failure to practice what she preached. As far as Stones was concerned she had known exactly what would happen when confessing her indiscretion. Reap what you sow was a harvest principle, a formula, which Stones was committed in his belief to. He would not regret any malaise or suffering caused to the mistress of his beloved college.

"If it pleases you, sir, I am ready, caned and most able. I would be honoured if you would apply your strap to my backside and assist in guiding me along the path to atonement and forgiveness, sir." Her voice was impressively steady and Stones nodded his approval, albeit to her quivering, tensed buttocks. He noted her head pressed hard against the table and the whites of her knuckles as she gripped the edge of the desk.

"Good girl, now hold tight and I will deliver you your dues, as you have requested. You say that you are able, let's see if you will be caned and able, after the strap, eh?" Stones chuckled as he swished his strap through the air, causing a loud gulp from his subdued victim.

As was his usual practice, he waited until her bottom lost its tension and she naturally relaxed and then swung down quickly with force and laid the strap at speed against the waiting fleshy globe. The crack of the strap landing was soon followed by a howl of surprised anguish. The strap rarely failed to catch its recipients unprepared; the sharp slap of the leather and initial pain soon followed by a quickly developing intense sting, was virtually impossible to prepare for unless you were an established exponent of taking high-level physical punishment. Dorothy was most certainly not, and to the best of Stones' knowledge had never received a punishment stroke of this level before. Her writhing bottom he found a joy to behold and he was delighted to see her display of her private parts was attestation of someone who had no longer held any sense of decorum or coyness.

"Oh dear, what a lot of fuss. That was just my practice stroke, my guide, a marker if you like. From now on they will be proper strokes."

As he spoke he slashed the strap back down. The second stroke was aimed deliberately at the very tops of her legs, his intention to cause her to lose control completely.

"Aaaaaarrrggghhh!"

The scream rendered in response was loud and despairing. Her resistance broken, any promise to bear her punishment with dignity blown away. Her legs buckled, her hands grasped her bottom, her body twisted away from the desk and Stones' position. To Stones this was a success but he waited, knowing full well that Dorothy would be devastated by her failure to retain some sense of control and self-esteem. He slashed the strap down again and then quickly again, producing howls from Dorothy that were both primal and full of despair. No part of her bottom cheeks were spared as he landed the next lash on the top of her cleft, adding to the bright red, angry welts raised already. Her body writhed and trembled as she hollered, her screams and garbled pleas and entreaties for mercy filled the air. Determined to ensure that she would know better than to cross the line again, he deliberately repeated the stroke, landing a stinging delivery on top of the already blistering upper buttocks. He decided to lay on more than he had promised, determined to break her completely, and was not at all surprised when she screamed her surrender.

Her hands deserted their post to try and block the anticipated stroke of the strap.

"No more, please Professor, no more. I cannot take any more, it hurts too much, oh no, it hurts so much, no more. I know we agreed that I would have no safe word at my insistence but I can't do this anymore. It hurts too much. Can I have a safe word to use now, please?"

Stones, of course, was as sanguine as ever at the reaction of one of the recipients of his devastatingly effective use of punishment instruments. He knew full well the effect, with his own urges meaning he had been on the receiving end of many a thorough thrashing, and so had little sympathy for the frantic reactions to those who felt his ire. Female tears moved him not a jot; he was an extremely good judge of the ability of each individual to withstand the anguish he unleashed and his enjoyment of the suffering caused was always equal in his mind to the act that created the response. Igniting the emotions of a miscreant was a duty as well as a pleasure and through pain and punishment came correction, redemption and enlightenment.

"Resignation is the word I have chosen for your safe word. Resignation! That's right, you pathetic creature, resignation. It had to be, did it not? Not prepared to take your just desserts, then you must pay the ultimate price for your cowardice. I will release your right hand and you can scrawl your words of disgrace and defeat. You are ready to surrender now, are you? Unable to take the punishment that you have happily overseen so many times without mercy or sympathy. Where's that moral toughness now? Where's that elegance and fortitude? Where's your dignity, you worthless hussy?"

He had hoped for, and to be honest expected, a positive and resilient response and was not to be disappointed as Dorothy brought her stoicism and pride to the fore.

"Oh fuck you, Edward, just get on with it then, you sadistic bastard. I am not giving you the satisfaction of breaking me completely. So do you worst, you heartless sod!"

"Ah-ha, she finds some courage at last. Fighting talk, my dear, fighting talk indeed. Obviously a few more punishment strokes earned with that little outburst, so let's have you on my special treats table, shall we?"

Dorothy sobbed in response as she yielded to his power and within seconds he had his contraption in place. The massage table concealed in a wall unit with its straps and pulley system that left his wrongdoers completely powerless and exposed. Dorothy's tear-stained face looked at Stones in horror as, laid on her back and fastened by hand and foot, he operated the system that lifted her legs and bottom clear of table of the platform before pulling her feet up towards her shoulders. The headrest was raised so that as he stood at the bottom of the table she was looking at him through wide open legs, her sex displayed completely to both of them. He ran a finger down her pussy to her arsehole and smiled wickedly.

"Oh no, oh no. I beg you please don't whip me there, please."

Stones raised his eyebrows.

"I may do, I may not. My little knotted lash has not been out for a while and I do like to keep my hand in."

"I will do whatever you say, Dean. Please do not whip me there."

Her pleas were becoming more desperate and Stones relented. He knew that there was an increasing likelihood that full sex was to be the crowning consequence of this liaison and was loath to risk spoiling that opportunity by overplaying his hand.

"Take a couple more with the strap well and then I will give you a taste of my longer knotted lash across these rather beleaguered cheeks to ensure that you have some long-term marking to remember your downfall. Chin up and look me in the eyes while I deliver the strap."

Dorothy gulped and let out a forlorn-sounding sob as she obeyed his instruction and met his steely gaze as he raised the thick leather above his shoulder once more.

Thwack!

"Yaaaaaaah!"

Her writhing body shook the table as Stones prepared to add to her agony.

"Eyes to me, Dorothy, eyes to me."

The weeping woman looked imploringly at Stones, earning herself a wide grin in return as he swung the strap hard against the very top of her raised bottom.

Thwack!

"Yaaaar! Yaaaar! Yaaaar! No, no, no, no, no."

Stones turned his back on her and went to his cabinet, hooked up his strap and turned back to her, holding the long leather lash with its tightly knotted strands prominently placed throughout even its length. Taking the handle in his right hand he began to swish the wicked-looking implement through the air as he returned to stand between her splayed legs. He crouched before her openness, peering intently at her ravaged buttocks before loudly sniffing at her crotch.

"Hmmmmm, you do smell rather nice, my dear. I do like to take in the scent of a nice vagina mixed with the aroma of fear-induced sweat. Lovely, lovely."

He flicked the knotted lash down her anal cleft, just catching the bottom of her labia. Her whole body jolted with the unexpected focus as her cheeks closed tightly in anguish and terror.

"Oh my, no. Please, Edward. Not there. I beg you, please."

His laughter was chilling.

"Just a warning, my dear. That was a tickle. Imagine, if you will, a full-blooded blow with the lash sending these tight little knots against your pussy lips. So behave now or that nightmare will come true."

He drew back his arm and then released a flurry of blows against the centre of her rounded cheeks. The knots and flared tail of the leather whipping hard against her blistered flesh. She screamed once more. Her whole body shook, racked with pain and he delivered twelve quick and accurate strikes.

He returned his lash to the cabinet and closed it with finality. Dorothy was still in the throes of the stinging agony as he moved beside her to mop her tears and wipe her brow.

"Hush, my dear, hush now and pull yourself together. Your atonement has been truly orchestrated and carried out perfectly. Your remorse is total. Your contrition placed on show. The naughty girl has received a fitting punishment as she deserved. All is forgiven. Hush, hush, my dear. There now."

He leaned in to kiss her gently on the lips, continuing to whisper his words that confirmed her ordeal was over and that she was pardoned for her sins. He unstrapped her and took her shaking body into his arms and held her tightly, stroking her back and placing delicate kisses on her neck.

She raised her head to his as her sobs subsided and he could see the ardour in her eyes. Her hand moved slowly and with great hesitation towards his tented trousers. With a loud sigh she ran her fingertips very tenderly down the covered length as she finally looked into his eyes, the apprehension leaving her face as she saw her longing reflected. She licked her lips and ventured:

"Oh my days, I can't believe how much I want you, Edward. I have been obsessing about seeing that erection in the flesh ever since the size of it first became apparent. I promised myself faithfully when I first thought to divulge my shameful behaviour to you that this was about punishment and justice, about guilt and shame, about the path I needed to tread to salve my conscience, to earn forgiveness and show true contrition. This was not to be about sex or longing or desire. Seems like I have failed again, Edward. I am struggling to understand what this means but to be blunt my sex is on fire as much as my poor bottom is. I have never wanted a cock as much as I want yours now. Please may I unleash this monster, Edward?"

He kissed her deeply, his hands, with fingernails digging into her back, urging her on as her fingers moved down to touch his erection. Wordlessly she sank to her knees, unhooking his belt and easing his trousers down. She reached to slip off his shoes, socks and remove the trousers completely from him before her hands went to the band of his pants and eased them over his throbbing cock. Stones slipped his shirt over his head, now naked, and he felt her hands tentative in their touch as she slowly encased his length in her hands. Dorothy bent forward to kiss his stomach and then his thighs as she worked her mouth around his groin. Her tongue flicked out and tickled the tip of his manhood, her reward a low groan and hands working their way into her hair. She teased him with light kisses and delicate touches with her tongue before licking her lips and then engulfing him into her wet, warm mouth. Her hands grasped handfuls of his buttocks as she forced him deeper inside before she slid him out. Taking him in one hand, she stood up.

"Bedroom?" she queried.

Retaining her hold on his cock she led him through to his bedroom, before climbing on and laying on her back with her legs wide apart.

"Take what you want, Edward. Do what you want and ask anything of me. You can have me, Edward, any way you wish. You are the master, Edward. I am but your slave, now a mistress in name only. A possession, a lover, a whore, a harlot. What you desire me to be, I am. Yours, Edward. Yours."

He climbed onto the bed and bent down between her legs,

grasped her upper thighs and breathed in noisily. He felt her legs tense but sensed no resistance as he slowly dipped his head down to the glinting slickness of her pulsing pussy lips. His nose nudged her clitoris, feeling the hard nub, and his tongue snaked out and he began to lap at her wet folds. For several minutes he licked her delicately, his tongue accepted and rewarded with a low continuous moaning and a body that gently writhed as she gave herself so willingly. He smiled at her acquiescence, her surrender, her acceptance of his control and her promise to indulge him. He raised his head and planted a kiss onto her parted lips, his tongue seeking hers, his fingers tweaking hard, erect nipples.

"Delectable, my dear, absolutely delectable. Pure nectar of the Gods, simply divine. Your pussy juice is sweet and tasty."

Dorothy responded to his kisses, words and manipulations, with a passion and enthusiasm that he found a real turn-on and for several minutes they moved together as their tongues explored every part of each other's willing mouths, their bodies grinding against each other. Once more their senses were ignited and mutually aligned, he heard her sigh of approval as he turned his back on her and placed his knees on either side of her head.

"Come to me, my darling, come to me." Her husky voice betrayed her longing as her mouth reached up for his throbbing erection.

He positioned himself to allow her lips to gather him into the warmth of her mouth. He placed his elbows between her legs before forcing them under her knees and lifting and widening her spread legs. As her tongue encircled his hard cock and her head gently bobbed, he dipped his own face down and rubbed his mouth and nose into the sodden gash below. She moaned loudly, the pressure of her lips tightening around his length, her movements less calculated now, more driven by her own desire as she welcomed his tongue delving deep inside of her sex. He pushed his face down so that his nose teased at her anal opening, his chin pressing hard against her pubic mound. He felt a wet finger circle around his own arsehole rim and paused in expectation. She plunged her finger into his arsehole and he groaned into her pussy, teeth nibbled at her erect clitoris as he pushed his whole face hard against her. The urgency of her sucking mouth increased and he judged their climactic moments to be close. He pulled back, completely embedding the full length of her finger into his bottom and eased his cock from her mouth. He grimaced as she whipped her finger free, the pain and discomfort of the exit an added element of his sexual pleasure. As he turned he took the finger deep into his mouth, his eyes thanking her and he positioned himself with his wet cock at the entrance to her fanny.

He finally entered her, driving into her willing wet warmth, his hard, rigid cock plunged deep inside of her. She accepted the thrust willingly, her body jerking forward to meet him as he forced his hips back, then forwards again. She convulsed against him, her body twitching and shuddering as he thrust again and again, each time more forcibly than the stroke before. Her body began to rise to meet his efforts as the two began to work in tandem as they searched for their moments together. Their fit seemed perfect, their bodies entwined, their limbs as one. His hands slid under her taut buttocks as her small hands reached to grasped his in their reciprocal lust. He took a quick glance at her face and was rewarded with a beaming smile before she closed her eyes as she forced her wanton body upwards to chase and encase his cock as he pulled back ready to pump into her once more. She worked her body simultaneously with his, moving with his thrusts, taking his cock inside of her wet hole, sucking him in. Her fingernails dug into his bottom as she pulled him deeper into her. He paused, held himself above her, almost flipping out of her as she desperately raised her flanks, screaming at him, clawing at his body, imploring him to feed her slick, wanton tunnel. He smiled knowingly as he began his journey of hard, rapid and deep strokes that would take him to climax.

"Yes! Yes! Yes!" she screamed. "Come in me, come in me. Give it to me, Edward. Fucking well give it to me. I want your spunk. Come in me, my love. Spunk in me, my darling."

Stones felt her arms move to his neck as she kissed him deeply and began to force her pubic bone hard against him to match his thrusting strokes. He sank his cock in as deep and hard as he could as he felt the sensation of his sperm travelling through his member seconds before it exploded inside of her. He groaned long and loud as she screamed in response, her body jerked and writhed to match his, her face a grimace as though in pain before her tension released and he felt her sprinkling inside as she came howling and sobbing. Her eyes screwed tight, her lips wide apart, her hunger obvious, her climax dramatic, as she convulsed, shuddered and then collapsed beneath him. Her hands pummelled his back and then grasped his buttocks once more, forcing him inside of her as deep as possible, seeming to Stones as if she was trying to suck his cock empty. He held himself still as she writhed and twisted, she rubbed her pubic bone hard against him once more before her body shook and tremored beneath him as she came again.

"That was most pleasant, most poignant and most passionate, my dear. Thank you for your time and the opportunity to enjoy you in the ways that so delight me. I hope your bottom appreciated receiving the thrashing as much as I enjoyed delivering it. The fucking was of the highest level also, I have to say. However, your time is up. I believe that you have a dinner to get to. So get dressed and get out."

He watched as she quickly threw her clothes on, undoubtedly conscious of needing to spruce herself up, waiting for the moment she spotted that he held her panties in his hand. Her voice when the time came betrayed her uneasiness in asking the question.

"Um, Edward, can I please have my knickers back?"

Stones smiled that renowned smile of his that brought no one favour.

"Absolutely not, my dear. They are my keepsake from tonight."

He held them up before inspecting them and then burying his face into the depths of the material, taking a loud long sniff.

"Lovely. I'll always remember what played host to these beauties when I finger and sniff them. No, Dorothy, not only do you leave here vanquished and without knickers, but you will now vow to me you will attend your dinner tonight with no undergarments on whatsoever. Let the air get to your most private parts whilst serving as a reminder of what you were doing before you arrived. The answer is, of course, to be in the affirmative, I take it?" Stones voice was at its most imperious.

She looked at the floor, a forlorn and accepting expression on her face.

"Yes, Edward, of course." Her shoulders slumped in defeat and she left his room without a further word.

There was nothing Stones could do to ensure her compliance but he absolutely, without any doubt whatsoever, knew that she would acquiesce. He had mastered the mistress and his sense of triumph was almost overwhelming.

CHAPTER 6

MELANIE NEEDS A WAKE-UP CALL

The message he received from Melanie, in response to his request for her and Emily Govan to attend his quarters for an unrelated disciplinary issue, had been full of woe. Although her diet and exercise regime had begun with great promise and much weight had been lost, her message was one of despair as the time had come for her to attend his rooms for a weigh-in to monitor her progress. In response, Stones had brought their meeting forward as he very much suspected what the outcome of her visit to the scales would lead to.

Melanie sobbed as she took in the scornful look from Professor Stones. The naked woman trembled all over, her vast breasts heaving as she gulped air. Much as she had quickly become very relaxed and unashamed in displaying her nude body to the professor on her regular visits, the thought of having incurred his wrath and disappointment brought her much chagrin.

"I am so sorry, sir. I have really let you down. I am such a weak useless specimen, aren't I?"

Stones continued to stare her in disapproval. He realised that this was a significant moment in not just the student's battle to lose weight but also in her quest for self-esteem and inner peace.

"You haven't let me down, Melanie, you have let yourself down. Now in a clear voice, announce this month's result so we are in agreement on that before we discuss any repercussions or action to correct and amend the situation."

The student took a breath, peered once more at the digital display on the scales she stood on and spoke the words she had dreaded saying ever since she had embarked on the quest to lose substantial amounts of weight. Several successive months of significant weight loss had followed her sessions with the Dean of Discipline and she seemed to have committed fully to the diet and exercise regime that Stones and the college nurse had set her. Until now.

"I have gained five pounds, Professor Stones. I am so sorry. I pigged out for a few days and just did not bother with my exercises and ignored my diet. It will not happen again."

Stones leaned over to check the scales before recording the weight on his laptop screen.

"To be fair, Melanie, this is your first step backwards and not a disaster. We will ensure it is just a blip by putting into play the agreed correctional treatment and you will commit to acting in a more disciplined manner going forward. Now I suggest that you take a seat and write me a short piece explaining in detail your disobedience, your lack of willpower and the behaviour that led to this unfortunate situation. You will also detail how you wish to pay your dues this afternoon. I believe that you do wish to be given the opportunity to find solace at least in receiving a deserved punishment and a chance to restore some pride and dignity by accepting your just desserts?"

The distressed student was only too pleased to pursue the route that would pacify her mentor and earn any crumb of approval that he offered.

"Oh yes, sir, yes indeed. I don't want to let you down again, sir. Whatever you think is best, sir. Yes, sit down and write, sir. Yes indeed I will, sir. Thank you, sir. Sorry, sir."

Her incoherent dabbling continued quietly before she composed herself at the desk and began to write.

"Get on with it quietly and quickly, we have a busy afternoon ahead and, all being well, an interesting distraction for you to follow once we have put your indiscretion behind us. That is, presuming that the next hour goes to my approval. I hope my trust in you to become Emily's replacement as my student carer in disciplinary matters has not been misplaced. We have a couple of first years to have a little chat with soon and I can see a role for you dependent on the choices they make and the route they wish to take."

Melanie's eyes lit up briefly as his words sunk in and a sly grin passed across her face before she returned her pen to paper with a touch more enthusiasm. Stones had earlier recruited her as a support student for disciplinary issues, alongside Emily Govan, and he could see from her application to the task with renewed vigour that she understood an opportunity to be involved in a punishment session could well be on the agenda.

The buzz of his doorbell caused her to flinch and a look of anxiety crossed her features before her previous experiences in the room caused her to maintain poise and continue her work as the door opened on Stones' command.

"Afternoon, Emily, welcome back to the college, thank you for attending. I hope that your guest room is to your liking and that all your needs are met. As I told you on the telephone, I wish for you to team up with Melanie here once again to aid in bringing her up to standard as my student support assistant. I thank you for agreeing to be available at my behest and hope that you will find your short stay back here rewarding. We have an extended duty today, as Melanie has let herself down somewhat with her weight-watching discipline, so I hope you are up for a double shift?"

The first look of gleeful anticipation was immediately followed by a frown and a decidedly more pensive look.

"Oh dear, if Melanie has let herself down then that means as her mentor I too have failed you, sir."

Her voice was servile, but clear and Stones knew that the prospect of being beaten was not unwelcome.

"That is a moot point, Emily. I have to say that I assumed with your mentoring that Melanie would have been beyond returning to her previous slovenly ways. I am not sure, therefore, that you are to blame in any way for her taking backward steps since you left the college. Do you feel that you are in some way responsible then?"

Emily's gaze lowered to the floor and Stones' mood lifted immensely by her next words.

"Sir, I obviously did not commit to training her as I should have. I am appalled at her failure to stick to her promised plan and certainly believe that she should be thrashed to remind her of her commitment and lack of will power. However, I must accept responsibility too, as it was my task to ensure that she understood that she faced repercussions for any deviance and I apparently have failed. I can only apologise and present myself in disgrace to face your ire. Any punishment due to Melanie must also be my cross to bear, sir. It is only correct and fair."

"Absolutely correct, Emily. So clothes off, and in the corner while we wait for Melanie to scribble down her apologies, her plea for assisted redemption and her proposed voluntary punishment. Obviously that will be for the two of you."

Emily's speed of undress was almost indecent. Stones hid his pleasure as he was once more rewarded with the sight of the stunning blonde's perfectly proportioned and gym-fit naked form. She had only been gone from the college for a matter of weeks but hers was company that he had never tired of, and had been delighted at her response to return when requested. He was far too long in the tooth to pretend to himself that Emily was not aware of his reciprocal attraction to her and the rather devious and cunning strategies she had employed, in the past, to tempt or manipulate him to do what she wanted. On the other hand they both were fully aware that he consistently outmanoeuvred her at every turn and Stones knew that she was well aware her feminine wiles had failed spectacularly to achieve her aims as far as her intentions towards him sexually went. Whatever her wishes, Stones was exceedingly grateful that her supposed opportunism led to him being able to feast on the sight of those twin globes of delight that never failed to arouse him. Regardless of how many females had exposed their buttocks to him over the years, he honestly could not name one whose wares had consistently stirred the passion in him in the way that a display of Emily's bottom did. His eyes feasted on her delicious globes as she, intentionally he had no doubt, took her time in unveiling and presenting her rear view to him. Not that he gave away those thoughts; the slightest hint of a sign that he thought she may have cemented a special place in his heart, he saw as an invitation to prove her wrong and keep her uncertain.

As she settled herself in the regulation pose that she knew so well, her hands on her head, her legs apart, Stones enjoyed the long, lingering moment contemplating the firm, rounded spheres of her flawless symmetrical buttocks. As his cock stirred his thoughts were interrupted by Melanie's apologetic words of contrition and supplication.

"So sorry, sir, I hope I have put into words my acceptance of my dereliction of duty and lack of control. I am happy to take full responsibility and ask that I take on Emily's punishment as the blame is entirely my own, pathetic specimen that I am."

Stones sighed as he took the sheet of paper from her hand and waved her to the corner to join Emily.

"So, young lady, you believe that a spanking followed by a dozen of the best with a cane of my choice is suitable punishment for your embarrassing weakness and inability to follow a simple and straightforward set of instructions regarding your diet and exercise regime. Obviously doubling that would be yours to bear if I was to allow you to take on Emily's share. Emily, do you have something to say? I assume you do."

Stones saw the glance between the two and the subtle smile and nod from Emily to the other.

"I absolutely must insist that I be allowed to take my share of any thrashing due, sir. May I add to Melanie's fine words by insisting that I need to accept my own misgivings and failures in this matter, sir? I also believe that a spanking and a caning would be appropriate to bring a resolution to this matter, sir, and would, hopefully, ensure that you have no cause to repeat this chastisement for a similar reason. To that end, I would suggest that the punishment should be severe to benefit both of us, sir. For me as a reminder to take responsibility more seriously and for Melanie to act as a warning that lack of commitment and poor application is not acceptable and bodes badly for the future. Nip this in the bud now, sir, and improvement will be realised."

Stones smiled at her use of words similar to ones he had espoused consistently over the years and handed the paper to Emily.

"Nicely said, Emily. Although please be aware that I intend to wipe the self-satisfied look from your face and make you regret your fine and supposedly unselfish words. Now put that into writing succinctly to confirm that you agree with Melanie's punishment and wish to be treated accordingly."

He took Melanie by the hand, led her to a part of his bookcase and revealed two sets of metal rings.

"I do not actually believe an over-the-knee hand spanking is the answer for persistent offenders such as yourselves, too comfortable for the recipient by half, so we will try something else to drive my message home. Take hold of the rings, please, Melanie, and shuffle backwards and push those buttocks out. Emily, put the paper on my desk and take your place alongside your fellow rapscallion, please."

The rings were positioned at a height that forced the hands and head down below the waist in a classic school caning pose with the bottom high and the cheeks rounded and tight. Stones opened his cabinet that housed his assorted implements of chastisement and picked out a thick rounded wooden paddle and his medium-thickness cane.

"Twenty with the paddle ladies and then a standard 12 of the best with the cane. I doubt that I will have any problems with you two old hands but just so you have notice there will, of course, be punishment strokes available for any non-compliance or further poor behaviour. I will alternate the strokes so that you both get a consistent level of force. Prepare yourselves. The first few blows will be quite a shock without a warmup from my hand. There's a reason why there is a sequence established in the use of thrashing implements and number of strokes. You are about to discover why a spanking is beneficial to all parties."

Stones positioned himself behind Melanie and addressed the two supplicants.

"Excellent presentation, Emily, everything displayed, good show. Now Melanie, with much less padding than you used to display I think we should be expecting to see that lovely anus of yours on full show. So one further step back, legs slightly further apart, buttocks pushing up at me. Success! There you go, one shy puckered rose gloriously peeking out from the darkness. Now concentrate on keeping that exhibited throughout."

As he finished speaking, the paddle landed against Melanie's substantial left buttock. A pause to enjoy the moment when the milky white skin turned a bright shade of pink as a perfect circle appeared in the centre of the cheek and, before her scream in reaction had time to form fully in her throat, he slammed down hard across Emily's buttocks. The stifled scream from one of his most resilient victims was music to his ears, although the noise emitted by Melanie would feasibly have drowned her out anyway!

The next six strokes were administered in a few seconds with Melanie's howling virtually unbroken and Emily grunting in a most unladylike manner as she fought to keep her response under control.

"As warned, my young beauties, a hand spanking is an excellent preparation to aid in withstanding the much harsher application that usually follows. It gets one acclimatised to the sting and pain, its warming effect has an element of comfort, the process of bare hand to exposed buttocks has that aspect of sensuality and, dependent on the relationship between giver and taker, can be erotic and sexually charged for one or both. The harsh slap of a thick paddle with no prior groundwork to lay a foundation for its receipt is a different kettle of fish. Funnily enough I have discovered that my recipients do not seem to find that the strokes get easier to bear as the chastisement continues. Presumably you two would not disagree with that from the sounds of it!"

Whether or not his question was rhetorical was not something that the two students appeared to wish to comment on as the paddle swept down again and again. Melanie's legs were buckling and Stones could see that her hold on the rings was close to breaking as he completed the 20-blow punishment.

Emily's recovery was impressive, a final moan, a few deep breaths and a long sigh.

"Thank you very much, Professor Stones. Thoroughly deserved and I am so sorry to have put you to the trouble. I would be honoured to take a damn good caning now to complete my retribution for my shame."

"For goodness sake, Melanie! If you could please desist with the wailing now, pull yourself together and get yourself back into the correct position for chastisement. If that is not too much trouble for you, please, Melanie."

Stones began to tap the cane against the quivering bright red bottom as he waited patiently for the snivelling Melanie to present herself correctly.

"Extra strokes coming your way unless those legs straighten and that backside is held correctly, buttocks nice and tight, and raised high within five seconds."

Melanie immediately took the correct position, adjusting her posture to present as he had ordered.

"Good girl, good girl. Hold tight and here we go."

The cane landed on his final syllable and was instantly repeated on Emily's firm and perfectly still bottom.

"Thank you, sir. Please can I have another one?" was the response.

"Oh indeed, my dear, but do be quiet. You were not invited to speak. Further words and your legs will be in receipt of my disapproval as an additional gift."

Stones smiled as Emily whispered her apology, and began to slash the cane down in turn on the exposed bottoms. The more fleshy buttocks of Melanie accepted the wooden implement as though wrapping it in her folds of more plentiful cushioning, contrasting with the tighter hard buttocks of Emily that produced an almost trampoline bounce effect as his cane landed and retracted instantly. In a short while the final strokes hit their targets, Melanie mewing loudly and jerking her bottom from side to side, Emily as stoic as ever, grunting quietly as each stroke landed but ultimately taking the delivery as her due and just punishment. Stones swung the cane back harder and harder; he doubted this was the last time he would deliver such treatment to Emily's beautiful bottom but it could be and he intended that she would remember the sensation. The sobbing of Melanie was inconsequential to him. Much as he enjoyed the application of a cane to any female's bare buttocks, she was a supporting actress in this play, admirable though he thought her acquiescence was.

Flattening the quivering cheeks of Melanie and the motionless buttocks of Emily for the final time, Stones stepped back to admire the view and his handiwork.

"Excellent ruby-red lines all down the buttocks, good pink background from the paddle, smarting sore cheeks for both. Job done, ladies. Rise and shine. In the corner, hands on heads, legs apart, rosy cheeks on show. Chop, chop."

Both students shuffled over to the supplicant positions, the discomfort of their throbbing cheeks very much evident, to face the corners of the room. Emily was quick to articulate her notion of what was expected.

"Thank you, sir. We both apologise for our indiscretions and weaknesses, sir, and appreciate you finding the time to help correct our poor performance. Don't we, Melanie?"

Melanie took her cue.

"Oh. Absolutely, Professor Stones. I am so sorry to have let you down and apologise profusely to Emily for causing her to be thrashed. My fault entirely, sir. Sorry, sir, and thank you."

Stones ran his hands over both sore bottoms.

"That will do. Quiet now. Stand still and contemplate your failings. We will wait for today's miscreants to appear before moving on."

It was several minutes before the chimes of the doorbell announced the expected visitors.

CHAPTER 7

FREYA AND NATALIE THOUGHT IT WOULD BE A LAUGH

The door opened and two nervous-looking students entered. Their astonished faces as they noticed the naked figures of Emily and Melanie delighted Stones. One froze in mid-step, her mouth hanging open, the other stumbled, as her eyes flashed between the naked forms with their bright red bottoms and the professor.

The two young women, both first-year undergraduates, both slight, with short blonde hair and very pretty to the point that they could easily be mistaken for twins or sisters haltingly gathered themselves and stood nervously before Professor Stones, glancing back at Emily and Melanie in comic amazement and bewilderment. He let the silence hang for a moment or two. Neither of the young women had been in the rooms of the much feared Dean of Discipline before and their demeanour rather suggested that they were not at all happy to be before him now. The sight of the two obviously punished students already in the room had clearly brought home the stark reality of the trouble they were in.

"Now then, Freya Barnes and Natalie Cornwell, just what have you two been up to that has caused you to need to visit me? Oh look, puzzled expressions and looks of pure innocence, surely I am not mistaken and you have been summoned here in error? I do not think young Emily and Melanie came to my rooms in error. I certainly hope not as I have just thrashed their bent-over bare buttocks as you can see. Freya, what have you got to say for yourself? I can see from the stupid expression on your face that your feeble mind is working and that you have got something you wish to voice."

Stones, of course, had all his facts assembled and was just going through a well-worn routine of seeing how far he would be required to lead these two before they buckled and admitted that they had something to feel guilty about.

"Sir, we really don't know. We are well-behaved and studious so really have no idea why we should have been called to a disciplinary hearing, sir."

Stones just raised his eyebrows at Freya, immediately identifying herself as the spokesperson of the two youngsters. First years, on the whole, tended to be less likely to get into serious trouble at college. Over the years it was an established pattern that the most troublesome students were second years. By now established in the college and used to its ways, more knowledgeable about the city and its attractions and with the big plus of there generally being no examinations of real importance in this year of their courses. A year older and possibly a year more streetwise with burgeoning confidence and assurance, but unfortunately as they often found to their cost, not quite as all-knowing as they first thought. These two were still not as worldly-wise in university time as they liked others to think and Stones, as worldly-wise as it was possible to be, saw through the bravado with no moment of doubt.

Professor Stones was proficient at using silence and he let Freya's words hang in the air as he adopted an expression that incorporated both doubt in the students' ignorance and growing frustration at their reticence in accepting that they had something to hide.

"So, nothing to see here is the stance you are taking. Let us see if you are so tight-lipped and oblivious of any wrongdoing once you are separated."

Stones told Natalie to step outside, into his secluded garden, and noted the clear glance of apprehension she directed at Freya.

"Come on, child, out you go. I will open the door automatically when I require you back inside for your version of events. I would advise that you take the time to have a rethink of your state of denial while you are in the fresh air. Then we will see if you have a tale to tell that matches what Freya is about to reveal."

Stones could see that his carefully chosen words had produced the intended effect as the darting eyes of the two students gave evidence to their growing unease and seeping confidence.

As a now decidedly nervous Freya stood before him, casting furtive eyes back at the two silent naked students, Stones worked the controls that allowed a screen to unravel slowly from its concealed casement in his ceiling. The screen flickered into life under the professor's administrations and a perfect view of the street in front of the college appeared. With a few deft movements with his hand the picture moved to focus on a close-up of the external windows of the first-floor student rooms above the college gates that overlooked the street.

"I can go closer and I can fast forward to the time that is most relevant, Freya. However, I do much prefer to allow the reprobates before me an opportunity to ease their consciences and begin the necessary steps towards acceptance of blame for misbehaviour, contrition and then correction and improvement. Now, young lady, would you like to talk me through what occurred and at least show some gumption and a bit of honesty?"

Freya seemed frozen as she stared at the screen. There could be no dispute that the close-up showed the main window of her bedroom and Stones rather hoped it was now just a matter of time before the student would realise that it would be judicious to come clean.

"I am going to give you a moment to contemplate and compose your thoughts. Emily and Melanie can get dressed, their punishment is over. You, Freya, can go and stand in the corner, face against the wall between the bookcases. I will give you five minutes and you need to appreciate that these are five minutes that will determine an awful lot that is going to happen in your life in the very near future. Do not even think to debate this with me as my patience is wearing rather thin. So take yourself and that petulant expression over to the wall as instructed this instance, girl!"

Stones' voice had risen as he spoke and Freya's resistance wilted, and with a shrug of her shoulders she turned and slowly made her way into the corner as instructed. The exchange of glances with the two released from the corner was telling. Melanie's expression was one of pity towards the young student replacing her, combined with self-pity as her tentative steps gave evidence to the success of the right arm of the Dean of Discipline. Emily locked eyes for longer and Stones appreciated the message that her raised eyebrows and nodding head were intended as encouragement to give the younger student strength to step up to the plate.

Stones smiled. He enjoyed these challenges and had no doubt that he would soon be dealing with two apologetic and contrite young women. Emily would be key to their transformation from deniers to apologetic confessors and he beamed at her, knowing full well that his approval was all the incentive she would need to play her part.

After Emily and Melanie were dressed and having obediently written their notes apologising for their misdemeanours, Stones asked Melanie to read hers out. Emily smiled, knowing full well that this was for Freya's benefit, to add to her turmoil as she stewed in the corner. Melanie was hesitant but the prospect of refusing an instruction from the professor was not something she would spend too long contemplating! She was eloquent though as she read clearly her words of apology, accepting blame, thanking him for his pearls of wisdom and for showing her the path to redemption with a thrashing of her bare bottom. Stones saw the flinch that passed through Freya's body as she processed those last words and suspected that hers was a bottom that would soon be exposed to his gaze. That it would be most appropriate given the student's conduct that had resulted in her presence in his room pleased him no end!

His connections within the city centre's CCTV operations, who worked privately but in association with the police, had alerted him to the goings on in the rooms overlooking the college's grand frontage. His patronage had been the reason that they not only had some of the best equipment in their field but also a well-furnished and spacious recreation room to spend their off-shift breaks in. In return Stones was allowed virtually complete access to any footage he required when dealing with incidents that concerned the college. Young drunken females pointing their naked bottoms out of windows overlooking the street fell exactly into that field. Stones could not actually identify the students, the footage mainly showed protruding white buttocks, but the two summoned girls were the sole occupants of the shared suite of rooms, and were not ruled out by their body shapes and skin colour, so were clearly chief suspects in anyone's eyes.

Stones asked the fully dressed Emily and Melanie to bring Freya to him as he sat at his console as though preparing to play his key card.

"So, young lady, have you decided on the course of action you will now take? Your punishment for your misdemeanour is not fixed. This is important as you do need to realise that I will determine the severity of your sentence based on your honesty with me over the next few minutes. Take this opportunity to purge yourself of guilt, seek redemption and forgiveness, and accept the consequences of your outrageous actions or choose to deny everything, play innocent and lie through your back teeth to me."

Freya blanched, her eyes fixed on the screen that showed a frozen image of the partially opened windows of the students' room.

"I. Um. We. Um. I..." Her attempt to speak was like a red rag to a bill to Stones, the arch manipulator.

"Speak clearly, young lady. You apparently are a bright spark with aspirations to follow in your mother's footsteps. A top legal career will require you to be articulate, eloquent and honest. I challenge you now to take a deep breath, engage your thought processes and display the character and backbone required in adversity. Then, and only then, young lady, can we move on and see if your time here at college can come to a worthwhile conclusion. I am hoping that you get my drift, Freya, and that in the next few minutes you come to your senses and admit your actions and possibly give me some sort of explanation. We can then hopefully move on to discussing the consequences of your behaviour. Those consequences are to a degree in your own hands, Freya. They can be long lasting and detrimental to your future or they can be very much under the category of short-term pain for long-term gain. So think on, my dear, and let us look for a resolution that can allow us to move on with no lasting damage." His words had the desired effect as Freya raised her chin and with a long breath in, spoke.

"I am so sorry, Professor Stones, I really do not know what made me behave like that. I know that we had been drinking but I have never done anything like that before. I am so very sorry."

"Not enough, you urchin. I want to hear you describe fully your actions. This is a confession that will determine your punishment and as such needs to illustrate a clear understanding of your disgraceful actions and a full description of your deed. In detail, girl, in detail. Your partner in crime will be back in here in a minute so do not leave a single detail out. I will not accept any vagaries in your tales, and there will be consequences if any are apparent," Stones barked at the trembling student, whose face now displayed the expression of a vanquished foe.

"Yes, sir. Sorry, sir. Well, what happened is that we were hanging out of the window, I think Natalie was sitting with her legs on the sill. We can do this safely as there is a little sort of balcony that you can put your feet down into. We were chatting to some friends in the street below originally but they had just left when a group of Hamilton College students came past. We had a bit of a fractious baseball match with them the other week, sir. We both play for the college in the inter-college women's league. They recognised us because Natalie and one of their team are on the same degree course, and there was a bit of banter and name-calling. One of them kept saying that they had kicked our backsides and, oh dear, er, um, Natalie said that they could kiss our backsides now, sir. I can't really explain why we did it but they made slurping and kissing noises, sir, and before I knew it Natalie had got up, pulled her trousers and knickers down and pointed her bare bum out of the window. I did not think, sir, and just automatically did the same. We were sort of taunting them saying things like only in their dreams could they kiss bottoms as beautiful as ours. Oh my, I am so sorry, it sounds so childish and rude now."

Stones fixed the now decidedly apprehensive student with his most severe gaze.

"Your confession does you credit although your actions clearly do not. So no shilly-shallying now, Freya. I believe that this act of degradation and outrage deserves a severe punishment and a one-term suspension, followed by confinement to college for a further term on your return. You have brought shame and outrage to the door of this institution. An unforgiveable offence. Freya, this proposed sentence would seem appropriate, along with a written apology to the shocked members of the general public that reported your offence. Obviously your withdrawal from all university social and sporting activities goes without saying. Oh, you looked surprised. What exactly did you think your obscene act, your disgraceful behaviour and your objectionable shaming of this noble institution would bring forth?"

"But, but, but sir. You mean we would be sent home? Our parents would be told? We would miss our lectures, supervisions and tutorials? Sir, no, please. That would be disastrous, sir. What about um, you know, sir? Um, other sorts of punishments?"

Stones' joyful inner emotions stayed just as he set his face with a look of query and lack of understanding. He saw Emily's grin out of Freya's eye-line and decided then and there that he would enlist both of his earlier victims as assistants in what very much looked like the upcoming thrashing of at least one unhappy young lady.

"Do please expand on your thinking, Miss Barnes? I am always open to considering viable options that have no detrimental educational impact on the reprobates of this college."

The contortions that the student's face went through as she decided exactly how she was going to phrase an alternative proposal were comical but her dilemma was fully to the approval of Stones. After a most unladylike gulp and long sniff, Freya said the words that Stones could never tire of hearing!

"Could we not have a thrashing instead, sir? I thought that was what happened if you misbehaved badly in college." She glanced around at Emma and Melanie before continuing, "Just like these two have had, sir."

Stones appeared to consider this as an unexpected option for a moment.

"Well, this is indeed possible although clearly a quite severe chastisement, and decided evidence of your contrition would be required for it to be considered appropriate. I would also expect your partner in crime, Miss Crawford, to be in favour of this route to finding a solution to the dilemma you have landed yourselves in. Do you think the two of you could be in accord with this option?" As Stones had expected Freya leapt wholeheartedly at the opportunity offered.

"Oh yes, sir, if I could speak to her I am sure we would both prefer this option to being suspended."

Stones decided that it was time to bring Natalie back into the room and sent Emily to collect her. Freya was ordered to the corner with her back to the room. The time spent outside had not aided Natalie's state of apprehension and agitation and when she spotted the frozen image of the windows on his screen, she froze.

"Please do come in, Miss Cornwell. Do join us. We were just discussing what occurred after this screenshot. I was rather hoping that you could confirm what your roommate has told us. So, young lady, would you like to enlighten us to your version of what happened next? That was both an instruction and a question, so do please speak." Natalie's mouth had been opening and closing quite comically as he spoke and now her eyes went desperately to her friend, seeming to attempt to read her mind as she stared at the back of her head.

"Oh no. You know, don't you? You know what we did. You know what we did. Oh no. What is going to happen to us?" Tears filled her eyes and her look of desperation. With a faltering voice she went on to give a more or less mirrored version of Freya's version of the flashing episode, her cheeks ablaze with embarrassment. When Stones proceeded to lay out the possible repercussions of their actions, Natalie interrupted him, waving her arms at the motionless figure of her roommate.

"Has she asked for us to be given a caning, sir? I bet she has, she's always talking about the girls who have supposed to have been caned. I bet she's volunteered us to be caned, hasn't she? Oh no. I don't want to, I don't want to. Please can I be punished differently, sir?" She spluttered to a halt.

Stones moved closer to her, causing her to wilt, his voice became harsher and louder as he faced her down.

"I will reiterate what I said to Miss Barnes. This act of degradation and outrage deserves a severe punishment therefore warrants a one-term suspension followed by confinement to college for a further term on your return. You would also be expected to compose an appropriate written apology to the shocked members of the general public that reported your offence. Obviously your withdrawal from all university social and sporting activities goes without saying. Oh, you look just as shocked and surprised as your partner in crime. Do tell me what exactly your obscene act, your disgraceful behaviour and your objectionable shaming of this noble institution deserves as a punishment?"

Natalie was sobbing almost uncontrollably now as the reality of her situation finally sank in.

"It does pain me that I continually have to remind you wretches what exactly you signed up for when you entered this marvellous institution. What I am now holding is an agreement that not only your parents signed but also clearly displays your own signatures accepting the conditions of entry. I will now read out the relevant words to remind you both and then I would suggest that we move things on and desist with this prevarication."

He loudly and dramatically cleared his throat before adopting a solemn tone as he read from the sheets in his hand.

"I undertake to, at all times, observe the orders and regulations of the College and pledge obedience and loyalty to the institution.

"It is my wish that the option of corporal punishment be applied if my indiscretions deem it necessary and appropriate.

"I undertake to accept disciplinary punishment in any form and as proposed by the College's Dean of Discipline and would welcome the opportunity to be educated and improved by such punishment as deemed fit.

"I request that the College accepts my signature as evidence of my commitment and I hereby authorise the said powers to carry out any requisite action to ensure compliance and obedience for the good and benefit of myself, and the College.

"Please accept my signature as my promise and commitment: To the aims and ambitions of the College; to my welfare, my education and my improvement through learning, mentoring and discipline."

He allowed the silence to hang in the air for a few pregnant seconds before pointing at Natalie.

"You have a couple of minutes to pull yourself together, young lady. But this is not a playground. You and Freya may go out into the garden for a few minutes to discuss the options open to you. Emily and Melanie will go with you to help you come to a decision. Rest assured that there are only two options for you to consider and this is your choice. Now get out, the four of you!" he barked.

When Emily led the group back in five minutes later, it was obvious from the subdued and reddened faces of the two young women under pressure, particularly Natalie, that a few home truths had been spelled out. Stones had full faith in Emily and Melanie's loyalty and commitment to his principles and philosophy and was confident that Emily's input would have been crucial to the chastened expressions on both Natalie and Freya's faces. He raised his eyebrows as the two positioned themselves before him, clearly having been schooled as to how they needed to behave at this point in their denouement. Nudging Natalie, Freya took the lead.

"Sir, we are both very sorry that we have conducted ourselves in a manner that has brought shame to the college. Our behaviour was childish, ill considered, offensive and demeaning. We are agreed that a punishment imposed and conducted immediately would be much preferred to any punishment that would be detrimental to our education, our extramural activities at college and extremely upsetting for our parents to have to cope with. Let alone shameful and embarrassing for us to live down at home as well as in college."

She halted as Stones raised his hand. "Thank you, Freya, most articulate and commendable but I do need to hear what Natalie has to say. I need convincing that you are both committed to the alternative route to correction and improvement through physical chastisement. Only once I have heard a convincing case made as to why I should allow you to take what is undoubtedly the more convenient option for you, will I consider that this is the route we will go down."

Natalie took a breath and Stones could see that she was steeling herself to make a statement she obviously would rather not utter. A discreet nudge from Emily, who had placed herself very close to Natalie and was looking at her with a look of exasperation.

"We, um, do not want to be sent home, sir. We are really sorry that we let ourselves and the college down by our actions. Could we perhaps have a spanking on our bottoms to teach us a lesson, sir?"

Stones sighed as Freya almost stamped her feet in frustration at her friend's reticence and Emily gave her another nudge. Stones decided to spell it out.

"Natalie, you are a wretched child and I am not happy at your reluctance to face up to the consequences of your actions. Freya, I believe that you would seize the opportunity for chastisement in the form of a bare-bottom spanking. All corporal punishment is taken fully naked and exposed to ensure full shame is experienced. Your spanking would be followed by a walloping with a leather paddle and rounded off by a 12-stroke caning. If this is what you are proposing then you may go over to that desk and write the confession of your misdeeds, the remorse you feel and the desire you have to be punished specifically as I have outlined. Natalie, you have five minutes to request a similar option for yourself otherwise we will put into process the formal documentation to suspend you from the premises and make contact with your tutors to see if your coursework can be reorganised, to allow you to continue with your degree. Sometimes, I am afraid, it is not possible, but hopefully in your case it will be."

His unemotional and matter-of-fact delivery had an immediate effect as Natalie suddenly found some survival instinct infiltrating her consciousness.

"I am so sorry, sir. I would also like to take up the offer of a thrashing as you have outlined, please. Oh, crikey. I want the beating, sir. Please do not suspend me. Yes, yes, yes. I will accept the beating, sir, please. Can I go and write my statement, please?"

Stones gave her a wry smile. "At last, sense prevails. Go on, get on with it, young lady."

Natalie scurried over to the desk where she received an exaggerated raised eyebrows performance from Freya.

With both documents finally written to Stones' satisfaction the students were sent back to their rooms accompanied by Emily and

Melanie, with instructions to be back in two hours, freshly showered and ready to take their punishment that evening. It suited Stones to keep his two young assistants involved and, aware that Celia had commitments that evening, he had jumped at the chance to bring Sara Morgan into the support role as he manoeuvred to establish the future direction of the disciplinary arena, with his coming retirement now public knowledge.

A quick spot of dinner, a glass of wine and he was ready and waiting well before his doorbell announced arrivals. The leather paddle and his medium-thickness cane were laid on his desk and two tables with attached seating benches were positioned to suit his intentions in the centre of the room. He had left his screen down with the frozen shot of the two exposed bottoms hanging over the window ledge. The four young women entered, Emily with a real spring in her step. Melanie had a more studied expression on her face, Freya looked resigned to her fate, while Natalie just looked plain terrified!

"Enough of today has been wasted on you two rascals, so let us not hang about. Time to face reality, ladies, clothes off and into the corner, hands on your heads, we all know you are keen on displaying your rear assets, don't we!"

Fully mentored by Emily for their ordeal, both students were quick to obey and avoid angering Stones any further. Stones had only needed a few words with Emily to make sure she was fully engaged in how he wished things to proceed, and had rather over-stressed to both of the second-years how their outcomes could worsen if there was any failure to fully cooperate with their agreed tribulation. Stones seated himself in his chair now placed in the centre of the room.

"Natalie, I rather feel we need to start with you before your bravado deserts you. Come here, come here. No avoidance and time-wasting tactics now. Over you go."

A quick tug of her arm and a hand in the back from Emily, and Natalie found herself facing the patterned carpet of the college's dean of discipline, her bottom raised over the substantial man's lap and tiptoeing on the floor as she struggled to get herself balanced. With Emily now moving around to sit before her, tissues at the ready, one hand gripping Natalie's wrists together, and Melanie sitting at her feet holding her ankles wide apart as Stones had prearranged, Natalie's courage went and she began to plead for mercy. She had barely formed her words, when the giant right hand of Professor Stones began a torrent of hard slaps on her tightly stretched, firm young buttocks. To no one's surprise the room was soon filled with yelps, cries and gasps from a student unused to physical chastisement. Eighty slaps and just a couple of minutes later, Stones reached under his chair to pick up the leather paddle. Waiting until, after quite a lot of ministration to leaking orifices, Emily nodded to him that Natalie was under control enough to take full notice that the next part of her thrashing was about to begin, Stones gently stroked the burning cheeks with the flat leather surface of the paddle. Never one to take the tender-hearted route when a more painful option was available, Stones laid the paddle on the, so far untouched, tops of her legs with some force. The screams were now of a different level, and when Stones began striking the same patch of the unyielding tight skin of her cheeks over and over again, she reached banshee wailing heights. Fifty strokes later, it was over and he rested his hands on the crimson bottom as it bucked and writhed in his lap.

"There, there, my dear. There, there. That's it for a while. Sadly for you, though, the worst is yet to come, but hush now and pull yourself together. Back to the wall now to think on your behaviour and perhaps listen to Freya taking a punishment with a tad more resilience and fortitude. All mopped up, Emily, at the front end? I would guess that there are no sexual juices leaking from your viewpoint, Melanie? No? Did not think so, but always like to be aware if I've caused more pleasure than pain to my miscreants. Young Emily here can give you more information on that front if anyone wants an example or explanation. Isn't that so, my raunchy young friend?"

Emily spluttered in total shock but earned herself a nod of approval from Stones by quickly regaining her composure and saying, "Indeed, Professor Stones. You have caught me and appropriately punished me for my injudicious and slutty tendencies. As I deserved and I thank you for highlighting my disgrace, I certainly warranted it."

Not that Natalie took in the exchange as she continued to sob loudly, causing Stones to push her off his lap onto the floor in exasperation. "Oh for goodness' sake, stop that nonsense before I decide you need to have another spanking. Help her into the corner, ladies, she can snivel away there for a while. Come along, Freya, let's have your lovely little derrière placed in the firing line."

Freya strode over without hesitation and draped herself over Stones' lap, spreading her legs and raising her bottom in preparation without delay or pause. As Emily and Melanie settled in their places, his hand began to pound the pert, rounded cheeks of Freya's bottom. Gasps and loud sighs were all he heard from the compliant student as she held herself almost motionless under the torrents of slapping blows. "That is the end of your hand spanking, Freya, so it is this leather paddle next." He slid the paddle up and down and then across the bright pink cheeks, allowing the edge to slide into her open cleft and running it down to her vagina. "How is she looking down there, Melanie, a bit damp I suspect?"

There was a laugh from Melanie. "Certainly is, Professor. I would say that she appears to have enjoyed her spanking."

Stones heard the groan from Freya that suggested she was well aware that this was not good news being announced by the older student peering between her legs, so close that Freya would feel her breath.

"Let us see if the paddle is as much fun."

The paddle landed over and over again on the tops of the young woman's legs as at last she began to move on Stones' lap in reaction to the stinging slaps. Directing the next series of blows at the untouched sides of her buttocks, he targeted mainly virgin skin that his hands had not marked. The yelps that this onslaught produced suggested that the experience was no longer as enjoyable as she had first indicated and after a few more hearty blows to the centre of the buttocks, now swaying rhythmically on his lap, he stayed his hand. Freya's weeping was evidence that his mission was successful and he jerked his thighs and deposited her unceremoniously at his feet.

"Up you get, hands on head, legs apart, facing me," he snapped. "Melanie, have a look, does she seem as excited now?"

Melanie dropped to her knees behind Freya and quickly gave her voice to words that caused Freya to visibly relax. "Seems to be a lot less moist in the pussy region now, Professor Stones, but her bottom is so red."

"Well no point wasting time, Natalie. Let's have you over here at my caning desks. Emily, I suspect it might need both of you to get this one in place. She's not very keen to pay her dues for such a naughty girl, is she?" Stones was in full tease, taunt and thrash mode as the reluctant Natalie was rather pulled over to the desk he waited at, now with a cane in his hand. "Freya can join you at the other desk now, if you please, young lady. I do not think you need assistance in taking your place based on your earlier bravado. Or has that all dissipated now that your bottom has felt what a real walloping really ignites?"

Freya turned a defiant-looking face to him and strode over to the other desk. "I am ready to accept the cane, if it pleases you, sir," said the determined-looking student.

"Clearly it would be highly appropriate for you to make a rude and blatant display of your naked buttocks as part of your denouement. So you will both climb onto my tables here, on your knees, legs apart and head hanging down while we wait for a further guest to join us."

Both women looked round at him with shocked and apprehensive faces but Stones could see the quick acceptance of their fates and resigned slump of both sets of shoulders, and knew that he had broken their spirit of resistance already. When Sara Morgan, the

Chief Administration Officer of the college, entered the room, she was greeted by the sight of two students, apparently just settling into position, kneeling naked and rudely displaying their private parts on desks. She took in, as nonchalantly as she could, the added fact that two clothed students, Emily and Melanie, were knelt on the floor before them. Professor Stones was bending and flexing a couple of canes, swiping them through the air in preparation for what Sara very much hoped was going to be a jointly shared experience.

Stones paused and stood back as though to drink in the glorious sight of the two young women, naked and bent over, their legs parted, their bright pink bottoms raised with cheeks parted. Almost identical even in this most extreme and exposed position, their pert white buttocks split to reveal the darkened skin encased in their anal clefts with small, discreet arseholes housed amongst downy off-blonde curly hairs leading down to their displayed labia. He noted with interest that Freya's most private of orifices was reminiscent of a cross, four distinct lines with the neatest of dark holes at the centre, while Natalie had an almost perfect round opening, a much brighter pink than her roommate's, with minor ripples of tight skin making a more prominent rim. He inadvertently licked his lips, annoyed to see Emily looking up at him from her position on her knees in front of Freya, a knowing smile playing on her lips.

"An enchanting sight indeed, ladies. What a lovely display. Two rather beautiful young bottoms, offered up for a chastising sacrifice. A pity to cause blemish to such outstanding loveliness, do you not think, Sara?"

As delighted as she was to have been called in to participate in a punishment session, Sara was understandably anxious that she played her role well. Celia and Jamie's unavailability at such short notice had led to this opportunity to prove her worth to Stones and she was so determined not to put a foot wrong. It had been clearly hinted to her by Celia that with the professor's approaching retirement her enthusiasm for involvement in corporal punishment situations had been noted and very much approved of. The suggestion that she may soon be trusted with an elevated role had made her day and she was desperate not to do anything that would cause him to rethink. Stones could see her grappling for the right response and he waited with interest to see what route she took. He was not to be disappointed with her considered response.

"Indeed, Professor Stones, indeed. I have to agree that this is a delightful sight but needs must, I believe, and the true path to forgiveness, redemption, contrition and ultimate improvement can only come from an honest but painful lesson. These two require processing in a manner that will give them food for thought for a long time. This is a simple, efficient and effective procedure that will serve due warning for their future behaviour and hopefully assist in guiding them onwards towards a more mature path for the future. It would be my honour, Dean, to assist you in their learning journey."

Stones laughed out loud. "Pompous and over-wordy, Miss Morgan, but fair. Do you not agree, rapscallions?" He tapped both young women lightly on their tightly tensed bottoms, causing both to flinch dramatically. Their muttered affirmations were not convincing but Stones allowed it since both had responded positively.

"Let us proceed then. Sara, you can have the pleasure of striking first. Alternate strokes to each bottom to start with, to get them both thinking about how they will ensure their disrespectful behaviour and poor judgement are never repeated and that lessons have been fully learned. Emma and Melanie will hold your wrists tightly whilst your buttocks are thrashed and will also wipe away any eye, nose or mouth leakage if your faces get a bit messy. I very much hope that will be the case. Tears are required to help wash away your shame. Any leaks from your lower regions will be dealt with entirely differently so I hope you are both in control of your bladders and any sexual desires that occur. I realise that some of you disgusting urchins get rather lustful whilst displaying yourselves thus and find being beaten an exciting sexual experience, but that is not something you would be advised to advertise during a punishment beating, I can assure you."

This was not the point for Natalie to make a snarky observation but, to the surprise of everyone in the room, she clearly could not restrain herself!

"Oh, really? Do we have to have this degrading commentary? It's bad enough we are treated like naughty children and have to display ourselves like this."

Emily broke the silence that followed the injudicious words.

"Well, Natalie, do remind me, who was it that was hanging her bare arse out of the window and displaying herself to anyone who happened to be in the street?"

"Indeed, indeed. Thank you for that observation, Natalie, and fair point made, Emily, albeit I do not recall requesting your opinion. Please remember your role here and refrain from overstepping the mark. I can always add a third table and duplicate the punishment about to be given to an additional bottom. A bottom that I expect is still rather sore so may not appreciate a severe caning to reignite its fire."

Emily dropped her head and muttered a quiet apology, not that Stones was convinced his threat was that much of a deterrent to the wilful and highly sexed student. The next words were directed to Natalie though.

"I wonder if you are not appreciating how disgusting your behaviour has been. I wonder if we need to have a thoughtful moment to consider the actual presentation you made with this display of your naked buttocks. Let us have a close look at how you are presenting yourselves now and take a minute to see how a punishment can so be made to fit the crime."

Moving to his desk and utilising his state-of-the-art CCTV equipment, it only took seconds for giant hanging screen to be filled with an extreme close-up of the girls' predicament. A couple of clicks later and the screen was now filled with Natalie's taut bent buttocks and her most private parts in intimate detail, as she was now displaying.

"I understand that you taunted your audience as to their honour in getting to view your backsides, as you considered them fine specimens that were beyond the reach and dreams of the young men. So you are very proud of what you consider to be your beautiful derrières. Well, no real harm in that but now is your opportunity to educate and enrich us here today by describing what we see in full detail so that we appreciate how wonderful they both are. Let us start with you, Natalie, since it is your bottom filling the screen. Please describe in detail what we are looking at so we can appreciate its beauty fully."

The sob from Natalie illustrated her regret at her remarks but she failed to respond, despite a hissing pointed whisper from Freya suggesting that she needed to watch her mouth! Stones let that go but the opening of his dreaded cabinet of punishment implements boded badly for the two malefactors.

"As you appear to need encouragement to obey the simplest of instructions, I am going to give you an example of what will follow if you continue in this vein of insubordination and waywardness. This is my thin whippy cane, ladies, and with it I will apply a fusillade of stinging swipes to these fine young buttocks. Nowhere near as painful and lasting in its effect as the bamboo that will shortly be introduced to you to properly amend, correct and improve your behaviour, but a unique experience when applied quickly as it has a real cut and produces a lovely thin red line that has a lasting sting."

His nod to Emily and Melanie was all that was needed for them to quickly move in and grasp the two students' wrists just before the cane landed on Natalie's backside. As promised the cane rose and fell rapidly and the swish through the air and slapping impact became the only sounds in the room, until Natalie registered the pain and began to cry out. Stones stepped to the side, saying, "Oh, and just to confirm what poor Freya must be dreading, any additional punishment imposed will be applied to you both regardless of whose errant behaviour has earned it. A tad unfair, possibly, but hopefully will assist in preventing any further disorderly conduct. 'Naughty girls get sore bottoms' is the mantra we agreed a few minutes ago, so surely you will not be surprised when I keep to my word as we try and educate you to reach the standards required from our students here."

To Freya's credit, she made no comment as Stones took aim beside her before whipping the cane down for the ten rapid strokes. No yells or struggles from Freya, her head down and her buttocks still as she squeezed them tight to receive the cane. A long breath out when Stones stood away was her only response.

"Well taken, Freya. A lesson there for you, Natalie. Hold your thoughts, prepare yourself and take your just dues without too much fuss. You may both thank me."

There was no hesitation as both students blurted out their thanks. Freya's gratitude composed and clear, Natalie rather spluttered and tearful.

"Now, young Natalie, take a breath and pull yourself together, we are ready now for you to describe this bottom you were so keen to put on public display. Both of you, heads up and study the screen, please. Note that I have the whippy cane still tightly ensconced in my fist and am leaving myself perfectly placed to apply a further ten strokes if you fail to comply to my satisfaction. A full detailed description of what we are looking at, please. Begin."

The gasp from Natalie did not give Stones any confidence that she could comply.

"Oh, no. I don't know what to say. It is my bottom, sir. My cheeks are quite full and they are pink all over apart from the bit between them and you can see much redder lines, which the cane made. Um, my legs are open, sir, so you can see my pussy. Oh dear. My bottom crack is on show, sir. Er, is that enough, sir?"

Stones did not speak but Natalie was made aware a second later that her response was deemed not fit for purpose, as the cane whipped into her bottom cheeks. Once more Natalie's screams rang out and continued as Stones took two steps to his side and flayed Freya's bottom, again to little reaction from the impressively stoic youngster.

"Emily, wipe the face of the pathetic specimen you are holding. I want her focus back on this lovely image of the bottom she was so keen to put on show. Now Freya, we will give Natalie a chance to learn how to carry out a simple task. I would like you to describe Natalie's vision of beauty for me and then we will concentrate on your own but with Natalie providing the descriptive commentary. Off you go, Freya." A sharp tap of the cane accompanied his request.

"Ouch! Thank you, sir. Well, Natalie's bottom is gorgeous, lovely round cheeks but pert and perfectly symmetrical. So sexy with her lovely unblemished skin now with really sexy stripes from your cane on top of the redness caused by the deserved spanking she received. She has nice dimples and a lovely set of creases that underline the prominent sweet cheeks above. She has a nice crack dividing her buttocks, sir, with the darker skin hinting at the secret intimacy of the pretty little rosebud of an asshole at the centre of the dark mass, like a hidden treasure in the depths of a secret dark cave. Her asshole is like a secret round entrance with a bright pink door, encircled by an intricate pattern of tiny twisted skin like a garland, sir. Beneath that there is the vision of absolute beauty that is her pussy, sir. Such delicious-looking lips, basically overlapping each other and coming together to form a gorgeous dish of delight for anyone lucky enough to get close enough to gaze at, smell or ultimately lick and kiss their wonder, sir. What an honour to be bid to describe her beautiful orifices, sir. Thank you for allowing me to see this vision of paradise."

Stones applauded her rites with great enthusiasm.

"Well played, Freya, well played. What a tribute to your most intimate and private quarters, Natalie. Your friend has done you proud. Now can you return the compliment as we bring into focus Freya's presentation of her private attributes?"

The screen before them now filled with a full view of Freya's current predicament, her open bottom and parted legs totally exposed. Natalie took a breath and buoyed by Freya's most complimentary description of her own display, made an effort to return the favour. "Er, sir, um, Freya has a lovely bottom. Obviously very red and covered in marks from the cane, sir, and they look ready to receive more strokes with your bamboo cane. I love the view of her cute cheeks all opened up so that we can see the dark skin that surrounds her little butthole with the field of little white hairs around it. Her hairs are much curlier than mine, sir, and go all the way down and round her pussy. Her butthole looks like a multiplication sign, sir, with little mounds around the dark hole, and bright pinkish bits inside that you can see when she clenches and opens. Her pussy looks like a damp sponge and I think it is really pretty and looks good enough to eat, sir."

Stones tapped the desk between Natalie's legs in appreciation, saying, "Well done, well done. See how imaginative and creative you can be with the right incentive. Fair play to both of you. Let us finish off with just ten strokes, a kindness on my part, with the bamboo, to seal the deal, so to speak. Sara, take position and follow my lead. We are going to cane these young reprobates alternately and change positions after the first five. Emily and Melanie will hold their hands tightly and both wretches will keep their legs wide apart on promise of additional strokes if they fail to comply. Here we go, young Natalie, see how this feels."

The bamboo cane swung through the air and landed with a resounding thwack on the taut buttocks of the terrified student. The scream was immediate and the reaction dramatic. Emily went sprawling as she failed to hold on to the wrists of the almost uncontrollable Natalie, as she flung her body off the desk, falling to the floor where she clutched her buttocks and howled in despair. Stones grabbed the desk to keep it upright before taking a handful of the wailing student's hair and dragging her back to the chair. If the paddling she had received earlier had caused her discomfort, it was nothing to the torment that the avalanche of blows to the tops of her legs caused her. Held in Stones' iron grasp, Natalie had to suffer for two long minutes as the paddle battered her sensitive skin 100 times with a ferocity that silenced the rest of the room. He rose with his hands under the arms of a screeching Natalie before depositing her back over the table, snapping, "Emily, Melanie, take one arm each. Sara, a change of plan. Please sit between this miserable creature's legs and hold them wide apart. I will teach her not to respect the process and give her a lesson she will never forget. I am absolutely not going to have this nonsense in my rooms."

The ten strokes promised were a thing of history and irrelevance now, as the cane bit deep into the writhing cheeks and even under the grip of the trio, Natalie continued to twist and fight her captors.

"This flogging will continue until your resistance is broken and compliance is achieved. I can do this for as long it takes, young lady. I also have my favourite thick, heavy leather strap hanging down in my cabinet that I can hear calling to me." The cane continued to ravage her bottom and legs, scarlet lines rising in weals, with Natalie's screams becoming hysterical although her movement was finally subdued and her lower body slumped on the desk. With six final hard strokes aimed vertically into the open cleft, Stones was mindful not to strike her open arsehole with his harsh blows. Throwing the bamboo down, he strode across to his cabinet, took out his favoured strap and marched straight back to deliver a stinging crack across the centre of the thoroughly beaten bottom. Five more times the strap cracked across the student's buttocks as she yelled in agony.

"Emily. The bath is partially filled with iced water. Please deposit her in it. Her buttocks will need some help. No talking but you are permitted to slap her face if there is any backchat or disobedience from this wretched scoundrel. Get her out of my sight! Melanie, take hold of Freya's hands while Sara now wallops this one's behind. I expect no repeat of Natalie's pathetic behaviour. Sara, be mindful that I am expecting a damn good job. You will give her all the hard strokes she has requested, please, laid in tramlines that are positioned evenly from the top of her cleft to that lovely painful area at the tops of her legs, just under her sweet bottom dimples. Proceed."

Sara took hold of the cane with a look that betrayed trepidation as well as determination. She tapped Freya's bottom several times and boosted by a wink and a huge smile of encouragement from Melanie, struck Freya hard across the very top of her buttocks. She paused as the angry red line slowly formed and laid the cane an inch under the line. The second stroke landed as anticipated and drew a welcome gasp from her victim. When the fifth stroke was applied, Freya began to sob loudly to the obvious relief of Sara. Her distress seemed to ignite Sara, as the sixth stroke carried extra force, eliciting a yelp from Freya who was now struggling to control her resistance and stay in place. Stones noted with approval the tenderness of Melanie as she wiped the distressed student's face and whispered words of encouragement and compliments at her performance in accepting the thrashing without complaint. When the final blow struck the tops of her legs in perfect symmetry with the previous ones, Freya was almost propelled into Melanie's lap as her lower torso jerked forward in response. Sara looked immediately to Stones, who moved in and placed giant open hands on Freya's beleaguered bottom cheeks.

"Yes. Yes. Very hot indeed and lovely lines. Excellent job, Sara. Duly noted, my dear. Stand up straight, Freya. Now touch your toes. One stroke with the strap, which you can thank Natalie for, and then Melanie will get you in the bath with your partner in crime."

To Stones' admiration, there was no arguing from the quietly weeping student. She sighed, sniffed loudly, bent forward and grasped her ankles.

"It is only fair that you have a notion of what young Natalie is suffering. It seems right that you have an appreciation of her suffering as well as a warning of what you can expect if you are misfortunate enough to be required to attend here for disciplinary reasons again. Hold still." The strap swung through the air at speed and landed with a resounding thwack across the centre of Freya's cheeks. The success of the strike was evident as the resiliency of the student was fully tested. She shrieked and her knees buckled. To her credit and Stones' further admiration, she kept her feet still and forced herself back into position as though ready for further punishment.

"You are a formidable foe, my dear. Well taken. Off to the bathroom and give these lovely buns a nice ice treat. Melanie, take her away. We will have them back before me in ten minutes, please. Same instructions as before, no talking or disrespect allowed. Permission to slap her face and bottom if there is any cause."

Stones smiled at Sara once they were alone. "Good job, young lady, good job. The Mistress has been watching events and is much impressed and is on her way to join us."

Sara beamed in pleasure. Stones knew that she had been plagued by her dangerous indiscretion with a student and, although he had made her pay with the most severe of punishments, he enjoyed the fact she seemed totally indebted to him that she was still in position and had not only taken her chastisement with humility, but appeared to hold nothing but respect and almost adoration for Stones since. His doorbell heralded the arrival of Dorothy Winslow-Bellingham, the college's Mistress. After the usual pleasantries were exchanged, Dorothy did indeed bestow her approval of Sara's role during the evening's events.

"Thought you were a bit harsh on Natalie, though, Edward. That was one hell of a beating."

Stones shrugged. In his final weeks in the full-time position of Dean of Discipline, he certainly had no intention of easing off or developing any leniency. "No regrets there, Professor Winslow-Bellingham. She dared challenge me and misbehaved in my rooms after her disgraceful display of her buttocks to the streets outside the college. I think she has learned a valuable lesson and we will have no repeat of any such episode in the rest of her time with us. Anyway, it is about time the rascals joined us."

He walked across to the bathroom, with its rarely closed door, and entered. Emily and Melanie were just wrapping the two subdued younger students in large luxurious towels.

"Ah, good timing, girls. Come along and join us. We have a visitor. How exciting, eh?"

Natalie and Freya's faces did not seem to share his enthusiasm for an additional witness to their shame, but Melanie and Emily hooked their arms and escorted them back into the room of their earlier most painful ordeal. Both gasped in horror to find themselves facing the Mistress. Their unhappiness increased no end as, on a signal from Stones, Emily and Melanie whipped the towels from them and left them naked.

Stones roared at both of them: "Hands on heads, stand up straight, legs apart. No courtesy given to false modesty here. Professor Winslow-Bellingham has been watching a live feed of today's events and felt the need to come and speak directly to you about your behaviour and subsequent retribution delivered and received. Now both turn around and bend over with your hands on your ankles, legs spread, to allow the Mistress to see close up that you have received your just desserts."

With cringing expressions, both young women turned slowly and dropped their upper bodies, hands encircling ankles, as instructed.

"Seems to be that you have got off lightly in comparison to your colleague, Freya. Although that stroke with the strap has given you something to dwell on for the future." She ran her fingers over Freya's round orbs with no reaction from the beaten student and her eyes met Stones in an acknowledgement of how she was also in admiration of the young woman's capitulation and total acceptance of the authority of the senior academics. Moving across to Natalie, Dorothy grimaced at seeing the blistered buttocks, their redness quelled by the ice soaking, welts raised by the cane, purple tramlines from the strap and half circles of crimson from the edge of the paddle. Natalie flinched and squirmed as Dorothy stroked her cheeks with some tenderness.

"Hush, child, stay still and quiet. It would be most unwise to cause ire to Professor Stones as you should well know by now. Have we got any cream to soothe this poorly bottom, Dean?"

Stones grunted as he turned to his computer screen. "Once they have written their formal thanks to acknowledge that they have received fair and appropriate punishment for their shameful misdeeds they will report directly to the college nurse to be checked over. After that they can return to the site of their disgrace and apply my soothing cream to each other's buttocks. Take this pot, it will suffice, Freya. Now both of you will stand at the desks and begin scribing and, assuming you are capable of writing acceptable notes of contrition, you may put your clothes back on and leave us. Emily and Melanie, I thank you for your assistance, it was a pleasure to give you your deserved thrashings earlier, which you received with dignity and courage. You may leave."

He ignored Emily's petulant look. Stones was confident that he would be seeing her naked form again in the not-too-distant future, and suspected there would soon be the opportunity for them both to satisfy their lust for each other on safer terms. As Freya turned to face the three seated academics remaining, she paused with self-assurance, saying, "I would be most grateful if I could read my statement out, please, Professor Stones."

Stones suspected that she was making an honourable attempt to give Natalie breathing space and an opportunity to heed the words she had scripted. Natalie's sheets had far fewer words than Freya's and Stones was very much of the opinion that Natalie lacked the wherewithal and creativity to recognise the route to take. Sensing that both Dorothy and Sara were not keen to see Natalie land herself in more trouble, trouble they correctly surmised could cause yet more harm to her poor, battle-scarred buttocks, Stones nodded his consent.

"I, Freya Barnes, would like to thank Professor Stones and Miss Morgan for the beating received in punishment for an appalling act of lewdness that brought shame and embarrassment to the college. I accept full responsibility for my actions, own up to my disgraceful behaviour with humility and thank the professor for allowing me to face my guilt and seek redemption through remorse and corrective treatment. I have been thoroughly thrashed as requested and deserved and it has been my fortune to have been allowed to assuage my guilt in this manner. I believe that this action taken will greatly improve my behaviour in the future and promise that I will never behave in such an atrocious manner again. Once more, thank you both for your fair and proper response to my disgraceful conduct. It was very much a learning experience that I welcome for both its severity and leniency. I am much humbled by the experience and my sore bottom pays tribute to that. Thank you both and I apologise for any inconvenience I have caused you."

The only sounds in the room now were the exasperated sighs and scribbling of Natalie's pen as she made numerous additions and corrections to her work. Stones rose slowly and formally shook Freya's hand. "Well said, well said, Freya. Very impressive choice of words. I hope you got most of that, young Natalie. You may dress yourself while we wait for Natalie's version of what you have just said." His chuckle suggested that Natalie did not need to worry about plagiarism!

A few minutes later a fully dressed Freya returned to face the corner without any instruction, earning further nods of approval from Stones. Natalie's words were delivered without the articulation and assurance of Freya's but the similarities illustrated her willingness to take on board the direction required and although Stones could find fault with her own lack of ownership and imagination, her inclination to follow Freya's lead and the desperation shown in her face to gain his approval swayed him to grant it. After a few seconds of silence as she dried up following a string of apologetic words, Stones made her turn and present her disfigured bottom to them.

"Tempted to make her walk through the college with these buttocks on show to help spread the message that unacceptable behaviour will receive appropriate correction." Natalie managed to constrain herself from reacting, sobbing but keeping silent otherwise as Stones continued, "Or possibly a poster campaign using these traumatised globes as a warning. Maybe, maybe. For now though, you may cover that mess up and get your dirty selves out of my sight." His teasing words created a certain amount of frantic hurrying as Natalie flung her clothing on and, grasping Freya's hand, the two left the room, Freya thanking them once more.

A laughing Stones reached for a bottle of wine, raised eyebrows suggesting Dorothy and Sara should join him. Another episode had been dealt with and put to bed.

CHAPTER 8

KERRY IS TOO OLD FOR A SPANKING

Kerry Lerner was not the average rebellious and arrogant teenage student rebel. A 30-year-old research post-graduate undertaking a Master's degree on the depiction of sexual abuse in literature. Recently separated from her affluent, well-connected spouse, and daughter of a well-remembered haughty young lady whose bare bottom Stones had beaten many moons ago in his early years as St. James' College's Dean of Discipline. Kerry had been involved in a hall formal dinner spat with senior staff that ended in her tipping a bowl of soup into the lap of one of the elderly esteemed academic teaching staff known as Fellows, causing pain and distress. Kerry was unrepentant; as far as she was concerned a sexist and offensive statement had been made and she was the wronged person, not the instigator.

"Let's get this absolutely clear from the outset, Professor Stones. I was on the end of out-dated and unacceptable language, my reaction was understandable and justified. Don't even consider that you are going to be asking me to suggest appropriate punishment. I am not cleaning bogs, I am not picking up litter and I am most certainly not dropping my drawers and going over your knee for a spanking. Are we clear here? Do we understand each other?"

"Oh, my dear. I hear you loud and clear. Now let us see what we have here, shall we? A 70-year-old academic and his brother are having their evening meal and a discussion develops along the subject of a woman's place in senior academic positions. In essence, you heard Professor Carling telling his brother that the title of 'Mistress' belongs in a bawdy scenario, principally as head of a brothel. You took offence and decided to butt into their discussion, highlighting leading women and their influence in fields such as academia, politics and business. They argued that you were mistaken in your interpretation of their conversation, and had not understood what they were saying. Your response was to refer to them directly and loudly using a very offensive and foul-mouthed manner. Understandably they reacted by telling you to mind your own business and stick to your earlier, overheard, rather loud and frivolous discussion with your cohorts, concerning which was the most popular colour of the sweets M&Ms and Jelly Babies. They also accused you of being drunk and told you that you had missed the precept of the conversation, and it would be best if you restricted your immature thoughts to the more trivial matter of preferences in children's sweets. An unconnected guest at dinner has made a statement to say that you referred to the professor and his brother as a couple of relics whose views belonged in a museum and that it was high time they were in bed as they needed their beauty sleep to recharge their feeble brains. I also have a statement that stipulates the use of the words senile, cunts and fuckwitted old fogies. When told that you were an impertinent and ridiculous girl you reacted by calling the professor a patronising, sexist old bastard and tipped his bowl of soup into his lap. You also stated that in your opinion the Mistress was lacking a spine, or she would have pulled her finger out, and got rid of all the old farts and dinosaurs in the college by now. I can report that you were also overheard telling your chums that the Mistress needed to grow a pair of bollocks. Anything you wish to dispute or are you happy with that precis?"

The pause was long and Stones knew that the balance of power was shifting in the student's mind and an anxious look flickered across her face. Not that he had ever entertained any doubt who held sway when it came to any cut-and-thrust power plays that took place in this room. He had never met a student who came into his parlour as well prepared as he was, and he had certainly not been outfoxed or outfought in any clash or dispute in his memory.

"Well, yes, we had a drink and voices did get raised but these people need to be challenged with their dinosaur views. Professor he may be in title, but his time is up and there is no longer a place in academic circles for entrenched, sexist, misogynist and outmoded opinions. Time for retirement and time for new blood and modern open views, I think."

"Well thank you for that. Your thoughts are now a matter of record. However, what you may like to consider is—" The professor was interrupted by the raised voice of Kerry.

"No, let's not. Fuck that. He is an old bigot and you are just covering his tracks now. I know what I heard and I am not gracing this meeting with my presence any longer. Good day, Professor Stones. I will leave you to resolve this, but without me. I am not playing your mind games anymore. Bye!"

While she had been speaking, Stones was tapping away into his laptop. He watched Kerry leave, fetched himself a glass of red wine, settled back in his seat and waited.

It was just over an hour later when the ringing of his doorbell coincided with a loud banging on the door. He watched on camera as a very perturbed and agitated Kerry was virtually hopping from one foot to another. Stones slowly moved his hand to press the button that would allow her access.

She marched in and waved her mobile at him.

"Was this you? Was this fucking well you?"

The professor fixed her with a fierce stare and waited for the woman to realise that this approach might not be the most successful.

"Sit down, my dear. When you are calm and ready we can have an adult conversation."

"The fuck? The fuck? I don't believe it. No. No. No." With that she burst into howling sobs of total despair.

Stones allowed her to weep for several minutes and busied himself on his computer. Unbeknown to the despairing student before him, he had just received confirmation that Celia Ford, the Senior Tutor, and Dr Philippa Stanford, the Graduates Manager, had accepted his invitation to attend his rooms to discuss her future at the college.

"You've done this, haven't you? You and those fucking old misogynistic bastards, those senile old gits. This is so pissing well archaic and self-serving and authoritarian and, and, and so fucking old boys' network, and disingenuous and, and, and hierarchical and just plain fucking unfair!" The tears restarted and Stones just sat, relaxed and calm. He let her vent and watched her outrage and despair cause her to become almost incoherent.

Seeing his guests arrive together on his CCTV screen he silently buzzed them access and they were beside Kerry before she had even registered their arrival.

Now real panic appeared in Kerry's eyes. As a graduate she knew that these three senior staff members together were a formidable trio for any student to face.

"Celia, Philippa. Welcome. As anticipated we have a seriously agitated young woman before us."

The two senior members of staff had moved to sit alongside the professor so Kerry suddenly found herself in the role of prisoner in the dock.

"Now you know the gist of it but I can confirm that young Kerry here acted on what she heard without knowing the context of the conversation that my colleague and his esteemed brother were having. This conversation concerned the use of the title 'Mistress' and how they both believed it was unfortunate that it had other connotations and were discussing other options for a female head governor or leader of a university college. Before you even dare to make matters worse and interrupt me once again, Kerry, I can assure you that this is supported unequivocally by others as a conversation that had begun earlier in the company of a tableful of people. So the facts are visible, supported and accepted, the jury is back, you have been found guilty and it's just the little matter of the sentence to be imposed now. What do you have to add, Kerry, anything pertinent or have you finally realised that your goose is cooked?"

The panic in the graduate student's eyes became almost traumatic and was so clear to the occupants of the room.

"But, but, but. Oh, shit! But I thought, oh dear. I didn't realise. It's not my fault, I didn't know."

Stones knew now was the time to turn the screw.

"Oh you didn't know, you didn't realise. Oh well that's alright then, is it? That means it's okay to be foul mouthed, offensive and act disgustingly towards senior members of the college, does it? You are a naughty, badly behaved, rude young woman and now you have to damn well pay the price!" Stones' voice rose as he stood up and towered over Kerry. "I very much doubt that a suspension from the college for a period will be an option that appeals!"

Kerry's face dropped dramatically as she finally seemed to realise how much trouble she was in.

"Oh my God, no, no, no, no, no! That can't happen, oh no, please sir, no, no, no, no. Oh no, please, please do not suspend me, sir. It would be a disaster, people would know. I would be a laughing stock. People would judge me. It could stop me getting the qualifications I need. That would be the end of my world, Professor Stones. Oh my, oh my word, oh no. Sir, please, I beg you, no."

Stones kept a stone-cold face. She was yet another in a long line of stroppy students who had thought they were beyond the reach of Stones and his particular brand of punishment.

"Interesting response considering your rudeness and arrogance earlier, young lady. Do you per chance have an alternative that you would like to offer?"

Kerry looked confused, but more importantly as far as Stones was concerned, looked hopeful.

"What? Sorry, Professor Stones, what do you mean?"

Stones toyed with papers on his desk and made her wait to prolong her anxiety.

"What? Oh, well you could always consider the option for the corporal punishment route that I see you did sign up for when you joined us. Obviously that is purely a personal choice if you wish to consider alternatives to put on the table for the three of us to ponder?"

Post-graduates, usually studying for a Master's degree or a doctorate, were accepted as full adults without the college being required to act *in loco parentis*. In these cases the students were still required to sign the disciplinary process and conduct acceptance document, although as older and usually wiser, although not always as evidenced by Kerry's behaviour, it was quite rare for them to be seriously chastised.

"Oh my God, seriously, you cannot really expect me, a 30-year-old woman, to submit to that sort of demeaning experience. I mean, seriously, Professor Stones, Dr Ford, Dr Stanford, it is a punishment for naughty youngsters, isn't it?"

Stones smiled as though in sympathy and agreement with her.

"Oh absolutely, Kerry. It certainly is for naughty girls who misbehave. Even though the undergraduates have to be at least 19 years old to enter this academic institution there seems to be a good many of them that require treatment of their behavioural faults for which only a damn good hiding is deemed a just punishment. Naughty girls who are drunk, foul-mouthed, aggressive, rude, you know the sort. They deserve a damn good thrashing and this is what they usually come to decide, and in fact are grown-up enough to determine, is what they deserve. Anyway, back to you, Kerry. A written apology to all concerned and your acceptance that it would be appropriate for you to be sent home at the end of the week and return at the start of the summer term would seem fair. So you are suspended for a term and a half and we need to consider if there is a real possibility that you would actually be able finish the work you need to do under these circumstances. I will talk to your tutor and see if we can save your position on this or not."

Stones thoroughly enjoyed the next few minutes as Kerry went through that nightmare scenario that had been outlined as the end of her academic career. Her face showed alarm, fear, intrigue and hope as she appeared to have run through the meaning of the professor's words and what the consequences of her next decision could bring.

"Hold on, sir, are you definitely saying that I could take the option of corporal punishment as an alternative to being suspended?"

Stones acted as though she was taking him by surprise and appeared to give her words due consideration.

"Well yes, that is feasible and is in the rules, of course. As I have intimated I do not usually flog graduates such as yourself, to be honest, as normally a more adult approach is applied to our more mature students and generally they do not misbehave in the manner that you have. However, yes, in theory if you were to make a case to be chastised in that manner I would certainly give it consideration to help you avoid the damage and shame of a suspension."

Hook, line and sinker, thought Stones as Kerry's face gave away her eagerness to seek and contemplate a fate more palatable than the ignominy of a suspension from one of the country's leading academic institutions and the repercussions to her future that may entail.

"What, um, exactly would this, you know, um, corporal punishment consist of, sir?"

Stones stroked his chin, playing along with the idea that this was a completely unplanned and off-the-cuff scenario.

"Well normally, Kerry, the reprobate due for punishment would be expected to offer herself up for chastisement and agree an appropriate response. In your case this would be discussed with Dr Ford and Dr Stanford and once we had all agreed on the justified and deserved sentence, you would document your request formally and then report on a date, set by myself, for the punishment to be dispensed. All application of corporal punishment is to the naked form, the buttocks and tops of the legs receive all blows, with assistants and witnesses present to endure all is above board and punishment is carried out as agreed. The process would be fair, and by necessity painful for you, but this would be a learning process. Contrition, remorse, atonement, absolution and improvement are the results we would seek to deliver. You will feel humiliation, degradation and shame during this process but you will almost certainly come out of it with a more humble, tolerant and kinder attitude to others. Lessons would be learned and you would move on, hopefully a wiser woman. Now, enough pontification from me, any further questions before we take this option further or should I just get the suspension procedure under way?"

As Stones talked, most of the colour had gone from Kerry's face. When Stones had casually mentioned that any punishment was carried out on a recipient naked, her mouth dropped open but he had been aware that she had stifled a response, and he knew then that the battle had been won and her acceptance of the outcome was almost sealed.

"Generally by now I would hope post-graduate students would have developed a thought process that encompassed a capacity for consequential thinking. You appear to be lacking that capacity judged on your current performance. Would you agree?"

"Oh, I er, um, I suppose that I may have acted without thinking it through. But do you not think corporal punishment is a bit beyond the pale for someone of my age? Is it not possible to impose a financial penalty, sir? A fine. I would be happy to accept that, sir."

Stones raised his eyebrows at that. It was not a unique offer but it had been a while since anyone had chosen that path. St James' was inclusive and did attempt to be diverse, but written into its constitution was a commitment to accommodate family members and referred students, which by nature of hereditary and economic advantage meant that a good proportion of the young women applying were from a wealthy background.

"Interesting point, Kerry. Would you care to fully accept

responsibility for your actions and then we could discuss this further?"

Less used to Professor Stones' inclination to allow miscreants to seek escape routes from their dilemmas, Philippa's face registered shock at his words, but Kerry was too preoccupied with her own thoughts to notice. Celia, well used to his devious ways maintained a poker face and showed no reaction, nudging her sharply, her eyes conveying a warning to keep any thoughts to herself.

"Yes, sir, indeed I now see that my behaviour was very poor and I willingly accept a financial penalty and I am also happy to volunteer to apologise to the professor and his brother, sir."

Stones raised his eyebrows, causing a flicker of panic which was not helped by his next words.

"What about your offensive remarks about the Mistress, Professor Winslow-Bellingham?"

Kerry gulped.

"Oh dear, yes, yes. Oh dear. Yes. I am prepared to apologise. But surely she does not know what I said, does she?"

Stones' laugh was chilling.

"Of course she does. We are a very sharing set of colleagues. Even if she didn't before, she certainly does now because she is currently watching a live feed of our proceedings."

The look of horror and shock on Kerry's face brought smiles to all three senior academics. Alarm followed as she scanned the room for cameras, quickly preceded by a look of suspicion.

"Oh don't bother, Kerry. They are very small and there are a multitude covering every angle, trust me. Or possibly not. Maybe I am toying with you. Now I think you were asking about making a financial donation to buy yourself out of trouble, were you not? What figure exactly did you have in mind?"

A look of hope and relief lit up her face as a way out of the predicament she had landed herself in suddenly seemed to open up.

"Oh, sir, I am not sure what would be appropriate. Perhaps £200?

What amount would you consider reasonable to impose, sir?"

"Interesting, Kerry. Well one million pounds would be considered reasonable in my opinion."

The look on Kerry's face made the Dean's day. Emotions displayed went from total incomprehension to shock to anger in a flash.

"What! What! What the fuck! No! No! Are you fucking mad?! Of course I do not have that sort of money. That is crazy. I haven't, I couldn't. Ridiculous! This is a joke. A fucking joke? Are you completely mad? Seriously, can we talk about this sensibly?"

Professor Stones glared at the outraged woman for several seconds.

"I am wondering whether to have a word with your mother. She was very invested in you finally achieving a place at St. James', particular after your failure to gain sufficient credits to enter at undergraduate level. She will surely be very disappointed in hearing that your Master's degree is at risk and that any plans for a Doctorate have taken a big backwards step."

Further horror crossed Kerry's face as she processed his words.

"No, please. Leave my mother out of this, you cannot tell her, I forbid it. You don't have the right. Dr Ford, Dr Stanford, why are you allowing this? Surely you don't approve? I am 30 bloody years old. Oh my God, you actually go along with all of this punishment crap. No, I will not accept this. I want to speak to Professor Winslow-Bellingham, the Mistress. I demand that I be allowed to speak to her and get this ridiculous nonsense brought to an end."

Professor Stones raised his eyebrows and leaned over his desk, tapping on his laptop.

"How is the stream, Professor Winslow-Bellingham? Are you catching all of this?"

The Mistress' voice came clearly into the room.

"Oh indeed, Dean, oh indeed. What a shameful performance, Kerry. It's embarrassing to watch and hear you behaving thus. I would suggest that you need to remove yourself from this situation for five days. You will consider your conduct and what has been discussed in this room today and then I would suggest that you return and throw yourself on Professor Stones' mercy. A plea to be thoroughly flogged to show that you have come to your senses and wish to remain a member of this college and complete your course would appear to be a good start, and one that I would heartedly support if you opt to request this path. If the professor deems that this would suffice then I anticipate this matter could be brought to an end assuming that you show true contrition, remorse, responsibility and shame. Your offensive behaviour and your challenge to the authority of this college has been noted and I therefore ask that Professor Stones relay to you the rights and belief that are ingrained in our constitution. Unless you accept this then I would have no option but to suggest that you return to your room and pack up your belongings before being summarily removed from our premises."

Tears now coursed down the cheeks of Kerry as her shoulders slumped in a show of abject surrender.

Stones moved to stand before her.

"Listen up, you miserable wretch. You heard Professor Winslow-Bellingham, listen and learn."

Stones took a deep breath and began a monologue that he was well-versed in, having written the words himself.

"The foundation of the jurisdiction of the Dean concerning the behaviour and conduct of students of the College is authorised and enforced by due governance and written into the College's statutes. This is supported and approved by the signed contracts, and given permission granted by both the students and their parents/guardians, when students formally join the institution. From this premise the approval and acceptance of the College's commitment to the future of each entrant is confirmed. Within this, agreed by entry into the College community, is an understanding of the options of degrees of punishment that are available to the Dean and authorised by the governing body. Corporal punishment is authorised within the terms of such agreements between the College and the students with the support and approval of aforementioned parents/guardians. The Dean is therefore empowered to dispense and administer such admonishment when students are deemed to have warranted such action. All corporal punishment however must only be administered with the agreement of the offending student. To this effect, any student receiving corporal punishment would be expect to make a signed, written statement to this effect; that the aforementioned punishment is just, deserved and appropriate. Corporal punishment is a voluntary endeavour for serious misdemeanours committed, and is an alternative to suspension or expulsion (formerly documented as 'sending down') which are deemed more detrimental to the student's education. The acceptance of corporal punishment is encouraged but therefore not mandatory and the right to opt out is available and optional. However corporal punishment is considered, unless exceptional circumstances are in play, a private matter between the College and the recipient, unlike suspensions and expulsion which are documented publicly and announced in formal proceedings. Unless it has been requested and accepted as a condition of enrolment, parents or guardians are not advised when corporal discipline is carried out. It should be noted that, as part of the disgrace and shame any miscreant should undergo as part of their chastisement, students will submit to punishment unclothed and chastisement would be administered to the general area of the bare buttocks. The aim of all such punishment is intended to bring shame, deliver penance, aid atonement and ultimately encourage improvement in character and behaviour to assist in the formation and building of a well-rounded, educated and moulded character that will leave this place ready for a successful future."

Stones paused before continuing.

"I believe this to be enough information for your tiny mind to cope with for now, Kerry. However I will continue with this monologue when you return to this room at your own request to bring this matter to a close. If, indeed, you decide to choose the sensible route to end this appalling situation."

He paused and reached over to lift the chin of the graduate student before him, who had virtually frozen in stunned silence as he lectured her.

"Young lady, the overarching aim of the University is to develop the minds of its student population and enable them to positively contribute to society through education, knowledge, learning and research, development of, and at, the highest level of excellence attainable. To this end, young lady, you will be punished severely for your unacceptable behaviour, if you so wish. This will serve as a fundamental lesson for you for the future. I sincerely believe that the benefits massively outweigh the negatives, and that you will come out of the process a better and stronger person. The time for discussion, however, is over. Please state clearly how you wish to proceed."

Kerry's demeanour, during his monologue, had lost the early shows of indignation and outrage. The haughty resistance had wilted away to almost nothing, and the picture now was of one of a defeated and cowed student, struggling to take on board that the acceptance of corporal punishment was the solution to the situation she had created for herself.

Stones let out a long sigh, purely designed to encourage the student to believe that he was patiently allowing her the opportunity to come to her senses. He adopted an air of the more mature and knowledgeable adult, carefully guiding his willing but thoughtless pupil to take the correct steps for all their sakes. It was a well-practised routine that, nearly always, produced the result he intended. Kerry, of course, in her state of discombobulated and bewildered confusion was not to know how she was being played.

"I would like you to volunteer to accept suitable and appropriate punishment and would quite like to hear a proposal of how you feel that you can make the best of the very bad situation you have landed yourself in. Come along now, Kerry, show Professor Winslow-

Bellingham, Dr Ford and Dr Stanford that you have some gumption and self-respect, and we will endeavour to support the case for you being able to continue your research as a member of this esteemed college." Stones' voice was now compassionate and calm as he eased her in the direction he wanted her to take.

"I will allow you a few more seconds to think this through while you have the chance, Kerry. Accept that justice is required to correct your disgraceful behaviour and then we can administer your dues and all move forward."

Stones watched the student's face become more stricken as he spoke and knew that the fight had gone and survival would now become her quest. Whether that meant she had recognised that a thrashing was the only outcome she had yet to vocalise, and Stones continued the process of leading another miscreant along the path towards submission and acceptance of her fate.

"However the clock is ticking and we all have work to do, so come along now, Kerry. Time to take a breath, get some gumption and begin the process of redemption."

"Is there no option other than this barbaric form of punishment? Surely, please, there is a way I can pay penance without a suspension that would do irreparable damage to my work and standing? Suspension or a vile, outmoded and humiliating thrashing on my bare backside? Please, is there no other choice? Barbaric corporal punishment should not be my only option. I beg you to reconsider." Kerry's plea was only ever going to produce a change of tone from him, and he duly obliged.

"You deeply offended senior and renowned academics, you were drunk in the dining hall and you physically assaulted Professor Carling, dangerously tipping hot soup into his lap and it is purely by luck that he escaped serious burns. Incredible behaviour. Now you need to learn what can happen when you breach college rules and act like a hooligan. My patience has worn out and I can no longer give you further time to come to your senses. Dr Stanford, as Kerry's mentor, will you please escort Kerry to Professor Winslow-Bellingham's office and I will electronically file the immediate suspension and we will facilitate her removal from the college with immediate effect. Whether that be temporary or permanently will be in the hands of the full council."

"No! Please. You can spank me! Yes! Please do not suspend me, Professor Stones. I am so sorry. Please, you can spank me now. Should I take all my clothes off? What do I do? Please don't throw me out. Please." Kerry's capitulation was hardly a surprise to those present as the screw was turned, but Stones would never countenance any attempt to negotiate a punishment at this stage. His bark was now fierce.

"Stop your nonsense. We have a way to go to decide what your chastisement should consist of but we are certainly far, far beyond a mere spanking as the solution. But yes, I accept that the gesture of removing your garments in readiness for a thrashing would at least show that the message has sunk in and that you are prepared to begin the journey towards personal improvement."

Kerry was in full panic mode now and discarded her clothing in seconds, standing naked before the three senior staff members, shaking and with wild eyes flicking from one to the next.

"Please Professor Stones, what do you want me to do now?" Kerry's voice was meek, all evidence of the haughty, arrogant student from minutes ago now gone.

Stones sneered at the student.

"Turn around, bend over, legs apart, grab your ankles with your hands, and present your bare buttocks to us. At the very least we seem to have made a start, so let us not waste any further time," he said in a seemingly disinterested tone.

Kerry immediately obeyed, all resistance gone, no argument left. Her firm, naked buttocks facing the audience of three senior academics.

"At last, success of a sort. Right, buttocks nicely rounded and spread, cheeks apart, point that cute little anus up at us. Ready to go. Hold that position while we discuss what would constitute an appropriate punishment to correct the error of your ways."

The sob from Kerry gave evidence to her broken spirit and utter capitulation as her whole body trembled, her buttocks squeezing tight together as she tried to preserve some sense of dignity.

Stones turned to his companions.

"Now ladies, now we can see the target fully, let us decide who applies what. Dr Stanford, I suggest that you fulfil your commitment to our graduate education and enhancement program and apply the leather tawse after I have delivered a good paddling to these fine buttocks." He deliberately ran his hands over Kerry's quivering bottom, allowing his fingers to flutter over her anal cleft. To his utter delight, she squeezed her cheeks tight together to close her most intimate orifice for a split second, before she realised that she had unintentionally trapped one of his fingers. He deliberately wiggled the finger and she immediately relaxed the tension to release his digit, causing her crinkled hole to open up obligingly. He smiled, thoroughly at ease with the shame and embarrassment that he caused as she whimpered in her distress and humiliation. The sudden ringing of his desk telephone made them all jolt.

"Stay in position," growled Stones as he took the call, Dorothy's name showing on his console. "It seems that Professor Winslow-Bellingham would like a private word."

He gave a couple of affirmative grunts into the mouthpiece before ending with the words that sent another spasm through Kerry's bent over body.

"As you wish, Mistress, as you wish."

"Get your clothes on and get out. You will return here in five days' time for your chastisement. At the Mistress' request, you will receive a paddling from myself, the tawse from Dr Stanford as well as a caning from Dr Ford. Professor Winslow-Bellingham will oversee your chastisement. The punishment is severe due to your loutish and offensive behaviour and due to your abominable performance in this room today. During the next few days you will make your apologies to the professor and his brother as well as the Mistress. You will also take this time to think seriously about your future. You will return here to take a thrashing at your own request. You will write to me to confirm that this is your wish and you will specify your willingness to undergo the corporal punishment that I have specifically detailed. Your punishment will be principally on your bare buttocks. Again, I would expect you to note that this is with your approval and at your bequest. You will come to my rooms cleansed, with empty bowels and bladder, and ready to take your requested chastisement. Do you understand?"

Frozen by his words as she stooped to draw her knickers up, she turned to stare comically open-mouthed before timidly nodding her assent. Realising that her breasts and pubic region were now facing the academics she squealed and covered herself before recognising the futility of her actions. Eyes full of tears and trepidation, she abandoned any sense of decorum and flung her clothes on as fast as possible before, muttering apologies, she scurried from the room.

CHAPTER 9

KERRY: FIVE DAYS LATER

At the appointed time Kerry returned to stand before the trio of academics. The challenge in her eyes, the belligerent demeanour, the feisty temper, all gone. Timidly she passed Stones a copy of the email she had sent earlier confirming that she had made the decision to volunteer for the option of corporal punishment rather than face a suspension from college. She had delivered accepted apologies as instructed, the Mistress having regaled Stones with the humiliation she had endured at the hands of herself and the elderly academics as they had forced her to explain in detail the punishment she was due to receive. Professor Carling, forewarned by Stones, had put Kerry through hell as he insisted on her retelling her experience at the interview, and then demanding the most intimate details of the punishment she was to receive. He had made her stress the fact that she would be naked, spread-eagled and thoroughly beaten on her buttocks by three different perpetrators. It had been belittling and highly embarrassing for Kerry, particularly knowing that far worse was yet to come.

As an older student there were higher standards of deportment expected and Stones had no hesitation in applying harsher rules to the post-graduates in the college, who he felt should know so much better. His intention was to cause shame as much as pain, the experience to be memorably demeaning and distressing mentally, as well as physically agonising. His approach was not universally approved of, even within the walls of the college. Some of his colleagues were of the opinion that the humiliation he dished out was too severe and belittling. He did not accept this argument, although it had never been put to him, with any conviction, that he should change his methods, as he was entrenched in his view that the punishment fitted the crime and that there was a lesson to be learnt through shaming. As his time to hand over the reins grew closer, he became more than ever determined to continue the way he saw fit. He often pointed to the extremely small number of repeat offenders he had to deal with, and would not accept that the humiliation of offenders did not play a big apart in the improved behaviour the vast majority of those chastised portrayed afterwards. With Celia almost certain to be confirmed as his replacement soon, he accepted that it would signal the end of certain disciplinary practices but until then he was most certainly not one for turning! He took a breath, fixed Kerry with a piercing stare and ordered her to strip naked ready for inspection and punishment.

With no hesitation Kerry removed her dress, revealing no other clothing except a pair of tiny briefs which she whipped off and stood naked before her audience. At raised eyebrows from Stones and a helpful nod from Dr Stafford, most definitely an opponent of his shaming process, she put her hands on her head and faced them with a look of acceptance of her fate very apparent.

"Right, young lady. I presume you are thoroughly emptied internally and cleansed externally? Yes?"

Kerry turned a deep shade of red, as shame and embarrassment were immediately brought to the fore by Stones. He noted Philippa's eyes cast down in disapproval.

"Yes, sir," she whispered.

"As promised you will be paddled by myself, a hard 20 with my thickest wooden version. You will be then given ten lashes with the leather tawse by Dr Stanford. The cane will then be applied 20 times by Dr Ford. A good 50 strokes in all to be delivered, hard and true, to bring closure to this sorry episode and hopefully will result in an enlightened and improved post-graduate student. There is a further option of six strokes from my favourite thick leather strap in reserve which will be brought to the table if there is any lack of compliance, offensive language or misbehaviour during punishment. This is what you deserve and this is what you have requested. Is this correct, Kerry?"

The weeping student's answer failed to be delivered in a clear and articulate manner, but Stones was prepared to forgive her that. He had received an email from her the day after their meeting and Stones had been impressed by her change of tone, in her request to be thrashed until the threat to her future at the college was removed. She had stated that she authorised Professor Stones' to punish her without mercy and until her sins had been cleansed and forgiven. He felt that it was a courageous email and hoped that this newly found acceptance and stoicism would be evidenced when the reality of the moment was faced. So far, so good, he thought. Her distress was apparent, understandable considering what she was about to endure, but the haughty attitude and sense of being wronged, seemed to have dissipated.

At this point the door buzzer sounded and there was no disguising Kerry's absolute horror when the original source of her current predicament entered the room.

"Good evening, Professor Carling, you are most welcome. Sadly the college Mistress is unable to join us currently, Kerry, but Professor Carling unselfishly volunteered to give up some of his valuable time to take her place. Hands on your head, girl. Do not want to deny Professor Carling a full view of your splendid nakedness all ready to receive its just desserts, do we now?"

Tears poured down the face of the distraught Kerry, her horror at being naked and exposed in front of the elderly academic so apparent. Clearly, as Stones had known full well, she was not delighted at the thought of her nemesis being a voyeur at her denouement. Again, he noted, Philippa's pursed lips and stony face. He would deal with her at a later date.

"My pleasure and my duty in the circumstances, Professor Stones. Happy to assist in any way you wish. Good evening, young lady. Although I do not suppose you were hoping to be in my company again so soon. Your description of what your punishment was going to entail was most heart-warming and I must say that when the opportunity to be present when you received your comeuppance came up, I found it hard to resist. The thought of being able to watch at close hand while your buttocks suffered a damn good thrashing from my three colleagues here was most inspiring and quite thrilling to be honest. As a long-time supporter of the college's commitment to apt and appropriate physical punishment to bring miscreants to task, I am rather looking forward to the experience I have to admit. Probably rather more than yourself, eh, young lady?"

Carling stood in front of the unfrocked student as he rambled on, his wide eyes and smirking expression rather illustrating his unconcealed joy and relish at her predicament.

A sniffle, a quiet sob, and a nod of acceptance was the only response from Kerry as Stones smiled with satisfaction at this extra twist he had added to Kerry's ordeal. Her demeanour was an illustration of total defeat and before a blow had landed, Stones knew that his desired outcome was already accomplished. He suspected that the process had already done a good part of the job of bringing Kerry into line. The humiliation and shame he could see her experiencing now was a true punishment in itself and possibly more productive in teaching the young woman the error of her ways than a red and sore bottom. Some might consider the thrashing itself now an unnecessarily tough and vicious act of vengeance, with the misfit having learned her lesson, apologised, been punished and disgraced and unlikely to repeat her offence. Some might indeed, but not the renowned Dean of Discipline at St James' College. Oh no, indeed!

"Right, you rapscallion. Let's have you over my lap in the old-fashioned manner for a damn good bare-bottom spanking. Come along now, Kerry, over you go. Let's have a good look at what we have to work on. That's it, over you go, hands grasping the chair legs, bottom up and stretch those lovely pins of yours out. Don't be shy, it's all going to be on show for a fair while, so do get used to it!" He taunted his victim as he tugged her over his lap, indicating to Professor Carling to position himself at the action end. At a nod from Stones, Celia moved, tissues in hand, to guide the discombobulated student's hands to the bottom of the chair legs, coaxing her to steady herself in preparation for her ordeal.

"Keep her steady if you can, Dr Ford, I intend to set these globes on fire soon. A quick 50 with my hand to warm you up and get a nice blush on these lovely cheeks before we start on your serious punishment. Any structure is assisted by having a good foundation before we apply a layer of hard core, I always think. Sound like a good plan to you, young Kerry?"

The whimper in response was not discernibly an affirmative or vote of confidence in any way, but Stones decided to be charitable and take it as an assent.

"I will take that as a yes and proceed in that case." His flat hand landed with a loud clap, accompanied by a squeal of protest and the start of a struggle from Kerry that was to last until Celia's firm hand held her wrists securely in place as the first 20 blows rained down. The slaps continued to ring around the room as Kerry proved to have the perfect rounded cheeks to bring out the best and most satisfying sound effects brought forth by a bottom spanking. The howls from Kerry varied in volume but consistently greeted each new spank as the professor methodically worked his hand over the fullness of her buttocks and the tops of her kicking legs.

"Now that's a lovely shade of pink. Time to begin with this good thick paddle which will be laid on with full gusto while I reiterate why we are here." *Splat!* "The purpose of corporal punishment," *Splat!* "is ultimately to ensure," *Splat!* "that any harm inflicted on the college," *Splat!* "including college society and personnel," *Splat!* "is limited and corrected where possible." *Splat!* "It is also to issue a," *Splat!* "learning lesson to the miscreants," *Splat!* "and encouragement to avoid future offending." *Splat!* "The improvement of said offenders," *Splat!* "is paramount to our thinking." *Splat!* "However, other values outside," *Splat!* "the narrow focus on the offender," *Splat!* "may play a role in sanctioning." *Splat!* "In some countries, the impact," *Splat!* "of a sentence on the family," *Splat!* "and the community of the offender," *Splat!* "will effectively play a larger role," *Splat!* "than in others, either with respect," *Splat!* "to the type of sentence chosen." *Splat!*

Each impact received a louder squeal than the one before and Stones could see the efforts being put in by Celia, as Kerry's head jerked and shook while she suffered in a manner that she had never previously entertained.

Laying the paddle down behind him, Stones nonchalantly flipped the sobbing woman from his lap, noting from the wide glistening eyes of Professor Carling that he was enjoying the spectacle immensely.

"Ladies, if you could strap her down over the desk, please. She is clearly not going to endure the rest of her dues without being fastened securely. No rush, I want her calmed down and in a state to fully appreciate her strapping with the tawse and then the caning. No point hurrying, the full benefits of a thrashing need time to sink into an individual's consciousness. The bite of the cane and the slap of a tawse need time to savour, I feel, for their recipients to truly respect and value the lesson being dispensed. Now Kerry, try and have a bit of dignity and pull yourself together."

The blubbing woman, barely holding herself upright even with Celia and Philippa's support did manage to direct a hostile glare towards Stones, indicating at least an element of self-respect remained. Stones acknowledged it with a grin.

"Ah, a spark of gumption remains. We will see if you can repeat that once Dr Stanford lays this rather fine piece of split-ended leather across those rather tender-looking scarlet buttocks. Get her secured please, ladies, we do not want her tempted to try and avoid her just desserts. Dr Stanford, if you please, administer the tawse. Ten strokes with maximum effort. I want to hear her screaming, please. Lay the foundations for the searing that her bottom will soon be receiving from the cane."

Now fully bent over and secured, Kerry was completely at the mercy of her tormentors and her weeping was indicative of the realisation of unavoidable physical castigation. Celia wiped her brow and began to whisper words of encouragement that Stones knew were shallow and fabricated, as she revelled in having the opportunity to deliver the grand finale to Kerry's denouement. He was more interested in whether or not Philippa would fulfil her duty and admonish Kerry to his satisfaction. Her first stroke was wild, catching Kerry full on her left leg with the split ends slapping hard between her legs, its forked tips catching her labial lips full on. The resulting screech from Kerry certainly backed up the assumption that it was not a tick of approval to Philippa's accuracy.

"Whoops," said Stones, his face a grin but his steely eyes causing a stuttering apology and a look of fright from Philippa. "Concentrate fully on where you intend to land the tawse please, Dr Stanford. Accuracy first, concentrate on exactly where you intend to lay the stroke before focusing on power. Sadly for Kerry, if the strokes are deemed not severe enough, I may consider repeating the dose."

Even in her distress from the painful blow, those words permeated her consciousness and Kerry howled in acknowledgement.

Philippa's face reddened and her face set in extreme concentration as she laid the tawse against the taut trembling cheeks before her.

"So sorry, Professor Stones, I will do my very best." With that she drew her arm back and taking a loud breath out swung down in a wide, slow arc. The leather landed full across the centre of the split orbs before her, the tip flicking around to whip her thighs with its deadly split end. A yelp from Kerry signalled accuracy but everyone present knew that this was a mild stroke, power lacking and sacrificed to ensure the target was well met.

"I will accept that as a marker, Dr Stanford, now strike in exactly the same place but with a lot more power. No hurry at all, Dr Stanford, take your time." Stones' voice was mild but no one in the room doubted that Philippa was on borrowed time and that a flawless third stroke was very much expected now.

With a look of terror in her eyes initially, slowly giving way to an expression of steely determination, Philippa's arm went back and then swung down with much more force. The scream from Kerry gave support to a much truer application, her body writhing pointlessly in her restraints, her legs and buttocks beginning the uncontrolled trembling oft displayed by vanquished young women under Stones' tutelage and corrective procedures. He nodded his approval, causing a triumphant grin to spread across Philippa's face as she raised her arm once more but now confident in her ability to inflict the torment ordained. For the next few minutes no other sound was heard in the room save the swish of air rapidly displaced, the slapping impact of leather on naked flesh and the resultant scream acknowledging the success of Philippa's endeavours.

Turning to the professor, as the tenth stroke and its response from a distraught Kerry reverberated around the room, Philippa's face was one begging for approval and acceptance. He looked into eyes that shone with pride, apprehension and no little desire and Stones felt that finally he was seeing evidence that Philippa was more on board with their ethos and methods than maybe she liked to admit.

"Well done, Dr Stanford. At last we see promise of the commitment that has sadly been lacking in your previous attendance in this room. Progress, my dear, progress shown and a return, at last, on our investment in time, energy and no small financial commitment. A decent job. No more, no less. Now Dr Ford will illustrate how to deliver a severe caning although we will give the recalcitrant a moment or two to pull herself together and cease that ridiculous keening. Be warned, Kerry, calm yourself down or I will feel obliged to strap your legs to remind you that there is always an upgrade available on any chastisement being dispensed."

Philippa's beam in response to rather backhanded praise from Stones, rather gave away her desire to earn his approval. He found it interesting how once they had taken part in a thrashing, quite a lot of reservations seemed to desert his helpers. A quick glance at Professor Carling to ensure that he was still enjoying the spectacle was all that was needed. He looked absolutely mesmerised, wide-eyed, open-mouthed and with an unmistakable look of unadulterated lust in his eyes. Stones doubted he would have anything other than approval and gratitude from him when they completed the corrective treatment of the errant post-graduate student. Stones' keen eye could see the tented front of his colleagues' trousers, unaware that he was in full view of one of the recording cameras always filming disciplinary processes, and filed that useful knowledge away, although suspecting that he would not require any material to ensure that Carling signed off his consent that justice and retribution had been accomplished.

With Kerry's noise reduced to a snuffling and gentle weeping, Stones judged it was time for her to receive the finale of her punishment.

"If Kerry could confirm that she is fully ready to receive the cane, Dr Ford, I think we should get this episode done and dusted. Kerry, please state clearly that you wish to proceed with your caning and state why you need such a harsh thrashing. I assume you do wish to accept this final part of your correction and improvement for the wilful disrespect, rudeness and appalling behaviour that was displayed so shamelessly."

Kerry seemed oblivious that a response was required and for a long minute silence hung in the room.

"Philippa, I suggest you have a word with your charge. I am not given to repetition but will allow that Kerry may be a bit distracted taking into account the state of these rather beleaguered buttocks." There was no reaction from Kerry as he ran his hands over her bottom whilst he spoke. All fight was gone, total compliance and obedience had been achieved, her submission complete.

Philippa bent down and raised Kerry's head, speaking quietly to the vanquished and clearly overwhelmed woman whose anguished response to Philippa's murmurings encapsulated her misery. After a few pleading words that fell on deaf ears, Kerry's shoulders slumped down once more as Philippa stepped away with a last few sharper words.

"I am waiting to hear from you, Kerry. Do you have anything to say?" Stones said, his voice just tainted with a tone of slight impatience.

In a voice barely recognisable from that of the contemptuous and disdainful woman of a few days previously, Kerry spoke with total servility.

"Sir, I am so sorry for everything and, and, and, oh no. Oh, sorry. I um, er, think that you should give me a caning, please. Oh no, oh help. Oh sorry, please cane me, sir, Dr Ford."

At a nod from Stones, Celia raised the cane high.

"As you wish, Kerry, as you wish." With that the cane fairly flew through the air before landing on the lower part of Kerry's bottom cheeks.

Whatever she had endured before clearly had not prepared the young woman for the initial shock of the harsh cut of the cane that preceded the dull throbbing ache. A strangled cry followed by a long pitiful moan as she rotated her hips in an attempt to absorb the blow. Celia proceeded to work her way up the squirming buttocks as she laid the next five strokes on in a consistent and thoroughly ordered manner. She allowed Kerry's squeals and writhing to cease between strokes, and Stones was impressed by her accurate spacing and intensity, the six stripes showing in fiercely red welts as if they had been painted on.

"Impressively laid on, Dr Ford. Now let us see if you could fill in the space between the lines. Nice and hard, I want to hear this reprobate sing out loudly in appreciation of your skilful delivery," Stones said, half an eye on Professor Carling, whose face betrayed the lust and satisfaction he was getting from Kerry's ordeal. Kerry herself was now just mewing quietly, a picture of defeat and resistance completely broken.

A smiling Celia, her face a picture of determination and satisfaction, raised her arm and proceeded to deliver six perfectly positioned stripes between the red guidelines she had already produced on the suffering bottom of the distressed Kerry.

Stones applauded her expertise, saying, "Give her two more on the tops of her legs, please, Dr Ford, and then I will apply the final six to the centre of her buttocks to give her a lovely sore point on her sit-upon. We do want her to remember her time here every time she settles those blistered cheeks down."

A nod from Celia before she applied two stinging strokes as directed, eliciting a screech from Kerry as the ultra-sensitive spot targeted produced the exact response Stones required.

He took the cane, swished it through the air a few times as he waited for the distraught student to settle and then raised his arm. It was doubtful Kerry had ever experienced the intense pain that the blur of the professor's arm created as he delivered six ferocious strokes of the cane with impeccable accuracy, to the centre of the beleaguered buttocks. The initial response of a sharp intake of breath was replaced by an agonising guttural groan of despair from a student who surely would think again before committing any further offence in her remaining time at St James'.

No one spoke as Kerry's very audible suffering filled the space in the room. Stones moved to his cabinet and stored away the cane, but to the surprise of everyone although to the obvious delight of Celia he unhooked his favourite thick strap and moved back behind Kerry.

"On the whole you have behaved yourself, young lady, and taken your punishment reasonably well and without too much complaint. However, to ensure that you do not return to my room I will apply one stroke only of the strap, with a promise that if these delightful buttocks were ever needed to be thus exposed to me again for chastisement, then you would receive a minimum dozen of my favourite enforcer here. Now take a breath and prepare yourself."

A babbling Kerry, clearly recognising that things were about to get worse, was apologising profusely as the wicked blow landed across the taut skin at the top of her bottom. The impact was loud but Kerry's howl drowned its echo as the tremendous stinging recrimination of the thick leather entered her consciousness.

By the time Kerry had reached a stage of awareness of anything else other than the fire burning in her bottom, a beaming and elated Professor Carling had taken his leave and she was being untethered and helped onto a bidet full of iced water.

Less than half an hour later Stones was ejaculating into the welcoming mouth of Celia, her own fingers frigging herself to climax as she swallowed his load.

A pat on her head as she milked the final droplets of his offering accompanied the words, "Good job all round today, Celia. Now knickers up and run along, my love, I have work to do."

CHAPTER 10

IN WHICH FELICITY WANTS HER MUMMY

"Mandy Coulson, as was, well bless my soul! Lovely to see you in my rooms again, lovely, lovely. Now let me guess, young Felicity here is about to discover what her punishment might be for her rude and inebriated behaviour outside a little gathering the other evening and Mummy has come along with her to plead her case?"

"A pleasure to see you too, Professor Stones, although I quite thought that I'd been in your rooms for the last time. Of course you're correct that I am on a mercy mission although if you'll hear me out I believe that you will be prepared to consider my proposition. Still is Mandy Coulson, Professor Stones, I have been divorced from Felicity's father for many years so I have reverted back to my maiden name."

Stones studied the couple before him. Young, frightened, timid Felicity Ferguson, petite first-year student, curly fair hair, nice figure, and very pretty. Mother Mandy, former student of this parish, a second-class honours degree in Land Economy, who, after graduating, went into a legal company specialising in agricultural issues and married a farmer, an affluent landowner. She had been an argumentative and feisty youngster, blonde, petite in height, albeit now with a few added pounds, but still as attractive as she had been 25 years ago, Stones thought. More importantly, she had twice been in his rooms bent over, naked and thrashed, and her presence before him today hinted tantalisingly at a possible third occurrence. Yes indeed, he thought, this could be interesting and his growing erection definitely seemed to agree!

"Well that's all very well, but I am not sure that I feel errant students deserve to have their mummies holding their hand when they face up to their disgraces. Sit down at the back of the room for now, Mandy, while young Felicity and I discuss her thoughts on her actions."

Stones just let the silence hang in the air. He could see a smile playing on Mandy's lips as she recognised this much-used tactic and it was not long before Felicity took the bait.

"Look, it was just a bit of fun that got a little bit out of hand, sir. No real harm was done, a little too much drinking, a bit too noisy and full of ourselves, although admittedly a bit too much lip at the porters. I am sorry, sir. I was drunk, I was loud and I did give those two porters a hard time. But that is all it was, sir. You know, hijinks and all that."

Stones just stared at her. She soon conformed to the norm: He waited, she wilted.

"Sir? I am sorry, sir, but I know that this is not the first time."

It was not news to Stones, of course, but it evidently was to Felicity's mother, whose jawline perceptively set.

"No, Felicity, not exactly the second time either, was it?"

"Oh my God. Yes, sir. But sir, the first time wasn't really me. I was just there, sir."

Mandy's eyes were blazing into the back of her daughter. *Well,* Stones thought to himself, *if you go into battle with back-up, it is not such a good idea if there is not really a prepared and discussed plan.*

"So the first time you and your cronies were punished with simple litter-picking duties, the second time you got toilet scrubbing and menial cleaning duties for a fortnight. Now do you remember what it was that I said to you, Naomi Emuah and Igraine Debussey concerning any further misconduct?"

Felicity grimaced.

"You said that you would stop playing with us, sir," she said miserably.

"Naomi and Igraine are not here. The reason being that they were not involved in this incident, were they?"

"No, sir."

"You were the vocal lead in the whole affair, were you not?" Stones was putting the miserable student to the sword now but felt she was still far from the point whereby he was getting total honesty and compliance.

"I suppose." Her sulky look and slightly defiant demeanour signalled that contrition and remorse were a few steps away, as far as Stones was concerned.

Her mother clearly agreed as he scowled and heard Mandy sigh, signalling her exasperation with her daughter matched his own.

"Hmmm. *You suppose*. And can you remember what it was you said to my colleague, the senior porter, when he said he would place you on report?"

"Oh I don't remember, sir, I think I was just messing around really. You know, sir, talking nonsense under pressure."

"Do the words *small man syndrome* and *fascist little Hitler* ring a bell?" His voice was gradually getting louder in contrast to Felicity, whose own voice was now rather impersonating a mouse. "Would you tell me what else you said, please?"

"That was it, sir. I am really sorry, I didn't mean it."

"Oh really? So if I was to inform you that the CCTV in that area is, like most around the college, an audio as well as a visual recording system, and your words are on record quite clearly, you would stick to your guns? Really? Last chance to confess or shall I play back the whole sorry episode for us to watch together. Just so you know, your ignorance and lack of co-operation is affecting the chastisement that I have in mind to impose. You are making things worse for yourself by the minute. Right, I have had enough."

Stones moved to his computer and began to tap. It was all an almighty bluff as the CCTV system had only very sporadic audio recording ability and none at all in this instance. As he expected, Felicity's mother took the bait this time.

"You stupid girl. What the hell did you say? For crying out loud, tell the professor now!" Mandy had risen to her feet and was shouting at her wilting daughter now.

Professor Stones adopted a weary expression as he played out the scenario to his own ends.

"Mandy Coulson, do I have to read you some rules of behaviour when in my rooms? You do not speak unless I ask you a question and I think I told you to sit down. Or did you want to leave? Because if you stay in my room, you stay on my terms and behave to my rules. Do you understand me or do you need a physical reminder of the manner in which miserable miscreants are dealt with in here?"

Mandy's shudder suggested that she did indeed, and she returned to her seat muttering rather grovelling apologises.

"Felicity, you have entered the last chance saloon and that door is soon going to close on you. Are you going to confess or not?"

Felicity took a big gulp, her eyes on the ground before Stones, as she confirmed the very words that had been reported to him.

"I am really sorry, sir. I did not mean it at all. I was just drunk and angry, sir. Oh, God, I am afraid that I called him a paedophile and a kiddie fiddler, sir. I am so, so sorry, sir."

A glance from Stones was enough to halt Felicity's mother in her tracks as she went to speak.

"Yes indeed. You clearly need to learn how much alcohol you can drink, don't you? You foul-mouthed, grossly offensive wretch. How on earth do you think I should punish you for this unforgivable and totally unacceptable behaviour, Felicity? Come on, girl, you are well aware that your stay in this hallowed institution is at risk. At the least a suspension would seem in order. What are your thoughts, Felicity? Please do not look at your mother, it is time for you to grow up and take responsibility for your actions now, young lady. You are nearly 20 years old for goodness' sake."

Unlike most other university colleges, St James' had a strict rule that all entrants at undergraduate level had to work for a year after leaving school, having completed their Advanced Levels and achieved qualifying grades. This was to ensure the young women arrived having, in theory at least, received a prior grounding of the real world, the college requiring approval of the chosen employment and a positive report of the potential students' performance. It was not a perfect system, but did mean that the students arrived having experienced 12 months in a working environment and had tested out earning a salary. They also were a year older and, it was to be hoped, more mature than they were at 18. Not always the case, Stones felt, but on the whole he approved of the policy and believed it meant he had every right to expect that these were young adults who should have learnt general societal rules of behaviour. Sometimes he felt very much let down by the students under his care and watchful eye and today was definitely one of those.

"Oh, sir, I am truly so sorry and will apologise and do my best to make amends with the porter, sir. Maybe there are some duties I could do for the porters, sir, as my punishment?" There was a look of desperation in Felicity's eyes now and Stones knew that the endgame was approaching.

He sighed loudly and at length. To the student it inferred that his patience was stretched, that he was tired with the exchange and disappointed with the responses received. It was tactical, and played to perfection by a master of his craft. All part of breaking down his miscreants' resistance and just a step on the journey to them accepting their fate and facing up to their just desserts for offences committed. He could see a similar level of exasperation cross Mandy's face and knew that he needed to cut to the chase with this student, who he felt had so far failed to grasp the seriousness of her behaviour and the situation she was now in because of it.

"Improvement, correction and purification is my aim, young lady, and often that calls for discipline via corporal punishment. I had hoped you would appreciate that a thorough, well intentioned and perfectly delivered thrashing of your bare buttocks may well serve to achieve that goal. This is my hope and my ambition in your case, Felicity. Would you please acknowledge that you recognise the position you have created and the only course of redemption open to you if you wish to avoid a suspension of a complete term."

His tone had become frostier and frostier as he continued.

"Suspensions, as you know, are not given lightly due to the repercussions they can have on your degree grading and standing within the college community. Please be advised that the disgrace of a suspension should never be viewed as an easy option, as it is one step away from being sent down. The clock on you would definitely be ticking then, young lady. However, if the idea of a short, sharp shock by means of a damn good hiding is that abhorrent and fearsome then let's not waste any more time here and get the paperwork prepared. Handily your mother is here, so once I have formalised your departure you can pack your things and get out. There's really no point in you seeing out this term. The sooner you get off, the better."

Tears were rolling down Felicity's face now, comprehension finally sinking in, as she looked beseechingly towards her mother whose own face was now a picture of distress.

"Professor Stones, may I offer an alternative solution, please?" Mandy ventured.

Stones nodded his assent while her daughter's expression showed desperate glimmers of hope.

"Yes indeed, Mandy. Maybe it is time for me to see the written work you have brought along? I have seen you fiddling with paperwork, and assume you have thought through the likely end scenarios of this meeting? I would hazard a guess that you have scribed the options that you can offer me to appease my ambition and intention to see justice take place?"

"Ahem, er, yes, Professor. I was wondering, would it be acceptable for me to give Felicity her punishment, as dictated by you, overseen by you and before you?"

Felicity's face rather gave away that this was not the alternative solution she would have chosen!

"Mum!" was her anguished exclamation.

Stones appeared to give very little consideration to Mandy's proposal, quickly discounting her plea.

"An interesting starting point in what I assume you believe is a negotiation, Mandy. Yes, an interesting proposal indeed, but unfortunately very much a lightweight option. It could be an unusual, and possibly enjoyable, option for me but I am not sure that you yourself are not missing the point. Your daughter is guilty of an abomination and this warrants severe punishment. What it does not warrant is her being involved in a negotiation to lessen the pain, distress, disgrace and humiliation of the corporal punishment that I believe is required to balance the books. So I thank you for your offer but respectfully decline it. Now I am presuming that given the choice, Mandy, you and Felicity would both wish for you to be present for her session? So if Felicity does come to her senses and opts for physical chastisement, then she may have her punishment tomorrow rather than wait the usual period to have to fret and worry. You may therefore stay in one of our guest suites overnight and attend here tomorrow, to view her flogging, if that is the agreed outcome. Have you anything else in your notes that would warrant further conversation?"

Felicity's mouth was just opening and closing soundlessly as he spoke, the dilemma of her situation evident in total fear shown in her eyes.

"Yes thank you, Professor Stones. I understand that you would insist on carrying out the punishment but I wonder if you would consider the alternative of myself carrying out Felicity's punishment before you, and then you repeat the thrashing to me. This, I believe, would serve the purpose of not only Felicity suffering the indignity of receiving her beating, but also you would bear witness to her humiliation. Following that, Professor, I would propose that Felicity watched as you then repeated the beating but this time applied to my own backside. She would then have to live with not only her own disgrace but also the consequences that I will have suffered for her misbehaviour."

Stones paused in contemplation. This was an option that appealed. The idea of a mature and willing Mandy being naked and voluntarily taking a beating had most definitely caused a stirring of the loins!

He turned his back on the two women to hide his physical interest in her words. As Felicity spluttered her objections, Mandy, thinking that he was dismissing her words, immediately continued with a pleading tone.

"Please, Professor Stones, if I could be allowed a moment with my daughter I think we can offer you an appropriate option." Mandy's voice carried such a level of desperation that Stones was moved to accept her request, and wordlessly left the two alone as he went into his lounge suite off the central room, taking the fortunate opportunity to adjust his clothing.

He allowed them ten minutes together, having left his door ajar so that the raised voice of Mandy berating her daughter was clearly audible. As expected Mandy bluntly explained the facts of adult life to Felicity, whose cowered response Stones could barely hear albeit she was clearly acquiescing to the rather threatening and berating tone of her mother. Mandy's rising voice brooked no argument and Stones smiled to himself as the unmistakable sharp crack of an open hand meeting a face resounded through the partially open door. He gave things a couple of minutes to calm down before re-entering the fray. A ferocious Mandy ceased her hectoring as he appeared and returned to her seat. "My naughty daughter has something to say, Professor," she stated.

Felicity took a deep breath before she announced her acceptance of her fate in a shaky voice, a single tear rolling down a reddened cheek.

"I am very sorry for my actions, Professor Stones. I do not want to be sent from the college and therefore... Poooh!" Felicity's voice broke and she dried up. Stones held a hand up to stem Mandy as she began to rise from the seat she had just retaken.

"Mandy, you will stay seated in silence unless you wish for me to increase Felicity's sentence for her heinous acts. I will have you escorted off the premises if I sense any further interference or intervention. Felicity, you can take a deep breath, make some sort of pretence at being an adult and continue with what I hope is a proper apology, an acceptance of your guilt and a proposal to satisfy me as regards the appropriate punishment you wish to undergo. Now damn well get on with it or damn well get out of this college!"

Felicity jolted at Stones' tone change. Her eyes cast down, she took the required breath and with an obvious effort at control began to speak. She was not to know that he was expertly accomplished at the roles he played to bend his reluctant misfits to his will.

"I apologise once again and most sincerely, sir. I would like to accept your offer of the option of corporal punishment. I realise that I must accept this punishment myself but hope that you can find it in your heart to allow my mother to be with me while I receive the punishment, sir. I do not wish my mother to receive any punishment, sir, and request that you please discount her previous offer to take my place or take any part of what is due to me. So, I would like to take whatever punishment you determine and wish to thank you for allowing me to remain in the college, sir. I am so sorry, sir."

Tears flowed freely now and the student's shoulders began to shake.

"You need to be far more specific in clarifying exactly how you wish to be punished. As you can see my cabinet here contains a good selection of items used to implement chastisement and improvement to disobedient and rude young students. Please take a moment to inspect the instruments that I hope will bring about your contrition and redemption. I would then like to hear what you propose as an appropriate chastisement for your despicable behaviour to a member of the college staff."

The horrified look on Felicity's face mirrored many that had stood in the same place before her. Her breathing rate increased and tears once more ran down her flushed face.

"Oh no. No. Oh my. Oh, Mummy. Oh I can't, I can't."

Mandy quickly moved in.

"I am so sorry about my silly daughter, Professor Stones. Is it alright if I assist her in her selection, please?"

Stones gave her a look of impatient disdain but relented to her request.

"Quickly now, and take into account that a damn good over-the-knee bare-bottomed spanking will be the precursor and should be taken as read, or should I say red?" His sneering chuckle, at his humour, caused both women to flinch before they turned back to the cabinet.

"A paddle and a cane, darling. Quick, quick. No, do not choose the ones that look least harmful, that just will not be acceptable. You need to show you truly regret your actions and require just punishment to show your remorse and contrition."

Stones smiled at her words.

"Ah-ha! Spoken like one who has learned a valuable lesson, Mandy. You see, Felicity, your mother knows the score. I am sure that she can offer tips on how to manage the process too, given her own history in this room."

Felicity turned immediately to her mother with an accusing look.

"You said that you had just had a bit of a spanking."

"Never mind that now, Felicity, just take these to Professor Stones and let us get this resolved as quickly as we can."

Mandy's attempt to brush her own indiscretions under the carpet were not to Stones' liking.

"Oh let us cut to the chase, shall we? Felicity, your mother has bent over, buck-naked on two occasions in my room. The first time she received a thorough spanking and a 30-stroke paddling for drunken misbehaviour at a college entertainment event, and the second time was for the ransacking of a fellow student's room after a disgraceful argument and a scuffle in the college bar. On that occasion, she received a longer and more intense spanking, a 30-stroke caning and a whipping of her upper legs whilst tied over a stool. All carried out in front of some of my senior colleagues, if I remember correctly."

Mandy and Felicity were not to know that Stones had watched a rather grainy recording of the events only hours before and so was very sure of his recollections!

Mandy's face was now bright red but she continued her selection and turned to Stones holding out a long, thick leather paddle and his medium-thick cane.

"Well, that was embarrassing to hear. Now you know, young lady. So maybe we can just get on with this, please. Is this sufficient, sir? I would suggest that her spanking be of 100 slaps, a 30-stroke paddling and 10 of the best with the cane to finish."

Felicity's face looked horrified but worse was to follow.

"Oh, I do not believe that a caning under 20 strokes fits the bill in this case, Mandy, so we can double that final flourish. Otherwise, I would agree that that is acceptable. Can you confirm that this is the form you would like your punishment to take please, Felicity? I would encourage you to be detailed and specific in your request."

The student's mouth just opened and closed wordlessly for several seconds, before a frustrated Mandy nudged her forward, whispering into her ear as she did so.

"Alright, alright, Mum. Sir, I agree to a beating, sir. One hundred spanks, 30 strokes of the paddle and 20 with the cane, sir. I am very sorry for the things I have done and do deserve my punishment. Is that okay?"

Stones looked at her with a certain amount of disdain.

"You will now sit down over there and write that down along with a full description of the actions that led to this decision and how you recognise the wrongs that you have done. I want to see full acceptance of the disgraceful behaviour that you have displayed, the remorse and contrition that you now feel and how much you wish to pay for your dues by requesting and receiving physical punishment to your bare buttocks to assist in your atonement. You will also remove all your clothing and write this piece of work naked as a gesture of your compliance and respect of my authority."

"What! Now. No. Surely not. Mum!"

Mandy spun round to glare at the professor.

"Christ! You are such a bastard!" Then a look of horror spread across her face as she looked into the impassive, granite features of her former mentor. "Oh. Sorry, sorry. So sorry, sir. Felicity, just get your clothes off and let's get this done with. Again, sorry, Professor."

As a reluctant Felicity began very slowly to disrobe, Mandy waited with trepidation as Stones moved to stand right before her.

"Mandy, that outburst is unacceptable. You will return to my room this evening to plea for your right to remain overnight and accompany Felicity tomorrow. I suggest that you spend a few moments contemplating your position and the consequences of speaking to me in that manner. Now you can wait outside while Felicity finishes her very slow striptease and gets around to writing her account and apology. Back here at 7 o'clock precisely and we will discuss the possibility of you being allowed to remain onsite. I suggest that you consider the problem that you have now created for yourself and think seriously about the action that may be required to realise your wishes as per the possibility of you attending Felicity's thrashing tomorrow. I can see by your expression that my meaning has been understood, and that you will make the necessary personal measures required for the meeting. Now get out!"

Her eyes dropped to the floor as she nodded her understanding, and, avoiding her daughter's despairing look as she stood in her underwear, Mandy all but ran from the room.

"Nice matching underwear, Felicity, but I would rather see it on the chair without you inside. Come on, off with bra and panties. Let's see what I will have to work with tomorrow."

Stones moved over to the chair and table he had indicated to Felicity to sit at and covered the seat with a small disposable sheet. With a twinkle in his eye, he explained.

"Obviously without forewarning you may not have prepared for exposing your naked glory today and therefore I will protect my furniture from any damage from your unclean lower regions. Now remove those skimpy bits of cloth and sit down!"

His voice rose as he spoke and despite the aghast look from Felicity as she processed the meaning of his words, she flinched at his growing anger and quickly whipped her underwear off. The scornful look she received as she covered her breasts with her arms and crossed her legs only cause her blush to deepen in her humiliation.

"If you do not get yourself seated and pick up that damn pen, young lady, I am going to upend you now and give you a spanking, a malodorous undercarriage or not!"

Felicity, clearly flummoxed, and now reduced to a squeak of mild protest, chose wisely to bow to his demands and scooted over to the chair, her hands now going to her backside in a pointless attempt to cover her bottom from his eyes.

"Your attempts at some kind of modesty are mildly humorous but also a tad annoying, young lady. I would suggest that you fully own your predicament that you and no one else has created, accept the blame, take the shame and come to terms pretty damn quickly with your situation. Please do not try my patience any further. Full confession and acceptance of guilt, desire to make amends by showing full remorse and volunteering for a beating to aid in your contrition and improvement in the future. As you have requested, a good spanking of 100 slaps, a 30-stroke paddling and 20 of the best with the cane seems just and fair. So get on with it and stop prevaricating. Any more nonsense and you might as well just add that you would like to volunteer for an additional good hiding immediately to assist in helping you focus and be obedient. Is that what you require to happen or are you finally of a mind to accept your just desserts?"

The gulp from a nodding Felicity suggested that she had finally taken everything on board and she picked up the pen and hesitantly began to write. Stones came to peer over her shoulder and guide the trembling student to find the correct words and tone, and was soon reading aloud a full admission, a cringing apology and a request for disciplinary action through the means of corporal punishment, stipulating the agreed sentence.

"This is adequate. I am glad you feel that this is the best opportunity you have to make good your appalling behaviour. As requested, I agree to flog your bare buttocks in an effort to assist you in making amends and seeing you on the path to self-improvement. You will return back here at 5pm tomorrow, freshly bathed, bowels and bladder empty, all ready to take your dues and begin the path to redemption. Dismissed."

His belittling words seemed to strip the last dregs of dignity from the stricken student as she fumbled with her clothes and rushed to get out of his presence.

When Stones responded to his buzzer shortly before the time he had proposed to Mandy, he was not in the least surprised to see a fresh-faced woman, pink cheeks and damp hair, dressed simply and with a look of mixed emotions on her face. He could see a certain amount of trepidation but it was decidedly conflicted by the sparkle in her eyes and a look of expectation.

"You are early which is forgivable and apparently rather eager as well. What do you think the result of your little outburst earlier should be?"

Always ready to fire the question that put any miscreant on the back foot, he smiled inwardly as the unexpected question took Mandy off her guard.

"Oh, sir. Well, um, er, I suppose that I should at first apologise and then request most sincerely that you allow me to make up for my rudeness and disrespect by accepting whatever punishment you deem suitable, sir."

Stones fixed her with one of his penetrating stares and kept silent, knowing that she would likely fill the void.

"Er, did you want me to suggest an appropriate punishment, sir? Do I need to apologise further, sir? I am truly sorry, Professor Stones, and really am ready to pay the price for my big mouth."

"Just meaningless words so far, Mandy. Please continue. I have noted the fresh summer fruit scent and damp hair and appreciate that you have come straight from your bathroom to stand before me. Let me hear what you wish to happen next."

Stones was just toying with her and enjoying the mature woman reverting to her former student-age self as she began to scrabble for the words to please and becalm the academic who had beaten and bested her years before. Like nearly all of the former recipients of Stones' particular form of punishment and improvement, all forms of rational thought, feminist principles and adopted behaviour went out of the window as the urge to win his favour and bow to his demands took precedence and became the paramount aim. It was most rare for any of his students to leave the college with anything other than, at the least, respect but usually admiration and a kind of love and even adoration for the masterful man who dominated and conquered their rebellious spirit. The college's academic records showed that there was no real argument that students, who fell foul of his old-fashioned and traditional disciplinary methods, went on to excel in their studies and indeed there were no real failures that could counter that he was successful in his aims and intentions to improve the individuals under his watch.

Mandy was a prime example. After the incidents, the second being a thorough thrashing and a most severe warning from Stones of stringent repercussions if she was referred to him again, Mandy had excelled in her studies and left the college highly qualified. This had led to her rising quickly to a senior position, eventually becoming a partner in a national recruitment company. Once the initial pain, shock and humiliation of their chastisement passed, virtually all of his malefactors mended their ways and looked back on their time in his rooms with some little misgiving, but an awful lot of gratitude and acceptance that the benefits had by far outweighed their shaming and discomfort. He watched with intrigue as Mandy thought through her next words, took a deep breath and set the scene for what he was always confident would follow.

"Professor Stones, I am a naughty girl who, evidently, still has not learned how to behave in front of her betters. I apologise wholeheartedly for my behaviour and respectfully request that you be gracious enough to allow me to attend my daughter's deserved punishment tomorrow. I believe that I also require a thrashing myself to ensure that I follow the good and noble lessons that the college taught me years ago, and which I have clearly flouted. I would therefore be most grateful if you were to take the time to assist me in correcting my faults by delivering a thrashing to my naked backside. I would suggest that a caning would be appropriate, and be very grateful for a hard spanking over your knee to remind me that I have behaved like a spoilt child. I have come prepared, hopefully to your satisfaction, sir, thoroughly cleansed and am naked under my dress, sir, to enable easy access. Shall I take my dress off, sir, to show you that I am ready and willing to pay for my sins, and seek your forgiveness?"

Stones almost applauded her speech. It was a pleasant change to get to the point of a usually unavoidable punishment, but he was also very well aware of the sexual longing now apparent in Mandy's eyes and confident he knew what the end point of this meeting would be.

His cock was throbbing quite pleasantly and he nodded assent to Mandy's undressing.

Her body was little changed from her student days, she clearly kept fit and healthy and the few extra pounds enhanced the fullness of her body in no bad way. She was confident in her nudity before him as she folded the dress and exhibited herself completely to his lustful eyes.

He dragged his chair out into the centre of the room.

"Select a cane from my cabinet and place it against the bookshelves there, where the rings are showing on the shelf. Then come and stand beside me, please."

Sure of the path this meeting would take, Stones had prepared in advance. The metal rings, normally hidden behind his stacked rows of books were exposed, several feet apart and were there purely for the act of a thrashing delivered with the recipient bent over and holding tightly to the rings with her buttocks left prominently displayed. He had an ankle cuff rod, which could be expanded, or contracted, to suit the height of his victim. This was intended to keep their legs spread, although in Mandy's case he suspected that her eagerness to please would mean it would prove unnecessary.

Stones noted that she originally chose the medium-thick cane but, after some hesitation, she selected the more wicked-looking, thickest cane. It would not have concerned him overly either way; the thicker one certainly caused longer term and harsher bruising, but the less thick cane moved through the air quicker and caused a deeper more stinging impact and possibly often more immediate discomfort. Inwardly he gave a nod of respect for her choice of the fearsome thick cane.

He tugged her over his knees, her hands automatically grasping his leg rather than the chair's as she favoured the contact directly with him as much as possible. She wriggled on his lap and he was certain that she was conscious of his erection. Her legs parted with no prompting from him, she thrust her buttocks up alluringly, her cleft parted, and a full view between her legs was presented to him. Her pussy was glistening and he could see beads of moisture all along her labia.

"I hope that this is going to be as much fun as you think it will be," he said as he raised his arm and slammed down hard. "But I do rather doubt it."

He rained down blow after blow, keeping his hand flat to deliver the biggest impact and hardest sting he could. The delivery was rapid and concentrated on the fullest flesh of her rounded cheeks, which turned pink then bright red very quickly. To begin with, her only response was a quickening of her breathing and muted gasps but before he was halfway through the spanking she started to cry out and twist and turn in his lap.

"Do tell me how you think this is going, my dear," as he paused and took a breath.

"Oh my, oh my. I had completely forgotten how much your hand stung, Professor Stones. Oh, wow, it really bloody hurts."

"Language, Mandy, language. I am sure you do not need me to remind you that additional strokes are available on demand."

"Oh, sorry, sir. Please, that was enough. Um, thank you, sir."

Stones laughed out loud.

"Enough. Oh please, Mandy. This is just me taking a pause to inspect the work done so far. My concern is that you seem to be leaking somewhat and I am concerned that you might drip onto my trousers. Let me just mop you up a bit."

With that his fingers delved between her legs, and he ran them from the top of her vaginal crack to her perineum. As she gasped and writhed on his lap, he glanced at the moisture gathered and wiped it across her red cheeks.

"You seem rather sexually charged, my dear. Are you perhaps expectant of closer contact between us? Do share with the room." He allowed his fingers to rest against the wet lips, making her squirm in response.

"Yes, yes, yes. Oh, don't stop, keep touching me. Yes, of course, I want you to make love to me. I've wanted that for the last 20 years, you sod. Don't be such a tease. You know damn well I want you."

"So it seems, so it seems." One finger had found her clitoral nub and was massaging it as she rubbed herself against him.

Snatching his hand away, he said, "Lovely as this is, there is a job to be completed," and so saying, his hand began to slam down onto already sore cheeks again.

The room filled with hearty cries in response and the sound of his flat hand slapping down onto her soft, rounded buttocks. He spanked her for two whole minutes, far more blows landing than the original intended punishment, as he reduced her to a sobbing, wailing misery, begging for mercy.

He stroked her blazing cheeks for several minutes as he waited for the howling to subside. The snivelling came gradually to a stuttering stop, and her gyrating body finally stilled.

"Fuck!" she breathed out gustily before a double strike to the tops of her legs pulled her up short. "Ow! Ow! Sorry, sorry, sorry."

"I believe in striking while the iron is hot, and certainly while the bottom is! Up you get and over to the rings. You know the drill. Firm grasp, head down, legs straight and apart, bottom up, anus pointing to me please."

Mandy's movements across to the bookcase were disjointed and uncoordinated as her hands rubbed furiously at her battered behind, desperate to ease the stinging sensation. She slowly took the position, her flanks rising almost reluctantly to expose her bottom to his gaze and the tapping of the cane he now held.

"Wouldn't you rather just fuck me now, Professor Stones? Can't you see how ready I am for you?"

"I can indeed, Mandy, your cup certainly doth literally runneth over. My, what a wanton creature you are. Take these strokes well and I may well grant your wish. As you have selected the thickest and heaviest cane, which delivers, as you must surely realise, the most painful and bruising strokes, I have decided to give you give you just a dozen strokes. However, these will be a dozen of my hardest, so I suggest that you take position, compose yourself, hold onto your ankles securely, and take a moment to prepare yourself. Please do not release your hold at any point. Additional punishment strokes are available, and will be implemented, in response to any failure on your part to behave in any form other than exemplary. Take heed and fair warning, young lady."

The air went still in the room as he raised the cane and held it there watching silently, as her bottom twitched and her legs trembled in anticipation of the fury he was about to unleash. His eyes focused on the tightened anal ring before him, before he swiped the cane down to land at exactly the moment she relaxed her muscle, and her cleft fully opened deliciously before him. The thudding muted thwack of the heavier cane emphasised its weight and thickness as her taut buttocks absorbed the blow. Seconds later the gasp that showed an appreciation of the power of the cane and the consequence that followed. The cry was of someone who had just felt a pain that was not anticipated or imagined. A pain that burned deep into the consciousness of the receiver and tested their every resolve. A loud intake of breath now as Mandy sought to control her reaction, the thick red welt seemingly paying homage to its maker.

Stones waited as her body twisted and squirmed although he was pleased to see that to her credit her hands and feet stayed in position. Mandy must have sensed that the next move was hers.

"Oh my, oh my, oh my. I never dreamed that it would feel like that. Oh, sir. Should I count? That was number one, sir, thank you. God, how many? How many can I take? Lord, give me strength. I suppose that I am ready for the next one, sir, please."

"There's a good girl. You see, you know exactly how to behave. A solid 12 will do the trick, I feel. The strap is always available if the cane does not deliver the message intended. Hold fast, Mandy, number two is on its way."

His arm was already swinging as he delivered that warning and caught her perfectly an inch beneath the first stroke. She grunted, she squealed, she writhed, her knees buckling but she held her position and Stones once more waited her out, enthralled in watching the red line form and then rise in a vicious-looking welt across the centre of her cheeks.

"Ugh! Oh, jeez. That was number two. Oh it hurt, sir. I don't think I can take many more. I never thought it would sting like this. Oh dear. I am sorry. I don't want…"

He delivered the next four strokes hard and fast, working his way down to the lowest part of the quivering cheeks. He knew it was pointless expecting her to recover and count the strokes, and decided that a quick flourish would serve best for him to master her completely. The screams were testament to his ability to lay on the cane to a degree beyond the expectations of most of his victims, and she was not to prove an exception, as the screams and wails filled the room. The six cane lines were artistic perfection, evenly spaced bright red tramlines and Stones' let a hand caress his throbbing cock through his tented trousers. It was an effort not to hurry the second half of her punishment as he recognised his eagerness to penetrate the moist full lips that were tantalisingly enticing. He took a breath and tapped the cane just above his first strike, paused as she let out a long, drawn-out sob and her body shuddered. Still she did not twist away or attempt to rise and he admired her submission and determination as much as he complimented himself on his skill in conquering her. He waited, to allow her to compose herself – she was sobbing with little reserve now – and the anticipation of the coming impact to build, and then he swung hard and true. Mandy stumbled, her hands reaching for the carpet to retain her position, a high-pitched squeal paying homage to the power and glory of the cane landing. Stones smiled as he landed the eighth stroke, just above the previous one. He nodded in appreciation of his own accuracy, the unblemished space left to the top of her bottom crack being perfect territory, and in his mind ripe, for the next three strokes, which he laid down quickly and with as much force as he could. This time, as he fully expected, she went down to the ground, her hands grasping pointlessly at her swollen, throbbing cheeks.

"Oh dear," he teased. "Extra strokes for not maintaining the correct position. It rather looks like you will feel the impact of my favourite strap after all, how delicious. Up you pop, my dear. Bottom cheeks bent over and properly presented. I am going to give you two diagonal whoppers to finish with. It is always aesthetically pleasing to have conformity, do you not think? Thirteen with the cane and a quick three with the strap should top you off well, I feel. Come along, Mandy, stop that pitiful noise and present yourself."

In truth he was very impressed with her fortitude in enduring 11 of his finest strokes but was of course as determined as ever to reduce his subject to the lowest level he could take her. In Stones' mind it was imperative that a punishment beating delivered by his hands should be a memorable event for its ferocity and comprehensiveness. No one should ever bemoan that he did not deliver what he promised!

As he watched the now heavily crying woman try to will her body to still and return to the position he expected, he touched her wet pussy with the tip of his cane, causing her to jerk forward.

"Still dripping wet, my dear," he taunted as he raised the cane high again. "Let's see if we can focus your attention away from that swamp of a vagina and give you something to savour in a different way."

The cane cracked hard against her quivering buttocks, a stark red line immediately forming across the diagonal. Her shriek was high-pitched and despairing and he paused to allow the line to swell up across the bent cheeks before Mandy took a loud, deep breath and stilled herself in anticipation of the final stroke of the cane. Seconds later a screaming woman was shaking and stumbling as he applied the stroke in the opposite direction to complete a perfect large cross on the dead centre of the beleaguered bottom.

"Hold still now while I fetch my strap."

An unnecessary statement he was sure, as her howls almost certainly drowned out his words.

Whop! Whop! Whop!

He applied the strap quickly and with full strength, the last stroke following her to the ground as she collapsed under the delivery of the fierce blows.

Mandy's howls were a joy for him to behold. Mastered and beaten but still enslaved to his wants and demands.

"I am sorry, please do not repeat it. Oh my. It hurts so much. I did not mean to move. Oh my. I am so sorry, please no more." Stones' enjoyed her entreaties and the pathetic pleading, appreciating that all shame and pride had long gone and she had truly re-joined the list of those vanquished by his might and power.

Stones contented himself with a walloping slap of his right hand, as he slung the strap away before grabbing her by the scruff of her neck and spinning her around to face him.

"On your knees and unleash me. I like to be wet myself before I indulge. Quickly, woman, the beast is ready and waiting to be served." Stones was confident that this authoritative and masterful approach was exactly what Mandy desired, the fact that it also turned him on was a bonus!

Within seconds her blazing backside seemed of secondary concern as she noisily feasted on his firm erection, her enthusiasm that of an experienced advocate of fellatio. With his cock buried in her mouth and a firm hand in her hair, he shuffled backwards in that ungainly manner men are reduced to, with their trousers and underwear around their ankles, until he reached his chair. With hands under her armpits he swept her up and onto his lap, Mandy reaching down with a fervent look of lust in her eyes as she took a firm hold of his pulsating cock, her saliva dribbling down its length, and positioned it firmly against her pussy. Their eyes met and Stones released his grip on her, enabling her body to settle onto his, her sex engulfing his erection greedily.

With his hands alternating between squeezing her breasts and gripping her buttocks, he thrust his hips upwards, a sustained rhythm soon established as both searched for their moments of sexual release. As Stones' groans became deeper, Mandy matched it with her yells becoming more and more high-pitched. Like seasoned lovers they climaxed together, both holding the other firmly and sealing their congress with a deep kiss.

Task completed to his satisfaction, he lifted her off his lap and pushed her dismissively towards his bathroom.

"Thanks for that, it was most pleasant. Now clean yourself up and get out."

Mandy smiled, wise enough to recognise the way he worked, and complied with his instruction. Within three minutes she was dressed and leaving his rooms. Her cheery wave and lewd wink receiving no response. She was dismissed.

Mandy may have hoped that her session with Stones had gone some way towards him acting leniently with her daughter. When they returned as arranged the next day, it was not long before she was disabused of her fanciful notion.

"Ah Mandy, Felicity, good to see you again. How is your bottom healing, Mandy?" Stones said.

Mandy's face was a picture of shame and shock. Felicity's face rather gurned in comparison as she slowly processed the professor's words. Bewilderment, amazement, horror and anger took their turns!

"Mum! Did you, did you really? What the fuck! Did you come back here for a beating last night? Was that why you went to bed early, and did not parade around naked, like you usually do? Did you let him beat you? Mum, what is going on?"

Stones cleared his throat noisily and Felicity's diatribe dried up.

"Do not use language like that in my room, please, Felicity. Do not speak to your mother like that. Do not question my actions. I would like to hear you apologise to both of us unless you would rather I dispense an additional spanking on the backs of your legs where you stand, young lady!"

The audible gulp from Felicity illustrated that he was quickly gaining control, realising that this was not the time or place to have this conversation.

"Sorry, sir, I did not mean to so rude. Sorry, Mummy, I was just a bit shocked. Are you okay? Did it hurt awfully?" Felicity quickly complied with the instruction from Stones.

"It is fine, my love. Yes, of course, it hurt, I got a thrashing on my bare backside. However, I deserved it and the professor delivered it as he should. Now it is your turn and I want to see you take it like a good girl without too much fuss. It will soon be over and you will have learned a valuable lesson without impacting on your education in any way negatively. I think the professor will concur?"

Stones was sure that Mandy's words were a rather desperate attempt to steer him away from giving any further detail about her presence in his room the previous evening. She need not have worried. A punishment was one thing and any embarrassment that caused Mandy was her problem to deal with, but the sexual joining was something between themselves only as far as he was concerned.

Stones turned to them both.

"A full confession has been received and a request made for improvement and correction by the means of physical chastisement. Felicity, you have commendably accepted your guilt and shown remorse and contrition, and you have come here today to attempt to make amends. I will shortly carry out the requested punishment of a spanking, a paddling and a caning. To this end I would like you to remove all of your clothing and go and stand in the corner facing the bookshelves, hands on your head, fingers knotted together. Mandy, you will stand facing the room in the opposite corner. You will observe, you will not comment unless you wish to receive a punishment yourself. I will also subject Felicity to any punishment that you earn and receive. This will, of course, be in addition to her own chastisement. So think on before you interject in any way. Now let us proceed."

There was a full-body tremble from Felicity as Mandy with a quick squeeze of her daughter's hand complied as requested. Stones put his chair into the centre of the room, positioned so that Mandy would have a full view of Felicity's behind over his lap. He waited patiently as a quietly weeping student reluctantly removed her underwear, exposing small pert breasts with tiny nipples, a coiffured pubic bush over discreet labial lips and a small, but nicely rounded set of buttocks, which she presented, as naked, she walked over to the corner he had indicated.

"Lovely. It is always good to have a proper look at what I will be working with before we begin. Yes, small cheeks but they look quite firm and rounded, so should take a good hiding well."

To the surprise of both women, the doorbell buzzed, and Stones moved to his desk and looked at his monitor.

"Excellent. Do join us, Sara." To the dismay of both mother and daughter, Sara Morgan, the college's chief administration officer, came into the room.

"I have asked Sara to join us, in the absence of Dr Ford, the senior tutor, to assist and monitor today's events. Your pathetic crying is trying my nerves, Felicity. I have not laid a hand on you yet and you are sobbing like a baby. Please desist, and thank Ms Morgan for giving up her valuable time to be here. Sadly, Sara, I think you may need to tend to this one's messy face before we even start."

"Thank you for coming, Ms Morgan," Felicity rather burbled out as Sara went straight to her with tissues and began to wipe her nose and eyes.

"Stop your nonsense now. I will help you get through this, but you do need to behave. Now pull yourself together." Her harsh tone did nothing to aid Felicity's demeanour and Sara was forced to assist in blowing her nose copiously to try and make her presentable to the professor.

"Enough," he barked. "Come over to me then. We ought to get this under way. Please drape yourself over my lap."

Felicity was understandably tentative as she walked over and stood beside Stones, her eyes flashing towards her stony-faced mother for one last hope of some kind of miraculous reprieve. A strong tug on her arm and she found herself putting her hands out on the carpet on the other side of the chair as Stones expertly flipped her over his lap. Sara had positioned herself to meet the bewildered-looking student, taking hold of her hands in the practised manner of one who had played the role before. Stones allowed Felicity no time to concern herself with the sight she presented, or how she was going to fare, as his meaty hand landed immediately on her right buttock. A half-formed scream was rudely interrupted as the left buttock received the same. The slaps came thick and fast as Stones held the wriggling young woman easily under his hefty left arm. He pummelled the young flesh over and over again, occasionally looking up to catch Mandy's eyes as she flinched in tandem with his blows.

"No more, Mummy, please stop. I mean, Professor Stones, stop please, I beg you, stop," came the sudden shrill cries from the suffering Felicity.

Stones was happy to pause in his work. He was halfway through her designated 100 strokes, so willing to take a moment to explore her words.

"So Mandy, it seems that Felicity is regressing. Do tell us how long ago it was since you delivered a spanking to this young urchin."

There was a sigh from Mandy and a low groan from Felicity, who Stones suspected was glad of the break, but not so pleased about the words that had caused it.

"I spanked her like this until she was 16 years old. At her suggestion, I hasten to add. I allowed her to take a spanking rather than be grounded during her teenage years. I am afraid that she was quite a wilful adolescent so there were quite a few spankings," Mandy explained.

"Well I have to admit to being a mite offended that you cannot tell the difference between your mother's much smaller and more refined, delicate hands and my great big slabs. I am evidently not smacking you hard enough. I will make good immediately."

As Stones' resumed, his hand came down faster and harder; it seemed that there was a competition in the room between the sound of his hand cracking against the tight rounded bottom and the screams of pain from the recipient.

In a short while, although Stones knew that Felicity would be thinking that the spanking had lasted forever, it was over and he unceremoniously flipped her off his lap onto the floor at his feet. Felicity's hands went to the bright red cheeks and began to rub most enthusiastically, giving Stones a first proper sighting of her very neat little arsehole nestling amongst a small smattering of curls.

"Oh, thanks for that view, Felicity. As your mother will be able to confirm, I do enjoy the display of a pretty anus."

Mother and daughter's groans matched each other at his humiliating remark and Felicity rolled over onto her back to hide the view she had inadvertently given them.

"I should not bother, sweetheart," said Sara as she moved to help her to her feet. "You will be showing us everything you have got without fear or favour soon, I promise you. The rings next if I remember, Professor Stones."

"Yes please, Sara. Your treat, I think. Let us see how you are with the paddle and controlling this wretch. I suspect we may have a bit more trouble keeping her in position than I had with her mother last night." Stones teased Mandy further and the older woman now seemed unable to meet Sara's eyes.

Sara fixed the pliable and acquiescent student's hands to the fixed rings, with the cuffs, before she could think of resisting.

"Now take two steps back, legs apart, and push that little bottom out please, Felicity."

No resistance, as a sobbing Felicity arched her back perfectly to present the small cannonball-like orbs, her head bowed. Even as Sara took hold of the leather paddle and positioned herself just behind and to the side of the student, she held her stance.

"Now Felicity, this is how it works. I am going to give you 30 hard slaps with this gorgeous paddle. I am going to strike your bottom cheeks hard and fast. However, and this is the important bit, if you move, sway, bend your knees or take any other avoiding movement and I hit another part of your body then the stroke will be repeated. This will continue until the set number of full-blooded strokes have landed on that sweet little derrière. None of the strokes landing elsewhere will count. They will just be extras. If you fail to rise and take position after a stroke, and I will allow a few seconds' recovery time, then you will be awarded a further two additional strokes. It is entirely up to you how long this punishment lasts and how many strokes you receive. Is this understood and do you agree that you have been given fair warning? To help you out the answer is, 'Yes, Sara. Thank you, Sara.' Now please respond."

"Yes, Sara. Thank you, Sara," whispered a snivelling Felicity, who still impressively held herself in the perfect position. It was not to last.

The resounding splat of the first impact, on her left cheek, knocked Felicity into the bookshelves. Sara moved forward and caught her right cheek perfectly. If the screams during her spanking had been loud, Felicity now moved up a level with a banshee-type screech. Sara was a sprightly woman and although Felicity was twisting and turning, to try and escape the harsh punitive blows of the leather, she was most adept and moving in tune with her victim and landing blow after blow accurately on the screaming student's bottom. A quick wink aimed at the professor and Sara bent low and landed a few quick stinging slaps on Felicity's upper legs. Yet again, the level of screams went a pitch higher.

"Those were added punishment strokes because of your constant movement and evasion attempts, Felicity. Now I would like you to get a grip, resume the punishment position, stop that nonsense and prepare for your last eight strokes. We will get that face cleaned up a bit," she finished as she spotted Stones moving forward with tissues in his hand.

One large hand clamped around Felicity's neck as a crumpled tissue was unceremoniously swiped across her face, before Stones pinched her nose, and added further to the tormented student's nightmare.

"Blow, child, come along. Let us get you sorted. Goodness me, what a performance," he chided. "I can see that you will need to be firmly strapped down for the cane."

That produced a wail of anguish from Felicity, which was soon followed by a stifled scream, as Sara brought the paddle down full across the centre of her bottom.

"Come along, wretch. Keep that position. Show some courage. Bottom up. Nice and tight buttocks, ready to receive what you have earned yourself."

With Stones standing beside her, still with his meaty hand holding her around the neck, Felicity's movement was restricted and she managed to hold as still as Sara required, to take a final onslaught from the paddle.

"Get her straight over to the tables, Sara. We will have her cuffed and ready straight away, I think. The lesson seems to be sinking in. I take it that you are going to be on your best behaviour at college from now on, Felicity?"

The compliance of the student as she allowed Sara to cuff her legs wide apart before securing her wrists, without complaint or resistance, was firm proof that she had been reduced to a contrite spirit, as her reply confirmed.

"Oh yes, sir. I am so sorry, sir. I will never do anything wrong again, I swear. Please, sir, do I have to be caned? I am hurting so much already."

"Still up for a joke, then. Very good. That's the spirit." His deliberate misunderstanding drew a loud sob from Felicity.

Sara went to kneel at her head and gently stroked fingers across her forehead, saying, "There, there, sweetheart. Soon be over. Professor Stones is just going to seal your correction and improvement, now. Take a deep breath and let it out slowly as the cane bites. It will soon be over and you will have learned a valuable lesson. Now brace yourself for the bite of the cane, my dear."

It might have been good advice, thought Stones, as the cane swished through the air before slamming across the centre of the rosy cheeks, but he rarely witnessed someone have a strategy that worked to contain the fire and distress his strokes brought forth. There was no slow expulsion of air from the recipient of an expert delivery applied by a master of the art, just a whoosh and then a yelp, followed by a long low moan as the pain sunk in. He liked to tailor his approach to delivering a caning to the individual and how he thought the impact would be best experienced and remembered, purely as a severe chastisement. He waited for upwards of 30 seconds before raising his arm once more as the moaning from Felicity gradually turned into gentle but despairing weeping. With the repercussions of the spanking and paddling having turned her bottom a rather scarlet colour, the cane strokes on top were quickly turning into rising welts that had a purple tinge. The changing hues and tones of redness on a miscreant's bottom cheeks had always fascinated and intrigued Stones and he enjoyed the effect as he laid on three quick strokes before waiting a couple of minutes to add further. He could hear Sara trying hard to calm and support the beaten woman, mainly to no avail, Felicity was in full banshee shrill mode again now and Stones doubted this would cease until he had completed the 20 strokes. Not that he cared. The crying, begging, screaming and groaning had no real effect on him. He expected it and saw it as evidence that a good job was taking place. Mandy had now just rested her head against his bookshelves and Stones was confident that he would have no further issues with her as his latest cut of the cane across the tightest skin on the top of her bottom cleft produced a desperate screech from Felicity. Stones fixed his gaze on her most discreet of anal openings as it squeezed shut and then re-opened every few seconds. She had a very different intimate layout from her mother, he noted with interest and fascination, as he peered between her legs at slim labia and a very neat vaginal slit. Distracted just for a moment, he corrected himself by flashing down three fast stokes at the very lowest point of her buttocks and enjoyed watching the writhing and contortions the blows induced.

A couple of minutes later, it was over and the small bottom was completely covered in vivid reddish-purple weals. He was confident that she would be feeling the discomfort from their work for many days. After he returned his paddle and his cane to his cabinet, he went over to Mandy and putting his arm around her, addressed her:

"Sara, please release her now. Mandy, you may take her into the bathroom and get her sat on the iced water bidet. I will call through when I am ready for her to come and write us a note of gratitude and make her final apologies. After that the two of you can leave. I very much doubt I will need to see either of you again in my rooms."

Wiping her own tears away, Mandy thanked the professor and hurried over to take her daughter from Sara, desperately trying to calm the sobbing student.

Final duties completed, thanks and apologies accepted, the mother and daughter were soon on their way from the room. Stones smiled as he saw the tentative steps Felicity was taking.

"Another good job, Sara. Well done. I think you are becoming a most valued member of staff."

Sara left the room with a spring in her step and a sense of relief that her serious misdeeds of the past appeared well and truly behind her now.

CHAPTER 11

LIKE MOTHER, LIKE DAUGHTER

Stones suspected that 20-year-old Veronica was feeling braver and more reckless than she had ever felt before as she stood before him. A shudder racked her whole body but there was no doubt, no hesitation. She seemed intent on pushing his buttons, to goad him on, to tempt him, to infuriate him like never before. To be fair, he conceded. She was doing the job quite well and he was having a job to keep his temper with her.

"You disgusting old man, you dare even think of laying your wrinkly old hands on me. I will have you drummed out of this college and forced into a retirement that should have happened many years ago. And that's if I don't decide to have you arrested, charged and imprisoned. You pathetic excuse for a man, your time is up, you are long past your sell-by date, the likes of you and your generation have no place in a working environment anymore, your time is done. You utterly ridiculous and dirty old man!"

Professor Stones waited a moment to allow the rage to settle. This young lady was definitely a challenge, but he had been there before with some of the students with pretensions of grandeur and misinformed opinions of their status within the college. He had long learned to quell sudden anger rising inside him and knew that an icy calm was often by far the best response to this sort of challenge to his authority. Veronica Corton-Blake may well believe herself to be one of the beautiful people and a member of High Society and her parents were undoubtedly supremely wealthy and influential, but she was certainly not a member of the aristocracy or landed gentry. Her status in her own mind, he thought, was profoundly higher than the reality and this was something that the professor would enjoy challenging and correcting. Veronica's education was about to start taking a different route, one that was going to take her through an unexpected turn of events. They may have been just pretentious and hopeful students during their time in college, but when you have spanked the wriggling bare bottoms of high-ranked members of the Royal Family of several countries over the years, it is hard to feel overawed at any response, from students with ideas above their stations. When you have taken a paddle to the wobbling buttocks of two current Members of Parliament and thrashed at least six civil servants in very senior positions, it is hard to take the threats of a single, silly young woman seriously. When you have caned and flogged senior police officers, heads of industry and commerce, prominent international sportswomen and some of the richest and most powerful women in the country and beyond, then you become rather comfortable in the power of your position and knowledge. Stones knew that the miscreants he had dealt with throughout his history in the position of Dean of Discipline recognised his place in their lives almost without fail, with a high degree of awe and respect and certainly in many cases with love and affection. He was a careful and cautious man, as his investments in technology and security proved, and he was as certain as he could be that within the boundaries he operated in, he was pretty much bulletproof insofar as it would certainly not be in many people's interest for him to be exposed in any way.

"Have you quite finished?" he asked the clearly confrontational and pugnacious student.

"You're the one that's finished, old man," she responded with some flourish and a total belief in herself and her position.

"One last chance to apologise properly and reconsider your decision. To reiterate, and I'll keep it concise since you seem to struggle to comprehend, you are guilty of being rude and insulting to several members of the Catering and Table Service team concerned with serving dinner in the Great Hall. You have refused to carry out menial punishment tasks in the kitchen to attempt to atone, you have refused to apologise to the staff concerned and you have turned down the opportunity to volunteer to be soundly spanked to bring this matter to an end. You have also compounded this by speaking to me in a very offensive manner, which I have recorded. Have you anything further to add, young lady?"

A supremely naive Veronica unwisely laughed in a taunting manner at a bemused Stones.

"Oh just do one, you filthy old pervert, you most certainly are not spanking my bottom!"

"Very well, you have left me no option, I am afraid." Stones sighed.

"It's about time you and your like realise that time has moved on, there's no place anymore for imperious and pompous old has-beens living in times long gone by. You're yesterday's man, time to be put out to seed. Done. Finished."

The professor let her words hang in the air as he looked at Veronica, taking in her audacious air of triumph and smugness.

"You may leave the room. I will contact you when I need to speak to you again. I will give due consideration to your attitude towards the reason you were here before me in the first place and I will give further consideration to your rhetoric whilst here. Goodbye." The professor dismissed her with the wave of a hand, knowing full well the likely impact this would have.

"Well…" she spluttered indignantly. "I certainly am going, I've had enough of you anyway," was her tame response before exiting and attempting to slam the door, not easy with the slam-resistant mechanism the professor had fitted to all the doors in his set.

Hours later Stones placed his mobile telephone back onto the desk and picked up the transcript of the audio link he had just sent to Lady Vanessa Corton-Blake, a very angry Lady Vanessa Corton-Blake indeed. He fondly remembered plain Vanessa Corton, as she had been during her time at St. James'. She had gone on to a successful career with one of the leading investment banks in London before marrying the boss and becoming fabulously wealthy. Nouveau Riche he may have been, thought Stones, but rewarded and recognised with a knighthood for creating and establishing huge foreign investment in these shores and, as goes without saying in these times, making massive contributions to party funds plus a good deal of charity involvement, mainly at the behest of Lady Vanessa. Her time at the college had been in the early days of CCTV, and the film that Stones had on file, although digitally enhanced and converted to modern formats, was a poor quality recording of her one and only thrashing for disgraceful offensive behaviour during a formal dinner. She had got a bit tipsy and told a senior college official what she thought of him and his rumoured wandering hands. Unfortunately she had made a serious error of mistaken identity which led her to be in serious danger of being sent down from college, a disgrace unlike any other and not one that would have been acceptable to a family of Veronica's standing. A very teary apology was followed by a humiliating afternoon spent begging the professor for any punishment other than the shaming of being sent home, as the professor manipulated the unsuspecting student to actually plead to be flogged. He had made her sweat, of course, waiting for his final decision as he supposedly thought very hard before reluctantly agreed to give her a second chance.

Professor Stones had enjoyed watching the recording back, enjoying the memory of her peachy bottom and how it had turned a brighter red than he had ever seen before, or since, as he had spanked, whipped and then strapped a screaming young lady. Stones smiled in recollection; she may have turned into one of the country's leading entrepreneurs and famed negotiators, but she had certainly met her match back then and the professor had enjoyed reminiscing with her as they chatted on the phone. She had surprised him by indicating that she would like to see the recording herself and a tentative date had been set for her to visit which had certainly tweaked the professor's interest. There had been a few visits from his girls, now in various stages of adulthood, over the years and they had usually disguised a yearning to revisit and replay their experience of the past. He had a couple of regular returnees and he thoroughly enjoyed these visits with such willing recipients. Although it would be true to say they often found the memory of their beatings had added a more romantic and sensual aspect to the reality of the occasion, and their wistful memoirs often turned from a soft-focus dreamland to a real-world nightmare!

Lady Vanessa, as he had anticipated, had been most perturbed to hear of her daughter's behaviour. Her solution had been to Stones' liking even if an element of this had come as quite a surprise. As usual Stones thought, this is going to end with one winner and it certainly was not going to be the arrogant and haughty Veronica Corton-Blake. He turned to his laptop and began to tap out an email to the recalcitrant young lady. By the time he worded it satisfactorily Lady Vanessa should have spoken to her daughter and he very much hoped that the air had been taken out of the sails of the troublesome student. He suspected that she would now be feeling rather fearful of the consequences of her earlier words and actions.

Just over an hour later an email popped into Professor Stones' inbox from Veronica requesting an audience as soon as the professor was able to see her. The short email stated that Veronica wished to discuss their earlier conversation and that she would in advance like to offer her apologies for her inappropriate language and attitude. It was not a surprise to him and a smile played on his lips as he made a quick couple of phone calls before replying to the student. He informed her that he could see her in an hour's time but that in the meantime he would like her to write him a formal apology for both her actions that day and previously, an explanation of her behaviour and a suggestion from her as to appropriate disciplinary action. Stones had never yet used corporal punishment on one of the students, or occasional staff members and colleagues, without them having first written a request to be punished in that manner. Well aware of the litigious behaviour of the modern age and the media thirst for any tale of perceived degradation or depravity, he was a very cautious and careful man.

An hour later she stood before him, on edge and without the confidence and haughtiness of her earlier appearance. As she stood in silence, her letter in her hand, her sense of unease was increased as the professor appeared intent on ignoring her as he rearranged the furniture, placing three chairs towards the back of the room facing a large screen that had dropped from the ceiling. He sensed that Veronica presumed this was nothing to do with her, and hoped she was thinking he was maybe entertaining guests with a film or slideshow later that evening. If so, she was shortly to have those thoughts enlightened!

"Let's see what you have managed to scribe, shall we?" Stones gave a show of satisfaction with his furniture reconfiguration and moved to stand directly in front of the now visibly trembling Veronica. "I am hoping that a chat with your mother has meant that you feel a little wiser and perhaps more philosophical concerning your views on your behaviour."

Veronica, keen to appease, quickly answered him.

"Oh yes, Professor Stones. I realise that I have acted unwisely and inappropriately. I would like to apologise again, if I may, please, sir."

"You can certainly keep apologising, but as far as I am concerned you need to direct that towards the staff you offended. You have apologised to me, and you now appear to be showing signs that you are ready to take whatever action is required to retain your place in college and accept a just punishment for your misdeeds. I presume that this is what you have to tell me when I read this."

He fluttered the envelope she had given him, in front of her nose, and turned his back on her to read what she had written.

"Oh dear, I thought that your mother had talked some sense into you, but not enough evidently. I can see that I may need to make another phone call." He reached for his telephone causing an instant reaction from the very flustered young lady before him.

"Oh no, sir, please don't do that. Please tell me what I needed to write. I did not mean to do anything else wrong, Professor Stones, sir. Please tell me what I need to do."

Stones fixed her with his most intimidating stare.

"It is now your last chance, young lady. Your route out of here is quite straightforward if you don't like the way we deal with scallywags such as yourself. I am sure your mother reminded you of the college disciplinary code that you both signed up to. I do have a copy and we can both read it together if you wish. I am also damn sure that you have been told exactly how to behave in this office. So maybe you should remind me what pertinent words of advice your mother imparted?"

Veronica now coloured completely, the blush spreading to all areas of her upper torso that were on show.

"Oh, sir, please, I cannot believe that you really beat students. I thought it was just a tradition to have that in the rules. You surely cannot possibly expect me to agree to let anyone beat me, sir."

The professor took a slow breath and then wearily sighed it back out.

"Not the question you were asked, not the answer you very much needed to give. So let us make it nice and simple for you, Veronica. You will rewrite this letter now, having recalled more accurately what your mother said to you, and you will detail exactly what form of punishment you are requesting. You will not write ambiguous sentences suggesting that you are happy to take appropriate punishment as determined by the disciplinary code. You will very much detail what a naughty girl you are, how you feel that the college should deal with this particular naughty girl and what precisely should be done to said naughty girl to ensure that she learns her lesson. You have precisely ten minutes and if you do not provide the degree of detail I expect, then you will go and pack your bags and I will telephone Professor Winslow-Bellingham and ask her to prepare your leaving literature, and contact your parents to ask them to remove you from the premises. Now think on, child. Here is a pen and there is a desk, so please start writing and stop snivelling!" His voice was like thunder by now and a sobbing Veronica visibly jumped as he finished. He was glad to see some kind of self-preservation instinct kicked in, though, as she took the pen and paper and moved quickly over to the desk he indicated.

Stones gave her about five minutes and then went and stood over her.

"Halfway through your time and you are nowhere near to the gritty detail that is required. I think you need to explain what you envisage I am expecting you to write, Veronica."

The girl blushed even deeper red before bowing her head.

"Have I got to say that I need to be spanked, sir?" was her tentative response.

"Oh, this is pointless, you are not accepting the gravity of the situation and clearly not deserving of the opportunity to extend your stay with us. You may leave that now and go and pack your things, I do not have the patience for this."

Veronica's face now showed blind panic.

"No, sir. Please, sir. I'll write whatever you want, sir. I'm sorry, sir, I do want to be beaten rather than be sent down. I do, sir. Seriously. I just do not know quite what I have to say."

The professor went over to his wall cabinet and opened the door, exposing his array of punishment implements or 'his improvers' as he liked to call them. Veronica's eyes opened wide in horror and fear as he turned to her.

"If your report does not say how you wish to be severely thrashed and flogged to atone for your sinful behaviour and does not include the names of some of my little helpers here, then this interview is over. You may also like to mention that you would obviously wish for the beating to be applied to your naked bottom, in the tradition of college formal corporal punishment. What you request of course is down to you, but you have only five minutes so I would suggest that you write quickly and concisely."

Veronica gave a long drawn out sigh but finally seemed to face up to the fate that she had been desperate trying to avoid. She raised the pen and gritted her teeth before starting to write. Moments later, she had clearly got into the flow, scribbling rapidly as the absolute seriousness of the situation seemed to have finally hit home. Stones watched the intense youngster and smiled as he cogitated on the comparison between the aloof and rude young woman who had stood before him, spouting a cascade of abuse, and the broken snivelling wretch he had reduced her to with words alone. He smiled, confident that he would enjoy spanking this one very much. He was looking forward to contacting Jamie, the Porter of Parkinson College and his right-hand man, to invite him to wield the cane and strap on the bottom cheeks of the contrary madam before him.

As Veronica laid the pen down and turned to pass it to him with a trembling hand, he moved his own hands away.

"Oh no, I think you should read it out, my dear," he said with a smile. "I will accept your full confession, acceptance of guilt and apology to those concerned. You just need to clearly state how you wish to be punished to show true penitence and draw a line under the matter."

Veronica struggled to hold it together as she looked imploringly at this man, finding it hard to believe that only hours before she had sneered at and taunted him. She was about to open her mouth and beg not to have to do this but then realised that reading out this letter was pretty incidental comparing to what she was actually requesting. Taking a deep shuddering breath, she stood up before the professor, who taken a seat, and read out what she had written.

"I apologise again to you, Professor Stones, for my behaviour throughout and accept that I should be punished thoroughly to ensure that I appreciate the offence and harm I have caused. I would like to offer to voluntarily submit to a beating using whichever belts, whips or canes that you deem appropriate. I accept and wish for the beating to be applied to my bare bottom." Tears were starting to roll down her cheeks as she rather stuttered her way through the final words, looking at the professor for his approval.

"At last it does seem that you have accepted the necessity of being subjected to a severe flogging to help you realise that your behaviour was totally intolerable and unacceptable. I accept your request and will now put in place the arrangements for this retribution to take place. For now would you please remove your clothing while I set up the process to begin your punishment with the initial assessment and formalities."

Veronica virtually froze in horror as what she had just agreed to had suddenly become a reality.

"Take my clothes off, sir? What, now? What for, sir? Oh no, sir, what do you mean, sir?"

"What you need to accept now, Veronica, is that you no longer have the right to question anything that is put to you in this room unless you desire your punishment to be increased. When I ask you to do something you do it, no questions, no argument and certainly no smart-Alec answers. I don't expect to have to repeat myself so will you remove all of your clothing, NOW!" The professor was well versed in dealing with young ladies such as Veronica and automatically knew the tone to adopt to force compliance.

Veronica found herself shedding her clothes as though hypnotised into doing the professor's bidding. Hesitating when she was standing in her underwear, she looked at this dominant man with desperate pleading in her eyes, but meeting his exasperated and penetrating stare, she quickly divested herself of her bra and knickers and stood naked in the room.

"Stand here, legs apart, hands on your head." Stones indicated a position just in front of the three chairs and was pleased to see Veronica obey without question.

"You will now just stand there until I say different," he ordered as he barely glanced at the attractive, naked young lady before him. Glancing at his watch, Stones smiled and proceeded to ignore Veronica as he tinkered on his laptop.

To a bewildered Veronica's consternation, he let her stand in absolute silence for fifteen minutes, noting though her rather agitated expression at being so ignored. There was a buzz from the door.

"Do not dare move and keep your eyes to the front," barked the professor as he flicked a switch.

Veronica closed her eyes in total horror as the door behind her clicked and swung open.

"Welcome, ladies, welcome. Mistress, Senior Tutor, take a seat. As I am sure you know, although not normally displaying her nudity so proudly, this is our latest miscreant, young Veronica Corton-Blake. She of the potty mouth and manners of a farmyard animal."

Veronica trembled all over and tears once again started to run down her cheeks. This was shame unlike anything she had ever experienced.

"Lovely plump buttocks, looks like they are built to take a good thrashing," said Celia, the senior tutor, as Veronica cringed under her close inspection.

"Indeed, Senior Tutor, indeed," responded the professor.

"Take your seats. My little film is ready to roll for our entertainment for the next 30 or so minutes. Veronica, come and stand just here, please."

The three of them seated themselves just behind where Stones placed the standing Veronica, but perfectly positioned to see the screen that was descending in front of the group. Veronica had no idea what was going on as the professor produced a handset from his pocket and the screen before them came to life.

Veronica gasped as, although the picture was a bit grainy, the film began showing the obviously recognisable figure of her mother standing stark naked, her back to the camera, in front of a much younger Professor Stones.

"No, no, no. Please, sir, no," she sobbed loudly and began to turn around.

"Stay exactly where you are, eyes to the front," warned the professor. "Part of your punishment is for you to fully understand that discipline in this college is as it is, for a reason. It will make you a better person, it will complete and fulfil you, and so will teach you a lesson that will serve you well in life. Your mother fully acknowledges this and is happy for me to show you how she learned her own lesson. Therefore you will watch every minute of her ordeal and appreciate the point of your punishment. Your behaviour has been worse than your mother's so do take on board that you can expect that your session will be more severe."

Veronica let out a loud sob at his words and watched with absolute dismay and total consternation, across her face, as the screen showed her so proper and elegant mother meekly obeying the command to bend over Professor Stones' knees. Her mouth dropped open as the screen showed his large hand start to smack down alternatively on her beloved parent's bottom cheeks. The slaps resounded in the room, soon to be joined by the sound of Vanessa Corton-Blake's cries as her resistance broke and her legs began the over-the-knees dance so often seen in this room. This continued for several minutes until her bottom was radiantly red and she struggled to her feet, a blubbering shaking mess.

"Right, girl, now I am going to give your backside a damn good paddling. This will be a proper whopping of those lovely cheeks. The spanking was to warm you up and get you used to the idea of having your naughty little bottie properly seen to. Now it is time to bend over and take your just desserts, young lady." The younger version of Professor Stones' voice resonated around the

room, the only other sound being the sniffling of Vanessa's daughter, suffering now, while watching the 25-year-old film.

The audience in the room watched, riveted, as a younger version of the man responsible for holding everyone's attention placed an ottoman in front of Vanessa, indicating that she kneel on it and bend over placing her elbows into the floor in front.

"Open your legs, dear, let's have a proper look at what's hidden between those thighs," he said.

There was a long pause before the student complied, opening her legs to bring into the shot a quite hairy bottom crack and rather prominent vaginal lips. Stones bent down, seemingly sniffing at the wide open legs before him. Veronica wailed as the professor's voice came through loud and clear.

"Ah, lovely, a nice aroma of honey blended with sweat. Presumably you creamed your bottom before coming today?"

Veronica's eyes were glued to the screen, with a face expressing morbid fascination, as her mother answered.

"Yes, sir. Thank you, sir. It's a honey and melon flavoured body cream, sir."

He leaned in again, now kneeling lower and quite distinctively placing his face close to the crack of Vanessa's bottom.

"Ah, yes, just get the hint of melon from your anus now. Quite pleasant, I must say."

Then he rose and walked over to his desk, picking up a thick leather paddle shaped like a small cricket bat and a medium-thickness cane. Without any issue he walked back to Vanessa's exposed taut buttocks and slammed the paddle down as he discarded the cane nearby. The first few blows drew only whimpers from his victim, but as the power and pace increased, Vanessa's howls began to resound around the room. Veronica's tears flowed freely as she watched the paddle swing down, over and over again, onto her mother's writhing bright red buttocks, until eventually the professor moved aside and that part of her ordeal had completed.

"Right, pull yourself together, stand up, hands on head, take a few deep

breaths. Let's have your composure restored please, young lady."

Veronica had to remind herself that she was watching something that had happened to her mother in another lifetime, a time before she herself even existed. She knew it was ridiculous of her to be feeling her mother's pain and shame now but she couldn't control the distraught emotional state she found herself in. On screen her mother stood quite proudly facing the camera, her body held straight, her prominent breasts jutting out as gradually the flow of tears ceased and her breathing quietened.

"Good girl, I am always impressed when I deal with a miscreant who at least knows how to take their punishment. I am going to reduce your caning to a mere six strokes in acknowledgement, presuming you can take them with the same stoicism displayed thus."

He indicated to Vanessa to turn around and moved behind her.

"Right, young lady, let's have a quick inspection before I apply the coup de grâce. Bend over, my lovely, legs apart, hands on your ankles. That's it, nice and wide now, open that bottom up." His hands caressed her red, sore cheeks and they could see him blow gently between the tops of her legs as he leaned right in.

"Right, I'll be taking this slowly as the strokes will be very painful. Please maintain your position, count the strokes, thank me for delivering each one and request the next when you are ready. I assume you are bright enough to realise that if you make me wait too long or fail to obey those simple instructions then there will be repercussions in the form of further strokes."

"Yes, sir. Thank you, sir. Should I say that I am ready for my first stroke now, sir?" Vanessa asked rather hesitantly, her head hanging disconsolately and her eyes squeezed tight in anticipation of the bite from the cane.

"Consider it said, Vanessa," answered Stones as the cane swung in a long arc before slamming into the centre of her buttocks.

Vanessa, as so many before her, had not been at all prepared for the wickedness of the cane's sting. Her screech filled the room, making Veronica gasp as her mother reacted instinctively, straightening up, with her hands going directly to the site of the burning pain.

Stones waited, tapping the cane against his leg and seconds later the reality of her actions breeched Vanessa's consciousness.

"*Oh, shit. Oh, sorry Professor Stones. Oh jeepers, I didn't think it would hurt like that, oh my. Um, thank you for delivering my first stroke, sir. Oh my. Oh, can I have my second stroke now please?*" She bent over back into position, grasping her ankles, in what looked a desperate attempt that her belated compliance would dissuade the professor from applying the promised extra punishment strokes for her failure to hold position. Any hopes she held were forlorn and the words she must have dreaded, were announced.

"*One extra stroke for failing to hold position. Further disobedience will carry higher penance but you will also receive a further additional stroke for your foul language. We will now both proceed to enjoy an application of eight strokes, at present. Now you may request the second stroke again.*"

Vanessa gulped loudly, albeit her emotion-filled face showed intense concentration as she fought to stifle the sobs, at least for the time being.

"*Oh, sir. Yes, sir, thank you. Please would you be so kind as to apply the second stroke to my bottom, sir?*"

It was no sooner said than done, and the resounding thwack signalled the cane landing barely an inch below the earlier stroke. Vanessa spluttered and groaned but with her hands attached to her ankles with a ferocious tight grip she managed to restrain any movement other than a rhythmic swaying of her hips and repeated tight clenching of her suffering buttocks.

"*Ooooh, sir. Ooooh. Thank you, sir. Ooooh.*" A quick gulp of air and she forced out the humiliating words. "*Thank you, sir, that was number two, sir, and I am now ready and waiting for my third well-deserved stroke please, sir.*"

The professor's smile on screen was matched by a similar smile in the watching room. But these were knowing smiles being exchanged, unlike the transfixed Veronica, whose gaze illustrated her struggle to comprehend that she was not only hearing her mother's meek and humble words, but also witnessing the pride and dignity displayed whilst taking her harsh punishment. Unfortunately for Veronica her mother's demeanour was about to change, her resolve and spirit about to be broken, like so many before her.

The cane flew through the air and landed just below the first two.

"Yaaaaargh! Yooo! Ow! No! Ow! Oh my. Oh no. Oh, oh, oh. Oh please. Oh no, oh no. I beg you, Professor Stones, no more, please."

Stones raised the cane and allowed the seconds to pass before warning Vanessa.

"This is your one and only pass. If I have to wait again then you will receive two further punishment strokes. So think on, young lady, think on."

Tears falling from her face into the carpet beneath her, Vanessa's voice now no longer carried the control that she had adopted to take the first strokes.

"Oh, sir, I am so sorry, thank you for the third stroke, sir. I am ready for the next one please."

The voice now just a whimper, her body losing its earlier tautness as the fourth stroke landed at a point above the others. Vanessa's knees crumpled, her torso shook with pain but she retained her hold on her ankles and quickly raised her bottom.

"Thank you, sir, oh my word, oh, oh. That was four, sir, thank you. I am now ready for the next stroke please."

This drew a smiling nod from her tormentor, as he tapped the cane against her lower cheeks.

"Excellent, Vanessa, well taken. These next two will be quick so no need to count until the sixth stroke has hit home."

There was no pause for Vanessa to consider or prepare as the professor's raised arm was already travelling fast through the air as he finished his sentence. True to his word the two strokes were rapid, landing centrally across her buttocks at the rounded point, one on top of the other.

Vanessa had started to cry out when the pain of the first of the strokes landed, but then found her breath completely taken away as the follow-up hit the same spot. The resulting noise was more of an inarticulate, long, despairing groan of agony than a shriek, fully appreciated by Stones as a firm believer that less is more when it comes to the vocalisation of true pain from his wrongdoers.

"Oh my, oh, oh, oh, yaaargh! Yah! Yah! Yah! Oh, oh, oh, oh. No! No! Please, no more. Ow! Ow!"

All resistance and composure gone now, Vanessa sobbed loudly, her hands hanging loose now as she released her hold on her ankles. Consequences of this were not something she was considering until, without a word the cane flew through the air twice again as Stones applied a reminder of the repercussions of not following his instructions. Vanessa's scream was heartfelt and long, filling the room and sending shivers through her weeping daughter's body.

"Extra strokes for poor compliance as promised. I am sure you agree that this is fair and deserved, young lady." He spoke loudly as he competed with the shrieks of the beaten young woman.

Vanessa was crying copiously now, tears dropping to the carpet as she struggled to grasp her ankles and resume the position instructed.

"Yes, sir. Sorry, sir. Oh, my bottom, it hurts so much, sir. Oh, sir, please no more. I don't want any more. No!" She released her ankles and stood up.

Hearing the sigh in response from the professor, she quickly tried to remedy her unwise words as she bent back down.

"Sir, sorry sir. Please, sir, thank you for those strokes, sir. I think that I have two left, sir, and am ready for my next well-deserved stroke, sir."

The professor allowed a pause to stretch out before speaking.

"Sadly I feel that you have abused the faith and trust that I had awarded you with. You still do not appear to have learned to be as compliant as required. So brace yourself for six rapid extra strokes starting now!" The cane flashed down and then was repeated five more times in the same spot towards the top of her cleft, before Vanessa could even consider taking action to avoid them. Her scream as the pain registered split

the air as her hands flew to grasp her beleaguered bottom. Stones paused before his cold voice penetrated Vanessa's subconscious and stilled his distressed victim's scream of agony.

"*Return your hands to your ankles for your final two strokes this minute. You will complete your punishment with a certain degree of decorum or you will return here next week for a full repetition.*"

Vanessa took a deep shuddering breath and then with a heartfelt sob she resumed her position, saying, "*Thank you, Professor Stones. I apologise for my errant behaviour and request that you apply my final two strokes. I am so sorry. Please complete my punishment.*"

Stones smiled and raised the cane high before whipping it down hard against Vanessa's lower cheeks.

A strangled yelp was the response as Vanessa used all her strength and forbearance to remain in position.

"*Thank you, Professor Stones, for my deserved caning. Please deliver my final stroke.*"

Stones' face showed that he was impressed with her compliance but not enough to apply any restraint or sympathy in his application of the final delivery. The cane whistled down and landed across the most tender skin at the very top of her buttocks where her crack began.

"*Yaaaaaaaaaaaarrrr! Yaaargh! Nooooooo!*" Vanessa's response brought a smile of victory to his lips as the student's legs buckled and her hands once more flew to her bottom, desperate to grasp the sore throbbing flesh of her beaten flanks.

Stones allowed her a few seconds to rub her bottom and gradually regain some sort of composure.

"*Well, that took a bit of getting through, didn't it, but I sense that you recognise you have been thrashed appropriately and deservedly. Is that so, Vanessa?*" he said.

The sobbing but resilient student turned to face him, answering clearly, "*Oh, sir. Yes, sir, absolutely, sir. Totally and completely, thank you for my thrashing, sir.*"

The screen turned blank and Veronica was jolted back into the present as the shock and horror of what she had witnessed sunk in. The silence filled the room as the screen rose into its fitments and lighting returned.

Stones fixed her with a penetrating gaze.

"Are you ready to be dealt with now, Veronica?"

Veronica stood as though mesmerised. She seemed incapable of speech, her eyes still riveted to the now blank screen, her mouth hanging open in horror and disbelief.

"I... I... I... But that was horrific... I... I..."

Professor Stones smiled as he enjoyed the stricken student's look of bewilderment and quite hopeless despair.

"Look at this as a big learning opportunity, my poor misguided child. Your dear mother did not put another foot wrong in her time at this establishment, after I gave her a bit of improvement and encouragement in how to behave. As you have probably surmised by now, our little film club episode here was with her agreement. Vanessa wanted you to fully understand that a price must be paid for misbehaviour and poor judgement, which, to be honest, is a very generous way of looking at the disgraceful attitude that has resulted in your attendance here today."

Veronica had now been rendered speechless, her mind whirling in its struggle to believe that she had landed herself in this position. Her face was a picture as Stones imagined the desperate escape and avoidance options flashing into her mind, as she tried to bring forth anything that would allow her some respite. An expert at manipulation, Stones recognised the turmoil of her thoughts and, in his own inimitable way, decided to turn the screw. To her credit there seemed to be an immediate acceptance that her mother had taken away the safety net she had clearly hoped would be supplied.

"We do have some free time, I believe, do we not, ladies?" he said in a contemplating way, as if this was of no real consequence. "In this instance I am prepared to allow Veronica the luxury of avoiding the long stressful wait to be punished. As long as she is a good girl now, then we can get this done and dusted, and it will all be water under the bridge. All in concord?"

Nods of agreement from the two senior female staff brought further consternation to the errant student as she fully realised that her fate in this room was sealed. Stones waited as she processed her thoughts. She had to take on board that she was going to receive a thrashing, completely naked, by the college's Dean of Discipline with an audience in attendance. Not just any audience but the actual Mistress and Senior Tutor of the college! She likely very much hoped that they were not actually going to participate in the dreaded deed, although, such was the state of flux Veronica had been reduced to, it would surely cross her mind that maybe they would be a softer option than that of the large, overbearing and frankly quite terrifying Professor Stones. Not only that, her own mother had made it perfectly clear that she thoroughly approved of the act, and she would do nothing to prevent it taking place. Dire consequences appeared to be the threat if Veronica were not to accept her just desserts in a manner that appeased Professor Stones. The matter in hand was suddenly brought back into sharp focus with the next words that were uttered disdainfully by Professor Stones.

"I am not sure that young Veronica will have realised the preparation I insist on before thrashing the buttocks of miscreants, Celia. Would you carry out the requisite odour checks, please? Unpleasant task though it can sometimes be, but you know how fussy I am. Armpits, feet and both cracks, please, if you will."

Veronica froze as Celia rather leapt to her feet and was suddenly beside her with her face close to her armpits.

"Stand exactly where you are, young lady." Stones' voice cut through the air. "One more act of disobedience from you and your punishment will be beyond harsh. You will allow Celia to carry out my request and you will stand absolutely still with your mouth firmly shut!"

Any rising thought of rebellious acts died in that moment, his icy tone causing her to close her eyes. She stayed stock still, and was a picture of someone trying desperately to disconnect from what was happening, as Celia then knelt down and sniffed at her feet. When Veronica felt hands on her hips as Celia moved her face to the level of her groin and inhaled loudly, she jolted but kept her mouth and eyes firmly closed.

"Bit sweaty under the arms, feet are okay, a little bit manky around the front entrance and…" Veronica let out a low moan as she felt Celia's hands on her buttocks and then her breath on her skin. "Not totally fresh and sweet smelling around either her front or back doors, Professor Stones, a bit sweaty and pongy. I think she could do with a bit of a wash and freshening up, to be honest."

Veronica gulped loudly, her face now a bright red, her hands clenching on her head and tears springing to her eyes. Luckily she was so stunned that she remained silent, which was just as well, as Stones was waiting to pounce on any adverse reaction.

"Right, Celia, pour the dirty rascal a nice bath and she can prepare herself properly. That will help take the time up between now and my own plan for a full team on parade for this one's denouement."

Mysterious and disheartening words from Professor Stones, who now tapped away on his laptop, for a clearly confused and flabbergasted Veronica, her head spinning with how surreal the occasion had turned out to be. Stones revelled in the bewilderment he could cause his victims and was well aware that Veronica was desperately trying to get her mind around the idea that she was to have a bath in Professor Stones' apartment, in preparation for what she was coming to accept would be the thrashing of her life. Her mother had let on to him that she was sure Veronica remembered a beating from her when she was in the early stages of a rather lippy teenage period, a hairbrush slamming against her bare backside for many, many minutes after she was caught stealing from her elder sister's money box. Vanessa had informed Stones that her daughter vowed then never to earn her mother's wrath again, but now she had to take on board that she had indeed allowed herself to be on the end of an impending and ceremonious beating.

Led by Celia into the bathroom, Veronica's face, as she cast a look behind her at Professor Stones, was full of apprehension and incomprehension, searching for any excuse or reason she could bring to mind that would forestall, at least, the impending horror. As Stones stood observing from the doorway, Celia looked up sympathetically at her as the bath filled, noting the trembling limbs and single tear sliding down a cheekbone.

"Come along, my dear, it will all be over in an hour or so but there will be no lasting damage. You will get a very sore backside, your pride will take just as much of a beating as your bottom, you will be humiliated beyond your wildest nightmares and you will be a bit tender for a few days or so. However, it will then be over, you will have a learnt a very good life lesson which will serve you well, and you will get a sense of achievement in having crossed a line that you should never have traversed and then been brought back onside. This may well be the breaking of you, young lady, but it should also be the making of you. Now do you need to empty, before you settle in for a nice soak in my bath? Because, trust me, you do not want your punishment with a full bladder!"

Her words, although quite disturbing, were strangely calming for Veronica, who was obviously drawn to her by this apparent show of kindness. She was not expecting the next turn of events.

"Oh thank you, yes, I could do with a wee, thanks. Give me a moment." Veronica's expectation that Celia would leave the room and allow her to lock herself in for a few moments were quickly dispelled, as a smiling senior tutor sat herself down on the adjacent bidet.

"Silly girl, you do not suppose that you warrant any privacy. Professor Stones, I presume it is okay for our guest to urinate in your toilet?" Veronica had paused in front of the toilet and then made to move away as Celia's words brought Stones to the doorway.

"Ah, yes indeed. Empty your bladder thoroughly, please, young lady, we do not want any mishaps while you are being beaten. Then you can enjoy a quick wash in my bath before we have everything in place for the main entertainment." His deep chuckle disconcerted Veronica so much that her resistance melted away and she allowed Celia to position her on the toilet like a child.

"There you go, my lovely, pee away!" Celia laughed as Veronica coloured up once more. Veronica's face illustrated the agony she was experiencing as she attempted to relax her muscles enough to empty her full bladder.

It was several minutes before Veronica managed to relieve herself, Professor Stones having apparently become bored of the spectacle and turned to talk to the Mistress in the main room. In reality he watched her from the corner of an eye as she squeezed her own eyes tightly closed as, to her horror and shame, her full flow noisily filled the room as she emptied. Her eyes soon snapped open as the voice of Professor Stones shocked her attention back to her predicament.

"Rather raucous, but better out than in!" his voice boomed from just a couple of feet away, where Stones now stood holding out folded sheets of toilet paper for her. "Wipe your drips off then let's pop you into the bath."

A red-faced Veronica's shame was clearly complete as she obediently dabbed herself and quickly flushed the toilet. Stones suspected that she felt she had also just flushed away the last remnants of her dignity, he hoped so anyway!

He was pleased to see evidence of all resistance now broken as she meekly accepted his offered arm to assist, and stepped into the luxurious rather grand bath and settled herself, eyes downcast.

"Now I am sure you do know how to wash and clean yourself properly, young lady, but be thorough or you will be back in the bath with Celia and myself showing you how to do an exemplary job!"

Stones made sure that any thought of relaxing for a few moments was driven out of her head.

Several minutes later she found herself being dried most intimately by Celia, whose fingers were noted by Stones as they delved supposedly perfunctorily into the student's most intimate areas.

"When you two can bring yourselves to stop what you are up to it would be nice to get on with things!" Stones' voice froze them both in their tracks and Celia's coloured cheeks rather betrayed her guilt whilst Veronica looked perplexed and horrified.

Moments later, Veronica stood naked, legs parted and hands on top of her head before a seated Professor Stones.

"Time for you to meet my friend 'Redemption', Veronica!" he snarled at the student who trembled, her eyes squeezed shut in shame and fear. "A hand spanking of 100 slaps to warm us both up, then a good 20 with my leather paddle, a dozen with the medium-thick cane and my favourite thick strap waiting in the wings to top things off. A good six of this normally ticks the penitence box for the more severe crimes but this may depend on your behaviour, so the number, for the time being, is not set in stone."

Tears coursed down Veronica's face as her eyes alighted on the instruments of her punishment on the desktop behind Stones. The shining eyes and beaming smile on the face of the college Mistress did nothing to allay her fears.

"Oh no, sir. Please, no. I cannot do this… oooh!"

Any further words intended were lost forever as the combination of a firm hand in the small of her back from Celia and the professor grabbing her left hand with some force propelled her expertly over his knees.

"Hands on the chair legs, legs apart, bottom up, that's a good girl. We will have those cheeks open. We do like to have the anus presented and the vulva and vagina on show, don't we, Senior Tutor? Come on now, my dear, we need to have a good look at those lovely labia. Show us what you've got now!" Stones chortled away, knowing exactly the belittling effect his words had on his victims.

"Of course, Professor Stones. That's it, Veronica, push that bottom up. Lovely, lovely. Pussy lips in view, thankfully dry, and a lovely open bottom cleft, all ready to go, I believe," responded Celia.

Whilst her full fleshy cheeks would provide a certain amount of padding, a pert bottom never being an advantage when receiving a thrashing, especially from a hand the size of the professor's, Veronica's bottom was nonetheless bright red after less than 20 hard slaps had landed. Stones smiled as he applied himself with relish to ensuring that this was young one lady who would think twice about crossing him again. The firm grip across her back was very much required, as she bucked and thrashed beneath him. Celia swiftly moved to hold her legs in position.

"Oh my, she's a wriggly one, isn't she, Dean? Calm down, girl, this is just the starter to warm you up. Professor Stones has not got serious yet!" Celia smiled up at Stones, as he resumed his hard spanking. The two shared a moment of sheer joy, both enraptured by the flattening of the battered cheeks being quickly followed by them springing back into fully rounded targets, as Stones' ministrations produced a flood of tears and a constant wailing from the distraught student.

Within five minutes Veronica was up and assisted roughly by Celia was pushed nose first against the bookshelves lining his walls. Her bottom was glowing bright red and her legs trembling quite dramatically as she tried to come to terms with what she had just experienced.

"Now take a moment to compose yourself, my dear, and then we will move on to the more serious part of your treatment. Think of it as a menu for redemption, Veronica. You have savoured the starter and now have a main course and dessert to follow. Perhaps not a meal to be photographed and posted all over your social media pages, but a satisfying and fulfilling experience regardless. Now take some breaths and pull yourself together while we prepare for your next course."

The increase in her sobbing distress was music to the ears of the audience. There would be no mercy shown in this room.

The three academics chatted quietly amongst themselves as they deliberately allowed the errant student to stand and suffer with her thoughts, and her stinging buttocks, before the buzzer at the door went to announce the next moment of despair for Veronica. The look of sheer panic she threw at them over her shoulder was reward in spades for Stones, who got almost as much pleasure from his piece-by-piece breakdown of a miscreant's dignity as he did from the impact of his hand on their bottoms. Jamie entered the room, his beaming grin as he took in the scene before him very much indicating his pleasure at the late invite he had received. His salutations to the current occupants was rather interrupted by Veronica's less than welcoming response to his added presence.

"Oh no, oh please, no. Aaaaarggh!" Veronica's words ended in a scream as she realised the figure entering the room was a male. She immediately turned and headed for her clothes. She was stopped in her tracks as the long arms of the professor wrapped around her and lifted her clean off her feet. Once more she found herself staring at his carpet as he deposited over his knees.

"Dr Ford, please to be so kind as to pass me the round leather paddle. This young scallywag is about to find out the meaning of obedience. Her next punishment has now been doubled to 40 strokes. But first, Veronica, you will greet my visitor politely and thank him for coming along to assist me. Then we will deal with your rather disappointing behaviour as he entered by room. Very rude, young lady, very rude."

"Oh no, sir. I am sorry but I did not think anyone else would come, certainly not another man. Oh my, this is so embarrassing. Please, Professor Stones, I am so sorry."

Stones sighed and tapped the paddle lightly against her bottom.

"I have asked you to carry out a simple task, Veronica. If I have to repeat that request then I will double your caning as well. Which will be a bonus for young Porter here as he is the person who will be administering that cane."

Veronica howled and through tears and sniffs managed to stumble out the words required, her eyes downcast as she half-faced Jamie.

"Hello, sir. I am sorry if I was rude and offended you when you entered the room. I am also sorry if I offended you by being rude to your guest, Professor Stones."

"That is an improvement. You appear to be learning. Now please tell us all how you feel about your punishment being doubled with my lovely paddle here, because of your rudeness. Please do not be concerned about showing your body to my colleague, I can assure you that he will soon be well acquainted with all of your most private places!"

The tears flowed once more, as Veronica took a deep breath in and sobbed out the supplicant words required, very aware as she twisted her neck to see that Jamie had taken a seat with the two female academics, allowing himself a full view of her beleaguered rear quarters.

"Oh, sir, I would like you to give me twice as many strokes with the paddle, sir, to teach me a lesson, please. Yaaaaaar!"

The first stroke landed full on her unprepared relaxed cheeks immediately followed by a fusillade of slaps as Stones gave her a quickfire 30, his hand a blur as he pounded the wriggling buttocks.

"I think the last ten should be on your legs, young lady. Fertile and virgin ground to harvest. Prepare yourself, my dear, this is going to be a painful lesson for you." Stones teased her as he and Jamie exchanged smiles, watching the legs and buttocks of Veronica tighten and then tremble as he deliberately made her wait for the next stage of her nightmare to continue.

Her crying went up a pitch, as the anticipation and dread defeated her, and he took the moment to slam the paddle down on her right leg. He allowed the scream to reach its zenith before matching the strike on her left leg. With her legs fully apart he was able to work the rest of the strokes around the insides and outsides of both legs until her presented target was just a complete mass of red flesh, the edge of the paddle creating mottled crescents of deep crimson ridges.

"Her mother took a beating with far more stoicism, Porter. I am afraid that you missed the showing of Vanessa's last visit to my rooms before she graduated and took the skills, discipline and mindset she had harvested here and used it to make her successful way in the big wide world, all lessons taken on board, I am delighted to report. Sadly, this offspring is not made of the stern stuff that Vanessa brought to the table. Hopefully our task today will go some way towards improving Veronica so that she can follow in her mother's footsteps."

Veronica was not showing any signs of appreciating the professor's efforts in that direction and Celia had been compelled to take hold of her head and attend to the fluid production from the howling student's eyes, nose and mouth!

"Dear me, Professor Stones. What a fuss. Goodness alone knows what state this wretched child will be in by the time she has received a damn good caning." Celia's words elicited the response that she had perversely aimed at, as Veronica's sobbing increased once more.

"Yes indeed, Dr Ford. I think we will have her cuffed and bent over the caning desk straight away. The sooner she gets to experience the cane the better. What nonsense, girl. Now up and over to the table with my colleagues, please."

Stones jerked her from his knees as he put the paddle down and Jamie and Celia immediately took an arm each and marched the distraught student over to the site of the planned final and most severe part of her punishment. The two worked quickly and effectively to fasten Veronica in the traditional manner for a caning at St. James', with her hands and ankles cuffed wide apart, her bottom forced up, and legs apart, by the moulded mound on the desk.

Stones took out the medium-thick cane and gently tapped it against his hand as he studied her splayed cheeks.

"Well, my dear. So far, a job well done. Apart from the stark whiteness of your anal cleft, we have a sea of many shades of red. A well-battered bottom, for sure. We now need a good set of red stripes to assist you further down the road to full contrition, a release from the guilt of your offence, a path of improvement set for you to journey on and full redemption. I do hope you appreciate the effort that we are making here. In fact, Veronica, I feel it is now time for you to illustrate that you are on the correct path. Please can you confirm you have accepted that this is a worthwhile process and you fully understand that the path of correction has been successful so far?"

There was a long pause and Stones noted that Celia had bent to face the still-weeping student. He gently stroked Veronica's twitching buttocks with the cane as he waited for Celia to finish what he knew would be a very stern wake-up call and lesson in the correct way to answer any questions that Stones put to her. Meanwhile Dorothy had moved her chair to sit just to the left of the smarting raised bottom of the suffering student, out of the line of fire but perfectly placed to see the application and after-effects of the cane.

"Lovely view, is it not, Professor Winslow-Bellingham?"

"Indeed, Dean, indeed. It is always a duty and a pleasure to watch close up when one of our miscreants is brought to book, finds remorse and takes big strides on their journey to success, improvement and inner peace."

Stones continued to trace lines on the red cheeks as he extended the wait, and the dread of what was to come very shortly for Veronica, as well as emphasising the humiliating position that his victim was in.

"I believe that you have an answer for me, Miss Corton-Blake. Hopefully it will not have any relationship to the offensive language you felt empowered to spout in my direction earlier on? What was it now? Something about being an utterly ridiculous, dirty old man with wrinkly hands, if I recall correctly."

His taunting words produced a howl of despair before Veronica could gather herself once more assisted by a pinch on the shoulder from Celia.

"Ouch! Oh, have been very badly behaved and I am being deservedly punished for my behaviour and my uncalled for insubordination. I am so sorry. Um. Um. Is there anything I can say to stop you using the cane please, sir? My bottom and legs hurt so much. I have really learned my lesson. I will never behave badly again. I am so sorry." The sobs that followed were loud and clear evidence of a distraught and subdued student, but Stones was rarely one to relent due to entreaties. His assessment of the pain and distress suffered, delivered and caused was the only real opinion that mattered in the room, and as far as he was concerned this young lady needed to be taken all the way in this journey of justice that he had set out. He began to tap the cane harder against buttocks that had seemed to develop a life of their own and were quivering uncontrollably now.

"Do not belittle yourself any further, Veronica, please. Enough of the begging and enough of the apologies. Dr Ford, please take the cane and deliver the 12 strokes she has volunteered to receive. Obviously Veronica needs to request that you proceed and to apologise to you for having to spend your valued time doing this. Veronica, will you please show us all that you have recognised that this is all of you own doing, or do we need to look at extending this caning somewhat?"

The yelp from Veronica rather indicated that she had finally caught on as she gabbled out the words that Stones had been attempting to entice from her.

"What! No. Yes. Of course. Oh my lord. Thank you and sorry, Dr Ford. Yes, yes, yes. I am so sorry that you have to cane me. Oh, and thank you for doing so. Oh no. Sorry. Sorry. Sorry. Please cane me, Dr Ford. Oh no."

Stones sighed theatrically.

"Good grief, I suppose that will have to do. Cane her hard, please, Dr Ford."

Celia swept the cane down, her face set hard and her teeth gritted together as she landed the first blow. To no one's surprise, Veronica's response to the cane stroke could only be described as hysterical. She jerked and twisted her body to the limit the restraints allowed and began a banshee of wails that would continue throughout her thrashing. Celia took not the slightest bit of notice and laid on the cane hard and fast until she had completed ten of the allotted deliveries. The dispassionate trio of Stones, Dorothy and Jamie all moved in to study the developing deep red lines and Stones nodded his approval at the perfection of the parallel spacing.

"Excellent job, Dr Ford. Give her another ten, please. I am not really that keen on this pampering of our miscreants with just a bare dozen. Not sure it does the job. A nice firm ten on top of those already received should help cement the lesson in her silly little head."

His words set off a fresh series of howling from Veronica, caught short as she took a sharp intake of breath as the cane flashed down once more. Stones was interested to see, or more accurately hear, a much more muted response from the recipient to the second round of her torment. He surmised that the searing pain of the wood repeatedly striking already sore and throbbing skin, had taken the wind out of her sails and she was now fully focused on somehow withstanding the sensation that her bottom was undergoing. Her head slumped and jolted up as each blow landed, the noise diluting to a whimpered cry of anguish each time a new pain registered.

As Celia stood back, Stones handed Jamie his favourite thick strap.

"Time for you and Jamie to become better acquainted, Veronica. He has a stronger arm than me, you see, so can inflict much harsher strokes to end your session with a flourish. Top things off, my friend. This is a reckoning she needs to remember. Concentrate on the tops of her legs and the strip across the very top of her buttocks. A final intensive branding iron experience for this young scallywag to compare and contrast with the other means that we have used to educate her. No mercy shown. Make sure the message is one that she will forever remember."

Jamie took hold of the strap with rather evident relish and within a split second the leather had lashed across the backs of her thighs and brought forth the most blood-curdling of screams from Veronica.

To Stones' approval, Jamie took his time. Veronica had just about returned to some form of calmness, at least within the context of what she was enduring, her breathing a rather unladylike snorting as she attempted to gain some sort of control, when the strap landed for the second time. Her struggles against the restraints started anew as she screamed desperately once more and again Jamie waited her out as Celia moved in to wipe her face and cupped it between her hands.

"Only four more, my dear. Not feeling such a smart-mouthed, smart-arsed, clever dick now, are we?"

The strap struck the backs of her legs for the third time and Celia held tightly on to her head, grinning into the wild, despairing eyes of the defeated student.

The crack that the strap made as Jamie slammed it down across the tight skin along the tops of her buttocks echoed around the room before being joined by the howls from Veronica.

"No. No. No. Please stop. It hurts too much. I have had enough. Please stop. Professor Stones, make him stop please. I do not want any more. I am so sorry. Please make him… aaaaarrrrrgggghhhhhh!"

Jamie, so well mentored by the professor, landed the fifth impact from the thick leather marginally below the former, the skin flattening and rebounding, before turning a vivid red very quickly.

"Last one just below the centre of her buttocks, please, Jamie. Just at the point of the most pressure when she sits down. It will help work as a reminder of the lessons we have taught her over the next few days. As hard as you like, my good man. Do us proud."

The stroke was ferocious and landed exactly as directed, covering two pronounced glowing lines from the cane and adding to the discomfort already established. A final long howl from Veronica before her body slumped in abject submission, all fight gone as she began the process of handling the burning fire that was now lit in her hindquarters. Her moans reduced to a helpless keening as she suffered the after-effects of a severe thrashing.

"You may remove the cuffs and place her in the iced bidet, Dr Ford. Might as well give the coming bruises a helping hand to develop. Do try and get a grip of yourself, my dear. It is over and the remedy to your appalling behaviour has been applied. Only good things to come now, I am sure, if you allow yourself to accept and come to appreciate the steps we have taken to assist your development, your improvement and your enlightenment. You will soon be very grateful for our intervention, and at that point you will be on a forward path that should lead you to a better life."

Stones thoroughly enjoyed his exaggerated pomposity and further belittling of the rascals that fell under his corrective tutelage. The glance from Veronica showed no challenge, no fight, no fire. There was awe, fear, despair and defeat in the cowed student, which suited his purpose in full. He had conquered another wilful spirit and he was convinced that she would grow to be a better and more fulfilled human being because of his actions.

"She can have 15 minutes sitting in the ice, while we have a glass of wine to pass the time, and then we will have her in front of us to thank us and apologise again for her misdemeanour. A moment spent writing out some suppliant, apologetic and grateful words to help her process and accept what has happened and why. Then, and only then, she can return to her room and call her mother to confirm that she has received her comeuppance."

CHAPTER 12

IN WHICH OLIVIA GETS A LESSON IN SPORTSMANSHIP

The one thing that the vast majority of University sporting clubs adhere to is that Corinthian spirit ideal of being seen to 'play the game'. Fair play is all and the concept of being a bad loser and labelled unsporting is just not tolerated. Therefore pushing the coach and captain in the river when you are informed that you have not made the team for the National University Rowing Championships is not likely to go down well in one of the most prestigious colleges in the country!

Whilst in most circumstances the discipline within team ranks is down to the overall coach of the University team, there is a limit to their power and in serious incidents the responsibility to deal with the errant student falls to the respective college to intervene. Therefore Olivia Harland found herself referred to the Dean of Discipline with the recommendation being that she should be subject to the college's own disciplinary process or face an automatic one year suspension from the team. Neither the coach nor Olivia saw a suspension as ideal because it would weaken the team somewhat. With most of the rowing first team consisting of students in their final year, Olivia, as a second year, had virtually been guaranteed a position in the following year's boat. Put to her the alternative punishment of a short, sharp thrashing, Olivia had been very quick to write a letter of apology to all concerned, in which she opted to undergo a beating to atone for her behaviour. As always that did not appear to be the soft option it might have been considered initially now the time had come for her face-to-face meeting with the fearsome Professor Stones.

"I have spoken at length to the University's Coach and Head of River Sports, Nina Sparkes, and your captain, Lisa Downes, and am happy that we all agree that a much reddened bottom would be the ideal way for you to embrace the guilt, shame and disgrace of your despicable actions. Your letter states that you have selected this solution to bring this matter to a close and once administered to the satisfaction of all concerned parties you will be free to return to the water with your colleagues. So, young lady, a lengthy spanking followed by a caning is the decreed punishment. I would ask that you strip those clothes off and let me see what I have to work with please."

Olivia's first moment of apprehension appeared as she hesitated.

"Now, please, young lady. Obedience and compliance are required to avoid additional punishment being dispensed. Come along, no false modesty, please do not be shy, put your naked body on show now, or face the consequences. It is time to illustrate your acceptance of punishment for your actions, it is time to embrace the opportunity to absolve yourself of the guilt and the shame. Clothes off, come along now. I have not got any time for juvenile games, the time for baring your buttocks has arrived."

Stones never failed to get great pleasure at this point. Turning the screw verbally, as his miscreants suddenly faced up to the fact that the moment of their chastisement was now upon them, was definitely one of the pleasures of his life.

With Stones staring at her with dispassionate eyes throughout, the cowed youngster began to disrobe. A powerful-looking woman with strong shoulders, he could see that Olivia had the build for the strenuous activity she apparently excelled at. As she dropped her sports bra Stones gave her sturdy, firm-looking breasts and pointed, long nipples a nod of approval. Not that it seemed appreciated by the red-faced student as she turned her back on him to drop her knickers. Stones assessed the firm, muscular buttocks displayed as she bent to slip the briefs over her feet and decided to make the most of Olivia's clear unease at displaying her naked body.

"Excellent, now while you are showing off those fine glutes perhaps you could bend over, legs apart, hands on ankles. Now let me inspect you to ensure that you meet the very high cleanliness standards required."

All her attempts at nonchalance and indifference had come to nothing as she obeyed without resistance, displaying buttocks that were more oval than round. Olivia presented a perfectly straight anal cleft, which opened to display a neat, short, vertical opening of a virtually wrinkle-free anus, and a minimal darker-skinned surround with a sparse amount of anal hairs, tampering down into a long vaginal opening, with hints of a bright pinkness and neatly cropped pubic hair. Stones bent behind her and took a perfunctory sniff close to her bottom crack which Olivia accepted with only a slight tightening of her arsehole to show awareness of her situation.

"Good girl," said Stones, using his most obsequious tone. "Lovely display and a strong scent of rose illustrating that you have complied with personal hygiene, pre-thrashing instructions. You have a good pair of buttocks for walloping that look well able to take a solid beating."

There was an audible groan from Olivia but she held her position and Stones moved into place and readied himself to give her one of his longest ever spankings.

"Right, young lady, I will have you over my knees now. Time for my right hand and your lovely bottom cheeks to become better acquainted." Olivia draped herself reluctantly over his knees as he continued to taunt her. "I hope you will be comfortable hanging down there, you will be in this position for some time."

She acquiesced meekly, but glanced back at him with a face full of trepidation, as the last dregs of confidence drained away. Stones stroked her globes for a moment, waited until the cheeks lost their tightness and her muscles began to relax visibly, before his large arm descended at speed. His hand started to bounce off her buttocks to the accompaniment of squeaks and yelps, which soon turned to longer screams and sobs, as he increased the pressure and speed of the blows. The tops of the backs of her legs proved to be her most sensitive spot and he landed close to 30 slaps on each leg, turning each one a deep shade of crimson. Stones was determined that Olivia would not be leaving him thinking that a spanking was the easy option punishment-wise. He kept up his assault on her rear quarters for 20 minutes, and was confident that he had landed his hand close to 1,000 times before he delivered a final flourish of six stingers on the top of her crack. Her bottom was a pleasing bright red all over, her sobs wracked her whole body, her breathing erratic and her legs kicking the air in some kind of frenetic spasm.

He was patient as he waited for her to calm, glad of the pause, his hand stinging and his own breathing heavy with the exertion. This was the longest spanking he had applied in memory and he could certainly feel the effects himself, albeit he was certain not at the discomfort levels of Olivia's woes. She was completely defeated and demoralised, laying across his lap, weeping noisily, her hips rotating, exposing her private places without any thought of personal pride or privacy now. He stroked her throbbing cheeks tenderly for a moment before hooking his arms under her pliable body and bringing them both to their feet.

"Time to put you in place for your caning, my dear. I am going to have you restrained for this as these strokes will be severe and I intend to take my time to ensure you suffer."

He grasped her upper arm in one of his giant hands and marched her across to his desks-cum-tables that he had especially designed for this process of chastisement. Her resistance as she reached the wooden platform heightened but he ignored her lack of willingness and with his brisk and brusque manner forced her compliance without ever allowing her to consider refusal an option. Stones soon had her face down, bent over, legs apart, bottom raised, cheeks open, buckled into ankle and wrist cuffs before she even began to wonder what on earth she was doing and why!

"Well done, good girl," he said as he ran his fingertips down her beaten flanks. "I will get down to business soon. Just waiting for the extra element to ensure that your caning is something you will fully appreciate and remember for a good while."

Olivia's composure was gradually returning as she clearly processed his words as raised her head.

"Extra element, sir. What does that mean?"

Stones smiled at the now rather disturbed and confused young woman.

"Patience, my sweet, you will soon be enlightened. Now hush and contemplate the actions that led you to this little situation. I have some work to do. You just be quiet and compose yourself ready for your thrashing."

Stones could feel the building anger and simmering resentment as Olivia adapted to the heat and sting of her spanking and began to think with a clearer mind.

"This is ridiculous. You have had your fun and your thrills. Now enough is enough with this charade, so can you either hit me with your little stick or let me go. You have given me an excessive spanking which I think is more than enough of a punishment. I am not sure that this is not enforced imprisonment, so I think you'd be best advised to release me and we can forget all about this meeting."

Stones sighed and ignored her; he had realised she had an impetuous streak but it tended to be one that led her to speak without thinking and then regret it in reflection. As the silence hung in the air he was almost able to count down to the moment she recognised that she had again done herself no favours.

"Um. Er. Sorry, sir, I did not mean to be so silly. Can we forget I said that, sir? Please do not add to my punishment. I am so sorry about my big mouth, sir. Sometimes I do rather run off a bit and let myself down rather, sir."

Again Stones let her words hang for a while. In reality he was quite glad of this little interlude to kill the time until the next part of his plan for Olivia's chastisement came into play.

"Far too late for apologetic withdrawals, my dear. Your 12-stroke punishment can easily be doubled, and the next injudicious statement that comes out of your poorly controlled mouthpiece will certainly see that happen. Now think on before you react. I can see the anger in your eyes and the irritation in the set of your jaw. To be honest, young Olivia, the way you are carrying on makes me suspect that you could even be heading towards a 50-stroke beating, and that, my dear, I can assure you, will not be an experience I would recommend. Now head down in submission and let's have a subdued and compliant young lady preparing herself to take her dues."

At that point the doorbell sounded indicating that the added element to Olivia's experience had arrived. As Stones opened the door electronically, her head came up, her face a study in panic and disbelief as she twisted her head round to see the college's senior tutor, Celia Ford, and a tall well-built man she did not recognise enter the room.

"What the fuck! No! No! Get them out! Fuck no! No! No! What in hell are they doing here? I do not want them here. Get them out, Professor Stones. What the fuck is happening?"

Stones greeted his two colleagues as though she had not spoken although his next words assured her that he most certainly had.

"As expected, your punishment has been doubled again. You have not really heeded warnings have you, Olivia? Next outburst and we move to that promised land of 50 strokes of the cane. When are you going to learn?"

Olivia's head went down again and she began to weep. It was to jerk up again moments later as she felt unfamiliar hands stroking and prodding her sore buttocks.

"Good job so far, Dean. These cheeks are lovely and rosy all over. All ready for a damn good caning, I would say. Is our friend here going to have the pleasure?" Celia continued her stroking of Olivia's bottom as she indicated the waiting Jamie, who had got across the city as fast as he could once he received the message from the professor that he had an opportunity for him to deliver a thrashing to one of Stones' misbehaving students.

"Yes indeed, she's built a straightforward dozen of the best up to a fully-fledged 24-stroke flogging with the cane. I thought I would give her the first half and Jamie could add his considerable strength and muscle to ensuring that this ends up being a session she will not want to risk ever repeating."

Celia had been involved with this part of tormenting the victim on so many occasions in the past that she knew without any communication with Stones where to take the process to cause Olivia the most shame and embarrassment.

"Do have a closer look, Jamie, she has an excellent backside for caning. Have a feel. Nice firm but quite fleshy buttocks. These should take a hard thrashing well. There's the bonus of the view as well. A jolly cute-looking arsehole with its surrounding sweet little curly hairs and a sumptuous set of plump labial lips. Look, I'll pull her cheeks apart to improve the view as the silly girl has gone all shy and is trying to close the gates on her guests! How rude!"

Olivia was making incomprehensible noises and trying pointlessly to move her lower body away from Celia's intruding hands. Stones appreciated that her lack of offensive swearing might now herald her understanding that she alone was the cause of her increasing sentence and that less would be more as far as contributing to their discussion went.

"Very nearly trimmed vagina, don't you think, Professor Stones? She's quite a peach all round, I'd say. I will tend to the speaking end while you gentlemen have your fun. I might at least be able to help her keep this punishment down to a level that she can bear. Trust me, sweetheart, no one wants to be leaving here on the end of a 50."

Olivia's body stiffened as the unmistakable sound of a swishing cane filled the room.

"This is my medium cane, young lady. It's got a lovely sting and doesn't bruise as much as the heavy cane. On the other hand it tends to be faster through the air so has a real bite to it."

Stones was fully aware that the recipients of his castigation were not the slightest bit interested in his commentary both prior to and during the event, but he was sure it gave them more unease and perturbed them further, adding to the overall devastation they were enduring.

"Oh no, sir, please no. I don't want it. I don't want it!" Olivia's voice rose as she sensed Professor Stones moving into position and she grasped the offered hands of Celia as she knelt before her and stretched to take her fingers between her own.

"Chin up and a deep breath, tense and relax those cheeks and embrace the pain, my dear. You cannot fight it so accept it and oh, here we go!" Celia squeezed Olivia's hands hard as the cane swung through the air before landing for the first time. Stones hit hard and low, deciding to give her a real tester across the fleshy lower cheeks before him.

"Yaaaaaar! Oh, oh, oh, oh, oh. Oooyaaaar!" was the response from Olivia, her already red bottom now displaying a scarlet red line that was quickly joined by a second just below the first, before Stones paused to view his work and allow the student to properly suffer the after-sting of his well-placed strokes.

Once her cries had reduced to distressed whimpers, Stones swiped down four times rapidly across the tighter skin at the top of her bottom where her cleft began. The screams filled the room and Celia's whispered words of support failed to calm the wriggling student as she desperately tried to move to escape the vicious cane strokes. The next six were all placed across the centre of her cheeks, a minute apart, as Stones waited for her to settle and encompass the pain of one stroke before he added another.

"My arm is tiring, Olivia, and I am concerned that I will not be giving you justice if I continue so my friend Jamie is going to do me a favour and take over now, so I do not let you down. I hope you do not mind, my dear, but it is time to hand over to the younger man."

Stones passed the cane to Jamie and ran his hands over Olivia's striped buttocks. Olivia, to no one's surprise, failed to respond to the professor's comments as she finally seemed to be showing signs of a broken spirit.

Jamie paused, just lightly running the tip of the cane on the inside of her parted cheeks, just gently scratching the pure white sides before they blended into the darker-toned soft skin surrounding her anal orifice. Olivia flinched as he touched it to the slightly opened slit and toyed with her anal entrance.

"When you are ready to receive your strokes from me please ask me for the first stroke, then acknowledge it, thank me and ask for the next one."

Stones chuckled. "Good ploy, young man. Let's find out if the rapscallion has received and understood the message. Flay her naughty backside, please, my friend."

Olivia sighed before she forced out the words required to begin this final round of her torment.

"I am ready for my first stroke, please, sir."

The swish of the cane was followed immediately by the crack of the impact producing a strangulated groan and a tight clenching of Olivia's cheeks.

"One, thank you sir. I am ready for my second stroke now, sir."
Swish. Crack!

A second angry red line joined the first on top of her already swollen and reddened cheeks. Again Olivia suffered the stroke in near silence with resilience and Jamie and Stones exchanged impressed nods of acknowledgement. "That's two, sir. Thank you, sir. I would like my third now, please, sir."
Swish. Crack!

The third was slightly harder and landed perfectly on top of a raised welt from earlier. Olivia's head shot up as she absorbed the painful stroke. A small yelp of pain escaped her lips.

"Oh, sir, thank you. Ow, ow! I am ready for my fourth stroke now, sir."

Swish. Crack!

The stroke landed on one of the few unblemished strips of skin left on the beleaguered bottom of the stoic student and she sucked in air noisily but again kept her position and a certain amount of dignity. Stones enjoyed the challenge of a hard nut to crack and always gave due respect to those who illustrated a capacity to take the extreme punishments he delivered or oversaw. He was always adamant that the wretches before him not only had to suffer, they had to be seen to suffer and they had to be defeated, all fight quashed, all resistance broken. He raised his eyebrows at Jamie and the unspoken words between them boded badly for Olivia, with Jamie's jaw setting as a look of steely resolve took over his face.

"Ow. Thank you. I am ready for my fifth stroke now, sir."

Swish. Crack!

"Yaa! Fuck! Ow!"

Progress, thought the professor. He had the knowledge of the number of slaps it had taken to break the spirit of this feisty and tough student with the ferocious and prolonged spanking he had administered, so was less surprised than Jamie at her resilience.

"Excellent. More of the same please, Jamie."

They waited as for the first time, Olivia needed to gather herself before volunteering the expected words.

"Oh my. Thank you. Can I have my next stroke, please, sir?"

Swish. Crack!

Olivia squealed and her body jolted as she fought the restraints for the first time.

"Ooooo! Sorry, sir. Ow. Thank you, sir. Ready for number seven, sir."

Swish. Crack!

This stroke landed low, at the point where her bottom dimples met her thighs, fleshy but sensitive generally and so it proved.

"Yaaargh! Fucksake! Yaaargh! Shit! Ow! Fuck! Oh my, oh, oh, oh. Oh hold on, shit, that hurt. Oh dear. Thank you. Yes, that frigging well hurt. Oh bugger. Ouch, ouch, ouch. Thank you. Yes, thank you, sir. I am ready for the next one, sir."

Swish. Crack!

"Ugh! Fucking hell! Oh, it hurts, it hurts. Can I have a break now, please, Professor Stones?"

Stones laughed out loud.

"No, of course not, you stupid girl! Request your next stroke immediately or I will award two extra punishment strokes.

"Oh no, sir. Thank you, sir, sorry, sorry, sorry. I mean, can I have stroke number nine please, sir?"

Jamie and Stones shared a satisfied smile.

"Of course you can, my dear. Jamie, deliver Olivia's final four together, please. As close to the same spot as possible and with all your strength so that we do not disappoint the young lady. Hard and fast, my friend, hard and fast. Olivia, you do not have to count and can save thanking me until after the twelfth stroke has landed. Proceed."

Swish. Crack! Swish. Crack! Swish. Crack! Swish. Crack!

Four rapid and vicious strokes followed as Stones had decreed.

There was a long pause before the sobbing young woman managed to struggle out the required acceptance and gratitude, but Stones was content that he had again produced a truly broken and repentant student with his methods.

"Oh sir, sorry sir. That is twelve, sir. Thank you very much, sir."

Stones joined Jamie. They peered at the heavily blistered buttocks swaying before them.

"There is just a narrow strip that we've left quite unblemished as you see, Jamie. Celia, do come and appreciate the fine artwork on display. Olivia, please relax your bottom cheeks, my dear, but mind that you keep that neat little anus and your lovely labia open and out on full display for us."

The distraught gasp from his tormented victim gave Professor Stones further satisfaction as he suspected that the discussion of her most intimate parts was causing Olivia almost as much distress as the actual beating. Olivia, being reminded of her totally exposed situation actually tightened her buttocks frantically as his words struck home, which caused Stones to pinch the white skin between her cheeks to nudge her to comply.

"I think that we should just match that white stripe up with its surroundings. One last stroke should do it, don't you think, Celia, Jamie?"

Jamie raised his arm high, paused for a moment and then whipped it down viciously across her waiting flanks. It struck home perfectly, the crack of bamboo against flesh resounding throughout the room.

Olivia's head rose but the stroke was to land before she could respond to the decision made, and any words planned were replaced by a full-pitched, unrestrained scream of agony.

"Yaaaaaaarggh!"

Olivia's body rocked and swayed, before she unwisely let loose a torrent of abuse.

"Fuck! Fuck! Fuck and bullocks, oh you cunt! You utter bastards!"

The word hung in the air amidst Olivia's further guttural moaning and complaining, before her own mind must have registered what she had said.

"Shit. Sorry, sir. I do apologise for my language. I was not expecting that. I am sorry, I do apologise. Please forgive my outburst."

Stones, never one to miss an opportunity, seized the chance to inflict further misery and illustrate his power and control on the unfortunate young woman.

"I am so sorry, Celia. My reprobate here has such an uncontrollable potty mouth, it seems. I feel that you should make the point here that we do not allow use of that particular word and fetch the strap. It would be appropriate for you to now join us in admonishing Olivia and administer further punishment to remind her of her duty to behave and accept her dues with more grace."

The distraught, sobbing student began to splutter further apologies and begged for forgiveness but Celia's enthusiasm as she skipped over to Stones' wall cabinet suggested that mercy was not an option that was ever likely to be on the table! She selected the thick strap and waved it triumphantly as Stones nodded his assent.

"Oh yes indeed, Celia. This should ensure that Olivia learns a further lesson. Over to you, my dear. Please deliver six of your finest to these naughty cheeks. Olivia, the senior tutor has picked my favourite weapon of buttock destruction, my lovely thick heavy strap, so please prepare yourself for six of best that I very much suspect you will remember forever."

Olivia was well beyond preparing for anything; her whole body heaved as she processed the effect of that final cut of the cane. Celia laid the strap gently on top of her buttocks, one hand gently stroking the twitching sore cheeks.

"Hush now, my dear. Let's have you all calmed down to ensure you fully appreciate the savage beauty of the strap. Hush there. Nice and calm, please. That's better. Nice and still now and I will try and do justice with this beast."

Olivia was now just a quietly weeping, subdued player in this performance who was about to realise that there were worse physical penalties than the professor's medium cane. Celia raised the strap and with the signal from Stones swung it down across Olivia's beleaguered bottom.

Thwack! There was a pause of five seconds during which a thick strip across the centre of Olivia's bottom appeared momentary starkly white before a bright red hue appeared; at the same time Olivia's weeping stopped and a silence hung in the air. Then, to the delight of the perpetrators of her punishment and pain, Olivia let out a scream of epic proportions as her muscular buttocks clenched dramatically, presenting her audience with the straightest and narrowest bottom crack they would have thought possible. As the scream began to peter out and the tension left her cheeks, Celia swung the strap again.

Thwack! Landing just below the previous stroke the result was the same, albeit the tone of the scream slightly lower and more guttural, the buttock clench not quite as dramatic.

Thwack! The third stroke went just above the first, the three stripes melding into one red raw, wide area across the fleshy middle of her cheeks. The accompanying scream did justice to the hearty effort of Celia's swing. Stones and Celia exchanged sly grins as she raised the strap high again, sharing knowledge that the next stroke would be on the underside of her buttocks where they met the upper thighs, and the pain of the earlier strokes would no longer be the worst that Olivia could experience.

Thwack! As the stroke registered, Jamie had to quickly step forward to hold the stricken young woman by the shoulders as her reaction to the stinging in her rear almost lifted the heavy desk from the floor. Stones moved around to stroke her hair as she tossed her head from side to side.

"Hush there, my sweet. Just two more to go. Admittedly the next one will be across the very top of your bottom where the skin is less fleshy and the protection minimal. So hold tight while Celia gathers herself to deliver one of her finest blows."

With a big smile across her face, Celia ever keen to win Stones' favour, landed a thunderous stroke across the top of Olivia's bottom.

Thwack! Celia was rewarded with the longest scream yet and again Jamie forced Olivia's shoulders down as the distraught student fought her bindings and unleashed her distress totally. Without waiting for her to settle, Celia took aim and laid the strap diagonally across the writhing scarlet buttocks for the sixth time.

Thwack!

Caught unawares, Olivia cut short one scream to let loose a real howl of pain. At a nod of approval from Stones, Celia returned the strap to the cabinet and joined Jamie and the professor in standing behind Olivia as her body gradually calmed to the point that her cheeks were now just squeezing tight and then relaxing every few seconds while she moaned and sobbed, breathing deeply with the occasional shudder wracking her body.

"Excellent, truly excellent. What a team we make, don't you agree, my friends? What a perfectly beaten pair of buttocks. Look at this as an example of a young lady that has been thoroughly thrashed and, hopefully, taken on board the lessons we have given to teach her the way forward. What do you say you say, young Olivia? Have you seen the error of your ways? Are you repentant? Are you contrite? Are you feeling corrected and improved? What would you like to say to us?"

Olivia responded with a quiet, spluttering voice, now lacking arrogance and confidence.

"Oh sir. I am so sorry for my behaviour. I am so sorry. Oh, it stings so much. Oh my, sir. I cannot believe how much it ruddy stings. So very sorry, sirs, Dr Ford. I am so, so very sorry. Yes, yes, thank you for my punishment. Yes, I am repentant, contrite, full of remorse, all of those things. Thank you for my correction. Please, sir, no more, I really am sorry."

Stones studied her beaten flanks, touched, prodded and spread her cheeks wide apart. Her compliance and lack of resistance was exactly what he wanted. He fully exposed her as he dug both sets of fingers into the impressively straight anal cleft, displayed her neat, vertical, wrinkleless arsehole with its dark-skinned surround and sparsity of anal hairs leading down into that long, pink vaginal opening and neatly cropped pubic hair.

"Dr Ford, what say you? Is our work here done? Have we accomplished what we set out to achieve, would you say?"

"Oh indeed, Professor Stones. A thoroughly deserved thrashing, taken fairly well. Excellent use of the cane and strap to serve our purpose and a necessary task completed satisfactorily."

Celia played her role perfectly with devotion to Stones' usual script and method for the humiliation aspect of Olivia's punishment, her hands running over the beaten flesh, prodding and squeezing as Stones had done.

"Lovely, you could see that as a lovely photograph framed and on display. Very beautiful bottom and vagina, my dear. Thank you for sharing. What say you, Jamie?" Stones directed his next comment to his erstwhile stalwart.

Jamie took his cue and added to the completely defeated student's audible distress.

"It has been an absolute pleasure to be involved in bringing justice to the situation and having the added benefit of seeing a beautiful set of female openings at close quarters. Some lovely markings here that should last and an experience that should remain with this misfit for a while."

Stones grinned, confident now that his task was complete and the situation resolved.

"Escort Olivia to the bathroom please, Celia. I think we can afford to allow her the merciful relief of the iced bidet for a few minutes."

Celia half-carried Olivia into the bathroom, assisting the weeping student, stooped over in agony and struggling to put one foot in front of the other. She gently helped her to settle onto the bidet of iced water, little resistance left in the broken-spirited student, and stroked her head as she whispered calming words.

Meanwhile Jamie made his exit, eager to get home where Sara was waiting to hear the details of the activity and he was confident that a session of lovemaking would follow his recounting of Olivia's fate.

Celia dried Olivia off, inspected her stricken buttocks, and then calmed and relaxed her with sympathetic words before she led her to Stones' chaise-longue and settled her face down before him. As the professor came over with his pot of soothing cream the two of them exchanged a look that Celia knew so well. Stones nodded his confirmation with no words spoken, as had happened many times in the past. His own arousal would need to be sated and Celia was always only too glad to be the one sharing that moment with him! Stones allowed Celia to work the silky cream into Olivia's burning cheeks, knowing that it turned her on so much to do so. She kept flicking glances at him as she worked her fingers into the young woman's open legs, exposing her vagina fully as she gradually parted her cheeks, her fingers grazing the surface of the crinkled hole, slipping down to the very top of the fleshy lips below. Bordering on taking liberties, she resisted the urge she always felt to delve into the revealed delights. One aberration was one too many and with Stones watching her every move, Celia was prudent enough not to risk his wrath again, and the grief that would bring after her last painful experience at his hands for her earlier misdemeanour.

At a sign from Stones she helped Olivia up and to her feet, before leading her still naked over to the table where Stones had left the documentation that she was required to complete. He watched as she read through the words that stated she accepted that her punishment was deserved and just, and formally signing off that she had acquiesced at her own suggestion and was appreciative of Professor Stones' actions taken to improve and help her with her remorse and contrition. She meekly signed and after taking one last inspection of her bright red, striped bottom, Stones instructed her to dress and stand in the corner for a moment of contemplation.

"I need to use the facilities, please, if you don't mind, Professor Stones." Celia slipped into the bathroom and Stones flicked at his controls to allow her to close the doors, granting her the privacy he denied to his miscreants. A smile played on his lips. Celia's words had carried a hint of coyness that he recognised, and he wondered what she was planning.

After a couple of minutes Stones called the thoroughly chastened-looking student to stand before him.

"Have you anything you would like to say for the record before you make your way back to your room, Olivia?"

The subdued student raised her head, her eyes still tearful, her face one now of remorse and regret.

"Just to say again that I am so sorry for my behaviour and that I have really learned my lesson and will not be coming back before you ever again. I promise that most sincerely, sir. Thank you, sir."

Stones waved her out and she scuttled away, relief all over her tear-stained face as she exited, her ordeal over.

As the door closed and Stones looked across expectantly, Celia lifted her dress over her head and slipped her knickers down, bent over and presented her naked rear view to him.

"Do you want to fuck me doggy style, Edward? I am wet and ready for that lovely hard cock of yours."

As she opened her legs and pointed her buttocks at him, Stones could see the ring handle of a butt plug peeking at him from between her cheeks. Stones wasn't totally surprised as he had guessed from her earlier demeanour that the hurry to the bathroom was not totally for purposes of ablution.

"Looks like you are a step ahead of me in preparation, my dear. Into the bedroom and on the bed, you wanton creature. Rest of your clothes off and we will actually start with you on your knees before me. I will allow you to give me a nice lick and suck before we possibly move on to the slap and fuck that I fancy next!" Stones chuckled, never one to not appreciate his own humour and blatantly oblivious as to whether or not anyone else acknowledged his, in his opinion, pithy jibes and often warped barbs.

Passing from his central room into his palatial main bedroom off a corridor that was accessed through one of the bookshelf-lined doorways, he pawed at Celia's bottom, twitching the ring of the butt plug as he guided her before him. Celia removed her brassiere and shoes, while Stones stripped naked, his erection half-formed but beginning to twitch and enlarge in anticipation. Climbing onto his huge emperor-sized bed, Celia returned to her pose of total submission and wriggled her bottom at him. He moved towards her, watching engrossed as he saw her fingers appear at her pussy and start to slide backwards and forwards down her glistening lips.

"So dripping wet for you, Edward, just stick that tongue up me, my love, and then slide that big cock right up my gaping hole."

Stones never tired of Celia's crude language when they made their congress and dropped down to engulf her waiting and ready fanny with his open mouth. His lips moved slowly and tantalising over her labia, he sucked in her wet juices, flicked at her clitoris with his tongue, teased and tormented her. His nose dipped between the hot dripping folds before him, her hips thrusting back, engulfing his whole face, the primal grunts and groans spurring him on. He gripped the handle of the butt plug between his teeth, pulling it smoothly out before forcing his wet nose into the crevice of her arse seeking out her dark, still gaping anal hole and sliding it effortlessly into her welcoming entrance. His hands cupped her breasts, teasing and caressing her nipples erect before gradually pinching them, exerting a little bit more pressure than she would ask for but taking her to that fine line where pleasure and pain merged so that the two became one. He forced the butt plug back into her arsehole as his tongue lapped up the drops from her aroused fanny. Her body started to shiver and convulse and Stones knew her first orgasm was imminent. She had never failed to experience multiple orgasms during their passionate sessions, so he was confident this would be the first of many as he gripped her thighs and she drove her body into his face as she strived for her personal moment. His nose forced the butt plug ever deeper, his fingers squeezed and twisted her hard nipples. He did not hesitate or stop his assault on her body, her emotions or her senses for one second as her body shuddered and she let loose a strangled, drawn out cry. Celia grabbed for the headboard, her eyes rolling in her head as she revelled in the bombardment of her sensual being by the experienced manipulations and perfected ministrations of her experienced lover. She yelled out as his fingers twisted and pinched her hard nipples and she convulsed again as another orgasm hit her, her juices drooling down Stones' chin as he licked and slurped at her sodden, drooling fanny and she slumped to the bed, totally sated and exhausted.

Stones climbed astride her, his twitching hard cock nestling between her buttocks as he leaned forward to caress her shoulders and back. His hands kneaded her muscles as his head dipped to place tender kisses between her shoulder blades and on the back of her neck, his lips fluttering along her skin, his breath so light that it raised the tiny hairs there. One hand slipped down and with the slightest pressure eased the butt plug from her arsehole, fingers running round her anal ring as he continued his soft-touch massage. Her body was now completely relaxed beneath him as he slid both hands onto her bottom cheeks, gently prising them apart before dipping his head down to the crevice and blowing onto her arsehole and vulva. Celia raised her hips expectantly and Stones knew that she was waiting for his tongue to slip back between her glistening lips. In one quick movement he released her buttocks and slammed a giant hand down firmly on her right cheek.

Celia, caught unaware, screamed in shock rather than due to the pain. Her capacity for taking high levels of corporal punishment were well established but the surprise element caused a reaction to warm the professor's heart. He released a torrent of blows, very quickly turning her white cheeks a deep shade of pink. Celia, having recovered her poise, took the spanking in virtual silence, her heavy breathing between the strikes of his huge right hand the only noise other than the resounding slaps of contact. As suddenly as he had started, he stopped and moved between her legs, his knees forcing them wide apart before his hands grasped her hips and brought her up onto her knees. One hand pushed her head back down to the mattress, her back dipping in learned submission to present her wide open legs and display her full pussy and open arse cheeks. Stones recognised that his love and desire for her was of such an intimate level that he could tell she had reached the moment of maximum arousal and she now yearned for him to complete her, to be entered and driven to orgasm. His hands caressed her shoulders and back before grasping her buttocks, parting them wide, he exposed her gaping anal opening and her swollen wet pussy lips. He prolonged the moment, his eyes as ever enjoying the beauty of her sexual being and shameless lewd display. He pushed a thumb deep inside her sodden pussy, twisted it around inside of her, before pulling it out and offering it to her arsehole as he simultaneously began to slide his cock amongst her wet folds. She screamed his name as his thick digit penetrated her, the scream stifled as he then rammed his cock hard into her and her breath was driven out with an audible whoosh as though he had applied a pump and funnelled air through her body.

"Oh my days, Edward. Yes. Yes. Fuck me. Ream me. Split me open, you beautiful bastard. Fuck me. Fuck. Fuck. Oh, you beauty. I love you, Edward. Make me come. Aaaaaarrrggghhhhhhhhh!"

She screamed as she came, her body shuddering as she babbled incoherently in her moment. She convulsed and took in huge gasps of air before slumping across the table before her. As she fell Stones increased the speed of his thrusting, alternating between slamming his dick deep inside her pussy and his thrusting thumb in her arsehole, driving on towards his own climax. Pulling his thumb from her, he wrapped his huge arms around her, and pulled her tightly against his chest as he spurted copiously inside of her. "I'm yours, Celia, yours, my darling, all yours."

Celia groaned as he pulled from her, hands scrabbling behind her at his body. He caught her hands and held them as he leaned forward and planted a kiss on the back of her neck.

He took a step back, dropped to his knees and gently licked her bottom, his hands now holding her hips.

"Enough, my love, enough. I have plans."

With that, he delicately placed a tender kiss on her dripping pussy, rose and walked into his bathroom. Celia was dismissed.

CHAPTER 13

PHILIPPA BECOMES ENLIGHTENED

In the small private room of the college, across the corridor from the Fellows' private dining quarters, the group of six academics were nearing the end of their sumptuous meal. Two waitresses and a Fellows butler looked after their every whim, attending to every detail and available to fulfil any request. These were comparatively highly paid, hand-picked staff that would have passed detailed scrutiny from Professor Stones and were now trusted and devoted to his service. He was not naive, they were loyal principally because he made it worth their while. Their positions were rewarded monetarily well above the going rate and their annual bonus was paid to them directly from his own pocket. That bonus was very much dependent on their performance over the year and they were very much aware that discretion and a total acceptance that anything seen or heard within the walls of the room was never to be discussed outside of the college environment. An annual reward of over a thousand pounds usually ensured that their discretion could be relied upon!

Tonight, in these most formal settings, with carefully placed nameplates dictating their position around the table, Stones was entertaining a select group of guests. Professor Dorothy Winslow-Bellingham, Mistress of the College, and Dr Celia Ford, the Senior Tutor, were seated either side of him. The other three seats were taken by Sara Morgan, the Chief Academic Administrator, Sonya Coombs, the Pastoral Care Tutor and Dr Philippa Stanford, the College Graduates Manager. The last three had entered the room to take their allotted place as a pre-dinner drinks reception in the foyer had come to an end. The three were all aware that under the conditions of their employment their continuation of their roles all demanded that extensions to their contracts were dependent on a unanimous decision by a powerful assembly of college senior staff. The decisions were always announced at a dinner, which followed the powerful council's meeting. All three were hoping for the best of three possible outcomes, which was a long-term, up to ten years, contract. This carried a substantial pay award and virtually secured their academic future for life, whether or not they stayed at St. James'. There was, however, also the prospect of a much shorter term with a promised review in two years' time or a complete pause in their contract unless certain conditions were met. There existed the final, and dreaded option of, and this was almost unheard of, the announcement of a cancelled contract with the unfortunate academic suffering the equivalent of the Last Supper as they were informed that they were to leave the institution in the morning. In reality, the only time this had happened before, the intended recipient of the news was told on arrival and left without attending the formal announcement at the end of the dinner.

All three were conscious that they had made unfortunate decisions and suffered Professor Stones' ire over the years leading up to the meeting, and there was a certain amount of anxiety in the air. Pure rumour added to speculation and gossip meant that the three women had some knowledge of each of their companions' indiscretions and possible shortfalls, which meant that they viewed one another almost as competitors in hoping to have overshadowed any adversity with excellence in other areas. The demeanour of the committee members, who had now left the six alone, had not helped quell any apprehension. Some pointed looks and a couple of frowns directed their way had caused disquiet in all three. They were aware that their performance, characters and reputations would have been discussed in detail and each had read the missive from Professor Winslow-Bellingham warning them that the discussions would have dug deep into all aspects of their record in college. Each one of them had moments in the past that they knew would have caused concern. Even though the email had assured them that there was no expectation of a blemish-free past and the college recognised that it pushed boundaries and had high expectations of its staff, they all had said and done things they wished they could remove from record.

The conversation so far had been convivial and wide-ranging if somewhat inconsequential but as the coffee was served and the remaining dessert plates removed, Stones cleared his throat.

"Now ladies, lovely though this evening has been, there are serious matters to take you through and announcements that need to be made following our meeting earlier this evening."

Stones allowed the pause to develop. Now appeared a clear and distinct division of the personnel seated around the table. Dorothy and Celia beamed at the other three women who all now shuffled uneasily, firing small glances at each other as they submitted to the nervous tensions that had been building in each of them as the evening processed. The sobering effect of Stones' words appeared to bring the three fully alert, and each one conveyed elements of apprehension as to what decisions may already have been taken out of their hands regarding their futures in the college. Of their wish to remain there was no doubt, each one of them had submitted extensive documentation to support their application for extended tenure and long-term contracts.

"Now Sonya," he continued to Sonya's clear consternation as her head dropped and she squirmed in anticipation. "We did have an issue with you and your inability to understand the way you were expected to behave, to set an example and to forge a clear path to success on which your students would follow faithfully. Our discipline policy is straightforward but I think it is true to say that we had to overcome some hurdles along the way. Do you not agree, Sonya?"

With her head still bowed, the lively personality of minutes before seemed to have completely disappeared, as she whispered her response.

"Yes, sir. I am so very sorry but I did hope that I had taken all the steps required, fulfilled all your wishes and followed every instruction from you, sir. I thought that you were satisfied with my performance, sir."

Stones exchanged knowing looks with Dorothy and Celia, both fully aware of the subterfuge and mind games that he had employed to bring Sonya to brook when she had severely transgressed a couple of years back. Both had watched the footage of her most intimate revellations and the highly explicit coupling between herself and her husband, Ian. Stones cleared his throat noisily and Sonya's head snapped back up to meet his emotionless eyes.

"It is very rude of you not to look at me whilst I am addressing you, Sonya. It is hardly surprising that your husband has contacted me quite recently requesting that the two of you should attend my rooms to discuss some recent concerns he has with regard to you slipping back into your old ways. Disappointing, but probably something that can be resolved if we nip things in the bud quickly. I assume you would agree that there is a need for some restorative, and possibly punitive action to be taken?"

"Oh, of course, sir," said the red-faced academic, her eyes now fixed on Stones' as though she had blanked the presence of the others from the room. "Yes, sir. Indeed, sir. I am very sorry Ian has seen fit to contact you and I will be open to whatever restorative action needs to occur to make good my faults, sir. So sorry."

To her absolute horror, Johnson as Head Steward, who held the most senior position of the stewards and butlers team, serving the needs of the Mistress, President and Dean of Discipline as their personal butler, stopped beside her and casually, and quite blatantly, ran his eyes over her body.

"Oh, I am thinking that we should tackle that issue this evening, Sonya. Nip it in the bud, so to speak. Everything is ready in this room, is it not, Johnson, if we need to address some disciplinary issues tonight?"

"Of course, sir, your wishes have been seen to as discussed. All is in order, sir." Johnson's face was as grave as ever and showed no response to or recognition of the air of panic that now surrounded Sonya. Philippa, too, had turned white, as though in shock. Apart from a small grimace, Sara had taken in the developing scenario without any obvious anxiety. Celia looked absolutely delighted at the atmosphere becoming quite charged, while Dorothy had a serene expression of contentment set on her face.

"Surely there is no need to make such a public show of this, Professor Stones. I am willing to admit that I may have transgressed and that a bit of a reminder is due, but can this not be a more private conversation? With all due respect, sir, surely we do not need to discuss this sort of thing in front of the staff."

Stones went through an act as though considering the validity of her words and watched, to his inner amusement, as hope appeared in the pastoral care tutor's eyes. He took a moment before he dashed her hopes.

"I have given your response due consideration and have decided that I find it argumentative and quite offensive." He indicated Johnson and the two young female waitresses that were now hovering in the background. "Your rather disparaging remarks about our little team working tonight are particularly problematic to me as it shows a lack of respect. It seems your husband is correct and lessons have not been heeded."

The look of panic that spread across Sonya's face as the possibility that her extended tenure was not the formality she had assumed, when the invitation for this meeting over dinner had arrived in her inbox, brought Stones much satisfaction.

"I am so sorry, sir. I did not mean to be disrespectful. I was just shocked that certain subjects were not off limits for more general discussion. I thought that these issues were more private and confidential, sir." Sonya's blustering words were causing Philippa obvious consternation although the other occupants of the room were clearly better versed in the renowned Dean of Discipline's methods.

"Did you now? Well, firstly you need to apologise to our friends here. Johnson, Tracy and Wanda. Secondly, you need to think very carefully as to whether you wish to continue in your role in this college. I would have expected that by now you ladies would all have adopted the disciplinary ethos of this institution in its entirety, and that there would be no questioning of policy or basic instructions. Your remuneration package is very generous but in return the college does expect full commitment and adherence to its established principles and rules."

The pause was far longer than Stones would have wished but he allowed Sonya the thinking time she apparently required before she came to her decision. It might have taken longer than he preferred but he could see the anguish that spread across her face before being replaced with what he could only describe as a mixture of resolve and surrender.

"Of course, sir. I do apologise to the room for my outburst and particularly for any offence caused to Johnson, Tracy and Wanda. I am very sorry and of course accept any stricture that you wish to impose. I do very much value my place at this wondrous institution, and bow to any judgement made upon me as to my behaviour."

She took a breath and stared over the heads of all present. But Stones was not going to let her off one iota of what he deemed total acquiescence.

"Accepted, Sonya. Now you do need to share with the room what you think an appropriate chastisement should be, and also whether you wish to pay your dues instantly."

The gulp from Sonya was loud and long, her face now almost purple with embarrassment and humiliation. But as Stones knew that it would, the prize at the end was far too enticing for her to resist.

"If it pleases you, sir, I think that a good caning on my buttocks would serve as a reminder of my duty and responsibility within college. If it suits you, sir, I am willing to take my punishment this evening." The tears in her eyes, and her stumbling voice, belied her words though.

"Excellent, excellent. I think we have enough witnesses to verify that you have volunteered for a beating and see no reason why we should not meet your request now. Johnson, if you could just prepare the table and assist in placing Sonya in position. Tracy and Wanda know the routine, one hand each, girls, and hold her fast."

Any hope Sonya had clung to that the punishment might take place after the majority of those present had left the room, dissolved, and her face gave evidence of the sense of woe she was experiencing. With a sigh, she rose and acquiesced as with all resistance gone she allowed herself to be bent over the table that had been brought forward from the wall. With the young waitresses firmly holding the trembling academic's wrists, Stones rose from the table and slowly took hold of the hem of Sonya's dress.

"Let us lift this lovely material up and have a look at our target. Oh I say, everyone, look what we have here. Not only suspenders but open-crotch panties as well. What a lovely show! Was this all for our benefit or were you preparing for some after-dinner activity when you returned home?"

The sob from Sonya rather suggested that she may have forgotten about the undergarments she had donned.

"Oh no! It was my husband's insistence, sir. Oh lord, I suppose that this means he knew exactly what I would be letting myself in for tonight."

Stones' chuckle did support her thinking.

"Well, much as you are giving us a rather erotic show with your bottom cleft and lower labium on display, I think we will have them down and off for our purposes. That is it, legs wide apart while Johnson just winches the table top up a smidgeon so as to have you on your toes. Excellent, excellent. Lovely view of a fine set of buttocks, a delight to see them again even if it is rather sad that you have let yourself down again so soon. Glad to see that you have kept that lovely jungle of hair in place around both orifices, Sonya. Lovely, lovely. Nice full, fleshy buttocks to land the cane on as you can see, everyone. Yes, delightful, utterly delightful."

Johnson had produced a long bamboo cane from a cupboard, and began swishing it through the air to the obvious chagrin of the fully exposed and vulnerable pastoral care tutor.

"A good dozen I believe would serve the purpose and then we can continue with the rest of the business of the evening. Do you agree, Sonya, and would you like to formally request your punishment?"

The sigh from the lowered head of Sonya signalled her submission.

"Thank you, sir. I would like you to give me 12 strokes of the cane, please, Professor Stones, and I am so sorry that I have caused any disruption to the evening. I again apologise to everyone present. Please cane me, sir. Thank you, sir."

"Would you like a quick spanking to warm you up and prepare these lovely orbs before you feel the cut of the cane, Sonya?" Stones' voice was as though offering her a cup of tea, but the smile playing at the edge of his lips was recognisable to those who had been on the end of his teasing playfulness before receiving their beatings.

"If that is what you think best, sir, then please do." Sonya's voice shook as she spoke but Stones was impressed that she had lost all thought of resistance.

He nodded to Johnson. "Warm her up, my good man. As many as required to give her a nice pink glow and a foundation for the main event."

The sob from Sonya confirmed her despair at the way things were going and her head dropped down further onto the table top as her buttocks tensed in preparation for the pain and humiliation she was about to be subjected to. Johnson took his position beside her, took hold of her hips in his hands and pulled her bottom up higher before raising his right hand and slapping down hard. It was a short spanking of high intensity, and Sonya yelped and cried her way throughout the application of this forerunner to her main chastisement. Once finished, Johnson stood away, a look of satisfaction of his face, and made no attempt to hide the rather obvious erection tenting the front of his trousers. Stones moved forward, the cane already held aloft.

"Many thanks. I see you enjoyed that, Johnson. Good man."

The first stroke cut deep into the lower more fleshy cheeks of her bottom, producing a shocked squeal. As a bright red line appeared, he applied three further stripes immediately above the first before standing back to allow a full view of the writhing cheeks and the blatant display of Sonya's most private places to a spellbound audience. Stones noted that Philippa although staring intently at the displayed bottom, was not showing the wide-eyed intensity and smiling approval of the rest of the room. *With good reason*, he thought. *With good reason*. She was indeed the next one on his agenda, and it was obvious she had her suspicions that she might be next, and was having some thoughts of dread.

As he laid the cane on again Stones intermingled some taunting words to his victim amongst the savage strokes.

Crack! "Interesting chat with your husband, Sonya." *Crack!* "Don't scream, please, I am talking." *Crack!* Her muffled yelp showed willingness to comply if not totally with success. "It seems you have slipped back into your old habits unfortunately." *Crack! Crack! Crack! Crack!* "I've added three extra there for making so much fuss. Now control yourself." *Crack!* "There you go. You can do it if you try. Wipe her face please, girls, I can see she's getting a bit messy at your end!" *Crack!* "Just two more to go, my dear. Please bear up as they will be the harshest. One to the tops of your legs. There we go." *Crack!* Her scream was full-blooded. "I will forgive that, Sonya. I can see that really stung but please hold on to your dignity for the final one. Then I will take some photographs, as I promised Ian I would send him the evidence of your apology to him in the form of some deep red lines!" *Crack!* The final stroke landed on the thin, tight skin across the top of her anal crack. Her response was a long groan followed by a series of little yelps as she tried forlornly to control her response. Stones had handed the cane back to Johnson and was already busy taking some photos with his mobile.

"All done, Sonya. You may stand up and face us. What do you have to say?"

The tearful woman, head bowed, stood on shaking legs before them, her hands automatically going round to rub her ravaged bottom under her dress.

"Thank you very much, sir, for my punishment. I have learned a lesson and will not give you cause to speak to me again about my behaviour. I am sorry that I have let you down and beg the college's forgiveness. Thank you, sir. Thank you Professor Winslow-Bellingham. Thank you everyone."

Stones patted her on the head.

"Well done, young lady, well done. If you could just slip your clothes right off now. I think it would only be right for your shame to be on show for the rest of the evening. Let us have you naked, with that beaten bottom available for perusal and examination for anyone who wishes."

There was a shuddering sob from Sonya but no fight left, and with assistance from the young waitresses she was unclothed and seated back at the table in seconds.

Following the lead of Dorothy, Celia, Dara and Philippa all congratulated Sonya on taking her punishment and made light of her nakedness as the evening resumed with after-dinner coffee being served.

After a quarter of an hour there was a discreet signal from Stones to Johnson and Wanda, who immediately left the room, returning with a large carafe of water. As she arrived at Philippa's side she appeared to stumble and emptied the whole jug down the graduate tutor's front and lap. Amidst much screaming and cursing from a drenched Philippa, flustered apologies and a pointless attempt to mop her down from Wanda. The volley of abuse from Philippa combined with a raised hand that looked for a moment as though it was about to be applied with some force to Wanda's face, was brought to a halt as the professor's voice boomed out.

"Tracy, take Dr Stanford into the alcove and get her stripped off so we can get those clothes dried in Housekeeping's wash room. I am sure that there is a cleaner's housecoat that she can wear for the time being. Wanda, stop your fussing. You must be dealt with straight away. We cannot have such poor standards as this going unpunished. Johnson, I want her in the corner naked ready for a thrashing unless she would prefer to leave our employ with immediate effect. I can see not."

Wanda, who had acted out her part, as scripted by Stones and Johnson earlier that evening, to perfection, was smiling as she quickly took off her skimpy uniform with no self-awareness whatsoever. A statuesque blonde, she possessed large, firm breasts with prominent nipples, and a forest of fine, downy, fair pubic hair. Turning to face the corner, she presented the watching group with a long sleek back that tapered into a perfect set of full dimpled buttocks and long, quite muscular legs. There was a collective hush in the room as the stunning body was viewed openly and with a certain amount of desire appearing in the eyes of Dorothy, Celia and Sonya. Sonya's reaction seemed more of relief to Stones' mind and he assumed she was just relieved that the attention had been taken away from her now that she was not the only unclothed person in the room.

"Well, Wanda. What have you got to say for yourself? It seems that you are becoming a bit of a repeat offender. I can still see some faint lines on your buttocks from your previous caning, which was only a fortnight ago, was it not?"

Johnson was the only staff member allowed to discipline his own team albeit only in the presence of Professor Stones. He had worked his way up to become the most senior member of the elite team that looked after the academic staff and students of the college. Their relationship had begun many moons ago when, as a young apprentice, Johnson had been dragged before the newly appointed Dean of Discipline after an altercation in the college's formal dining hall between a gregarious old academic and the young whippersnapper who had retaliated to belittling remarks. His superior had wanted very much to keep the keen and enthusiastic young man in his employ, and an agreement had been made between all concerned that he could keep his job on condition that he accepted a caning on his bare behind in front of the aggrieved scholar. Stones had thrashed him hard and been most impressed by the young man's resilience and polite acceptance of his fate and his fortitude in taking his beating with no complaint or fuss. A further, and harsher beating followed when Johnson had again fallen foul of a senior scholar, but that served as a final warning, which had been heeded well by its recipient. Ever since then the two had developed a working relationship that assisted in Johnson's stellar climb up the ladder of seniority in his chosen field.

A few years ago, Stones had been called to deal with a staff dispute between the table service team that had been quelled by the threat of dismissal. Johnson had handled the situation perfectly and three very subdued young ladies, full of regret and pleas for mercy, had, prompted by Johnson, volunteered to opt for a corporal punishment alternative to losing their positions at an employer renowned for their high salaries and excellent working conditions. The resulting three well-thrashed and bright red bottoms were the beginning of a joint venture that had served them both well. Mainly exemplary and obedient staff, it just needed the occasional severe chastisement to serve to retain the best personnel. Already trained up and of proven quality, the staff were generally compliant and on their toes at all times. The vast majority soon showed a preference for a short, sharp shock punishment to the alternative of dismissal from such well-rewarded and much sought-after employment. Stones and Johnson had shared the actual application of cane or paddle, the occasional strap in use for the most serious cases, to the mutual enjoyment of both. If he was honest, Stones had long realised that certain members of staff, and this included both Tracy and Wanda, were young women who seemed keen and eager to cause these events and happily suffer the consequences. The punishments were conducted without the ritual humiliation and embarrassment he deliberately forced his students to undergo, and were more perfunctory and immediate. There was no education and process of improvement applied with these errant staff members as Stones did not see it as part of his mission to educate, improve and grow the characters as he did with his students. Stones knew from his own involvement that the punishment sessions were often forerunners to sexual liaisons and was perfectly content to be the catalyst in these situations.

They had not agreed Wanda's response specifically, in advance, but Stones had full confidence that she would play her role perfectly, and so it proved.

"I am so sorry, sir, my ladies, Mr Johnson. I have been so clumsy and clearly was not concentrating on the job in hand. I welcome being taught a lesson, sir, and would agree that a damn good thrashing of my bum is the answer. I apologise to Dr Stanford as well, and wonder if she would like to add a few strokes of the cane herself, sir."

At that point a hesitant and red-faced Philippa returned to the room with Tracy, stopping dead in her tracks when she saw the naked Wanda.

"What is going on? Why do I have to wear this outfit which is clearly too short and barely decent?" She was pulling at the hem as she walked, trying desperately to keep her groin area and lower buttocks covered as she took tentative steps.

"It is perfectly adequate and all that you require for the time being so hold your tongue. Wanda here is naked because she is about to be thrashed and you, my dear colleague, are going to have the privilege of applying some strokes of the cane yourself. We do need to involve you more going forward. If you are to be granted extended tenure, and it very much is an if at the moment, then you need to be careful how you conduct yourself over the rest of the evening. I need to see evidence of your commitment to the cause. However, there is time for that discussion and any necessary actions to assist in the decision-making process later. For now this clumsy and irreverent young pup needs a damn good thrashing of her bare backside to make her buck her ideas up. In fact, take a seat please, Philippa, and we will have her over your lap for a spanking before she tastes the cane."

As often was the case when the professor went into one of his oratories, the person being manipulated found themselves having acquiesced without thinking. Philippa was seated with a naked waitress draping herself over her knees before she was really aware of how it had happened. Standing before her, Stones had a perfect view then of her rucked-up housecoat as Wanda wriggled around and adjusted her position. Bending now and peering intently between her legs, Stones adopted an admonishing tone.

"Goodness gracious, you silly woman, you are still wearing wet underwear. Up you pop, Wanda, let have those knickers whipped off, please, Philippa. We cannot have you in wet knickers now, can we?"

To Philippa's utter horror, both Celia and Dorothy moved forward and took an arm each, leaving her unable to resist as the professor leaned in, lifted her housecoat and slipped her knickers down her legs.

"I don't, I won't, this is intolerable, Professor Stones. But. But. But." Her arms released, her hands went straight to pull the housecoat down to cover her exposed lower regions, before Stones' harsh words pulled her up short.

"Dr Stanford, this is your last chance to convince everyone here that you have the commitment and will to become a fully adopted senior member of this college, particularly in regard to the part of your role that requires shared values and 100% allegiance to our joint aims. As such, your ridiculous unease in the presence of nudity, your seeming shame at the possible exposure of your own body and the reluctance to fully engage in the corporal punishment process is concerning to a point that we do need to consider whether you should perhaps call it a day and leave this room now. Please take note that we were all witnesses to the torrent of abuse directed at Wanda and the obvious intent to strike her. But we will deal with that later."

The emotions on Philippa's face as she ran the gauntlet of Stones' fury and disdain were of great entertainment to the other occupants of the room, all too used to his calculated cunning. She went from a look of petulance at her apparel, horrified when she saw Wanda naked, confusion as she found herself seated with a naked form draping herself over her lap, anger as Stones' bent down to look between her legs, absolute despair as her wet knickers were removed while she stood helpless in her colleagues' grasp, denial as all control seemed taken from her, to finally outright devastation at his last words.

"No! No! Please, Professor Stones, Professor Winslow-Bellingham, Dr Ford. Please give me a chance. I can do this. I can do this. I want to do it but it just does not come naturally to me. I do not have this casual acceptance to be so comfortable around nakedness but I am trying. I can be an asset, sir. I am good at my job, I just need a bit more time and training to become as amenable and accepting of the punishment regime. Please give me a chance. I can do it. Let me spank and cane her, sir. I can do it, sir. Please let me show you how much I think she deserves a thrashing."

Her air of desperation was all-apparent and Stones fixed her with an unerring stare.

"I have two letters in my folder with your name on them, Dr Stanford. One extends your tenure for a limited amount of time to give the college longer to evaluate your suitability for your position. The other brings it to an immediate halt. One gives you a substantial raise while we commit and invest in you. The other gives you a generous settlement, upon your signature on a confidentiality clause, and an immediate end to your contract. Now we are rather jumping the gun with this discussion, it was due to be on the table a little later. However, you have forced the conversation to take place earlier than planned, so let us take this as an opportunity for you to dispel any miscomprehension about your levels of commitment and loyalty. To begin with you can remove that ridiculous garment, it was intended to get a reaction from you as was the whole planned episode with the water spill. Yes. Yes. It was all planned, Philippa. Try and keep up! Now hurry up, off with the housecoat and the bra, and let us begin our examination, literal as well as figuratively, of your allegiance, dedication and adherence to our cause. Naked, Philippa. Naked, please."

A red-faced Philippa spun around, meeting the eyes of her audience. Dorothy, Celia and Sara all met her gaze with smiling encouragement, Sonya was fighting to contain her pleasure that the focus had switched to her colleague, and Johnson and Tracy had impassive but clearly intrigued expressions as they eyed her unbuttoning of the housecoat. Wanda made no attempt to disguise her amusement at the rather serious senior academic's discomfort and seemed completely unconcerned that the moment when Philippa would be given the opportunity to take her revenge was rapidly approaching. Philippa took a deep breath in before she discarded the housecoat and reached around to unclip her bra. Fully aware that she was presenting her naked backside to the occupants of the room for the first time, she tried hard not to clench her buttocks. She had never been one to concern herself with grooming downstairs and was suddenly very conscious that the bushiness of her groin and anal cleft might be cause for comment. She closed her eyes as her pendulous breasts swung free of their trappings and she turned naked to face Professor Stones.

"Well done, Philippa. This is a start. Please let your arms hang by your side and see if you can adopt a more relaxed approach to the display of your lovely breasts with those extremely attractive areolae and long nipples. Your body is beautiful and you have an appreciative audience that accepts all shapes and sizes. Your buttocks are a perfect match for your breasts, very full and rounded and it is a pleasure to see someone not ashamed of their hirsute appearance. Clearly you believe in letting it grow free and wild down there."

It must have been doubtful from her expression that Philippa had ever been more embarrassed or consumed with shame in her life so far. The redness of her face spread down her chest almost to her stomach as she wilted under Stones' intense inspection.

"Try and relax, Philippa. If you have achieved one thing, it is that you have succeeded in making Sonya here feel a lot more comfortable in her nudity. Ho-ho!"

The confusion in Philippa's face when Stones' chuckled only succeeded in making him laugh further. Sonya, however, squirmed with embarrassment as everyone's attention reverted back to her nudity.

"Anyway, it is not about you for the time being, Philippa. We will come back to you for a deeper and more intense examination later on, as I am sure you have suspected by now. Get yourself seated, Wanda is waiting patiently for her beating which you now know that she thoroughly deserves since she soaked you on purpose. At my request admittedly but I think you can tell how much pleasure she got from her little role play, and indeed continues to exude an air of rather self-obsessed amusement still. Here is a nice thick wooden spoon from the salad bowl. Why don't you turn those quite nicely tanned buttocks a shade of red to match your face, Philippa? Give her hell, Dr Stanford, show us what you can do. Do not hold back, lay a nice foundation for the cane strokes she has to follow."

Distracted by the rather veiled threat to herself, Philippa dropped the wooden spoon at the feet of a not overly impressed Stones.

"Please get a grip, Philippa. This is your opportunity to illustrate your commitment to the cause and your chance to convince us all that you are truly a team player and one of us. Now pick that up and wallop this young minx's gorgeous bottom cheeks." Stones fixed her with a steely glint that brooked no argument and as if transfixed, Philippa picked up the implement and faced Wanda.

"Turn around, bend over and grip your ankles," she ordered, with a rather desperate voice that lacked the authority she had tried for.

She raised the spoon, and with a sudden gritting of her teeth and her face now set with a quite furious expression, she slammed it down on the rounded young buttocks before her.

Stones, like the more senior members of staff in the room, was fully aware that Wanda and Tracy were an experienced couple and very active sexually, with a bent for bondage and punishment role-playing games. Most people would be surprised to learn that Wanda, the confident, loud and more outgoing of the two, was the submissive in their relationship and Tracy, the reserved and quieter of the two, the dominant, who regularly thrashed, tied, manacled and blindfolded her compliant partner. A beating with a wooden spoon, however hard Philippa could apply it, was no real hardship to Wanda and a frustrated Philippa found her strokes losing strength as she failed to force a single cry from the thoroughly beaten young woman. Stones stayed her hand.

"Enough with the spoon, Dr Stanford. I think this young pup needs to feel the cut of a good cane for her to appreciate her punishment and honour your efforts with some sign that you are causing her discomfort. Don't look too disappointed, she is a hard nut to crack and rather enjoys her backside being heated up. A few strokes of the cane on her legs and across this tight stretch of skin along the top of her bottom crack should do the trick. Drape yourself over the table, Wanda. Hands gripping the edge and feet on the outside of the table legs so your legs are wide apart. Lovely, and we can all appreciate the sight of that open cleft and the rather moist-looking labium peeping out below. Take the cane, Philippa, and give her 20 strong strokes. Show us what you can do. I want to see that you really mean this. Although to be fair, there is another option you may consider."

He paused as Philippa's face betrayed the apprehension that his words could bode ill for her.

"Do not look so worried, my dear. I was just thinking that maybe this is a bit unfair on Wanda as she was actually just obeying my instructions and actually bears no real blame for the little water incident. It was all my doing so maybe you should have the option of punishing me. Then I would really know whether or not you can brandish the cane with the passion and commitment I expect from my teamsters."

The whole room was transfixed now as the appreciation of Stones' offer sunk in. Dorothy, Celia and Sara all looked as though it was an opportunity that they themselves would gladly take up! Tracy and John exchanged a glance that gave away that this was not in the discussed plan, while Sonya's expression was one of disbelief. Philippa herself looked absolutely horrified at the idea as her mouth opened and shut without any sound.

"It would seem only fair," said Stones as in close proximity to Philippa he unbuckled his belt and began to lower his trousers, exposing shorts that did not disguise the erection within them. "Please let me take Wanda's place and you can give me whatever punishment you think I deserve. I will strip off as quickly as I can and place myself at your disposal and under your full control, if you please."

"No! No! Stop. I do not want that. I am sorry, sir, but I could not beat you. It would not be right. I hold you in far too high esteem, sir. I am not worthy or capable of doing such a thing. I am so sorry if this means I have failed, sir." Tears were falling form her eyes now and Stones stopped undressing and put his hand under her chin, bringing her face close to his.

"Fair enough, Philippa. We will continue as arranged. This is not a failure, it is merely a factor. Do a good job of caning Wanda and we will speak more. For now, at least, I will remain clothed but you have missed an opportunity granted to few and I suspect have disappointed some of your colleagues in this room who would have enjoyed watching you flog my bare backside. Onwards, Dr Stanford, onwards. Concentrate on performing this task well and put aside your other concerns."

The chuckles from Dorothy and Celia were to disconcert Philippa more, and her first swing of the cane landed poorly and low down across the backs of Wanda's knees. The fear in her eyes as she looked at Stones, expecting castigation, suggested that she was struggling for control of her emotions but the shrug he gave seemed to provide her with a more resolved state of mind as the cane landed in a perfectly straight line across the tops of Wanda's thighs.

"Again." Just the single word from Stones inspired her further as she laid the next stroke on top of the last and was rewarded with a little squeal from the recipient. They all saw the transformation happen in Philippa then; the cane rose higher and came down faster, as she applied it to the top of the now squirming buttocks again and again. Each time the cane landed on an angry red line from a previous stroke, Wanda cried out, and each time she cried out a more triumphant look crossed Philippa's features. Her heavy breasts swung dramatically as she applied more and more effort into thrashing the ravaged bottom in front of her. As the red lines grew angrier looking and welts began to rise, with Wanda now openly yelping and audibly sobbing, Stones stepped in and took hold of the cane.

"The punishment has now been applied appropriate to the misdemeanour. You can see that your torrent of stinging blows has caused impressive weals that are close to blistering. We do not break the skin or do lasting damage to the buttocks and legs of those we thrash, and you will be tutored and instructed, so that you learn the correct application of our instruments of chastisement as we progress your involvement. Obviously this is subject to your, as yet, unclarified extension to your stay with us. Now you may take a break. We can all see by the rise and fall of that impressive bosom that you need to catch your breath. I will allow you one second chance to take up the option and beat my naked buttocks in a similar fashion to what you have just applied. I know the rest of the room would find that an added bonus for the evening." The smiling faces of all but Sonya, who looked totally bewildered at the turn of events, supported this assumption. "Have you had a rethink at all?"

Philippa's flustered look returned once more and her eyes lost the lust and spark portrayed as she had beaten the still quietly weeping Wanda.

"Sir, I would do so if it was a condition of my attaining the tenure extension, but I do not think I would do a good job and my heart would not be in it. It just wouldn't be right in my mind, sir. I think I would prefer for you to beat me than the other way round." She paused, her face now adopting a picture of panic. "Oh my word, I did not mean to say that. Oh my goodness, no, sorry. Oh dear, I am just not saying the right things at all, am I, Professor Stones?"

He took pity on her.

"Actually, Philippa, my heart has warmed to you over the last few minutes. Please relax, you have said nothing that harms your prospects of remaining with us, I can assure you."

The beam that filled her face gave Stones total confidence that his plans for the rest of the evening were going to come to fruition. Philippa might have thought and hoped she would leave the room with an extended tenure and an unblemished bottom but that was not what Stones had in mind!

He turned to the others, speaking in a mocking tone. "Sadly for you lot, my backside is not to be beaten in front of you. I appreciate that this is a major disappointment for most of you but never mind, you can all live in hope. Tracy, take Wanda away. I suggest that you both go home now and you can finish off this episode in your own special way. Johnson and I will see to clearing the last of the detritus from dinner. Off you go and thank you for your time. You will both be rewarded for your excellent service tonight."

As the young women left the room, the raised eyebrows of

amusement were almost identical from Dorothy, Celia and Sara. Sonya continued to look as though she had not fully subscribed to the happenings she was caught up in! Stones picked up on this immediately.

"Sonya, my dear. You must relax and enjoy yourself now. There are no plans for you to be the subject of any further punishment, and I can now formally give you your written confirmation that your post has been extended for two more years. You also have an option for a further five more years to be formally contracted, which the college is graciously suggesting can be put into place in 12 months' time, assuming that you do not blemish your record in the meantime. Congratulations are in order, this is an excellent result, well deserved. Your willingness to learn, face correction and improvement, and positive approach to college policy does you credit. A sore backside you may have, my dear, but think of it as a badge of honour. It is a glowing beacon of tribute to the efforts you have made and the lessons you have taken on board."

To Sonya's amazement, the venerable and much-feared, especially by her, college's dean of discipline leaned forward and kissed her on the lips. The grin that spread upon her face as he had spoken the words that she had longed to hear, became even wider as she met his eyes full of approval and apparent kindness. Stones, of course, knew exactly what he was doing and was confident that, yet again, he had converted a senior member of staff into a devoted disciple, and he could see from Celia's expression that she too was relishing the moment. As his replacement in waiting, it was important for both of them to establish a team of supportive and loyal colleagues to ensure the college's principles and aims of a disciplinary nature were protected and adhered to.

"I would like to add my congratulations, Sonya, and confirm that your behaviour here this evening has been impressive and heart-warming. You have shown yourself to be a devoted servant to our cause."

Dorothy's words brought tears to Sonya's eyes and when she too leaned in and kissed Sonya full on the lips, it looked as though the pastoral care tutor's heart was about to burst with pride and joy!

"You may get dressed now, Sonya, unless you prefer to remain naked, of course." Stones was teasing but the hesitation shown by Sonya before she tentatively reached for her clothing confirmed that she was fully under his control.

"Oh, um, well thank you. If you really do not mind, I would feel more relaxed with my clothes back on," she ventured, looking most relieved as Stones' nodded his consent, before adding, "Sorry, Philippa."

The rather apprehensive look on Philippa's face deepened somewhat at the realisation that with Wanda's departure and Sonya now hurriedly dressing, she was the only naked person in the room.

"So colleagues, as you are aware I am relinquishing my role formally at the end of term and although I will remain in a support role to help Dr Ford here grow into the role as the dean of discipline, I will be taking on the role of college president and as such will act in a more ambassadorial position. My time in college will be limited but I hope my influence will not be!" The smile from Dorothy rather cemented that thought in the others' minds. "All this will be formally announced via the governing body after the final council meeting of the year. So Celia, on behalf of myself and Professor Winslow-Bellingham, I am delighted to hand you the formal confirmation of your role as my replacement as dean which you will take on combined, for now, with your position as senior tutor." He handed Celia one of the two envelopes in his hand and kissed her on the mouth. It was doubtful that anyone noticed her lips part and her tongue snake out and Stones disguised the contact well, allowing the kiss to linger. She immediately moved across to Dorothy and the two embraced and kissed.

"Sara, you have been an exemplary member of staff aside from one blip in your behaviour. Unfortunately that was of a most appalling act of misjudgement that breached college policies and regulations and had serious repercussions." Stones' voice had become quite curt as he addressed the red-faced Sara, whose face betrayed the shame that she was feeling. "You are a lucky lady in so much that the institution was able to correct the problem and remove the risk you had placed against it. To this end, you were called to account. Your full confession of your misdeeds, and your subsequent willingness to make amends by facing the music and accepting appropriate but the most severe corporal punishment, showed us that your spirit was in the right place and your loyalty not under question. No member of staff has ever been subjected to the chastisement that you faced, but you took this without question. Since then you have been the perfect team member and with that in mind the decision has been taken to extend your tenure by the maximum ten years and raise your salary level to the highest point on your graded level. I am also happy to inform you that you will be the appointed deputy to the dean of discipline, will assist Dr Ford, when available, in dispensing corporal punishment, and you will stand in for her when she is absent. As such, you are now granted full rights to determine punishment and chastise both staff and students for misbehaviour under the terms and agreements in place. I have no doubt that you will continue to serve the college well and congratulate you on your elevation." Before Stones could move towards her, she had almost leapt into his arms and kissed him with some force as she thanked him repeatedly before hugging and kissing both Dorothy and Celia.

"Enough, already, young lady. We need to move on. Now for reference, hands up if you have caned a bare bottom in the grounds of this college. There was some hesitation from Sonya and Philippa followed by open-mouthed gasps as they realised that Dorothy, Celia, Sara and Johnson had all immediately raised their hands, as well as Stones himself, before they both raised theirs.

"Excellent, excellent. All of us. Now keep your hand raised if you have been on the receiving end of a damn good bare-bottomed caning from someone in this room."

The only movement was as Philippa dropped her hand, and then whimpered in despair as she realised she was faced with six grinning colleagues still with their hands raised.

"So, we now move on to the final issue to be resolved. We have one, aptly naked young lady here who, it would appear, does not know what it feels like to receive a flogging. This is unfortunate, I feel. Hands down, the rest of you. I can see the question in your eyes, Philippa, and I assure you that I can vouch for the fact that everyone in this room has been caned, because the person wielding the cane is also present. Is this not true, my friends?"

The nods around the room supported his statement albeit a couple of enquiring looks were directed at Dorothy and then Stones as the implications of what had been said were processed. Celia in particular was not looking that happy. The thought of Dorothy being caned by her erstwhile lover, and therefore naked in his presence, was not something that seemed to have amused her. The wink directed towards her by Stones did nothing to calm her discontent. His next words brought her up short though.

"Unless you wish me to make an example of you, Celia, and give you yet another thrashing of your bare backside in front of everyone, then you had better wipe that sullen expression off your face and get with the program!"

The option was not to Celia's liking as she stuttered an apology straight away and forced a smile onto her face.

"The issue at hand is whether or not Philippa's tenure should be extended and her authority to carry out corporal punishment on a more regular basis be increased. I believe that in future, as holding the senior position of Graduates Manager, Philippa should share all punishment duties when a post-graduate student is involved. I also strongly believe that one should not wield the cane, or indeed, other implements of punishment, unless one can fully appreciate and understand the effects that they have. So, Philippa, are you ready to show us that you are totally committed to our joint venture and fully qualified to apply the college processes as discussed?"

"Sir, this is the most dreadful position to put me in. I really do not see why I should be humiliated in this manner. I am sure that there is no need for me to be beaten in front of my peers and close colleagues, to prove some superfluous point. Surely my performance in my job here is what I should be judged on rather than this ridiculous and rather manufactured premise of proving a point. As to why I should be subjected to this in front of a college servant, I do not know. I respectfully refuse."

Her jutting chin and straightened back that became more pronounced as she spoke only held firm for a few seconds as the silence following her response hung in the air.

It was Dorothy who broke the stillness.

"I did not hear any respect in that outburst, Philippa. Mr Johnson is here with permission. I would like to point out that the quite offensive term of college servant was long ago outlawed in this college. Mr Johnson is to be addressed as a staff colleague. It is Mr Johnson's wish that Johnson is appropriate on formal occasions and when senior colleagues are present. A show of respect that you do not deserve, Philippa, based on those unfortunate words. You may take a couple of minutes to reconsider those fiery words. I rather hope that they were just part of an injudicious outburst that you are already seriously regretting, and that it was an aberration caused by nervousness rather than an entrenched viewpoint. You may well wish to offer Johnson an apology. I fail to see how you have not grasped that there is an element of doubt that you have adopted the principles and intentions of this college. For the present we are allowed, with our recipients and those of their parents and guardians, permission to dispense corporal punishment to enforce a high level of discipline. This is to ensure that our students graduate from here with any identified behavioural concerns corrected and their characters enhanced and improved. There is absolutely no intention to humiliate you in the manner that we believe serves well in dealing with recalcitrant young women. What has happened here this evening is a test of your mettle. Yes, you were on the receiving end of quite an entertaining little role play featuring Wanda and subterfuge was used to get you naked before us. Again I repeat that this was not intended to humiliate but to challenge and put into place an opportunity for you to wield the cane and carry out a punishment to our satisfaction. You passed that test once you had managed to accept that being naked before us, admittedly by an element of deception, was not the most appalling thing that had ever happened in your life, and probably thanks to Sonya having already set an example. However, let us not dwell on this. If you stand by your words then I authorise the handing over of the envelope that brings your time here with us to a swift and less than noble end. Quite simply, Philippa, I have never heard anyone make a case for needing, and deserving, a thoroughly good thrashing as you. I will grant, however, that you spoke without thought and therefore I will allow you one opportunity to make amends. Do you wish to accept this opportunity?"

The gulp from Philippa was both visible and audible. The tremor that ran through her body clear evidence that she was cowed by hearing the wrath in the head of the college's voice. The reddening of her face a sign that she was now regretting giving vent. They all watched intently as she struggled to gain some control of her emotions before speaking.

"Oh my word. I am so sorry. I apologise profusely. I am not used to this. I will learn and I promise that I do love my position here and want very much to stay. Please forgive me. What do I need to say and do, Professor Winslow-Bellingham?"

Dorothy signalled to Professor Stones that she was deferring to him now that it had been established that a punishment was to take place.

"You will first apologise to Johnson here, for your disrespectful words, and I would suggest that you ask him if he would allow you to submit to a chastisement to make amends. That would be a start." His tone brooked no argument and the hint of rebellion that flared briefly across Philippa's face was quickly quelled as she finally acknowledge that compliance was her only route to a future at the college.

"Johnson, I sincerely apologise for the disrespect I have shown to you. Please forgive me. I, er, I, um, would like to offer you the opportunity to set a punishment to help me accept my just dues for my disrespectful words. If you think that is appropriate," she said, the final words displaying her last vestige of hope that the inevitable was about to happen.

Johnson was a man who had worked alongside Stones for many years, occasionally being given the lead role in the corrective thrashing that had been applied to the bare backsides of his female assistants. He was not a man likely to turn down a chance to repay some of the poor treatment he had received from scholars during his time at the college, and reading the professor's intentions correctly, picked up the cane.

"Thank you, Dr Stanford. Apology accepted. If you would like to bend over the desk, bottom up, hands clasping the far edge, I would be honoured to apply the cane to your buttocks. I believe that together with your words of repentance this would be appropriate and personally satisfying."

Philippa's face turned a deeper shade of red and a single tear ran down her cheek, the undisguised pleasure Johnson was feeling adding shame upon shame to her expression, but she rather unsteadily moved to the desk and bent over as directed. Johnson swished the cane through the air several times, causing Philippa to flinch and tighten her cheeks quite dramatically, before unleashing a vicious stroke that landed squarely in the centre of the proffered flesh.

"Ooooyah!" Johnson paused as the audience automatically moved closer to see the impact of the stroke. As one red line formed it was soon joined a fraction lower on Philippa's bottom by a second.

Thwack! "Ooooyah!" And quickly by a third. *Thwack!* "Ooooyah! Oh! Oh! Oh!"

Stones leant in to study the effects. "Very good, Johnson. Keep them grouped there nice and centrally, please. Three more," he said, a sob from Philippa indicating that she had heard the news!

Thwack! "Ooooyah! Oh no, no, no, no. Oh please stop, no more. I am so sorry, everyone."

Philippa's response brought nothing but amused smiles from the watchers, albeit Sonya's face betrayed much more sympathy, Stones noted. Considering it was the sympathy of one who had rather recently undergone a similar experience, he was content that it was not misplaced. He wondered if she realised that she might soon be passed the implement that was causing Philippa's distress!

Thwack! "Oooyah! Yikes! Oowee! Stop it, please."

"Final one, make it nice and memorable, Johnson," Stones interjected.

Raising it high above his head, Johnson brought the cane swinging down at speed to catch Philippa's writhing buttocks just under the five closely grouped bright red lines already established.

Thwack! "Yaaaaaaarrrghh! Oh, glory. Oh no. Help me. Stop it. No. Please."

"Excellent job, Johnson. Please desist, Philippa. You may take a moment to rub your bottom but do not rise off the desk, please," Stones said.

He leaned in to inspect at close quarters just at the moment Philippa's hands grasped her throbbing cheeks and pulled them wide apart before his face. There were amused sniggers from Celia and Sara as Stones was quick to react.

"Oh, what a treat. Thank you. Now hold them there like that. I do enjoy the chance to study an open anal crack to see what treasures are hidden beneath, especially when there is a veritable jungle growing around the buried treasure!"

Her resistance broken, Philippa obeyed without hesitation, and held herself as though frozen in time.

"Beautiful, beautiful. Like looking at a crater in a volcano, almost a simmering heat at the heart of your glorious bottom. Intertwining ridges of flesh and a dark hole of promise in the epicentre. Very nicely designed labial lips beneath, what a lovely treasure trove. Thank you for that, Philippa. What a lovely treat. Time to move on, though. Johnson, if you could hand the cane over to Sara. Your turn next, my dear. How many do you think you would like to give her?"

Philippa's initial instinct to try and raise herself up met with a firm hand from the professor in the small of her back.

"Where do you think you are going?" he snapped.

"But I thought it was over. Please, I cannot take any more, Professor Stones."

"Oh indeed you can, indeed you can. However, you have reminded me you do need to thank Johnson for his offering. You may stand and face him to do so, but hands on your head. Forget the false modesty after that display of your open orifices."

The look of despair, total embarrassment and defeat on her face as she obeyed the instructions was warmth to Stones' heart. He was confident that her outlook on the punishment and disciplinarian methods of the institution were being challenged in a way previously unimaginable to the beaten academic, and that she was successfully on the journey to a conversion of considerable proportion. She stood before Johnson and spoke words that she would never have even dreamed of uttering in her worst nightmare:

"Johnson, Mr Johnson. Thank you very much for caning me. I did thoroughly deserve it, and am most grateful for your efforts. Thank you, and I again apologise unreservedly for any offence caused you."

Possibly not the clearest and best articulated apology he had heard as she sobbed and sniffled throughout but Stones applauded her words.

"Excellent. You may take your leave from us, Johnson. I will lock up. Can you leave Philippa's dried clothes out? They should be dry soon, I hope. It will not be too long before she needs them. First though, we have a few more strokes of the cane to dispense. Back over on the desk, Philippa. I think three or four each from Sara, Sonya, Celia and Dorothy should set you up nicely for a final six-stroke roasting from myself. Bottom up, Philippa. Embrace the cane!"

Nodding at Sara, Stones indicated the area just below where Johnson's last stroke had hit.

"Three tightly grouped stripes just there, please, Miss Morgan. I trust you and Jamie have been keeping your eye in. Presume you have laid on, and received the cane fairly recently?"

Sara took the observation in good humour, although a slight pink flush came to her cheeks.

"Of course, sir. We have both been taught by the best, sir. I think we are probably both carrying the bruises to prove it," she responded with a smile, and a twinkle in her eyes that brought an approving grin from Stones.

"Do not get too cocky, young lady," Stones said. "It is not too late for me to suggest that you need to give us some evidence of your claim."

Sara's expression showed her regret at her adventurousness in exchanging quips with such a master of the art, but well versed in his ways, she bowed at him, saying, "Whatever the professor wishes." Then she turned and tapped the target area of Philippa's bottom several times, causing her victim's cheeks to tighten as she anticipated the coming contact, before raising it quickly and slashing down hard and true.

With unerring accuracy that gave evidence to her experience in wielding the bamboo, she whipped the cane back down two more times very quickly, the strokes landing very close to their predecessors.

Philippa's first howl developed into one long scream in reaction to the speed of the strokes, causing Stones to march to her head and put a giant hand on the back of her neck.

"We have had enough of your histrionics now, Dr Stanford. I

would like to see a bit more fortitude and grace from you while accepting this punishment. Think of this as both a test of your character and an initiation into the disciplinary team proper. I want to see a bit more of a brave face put on, more courage and a bit less self-pity and theatrical behaviour please."

Philippa's reaction was to cut the scream immediately, and her shoulders slumped and she began to weep quietly.

"Now you may rub your bottom for a moment if you wish and then you will rise and thank Sara. I think she deserves thanks, with a kiss and a hug for a job well done. Do you not think, Philippa?"

To no one's surprise, Philippa refrained from rubbing her bottom this time, but with a tear-stained face, she rose and went to Sara.

"Thank you, Sara. I hope you won't need to do that to me ever again but I recognise the lesson I am being taught and thank you for participating." Her arms went around Sara's neck and she kissed her rather tentatively on the lips.

"I think we are getting somewhere, now. Sara, pass the cane to Sonya. Philippa, back over the table and give us that splendid sight of your raised buttocks once more. Sonya, as least experienced with the cane, as far as I am aware anyway, you have the bigger area of the top unblemished half of this magnificent bottom to aim for. Try and keep them close to the centre and go for accuracy rather than power. You will need to step up next year once I have gone, as Jamie will no longer be at the disposal of the team. Celia is planning to have an all-female disciplinary team, with a slightly different approach to chastisement going forward and as such, we need you all to be available to partake on a more regular basis. So give us a show of what you can do. Three strokes closely grouped, please. Fire away!"

The tilt of Sonya's head as she stared intently at the area of Philippa's bottom, and the fiery look that came into her eyes, suggested that she could well be a welcome addition to the punishment-dispensing team. Her first stroke, however, suggested that she had a lot to learn. Her aim was wild and landed diagonally across Philippa's right cheek, missing the left one entirely, the tip wrapping around the graduate manager's thigh and hip bone. It was a sensitive area and Philippa reacted with a high-pitched screech, her legs buckling, her hands flying behind her to grab the site of the pain.

"Oh dear, oh dear. You do need some practice and possibly a lesson in concentration and comprehension. I have just told you to aim for accuracy and not power, and your response has been to slash wildly. I am afraid that a just response and some apt correctional lessons are necessary. I assume that you agree and recognise your transgression."

Stones' smiling face as he spoke did not fool Sonya for a moment. The fear and panic in her eyes was acknowledgement that she well understood the consequences of her action.

"Philippa, you may rise. Sonya, you will need to undress once more and take your colleague's place. You will remain naked for the rest of the evening so that your shame is on show to all. This should serve as a reminder that you need to make progress in this sphere. Several licks of the cane to whip you into shape and improve your compliance will do the trick, although really we could do with another bottom for you to practice on. Any volunteers? No? Well give it some thought, ladies, while we get this part over with."

Several pairs of eyes failed to meet the professor's as he looked at them eagerly. The shake of the head from the Mistress suggested that she thought he was possibly taking this a step too far, but Stones could see that even she was loath to put herself in the firing line when he was on one of his missions! As Philippa stood with one hand over her impressive bust whilst the other continued to rub her stinging thigh, Sonya obeyed without a word and dutifully laid across the desk top vacated by Philippa.

"Hands off your breasts, Philippa. No room in this room for false modesty, let those gorgeous globes swing free. All friends here, after all. As you were the victim of Sonya's poor execution, I think you should have the honour of giving these lovely red cheeks a few more stripes. Six hard and true across these nice tight buttocks should bring her into line, I should think. Do you agree, Sonya?"

Sonya was quick to respond, completely pliable in Stones' hands now. "Certainly, sir, thank you. Thank you, Philippa, and I am very sorry for the rubbish stroke."

Philippa stood to her full height and the room hushed as they became aware of the gradual transformation of the previously stand-offish and reserved woman. With her chin jutting forward and concentration written all over her face, she swung the cane back and in a few seconds had delivered six searing strokes on Sonya's already swollen and disfigured bottom cheeks. Six bright red stripes stood proud of the paler reddened skin beneath, laid expertly almost parallel with each other. She nodded as thoroughly satisfied with the job she had done and offered the cane to Stones.

"Oh no, you need to give it back to Sonya now, once she stops that squealing and rather rude display of her anus and vagina. Notwithstanding that, I have to say those were an impressively delivered set of strokes. Good show, Philippa."

Sonya's legs immediately snapped together and she slowly pushed herself up from the desk, tears flowing from red eyes. Biting her lip, she turned to a beaming Philippa, who had made no attempt to disguise her pride and delight in receiving Stones' approval.

"Thank you very much, Philippa. I promise that I will do better now."

Stones was interested to see, as Celia stepped forward to wipe Sonya's face, that Philippa went straight to the desk and presented herself impeccably, lifting her bottom up to await the torment that she had still to receive, without a word. *Making very good progress*, thought Stones.

"If you feel the need to practice getting your lines straight, Sonya, I am sure Sara or Celia would volunteer to drop their panties and drape over the table for you. Neither of them is a stranger to the cane, I can you assure you of that."

Celia looked as though it would be way down her list of things that she most wanted to happen, but kept her face impassive, knowing Stones and his games. Sara, however, had decided there was little point in trying to outguess or outmanoeuvre the arch manipulator, and earned his admiration by pronouncing: "Absolutely no problem if that is what you wish, Professor Stones. Happy to take six for the team if it would help out Sonya."

Stones nodded his assent and if Sara had hoped that just the offer would suffice she showed no sign of it as she very quickly lifted her dress up and peeled down miniscule string panties. She bent over the dining table, all eyes swivelling to appraise her naked orbs with, as she had earlier hinted, light lines of dull bruising giving evidence of a recent beating.

"Lovely," said Stones. "I had almost forgotten what a beautiful bottom you possessed. Lovely, lovely, lovely. Now take your time, Sonya, Philippa can wait. You may stand up to watch this, Philippa. No need for you to miss out on seeing how Sara takes a good thrashing. Now aim, tap her lightly and draw your arm back. Not too far, and bring it down in a swinging arc."

The stroke landed centrally and almost straight, but very lightly. There was no reaction at all from Sara.

The next stroke was slightly harder and a pink line appeared instantly but again, there was no sound or movement in reaction from her colleague. The third stroke was harder still and an intake of breath from Sara paid a note of approval. The stroke was not so straight, however, and Stones reacted by pulling Sonya by the arm as he traced the almost diagonal reddening line with a thick finger across Sara's prone bottom.

"Now you can see how your accuracy has failed you as you got carried away and used more force. You need to ignore the fact that your target is not responsive, as I can vouch for the unarguable fact that these fine cheeks can take an awful lot of beating before you will get much response."

A tut from Celia earned her a glare from Stones and she quickly looked away from him.

"Please concentrate on delivering three straight lines, Sonya. I will have no option but to assume you are deliberately being disobedient otherwise and will take appropriate action against you."

His words caused a tremor to shoot through Sonya's body and with a chastened expression on her face, she began to measure up her next stroke and tapped Sara's buttocks multiple times before she applied a stroke of reasonable force to the top of Sara's bottom cleft. Whether or not it really caught Sara unprepared or whether she was trying to help her colleague out, there was an audible sharp intake of breath heard by all. Stones hoped that the placement was as deliberate as it appeared. It had certainly landed just about where she had tapped, so he assumed it was. Whether it was deliberate or not, Sonya had left a perfect area of skin between the last two straight strokes in which to place her final ones. With basically red marker lines above and below the obvious target area, Sonya now had perfect guidelines in place. Seeing her now tapping the cane just below the last delivery, he decided to allow her the benefit of the doubt and catching her eye, granted her a nod of approval. The instant relaxation caused by his gesture appeared to assist in Sonya's aim as the fifth strike struck an inch below the previous and was as straight as a die. Clearly confident that she had conquered her anxieties and with a steady hand holding the cane she swept her arm down in a wide arc before slamming it down hard across Sara's taut buttocks.

"Whoa! Felt that. Ouch! Ouch!" Sara's shuffling lower body rather supported the obvious conclusion that Sonya had caught her perfectly.

Stones reached out for the cane, giving Sonya a wink.

"Took a chance with the power but a splendid finish. Sara, thank you for participation, most appreciated and very enjoyable to see those lovely cheeks taking the cane again. Knickers, well what there is of them, back on, please. Philippa, back over the desk and let us continue. Sonya, please give her four similar to those strokes we have just seen."

Stones was delighted to see that Sonya took the cane back with an eagerness that came from self-belief and a new sense of teamwork and belonging. She began to tap the cane on Philippa's bottom before striking hard and low. The bended knees and raised head of the receiver suggested it was a worthwhile punishment stroke. The next three strokes were testament to the success of the practice and tutoring as they landed parallel to the first delivery and formed a well-grouped quartet on the lower half of the generous cheeks before her. Philippa's squawking response to the blows were convincing as far as the watchers were concerned, with Stones taking the cane and granting Sonya a look that portrayed his endorsement.

"Professor Winslow-Bellingham, would you like to apply the next four strokes?"

Dorothy took the cane, strode to stand beside Philippa and unleashed four identical strokes just under the still reddening lines produced by Sonya, with a matter-of-fact manner that belied the searing pain that Philippa's yell of agony indicated.

"Job done. Celia's turn now, I presume?" Dorothy said, as she turned dismissively away from the college's sobbing graduates manager's writhing body.

Receiving Stones' acknowledgement that it was so, Celia took the cane lovingly and moved in to peer closely at the rather mottled flesh of Philippa's well-beaten buttocks. Running her fingers over the various welts and weals that twitched beneath her touch, she commented: "I think I will go high, Professor Stones. I enjoy striping the top of a nice plump bottom crack. Good territory, with nice tight skin and less protective fat. I do this to you, Philippa, for fun and with a certain amount of malice, rather than as a duty. You have been in need of this from the day you and your snooty nose crossed the line that divides this hallowed institution from uncivilised outside world. Please know that I mean these lashes, Philippa, and each tear you shed, each scream that passes your lips is like golden nectar to me. This is your well-deserved comeuppance. This is where my strokes will land."

Saying that, she dragged her fingernails, digging forcefully into the tight skin, in slow and deep scratches across the top of a protesting Philippa's bottom.

"Just cane her please, Celia. Much as I am happy for you to enjoy yourself at Dr Stanford's expense we do not want to be here all night." Stones interrupted her harsh reverie.

Celia responded by raising the cane above her shoulder and swinging down with savage pace and power. The shriek it produced made Sonya and Sara both wince, Dorothy and Stones remaining impassive. Celia waited until Philippa pulled herself together, her hands having automatically grabbed her bottom.

"Please make some sort of effort to maintain position, Philippa. I will allow that indiscretion this once. Any further indiscipline and you will receive punishment strokes to the backs of your legs. Do you understand before I blister your backside again?" Celia said waspishly.

Philippa let out a despairing sob and took a spluttering long breath in. "I am so sorry, Dr Ford. I do apologise but you really, really hurt me. I am ready to take another stroke now and promise I will do my best to behave with more dignity. Thank you, Dr Ford, thank you for beating me so well."

Stones and the others exchanged looks. It was a brave statement but he hoped that Philippa did not think she was appealing to Celia's better nature. He knew her far too well! Celia's second stroke caused Philippa to drum her feet and toss her head as her scream filled the air in the room, but she held firmly onto the sides of the desk. Once more, Celia bided her time, until Philippa's body first slumped then shuffled properly into position.

"Good girl," said Celia in a patronising tone as she brought the cane down for a third time and then immediately whipped it down again. Philippa's knees buckled and her head began to thrash from side to side as she screeched and wailed. Her bottom mesmerised her audience as the four strokes stood out with their vivid red colour and the rising ridges paying testament to her delivery of power and expertise.

"Impressive, Celia, a very good job. She will be feeling those for days. Also impressive was your control and compliance, Philippa. So impressive, in fact, that I am only going to add three quick strokes across the middle of your buttocks to complete your punishment as I think you have proved your commitment already. The bad news is I am going to lay the strokes on top of each other, which, hopefully, will produce a welt that will give you quite a long-lasting reminder, every time you put that splendid rear end down, of your time here tonight. A sore bottom, uncomfortable and unforgiving, I do hope. Give her face a quick wipe please, Sonya. Enough of that blubbering now, Philippa. Just take these final three with some dignity."

When Philippa had control again, Stones placed the cane on cheeks that immediately tightened to their limits. Stones waited with the cane raised knowing that the clench could not be held indefinitely. As the whistle of the air heralded the bamboo's approach the globes relaxed and the wood bit deep into the flesh. Two more followed in quick succession, landing exactly as promised and resulting in the most heartfelt scream of the night from Philippa. Stones dropped the cane and placed his hands on the punished orbs of Philippa's battered bottom, squeezing hard.

"Embrace the sting, my dear. Soak it up. Breathe slowly and try and welcome the throbbing pain as a heart-warming glow. Feel the heat and accept it. You have done well, Philippa, very well." He patted her rotating bottom cheeks and drew back. "Look on and appreciate a fine job, and excellent teamwork, my friends, as we truly welcome Dr Stanford into the fold. Please help her up and show her your support and love."

Dorothy was first, embracing Philippa in a hug, congratulating her on her supplication and obedience, the full kiss on the lips bringing a sparkle to Philippa's eyes as she tried to stand erect and keep some degree of composure. Sara, Sonya and Celia followed suit, a particularly long hug from Celia who gave her bottom a rub with both hands as Philippa relaxed into her arms.

"I am glad to see a sign that the two of you are finally bonding. This was partially a punishment thrashing and partially an initiation into the ranks, so to speak. Consider yourself qualified to deliver severe retribution now, Philippa. Your bottom is a picture and you will do well to think back on your feelings during this session, when your opportunity to dispense justice in our favoured style presents itself in the future."

A knock on the door and Stones turned to allow Johnson to re-enter to drop off the keys.

"Ah, thank you Johnson, leave them on the punishment desk there by Philippa. I believe we have finished with it for the evening. As you can see from Dr Stanford's rather red and blistered buttocks, Johnson, we have continued from where you left off. Please do not be shy, Philippa, we are all friends together now. Let my friend here inspect your lovely bottom. He has already seen you in all your glory, wriggling buttocks, screams and howls included!"

Philippa's initial response was to cover her breasts and pubic region but as soon as Stones spoke she dropped her hands and pulled her shoulders back in a confident manner. The professor noticed the look that passed between Johnson and Philippa as she turned rather nonchalantly and almost pointed her battered bottom at him. Celia's raised eyebrows suggested she had seen it too and her querying look to Stones confirmed it. *Watch this space,* he thought, as Johnson muttered appreciative words to the others whilst running his fingertips over the most obvious welts. There was absolutely no resistance from Philippa as his fingers strayed between her cheeks for a moment and Stones pondered as to whether they had just set the foundation for an interesting coupling.

As Johnson left the little group of academics alone once more, Stones invited everyone to take a seat around the table, allowing Sonya to dress first but leaving Philippa naked. He then asked Philippa to stand and inform the group of how she felt.

"Professor, colleagues, friends if I may. I cannot believe how liberated I feel. The fear and dread of being exposed like this and taking any form of beating has lived with me since I started at the college, and I have allowed it to cast a shadow over my time here so far. However, now I feel released, relieved and, in truth, ecstatically happy, to have unburdened myself of the terror that has dogged my days. Yes, it felt shaming and demeaning to be naked before you all, and yes, being caned was one of the most humiliating things that has ever happened to me, and yes, it was a mind-blowing and unique experience feeling the cane bite into my bottom over and over again. But I honestly feel wonderful now, despite my stinging and sore backside. Not entirely comfortable being naked before you all, but I do feel freed of anxiety and worry and I can honestly say that my feelings towards you all are ridiculously close to adulation and love. Oh. I am burbling on and talking nonsense, but thank you, thank you all. I feel as happy as I have been for years. My sense of belonging feels established and I do believe that I have fully embraced the ethos of the college. It has been an honour to be accepted by you, and yes, to have been beaten by you, however painful. I truly feel that I have unleashed feelings inside of me that I have held deeply locked away. I know I am talking without making much sense now but can I say what a blessing in disguise this evening has been. Thank you, thank you."

It was the most that anyone present had ever heard uttered from the senior academic in their time working with her, but her words had the effect of a significant uplifting speech and all were beaming their approval of her confessional words. Stones was taken aback at the turnaround the evening had produced and was delighted to see this newly charged positive personality emerge. This was probably going to go down in his mind as one of the most successful punishments he had ever been in charge of administering, and certainly applied a huge tick to the process of corporal punishment to improve and correct behaviour. He suspected that they may have unleashed previously hidden inhibitions, but insofar as the required adherence to the college's philosophy and commitment to corporal punishment went, they might now have a rather enthusiastic addition to the support team required for formal punishment sessions.

"Well done, Philippa. This is a very good start to what I hope will be the new you. Please remain naked before us, this is an appreciative audience that accepts all shapes and sizes. Please learn to be comfortable in your nakedness. Your buttocks are a perfect match for your splendid breasts, very full and rounded and I repeat that it is a pleasure to see someone not ashamed of their hirsute appearance. Clearly you believe in letting it grow free and wild down there and it is truly a magnificent spectacle, and creates a lovely frame and backdrop to your most intimate area."

They could all see from the bewilderment, shame, gratitude and pleasure that fought for a place on Philippa's face, that she had very mixed emotions but the smile that stayed playing on her lips as she took a breath in to speak, spoke volumes on its own.

"Thank you, Professor Stones. Maybe I am starting to appreciate the way you do things and that there is a very good reason for everything that you say and do. I thank you all for your patience with me, I know I have perhaps not been the most supportive colleague and I give you my promise now that I will commit myself to you here and will prove that I am a worthwhile team member. I am happy to volunteer to be called to attend and dispense punishments whenever you wish in the future."

The evening came to a close as Professor Winslow-Bellingham formally confirmed that Stones was to receive his life presidency, Celia would be promoted to the permanent position of dean of discipline, combining that with her senior tutor's role for the time being. Sara's role would become elevated to Chief Academic Manager granting her status of Fellow within college. Sonya would take on additional responsibilities under Sara as well as maintaining her main role as the pastoral care tutor, and Philippa was confirmed as the graduates' manager. Sara's elation at receiving full tenure was tempered in the room by Philippa and Sonya receiving two-year posts, with a review for extension to five considered in 12 months' time. All present were advised of substantial salary increases so there was hardly likely to be any quibbles and all thanked Dorothy and Stones enthusiastically.

The further announcement that the head porter, Ronald Beaumont, was also retiring and that his replacement was to be female, a retiring police superintendent and graduate of the college, met with the approval of all. Dorothy confirmed that Mrs Sylvia Emerson would be invited to join the disciplinary team, subject to a meeting with them, when she commenced her role. It had been Celia's wish that her disciplinary team be a fixed tight-knit group, female and staff only, with no student support. Part of Stones' planning for the evening had been in aid of firming up Celia's options for taking on the future corporal punishment duties, to ensure that what was not a universally popular or approved process maintained standards and practices that were legally acceptable and defendable. Stones had given his full support to Celia's proposals, acknowledging that both she and Dorothy had become uneasy with his focus on giving equal prominence to the humility and shaming of recipients, rather than prioritising the actual physical chastisement. Stones had gracefully accepted that if Celia wished to allow the misbehaving students more dignity than he felt they deserved, then that was her call as dean of discipline. He had enjoyed his belittling of the students and the embarrassment he caused and felt that it was an essential part of the punishments he dispensed and a learning experience for the recipients, but had no desire to stand in the way of any reforms and amendments that Celia wanted to impose. So no more intimate inspections, no more commentaries concerning the women's private parts and no more spread legs when presenting their bottoms for chastisement. Celia's promise that she, personally, would submit to any of his desires whenever and wherever he wanted had given him food for thought, however. Her reiteration that she was, and always would be, his devoted and compliant servant, was not exactly unexpected. She claimed that her acquiescence had no boundaries. He had plans to challenge her in that commitment!

An excerpt from
The Dean of Discipline 5:
EMILY'S BRAND SPANKING NEW LIFE
to be published in 2024

CHAPTER 1

EMILY AND

THE RECRUITMENT AGENT

Deciding that she should make the effort to get a job and begin earning a decent salary to satisfy her parents' wishes, Emily had to try and ignore the fact that she had far more money than she really knew what to do with. Her trust fund was now available to her, but set aside until she decided where she wanted to buy property and settle down. She decided that she would at least earn a salary that was more than adequate to pay the rent of her flat on the edge of London, and allow her to live a comfortable although not extravagant lifestyle. Aware and astute enough to realise that she needed to look to the future, she had looked at the many options to invest securely and wisely. Much as the process bored her, Emily decided that she would pacify her mother and father, do her own homework and find a suitable position and source an ethically sound depositary for part of her rather impressive financial sum.

At her parents' behest she had agreed to look for a suitable city-based employment while she pursued her dream of becoming a physiotherapist, running her own practice, by studying for her qualifications in her own time. To this end she had initiated contact with a head-hunting recruitment agency experienced in placing high-achieving university graduates. Her family background was also a massive advantage and for someone as grounded, and indeed rebellious, as Emily, a lot of the privileges she received did rather jar. However, she was well aware that until she succeeded in her end goal of setting up her own business she must at least make a pretence of standing on her own two feet, albeit with a healthy fortune rather removing the element of danger and risk normally associated with broaching out into the cutthroat business and commercial world.

She had investigated several agencies before settling on a small business operating from a discreet office on the edge of the financial centre within the City in London. She had been treated really well by the initial administrator she had spoken to and transferred quickly to one of the partners once she had outlined her circumstances. His name was Luke, a recruitment consultant, and he had seemed earnest and humorous on the phone rather than slick and smooth like the last two company representatives she had checked out. His honesty had been refreshing, making no outlandish claims or detrimental remarks about rival firms. He had not promised her riches or rewards, but talked with complete candour about the basic similarities between most of the top-rated companies and the deals they offered. His voice had seem caring and truthful and Emily recognised that she found herself intrigued enough to want to see him face to face. There had been none of the slick sales pitch or underlying flirting that other calls had revealed, and she was keen to meet the person behind the attractive and rather hypnotic voice on the phone.

Within minutes of meeting him, Emily was fantasising about seeing Luke naked. She had to admit to herself that she was at times worried that she lacked pure and emotional depth. It was not her heart that ruled her head, she realised, it was her wanton lust and desire and maybe a pussy that moistened seemingly of its own accord! As Luke ran through her options she stared fixedly at him, aware that he was beginning to stumble over his words and that her attentive gaze was causing him some discomfort. She decided to take the bull by the horns, and with lunchtime approaching, suggested that they continue their conversation in more convivial surroundings.

The lunch flew past amidst much flirtatious exchanges and it was no surprise it ended with an agreement to meet after work for a drink. The drink resulted in an invitation back to his nearby flat which Emily took as a virtual guarantee of sex. Emily had discovered that, although Luke was in a relationship with a young lady called Charlotte, it was a pedestrian affair with no weekday contact and a twosome that seemed to continue because neither individual could commit totally or agree to part. She had allowed him to make the decision to take their meeting further and had assured him that she was not looking for love or commitment. His excitement at this opportunity to spend the night with a beautiful and quite eager young woman, with no strings attached, was palpable. Soon he was recounting his disappointment at foiled sexual adventures with Charlotte as alcohol loosened his tongue and his frustrations with his sex life were detailed. His excitement when she whispered that she liked to be dominated and that she was partial to spanking and bondage was barely contained. His erection rather obvious when they made a rather hurried exit from the bar they were in.

His flat was close by and they were barely inside before he began to claw at her clothes. Emily decided that she needed to exert some control.

"Whoa, stallion. Slow down. Why don't we have a shower together first? I could do with freshening up."

His eyes lit up at her suggestion.

"Let me undress you, Emily. I cannot wait to see you naked. You are so gorgeous."

She smiled at his enthusiasm and held her arms out to assist him in removing her clothing. She smiled as he trembled while he unclipped her bra and gasped when her breasts swung free. Her nipples were ready erect, her breathing getting faster as she relished his palpable excitement. He dropped to his knees before her, licking his lips as he slid his fingers under the waistband of the silk panties. As her mound came into view he buried his face between her legs, his nose up against her sex as he noisily sniffed her musty aroma.

"My turn, tiger," she said as she slipped out of her panties. She expertly unbuttoned his shirt, her fingernails scratching his back as she dropped to her knees to face his tented trouser front. She unfastened his belt, staring up at him as she looped it and pointedly held it in her fist in an unmistakable charade suggesting its use as an instrument of discipline. Trousers around his ankles, his eyes squeezed close as Emily's fingers moved over his shorts, skirting his erection as she teased him. With a sudden movement, he was exposed, as his shorts joined his trousers and Emily took his cock in one hand. Kissing the tip lightly, she rose to her feet and their tongues found each other's in a deep passionate kiss.

"I think you need to wash my dirty body and make it clean enough for you to eat, sweetheart," Emily said as she turned away from him and presented her rear view to his lustful eyes for the first time. Proud of her firm round buttocks, she was delighted to hear him draw his breath in, before he hooked her arm to lead her to the bathroom.

She took the lead as they stood together under the spray. Her soaped hands covered his body and despite his unease at her confidence, he allowed her to turn him and soap his buttocks, gasping as he took a female finger up his arsehole to massage his prostate, which she suspected was for the very first time. Her other hand ran up and down his cock, not that she was overly impressed at the short, thin rod, but was intrigued to know what it would feel like with closer contact in comparison to the rather more well-endowed lovers she had enjoyed before. To his absolute embarrassment and

Emily's annoyance he suddenly spurted in her fist, his spunk flying through the air and decorating the bathroom wall with his thick creamy liquid.

"Oh no. I am so sorry. That was just too much."

Emily laughed scornfully. "I will give you sorry, you naughty little bitch! Now clean me up and we will find out what it takes to get you your second orgasm."

She turned him round and encouraged him to soap her breasts as she squeezed the last drops of his come from a rapidly shrinking cock. To his credit he soon had her nipples erect and she could feel the juices being generated in her pussy. She allowed him to finger her for a few moments before she presented him with her open buttocks.

"You now know what to do, bitch. So clean me up."

Part of her hoped for a stinging slap on her backside to remind her to watch her mouth, but Luke just muttered a quiet subservient apology. The fingers returning to her pussy, though, were hitting the spot and her head bowed as he brought her towards the point where a climax in the near future was a distinct possibility. One hand soaped her back and she yearned for the moment when his fingers would probe her bottom cleft. Keeping his fingers twiddling away on her clit and pussy lips, his other hand soaked her buttocks until finally fingers ran down her crack and tentatively a finger circled her arsehole. With her bottom jutting back at him and no word of objection from Emily, a finger ventured to probe her opening, and finally a digit tentatively breeched her dark recess.

"Ooh, baby. That's nice. In and out, in and out. Love your fingers in my hole, Luke. Finger fuck me now! Yes. Harder! Push those fingers inside of me. Rub my clit. Come on, you bastard, fuck my holes. Yes. Yes. Yaaar! My pussy loves you. My arsehole loves you. Coming! Coming! Harder! Deeper! Fuck! Yaaar! Whoo!"

She dropped her head into the water spray, as her body juddered in her orgasm, with Luke proving himself a very proficient pleasure giver. Taking the actions of a tender and sensitive lover, Luke wrapped his arms around her and held her tightly as she slumped in her recovery from her climax.

"That was really good. Thank you, Luke," she said, feeling that he needed recognition of his proficiency. "Oh yes, what's this? On the way to being nice and hard already. Maybe I am going to get a proper seeing to as well. Let's get out and dry off." Her hand had wrapped around his twitching cock and she was impressed by his recovery rate.

"It's you doing it to me, Emily. You are just so damn sexy. I want to suck you and fuck you, my love." He slung on a dressing gown as she wrapped the bath sheet around her.

"Well maybe you should show me what you are made of then. Looks like there is a real man waiting to give me a good sorting out," she said coyly.

Luke finally took the hint and believed what she had been telling him. She had made it so obvious that she wanted him to take control that he would have been beyond foolish if he had not sought to take advantage. Minutes later he threw off his dressing gown and exposed a cock that was fully hard once more. He pushed her back onto the bed, pulling the towel from her and mounting her so that his cock stood proud and throbbing over her wet pussy. He positioned it between her thighs, clamped in his fisted hand, nudging her moist vaginal lips, parting the folds and probing her entrance. Releasing his cock wedged just inside her entrance, his hands moved up to her breasts and simultaneously and with precision, he pinched her nipples gently between his fingers as he massaged the orbs, using the flat of his hand to good effect. He kissed her passionately on the lips, his tongue easing between and flicking at her own before he dropped his head to lick and nibble at her erect nipples. As Emily sighed and closed her eyes, content to let him finally lead, he suddenly lifted his body above her, his cock slipping out, and used his hands to encourage her over, onto her front...

PREVIOUS BOOKS IN THE SERIES,

AVAILABLE THROUGH AMAZON:

THE DEAN OF DISCIPLINE 1:
DEGREES OF PUNISHMENT (2020)

THE DEAN OF DISCIPLINE 2:
STRAPPING STUDENTS (2021)

THE DEAN OF DISCIPLINE 3:
CANED AND ABLE (2022)

ABOUT THE AUTHOR

Dee Vee Curzon is an author with a fascination for the world of corporal punishment, especially the joint entwining aspects of domination and submission. Dee has used the world of academia to explore themes of misbehaviour and issues of discipline and plain naughtiness that results in comeuppance and chastisement. Punishment, fully deserved of course, is combined with ritualistic humiliation through exploitation of power and control. These themes run through her work focusing on underlying sexual tensions and barely controlled fetishes in a variety of encounters. Building towards erotic conclusions and sexual couplings of the exponents and main players in her dramas. The stories are all very much adult based and contain scenes of graphic sex and strict disciplinary sessions featuring consenting adults. All the stories are imaginative fantasy allowing readers to escape and delve into a world they may secretly long to be a part of. Adult only content and highly erotic elements of sexual adventure and humiliation are very much incorporated in the writing.

Printed in Great Britain
by Amazon